D0366903

more . . .

In A Heartbeat

Tina Wainscott

St. Martin's Paperbacks

IN A HEARTBEAT

ISBN: 0-312-97008-0

Printed in the United States of America

St. Martin's Paperbacks edition/June 1999

St. Martin's Paperbacks are published by St. Martin's Press, 175 Fifth Avenue, New York, N.Y. 10010.

10 9 8 7 6 5 4 3 2 1

To my long-time writing friends, Sandy, Linda, Laura, Judy, Betzi, Val, Rosemary, Nancy, Mary, and to my writing partner in crime, Marty.

To my grandfather, Max, who always lets me know how proud he is of me.

And especially to the memory of his sister and my great-aunt Vie, who I know still reads my books, even if she does it as an angel reading over my shoulder.

Sigrun —

It was great to meet you at RT!

Dina Wainscott

Acknowledgment

The ideas for my books come from real people and real mysteries. The inspiration for *IN A HEARTBEAT* came from a woman who went through a very real ordeal that became something extraordinary. From the amazing details she was brave enough to share spun the "what if" that became this book.

gaze
s trans-
 cked. . . .
clutched to her
she ran to the bed-
when she breathlessly said,

n." His voice usually sounded
certainty ran through it.
Not Paul's voice. Then elation
or. If they had a heart for her,
ston immediately. Where was
ly needed him?
sounding even more unsteady
crushed by anxiety, and she
. ." She couldn't even say the
ng her throat.
is voice broke off sent a shiver
he transplant coordinator just
art for you."
Her knees went weak, and she
t Paul's not here. He has the

lance for you. I want you to

Jenna

No, not Paul,
on a dusty street i
had. He wouldn't die o
wasn't going to lose him lik

Jenna pushed those thought
mind. Paul would come hom
enough to be reamed out for w

The house was dark but for t
that snaked down the hallway
door frame of the nursery, con
a baby cooing as it played wi
the crib. Would the baby have
eyes or Paul's brown?

In every house that she an
he let her create a nursery in o
whimsy, for they only stayed
year before moving on to the

And before she could have
She'd been on the waiting list
walls of her heart inexplicably

She pressed her cheek agai
needed staining. The trim wo

Prologue

Where are you Paul? He was never late like this. He always called if something had detained him, even for a few minutes.

Something's happened to him.

Elliot tried to still the doomsday voice in her head. *not her husband.* He wouldn't get shot down in a godforsaken country like her parents f cancer like her grandmother. She e she lost everyone she loved. to the far recesses of her 'e'd be just fine, fine this restoration project. Paul was already out scouting a home in Maine, the very task that had taken him away that day. She hadn't been up to the car ride, though he'd insisted she stay home and rest anyway. She hadn't told him about the pressure she'd been feeling in her chest over the last two days, the increased weakness.

Beyond the crib, moonlight spilled over the water like shattered crystals. In the distance, a lighthouse warned of danger with its beacon. The beam of light kept flashing, round and round. Her uneasiness mounted. Why hadn't he called? Paul was always considerate, careful not to upset her. He did his best to protect her from the harshness of the world.

Jenna shivered, wrapping her arms around herself, keeping her eyes far from the ticking clock. Instead, her ga___ strayed to the beacon, warning, warning. Uneasines___ formed to dread as the clock ticked, ticked, tic___

The phone splintered the silence. Han___ nightgown, chest tight from exertion___ room. Her voice sounded thick___

"Paul?"

"Jenna, it's Dr. Sh___

steady___

get ready, call a friend or relative to come with you."

"But Paul . . ." She let the sentence die. Paul was her friends and relatives wrapped up in one. "I'll be ready."

"Good. I'll be waiting." He paused, then added, "And I'll be here for you. Remember that." '

She hung up and readied the suitcase she kept packed for this occasion, then waited in the darkened parlor. Her fingers incessantly tapped the arms of the rocking chair. Dr. Sharidon wasn't telling her something. That knowledge revived her earlier dread. Why hadn't the transplant coordinator called her directly? That's how it had happened on the near-miss a few months ago.

She found her gaze returning to the lighthouse. "Oh, Paul, where are you?"

One

NINE MONTHS LATER . . .

The sun rose in brilliant splashes of color over the Atlantic Ocean. Like the sun, Jenna was also released from another endless night. The summer sky would soon be bright blue, the air warm and salty. Jenna drew up her knees and curled her arms around her legs. The gazebo near the rocky beach was her favorite morning place where she sipped her coffee and nibbled her bagel. And watched as the first child found her creation.

The state park ended several hundred yards away, where the beach was less rocky. In the predawn hours she wandered like a woman waiting for her sea captain to return. Before returning to her house, she arranged shiny brown stones into a smiley face. Later, she delighted in the children's fascination, reveled in the words "fairy" and "mermaid" floating over the wind.

She turned back to the turn-of-the-century house she had come to love. It was the longest time she'd ever stayed in one place, and she felt comfortable in the New Hampshire community. But her home lacked the two things most important: Paul and their baby. Why hadn't she thought to have him donate sperm so she could someday have his child?

That's easy, Jenna. He wasn't supposed to die; you were.

She shivered, blaming it on the chill morning air. Her hand went automatically to her chest, covering the place where Paul's heart beat inside her. Irony was cruel. Paul had often said he'd do anything to get her the heart she needed, but he probably hadn't counted on sacrificing himself. Yet, he had made arrangements, unbeknownst to her, that she get his heart should something happen to him.

She'd never heard of the ability to will one's organs to a specific individual, but apparently Paul had. He'd had his blood tested to see if they matched, then had signed his heart over to her. The transplant surgeon had trimmed the heart to fit her cavity, and as he'd told her in the recovery room, "You're off and running now."

Her sense of peace evaporated like the early morning mist. She gathered her dishes and the note pad covered in her flower doodles and left the gazebo, stopping at her shed-turned-workshop to start airing out the paint fumes. When once she and Paul had renovated houses for a living, now Jenna refinished furniture. Alone. The way she did everything these days.

The loneliness made her blood flow thick and heavy. She was tired, so very tired of feeling alone, but she didn't have the courage to remedy the situation. Making friends wasn't a skill she'd had the opportunity to learn. And the thought of opening herself up for any kind of friendship, to depend on someone who would let her down again . . . no, she couldn't do it.

She walked across the half-moon patio and up the wooden steps. The kitchen was bright and airy, sparkling with the sun catchers hanging in the windows. Little things made life bearable, like the children on the beach and the cardinals that visited her bird feeders. But was she making the most of her precious second chance? Last year she had been on the edge of death, struggling with even the most simple tasks—like sanding, painting, or making love. There were days she couldn't muster energy enough to get out of bed in the morning.

Jenna now thanked God for each step she took on her treadmill every evening, for every day she'd been allowed to live. She was grateful, yes, but her second chance had come at the expense of her dreams, of all she held dear.

Jenna thought she'd die from Paul's loss alone, never mind
the surgery or threat of her body rejecting his heart.

She told herself, as she always did when a bout of loneliness washed her in blue, that she didn't need anyone else
in her life; she had a part of Paul with her always. Not only
physically, but . . . spiritually. Sometimes his presence was
so strong, she would actually turn around and expect to
find him standing there. Jenna had dared to ask Dr. Sharidon about the sensations she'd experienced since getting
Paul's heart. She now craved the jars of tamales Paul used
to devour, and she was a sleepwalker, as he was, waking
to find herself in the living room or even outside.

Her doctor said he'd heard of instances where an allergy
had transferred from the donor to the recipient. But pres-
ences, cravings . . . not likely. The heart was only an organ,
nothing more. She should concentrate on the future, on a
life that, besides her medications and suppressed immune
system, was now much like everyone else's.

Dr. Sharidon thought most likely that Jenna was mourning Paul so deeply, she was conjuring the sensations. He
said she had to heal, both physically and emotionally, before they would go away. But was she ready to let that part
of Paul go?

No, she decided, heading to the office they once shared.
Her memories with Paul were all she had. Were, in fact,
the most important thing in her life. She was healing in her
own way, sealing herself in her world of memories. There
wasn't anything wrong with that. Was there?

The office was dark, rich with the scent of the wood that
covered the floors and made up the built-in bookcases. This
was Paul's place, where he'd managed the financial details
of their lives. Now she used the large oak desk and the
leather chair she slid into.

Framed pictures lined the back edge of the desk, from
their simple wedding ceremony to a recent photo of him
scraping paint from this very house. She found herself smiling back at him, but her smile faltered. She looked at each
of the pictures in turn, studying them. Paul was smiling in

most of them, but the smile never quite warmed his eyes.

Jenna blinked, picking up one of the brass frames and looking closer. Something thrummed in her chest, not the ever-present ache of loss, but something she couldn't identify. She quickly set the frame down, licking her dry lips and dismissing it as a by-product of her grief. Of course Paul was happy.

You make a good man of me.

His words echoed in her mind, fading into the quiet of the dark-paneled room. He said that a lot, though she knew his goodness had nothing to do with her.

I've never been happier in my life, Jenna.

Those words echoed, too, and faded. That's what he'd said, time and again. But was he truly happy?

"Why am I thinking this?" Her voice sounded thick in the silence, and she ran her hand over her shoulder-length hair, pulling it away from her face. "We had the perfect life. We worked together, loved what we did . . . loved each other. We . . ."

Her gaze drifted back to the photos. It was her imagination that made his eyes look . . . empty. They had been each other's first loves, drawn together by their loneliness and the ghosts of their pasts. She shared the tragedy of her parents' murders, and he shared the sadness of his cold childhood and his parents' deaths. Neither had siblings, though Paul had mentioned relatives who may as well have resided on some distant planet. It was just the two of them, and that's how he wanted it.

For the first time in her life she'd been protected, cherished. She would have lived in an igloo with him if that's what he'd wanted.

Jenna wrote out two checks and two invoices. Sometimes it seemed that all of her newfound energy went into worrying about paying the bills, keeping the house. As if to punctuate the thought, the stamp holder was empty.

She pulled out the drawers in the desk, each one moving like silk after hours of sanding and finishing. When she searched the middle drawer, her mouth went dry. Behind two boxes of pens lurked a plastic bag: the jewelry Paul had been wearing when he died.

She sat back in the chair, feeling as exhausted as she had in the days before her transplant. She had brought the bag home and stuffed it away, never giving it another thought.

She crossed her arms over her chest and stared at the bag. "Why were you driving so recklessly, Paul? You never broke the speed limit, always wore your seat belt." There was the other question, too, but she held in that one. She would never know the answers and, frankly, wasn't sure she wanted to know.

Before she even realized what she was doing, she'd pulled out the bag. "All right, so it's out. I can put it away just as easily."

But she couldn't.

The plastic unfurled slightly, inviting her to be brave and open it. She'd be the first to admit she wasn't brave. Not brave enough to look at their totaled car, not brave enough to delve into the questions surrounding Paul's accident. And until now, too much of a coward to open the bag.

Once again, her hands moved of their own volition, unwrapping the bag and spilling out its contents. Her gaze riveted on the watch with the cracked lens.

Ponee.

Jenna jerked around, though she knew the word had originated in her mind. It was Paul's voice, yet she'd never heard him say it before.

Ponee, Texas. Go, Jenna. Go to Ponee.

She sat very still, concentrating on every sound. In the distance, a lawnmower droned, a seagull screeched indignantly normal sounds. Sane sounds.

Maybe the grief was getting to her, that and the solitude. She often heard Paul's voice inside her head, memories of their conversations. But she'd never heard of any Ponee, Texas. Paul hailed from Philadelphia, and neither had ever been in Texas.

She waited for her heart rate to slow again before turning back to the watch. Paul had died at ten-thirty, or at least his brain had died then. His heart had kept beating for her, strong and healthy, and the rest of his organs had gone to others in need.

She reached out, fingers hovering over the timepiece, the symbol of time and love shattered in one instant. Her breath hitched, and slowly, she lowered her fingers to touch the cracked glass.

The room went black. Panic and fear froze her body. The sound of glass shattering and metal screeching filled the car . . . *the car?* The steering wheel was slippery beneath the desperate grip of damp hands as the car careened into a telephone pole. It was Paul's scream she heard as she sucked in air and wrenched her eyes open.

Jumping to her feet, she swiveled around. Nothing looked out of the ordinary. All she heard was the sound of rushing blood in her ears. What was happening to her? Was she going mad? Her fingers gripped the back of the chair. She did not—could not—smell blood. The coppery essence lingered, an aftermath as real as the sounds and the fear of the car accident.

It took her several minutes to regain her balance. She kept looking around the room to assure herself that she was indeed there. Her gaze drew back to the watch and then the ring that gleamed dully in the morning light.

She found herself sliding back into the chair, though her whole body trembled. "Paul?"

The word sounded jarring, ridiculous. She didn't believe in ghosts or things supernatural, but what she'd just experienced was not her imagination. She'd never been in a car accident but now she knew exactly how it felt. Not just any accident either, but the one that took Paul's life.

A glass dome clock on the bookcase ticked loudly, as though urging her to again touch the watch. She sat staring at it for a long time, trying to talk herself out of it. She had no will of her own. Invariably her hand reached out once more.

The moment the pad of her finger grazed the surface, Jenna was again enveloped in intense fear. The car took a turn too fast. Paul overcorrected, his hands too slick to grip the wheel. The back end of the car slid to the left. The headlight beams zigzagged across both lanes before spotlighting the telephone pole. *Nooooooo!* The horrible sounds crashed through her mind. Jenna's body shook at the moment of impact, and she fell back against the chair like a rag doll.

When she finally had strength enough to open her eyes, she again looked around the room. Nothing out of the ordinary, nothing but what had gone on in her mind.

Not my mind—my heart. Paul's heart.

"It's just an organ, a pump." She recited the doctor's words in a faint voice, believing them no more now than she had then. Her gaze went to Paul's wedding ring. She reached for it without giving herself time to fear what it might bring. Ready for more terror, she was surprised to be swept into an urgency . . . *Do the right thing. Find the truth.* It swirled around her like purple smoke, engulfing her with a purpose she had not felt in a long time. And then it was gone. She opened her eyes to find the ring clutched in the palm of her hand. Her fingers unfolded, and she stared at the simple gold band.

"Paul, what does it mean?"

He didn't answer, but the sensation echoed through her as she continued to hold the ring.

And then, several minutes later, his voice said, *Ponee, Texas. Go, Jenna, go.*

"What kind of answer is that?"

Jenna tilted her hand, and the ring rolled across the leather pad. She pushed herself to her feet and walked over to the bookcase. The atlas was tall and unwieldy; ten months ago, lifting the book would have been a struggle. She stood in the filtered slice of sunlight by the window and opened it to Texas. Ponee was a small town in the upper east corner; her finger went right to it.

"This is crazy."

Jenna returned the atlas to the shelf and sat at the desk. She didn't want to touch the ring or the watch again. She scooped up the plastic bag, clutching it tightly as she stared at Paul's smiling face in one of the pictures. The almost, sort of, *mostly* smiling face.

"Why were you driving recklessly? You were afraid of something," she found herself answering, remembering the fear even before Paul had lost control of the car.

And what about the biggest question? Where had he gotten the four hundred thousand dollars in cash found with him?

Jenna had given the police an answer that had satisfied her, at least for the most part: Paul had been on a house-buying expedition and had taken the cash to bargain with. The police had bought that after hearing that she and Paul renovated old houses for a living. But Jenna had been left with one niggling question: where had he gotten that kind of money?

She wadded up the plastic bag. There was something else in it.

For several minutes she was afraid to look. Paul wore only the watch and the ring, nothing else. She wanted to throw away the bag without looking. Even as she decided this, she dumped another wedding band onto the desk pad.

This one was more intricate than Paul's, embedded with clear, perfect diamonds all around. It was also at least two sizes larger than Paul's ring, with the minuscule scratches of many years' wear.

She picked it up between her thumb and forefinger. This time startling anger engulfed her. The air was salty, like the ocean breeze at her house. And all around her was an inky night sky.

Jenna dropped the ring. She had never seen Paul angry. His moods were steady, subtle. Whether he'd just smashed his thumb with a hammer, grieved over her damaged heart, or celebrated finishing another house, he remained calm and unemotional. Sometimes he would sink into a melancholy where she couldn't reach him. Eventually he would come out of it, and then he would make love to her, but he never revealed what troubled him. She figured Paul was trying to protect her from whatever it was. Maybe her illness painted him blue.

So why was he doing this to her now?

She had no doubt it was Paul. Where this knowledge came from, she didn't know. She wasn't frightened. No, not exactly frightened, but . . . concerned. All this meant that Paul had kept something from her. That meant she didn't know him as well as she thought. The memories of the man she'd married kept her going, and if he wasn't what she thought him to be, what did she have?

Nothing.

Sure, she had questions. But if the answers jeopardized all that she held precious, she didn't want to know.

She scooped up the pieces and put them into the bag, which she stuffed back in the drawer. And that's when she saw the folded newspaper pushed to the back. When she pulled it out, she recognized it. A reporter from the Maine paper had come to the hospital, bringing a copy of the article he'd written about Paul's car accident. He'd wanted an interview with the grieving widow who had received her husband's heart. A great human-interest story, he'd said with a smile as dazzling and phony as a cubic zirconia. She'd declined, but somehow couldn't make herself throw out the newspaper.

Paul's crumpled car made the front page, and Jenna shivered as she took it in. Her eyes clouded over, and she blinked to clear them.

The article had scant information about Paul, before they even knew the cause of the accident. Her gaze strayed to the headline article about a woman's body found at the bottom of a cliff. Details were even sketchier about that accident.

She started to fold the newspaper and found beneath it another dated two days later. This one included information about her transplant. Just as she started to throw away both newspapers, another article caught her eye. They'd found out who the dead woman was: Becky White. There was no evidence of either foul play or suicide. The nearby inn had been closed for the winter, and the woman had no business being there.

The strangest part was, the woman had no business even being in Maine. Jenna dropped down into the chair, legs weak as she blinked to make sure she'd read correctly. The words were there in black and white.

The woman had no business being in Maine because she lived in Ponee, Texas.

When Jenna rested her head upon her pillow that evening, it was with thoughts of the baby she and Paul could have had. Those were the thoughts that kept her sane. She dreamed of her gray eyes and Paul's sensual mouth on a little girl who laughed as she ran around the gazebo, or delighted in the smiley faces on the beach left by mermaids.

When Jenna woke suddenly, she found herself down in the office, phone clutched in her damp palm. The Yellow Pages were splayed open to travel agents, and a woman on the other end of the line was saying, "All right, Mrs. Elliot, I've got you on a Delta flight at eight-fifty this morning into Dallas–Fort Worth. According to my map, that's just a few hours' drive from Ponee. A rental car will be waiting at the airport, and your plane tickets will be ready at the counter in Boston. I believe everything's in order. Thank you for calling Twenty-Four by Seven Travel, and I hope you have a pleasant trip."

Two

Jenna could feel Paul guiding her through the motions as she made the early morning drive to Boston, the same way he'd guided her into making the reservations. No one even knew she was gone. There was no one to tell, no one who cared.

At the airport, she felt slightly claustrophobic among the crowds. When was the last time she'd been around so many people? She tried to casually wipe away the light sheen of perspiration on her forehead.

Jenna picked up her ticket and hurried to the gate. She could remember when just getting through a day had required this much frustration and effort, but back then she could blame her failing heart. *It's only a plane trip. Just a ride in the sky.* She shook her head. *You were never a good liar.*

While she waited at the gate, a man struck up a conversation, but she made an excuse to move away. She didn't do small talk, had little experience with it. Instead she busied herself with her doodles.

A while later, she settled into her window seat on the plane, taking in all the unfamiliar smells around her: the musty scent of the upholstery, coffee brewing in one of the alcoves, and the mix of perfume and sweat. Flying had never been a pleasant experience. It always meant she was going somewhere strange, someplace she didn't want to go.

She closed her eyes, fourteen again. As the imprint of her parents' murders filled her mind, the people in the remote African village had packed her scant belongings and taken her to the tiny airfield. Being an American there was dangerous, they'd told her. That was why the renegades had killed her parents. Jenna had escaped in a cargo plane so old it rattled and squeaked.

That distraught girl sat with her knees pulled up against her chest, arms coiled around them, as though she could curl into a ball and disappear. She didn't know what would be waiting for her at the other end of her long journey. Fear and anxiety mingled like a sour ball in her stomach.

"Afraid of flying?" said a man with a sympathetic chuckle as he took the seat next to hers.

Jenna noticed her drawn-up posture and placed her feet on the floor. She met the man's gaze briefly, but looked out the window. "I'm more afraid of landing."

The drive to Ponee was uneventful, but the closer Jenna got, the more tense she became. She'd traveled halfway across the country to a town she'd never heard of for a reason she did not know. But Paul knew. She hoped he would continue to guide her, because once she arrived, she had no idea where to go.

Jenna had always pictured Texas as flat and dry, barren like the deserts of Arizona. Here the road wandered through rich green pastures and trees. She saw no cacti and nary a cowboy hat anywhere. The sky was a brilliant blue speckled with dots of clouds reminiscent of whipped cream. She took a deep breath as she passed the sign welcoming her to Ponee, population twelve thousand nine hundred.

Pastures turned into residential, which then turned into a quaint downtown area. Some of the side streets were actually made of red bricks, harkening back to a simpler time. A time before heart transplants. Before car accidents.

Was she being led to Becky White's family? That was the only connection Jenna had to this place. One thing she did know: she was definitely being led. Her hands held steady on the wheel, driving straight through town with a purpose she did not feel.

Every time she thought about turning around and high-tailing it back to the airport, she felt a stronger urgency to keep going. Along with that urgency came the fear of what she might find. She knew, somehow, that it wasn't going to be good, could feel that her memories of Paul were in jeopardy.

Didn't he realize what he was doing to her? What had he thought about in those last few seconds when his life had flashed before his eyes? What unresolved issues did he now want her to fix? Whatever those thoughts had been must have lingered in his heart, to be transferred to her.

He should have been thinking of his life with her, of keeping whatever secrets he'd harbored from her just that— secret. Obviously he had not. Instead, he'd been stricken with this sense of doing the right thing.

Her mind played cruel devil's advocate games with her as she drove. Had he met with this Becky that day, and had she given him the money? Had Paul lied about looking at a house so he could meet this woman?

The stores thinned out, and Ponee once again became rural. She passed more pastures dotted with cows and bordered with Texas bluebonnets and purple verbena.

Jenna blinked. How had she known what those flowers were? Anxiety tingled through her. What was she doing here, anyway? She was a coward, content to never know the truth behind Paul's accident or the money found with him. Unbidden, the sense of doing the right thing swirled through her the same way it had when she'd touched Paul's wedding ring.

"Who am I doing right for, Paul? This woman's family? What can I possibly tell them to make things right?" What *would* she tell them? "Maybe I'm just going crazy. I wonder if Ponee has a sanitarium where the loonies can sit out on the porch and count the cows all day."

Her hands turned the wheel to the left, leaving the highway for a narrow ribbon of road. It was freshly blacktopped and created mirages of puddles that were never within reach. Stands of scrub oak lined the road, and on the right, acres of bright green pasture coated the land. Horses grazed on the vegetation, their brown coats shining in the mid-morning sun.

Jenna's throat started going dry. The more she swallowed, the drier it became. But her hands were moist, reminding her of that awful vision of Paul's accident and the way his hands slid over the wheel. She wiped trembling hands on her khaki pants. A low thrumming sensation started in her chest and swirled lower to twist her stomach.

I can't be getting carsick. She and Paul drove for miles, hauling their furniture with them, whenever they moved to their next project. Jenna had never experienced the faintest bit of nausea, even when she read.

She hadn't realized her foot had eased off the pedal until she noticed the car slowing. Just ahead, elaborate arches announced "Bluebonnet Manor" on her right. A paved one-lane road snaked beneath the arch and between two sections of fenced-off pasture. The car eased into the turn-off and stopped beneath the arches. It was the most beautiful, peaceful scene Jenna had ever laid eyes on: blue skies, green pastures, gentle breezes caressing the wild flowers flanking the drive.

She opened her car door and leaned out to wretch.

Nothing came out but the horrible sound of dry heaves. Jenna regained control of her stomach and righted herself, dabbing at her watery eyes. The air outside was hot and smelled of grass and earth. Now she recognized the tightening sensation as dread. The same way she'd felt the night Paul died as she'd watched the beacon warning her of trouble. Only this was ten times worse.

"Why are you doing this to me, Paul?" Her voice sounded hoarse. "Why couldn't you just leave me to live in peace with my memories?"

In answer, her foot lifted from the brake and depressed the gas pedal. She slowly moved down the winding road. Ahead and to the right a group of young men were playing football. Their field was partially hidden by trees. A road led off to the right and past them to a huge, T-shaped barn.

She looked to the left, at the immense brick home and found herself heading to it.

An odd sense of familiarity curled through Jenna. Home. A place of history and happy memories. It was not the same feeling she got when she stepped into an old house and sensed the history of it, wondered at the people who had lived there. Bluebonnet Manor, with its formal arched entrance and garden terrace, its steeply gabled roof and massive chimneys looked like nothing she had ever lived in or wanted to live in. But it welcomed her home just the same. Jenna had never felt anything so strong and sure. It pulled at her and scared her to death at the same time.

She'd never had a home, not in any real sense. She'd grown up in huts and tents, moving on when her parents' missionary work was done. With Paul, the place they called home was temporary, only home until it was finished and put on the market.

Paul had grown up in an upper-middle-class neighborhood in Philadelphia. He'd shown her old black-and-white pictures of him and his parents in front of their modest wood-frame home.

"I don't want to do this. Paul, you know I'm a coward. Please let me leave."

She had paused just beyond the bank of trees that blocked the house from the barns and the young men playing football. She parked behind the triple garage.

Her stomach twisted again as she palmed the keys and stepped out into the warm air. From somewhere behind the house, a plume of aromatic smoke curled up into the sky. She felt frozen for a moment, looking at the red brick wall that rose up two stories, bisected by a chimney. Upstairs a deck stretched out from what looked like a bedroom.

Pain and fear ricocheted through her body. She walked away from the house toward the small forest. It sounded like a perfect Sunday afternoon—men laughing, a dog barking, music. If she were watching this on television, she'd be soaking up the atmosphere of true-blue America.

Instead she was meandering through the throng of trees

with mounting dread, body growing stiffer as she neared what she now saw were grown men playing football. No one had noticed her yet, this interloper who moved steadily toward them. She was trespassing, yes, but that sense of being home prevented her from worrying about that aspect. Being arrested was the least of her worries.

She moved to the edge of the trees, clinging to the rough bark of a slash pine as though that could keep her from being pushed out into the open. Rock-and-roll music pounded from a huge boombox. The barking belonged to a monster black dog who ran back and forth on the outer edge of the playing field as though he fancied himself the coach.

Jenna had heard that things were bigger in Texas, and so it seemed thus far. Even the white barn was immense; beyond that was a large ring where two people worked with a jittery white horse. A chargelike scream pulled her gaze to one of the men who stormed through the brigade of men with such exuberance, she was riveted by the grace of his backside—until he was buried in a mass of testosterone.

Her fingers tightened on the tree even as she felt urged to step forward. Was she to continue on to the barn? What would she say when inevitably someone asked her business? She had only the name of Becky White. A deep breath didn't ease the anxiety swirling around her insides like a tornado. She wanted to turn and run back through the trees, back to her car. Instead, she took two steps out and clasped her hands in front of her, fingers twisting around each other.

The men were hunched over in their positions, watching each other, not her. One shouted out a series of numbers and hiked the ball between his legs to the one with the graceful backside, who took several steps back and readied himself to throw before the stampede of men reached him.

That's when she saw his face.

Jenna's mouth dropped open. At that instant, the man looked over at her and froze. Their eyes connected just before six men buried him. Jenna sank back against the tree, legs unable to hold her weight. Her hand covered her mouth, the other arm went around her middle. It couldn't be! No, no, Paul was dead. She had scattered his ashes along the rocky coastline by their home in New Hampshire. He couldn't be here in Texas playing football!

The man who looked like Paul, so much like Paul, fought his way out of the tangle of bodies and ignored the teasing of his friends. His gaze went immediately to her, and tossing the football behind him, he walked over. His dark blond hair was longer than Paul's, long enough to be bound in a ponytail. Several strands had broken free, and one damp lock of hair hung over his forehead. He wore a gray jersey shirt with the sleeves cut away, the bottom shorn off at the midriff. His muscles glistened with sweat as he moved purposefully toward her, brown eyes filled with an almost startled curiosity. Jenna managed to stand on her own, though it took every ounce of strength within her.

They made a mistake at the hospital! They had the wrong man, only thought it was Paul. He's been living here all this time. Maybe he lost his memory, and whoever's heart I received led me to him. She didn't want to know the whys, she only knew that Paul was alive; somehow, someway, he was alive and everything was going to be all right again.

She pushed away from the tree and hurled herself at him, enveloped by a rush of scents: sweat, deodorant, and the earth that smeared his knees and elbows. Her hands bracketed his face, fingers moving over his slick skin, daring him to disappear. But he was real, as real as she was.

"Oh, my God, I don't know why, I don't know how . . . but you're here. You're alive." And then she kissed him, her heart bubbling over with joy. She was instantly lost, dizzy as their mouths connected, as his mouth slowly came to life and took control.

The hoots and hollers of the men nearby penetrated her joy first, but she pushed it away. How could she have been afraid to come here, when her love was waiting? Something about him felt different, that was the next thing to push against the delicate bubble of joy. It had been nine months since she'd kissed him, nine whole months, she reasoned. That's why he felt different. Paul's hands circled her wrists and lowered them, and then he pulled away. Not even that penetrated her haze fully, as she just leaned forward to try again.

After a moment, he pulled away again. His lips were pink and moist after her assault on them, but it was the questioning look in his eyes that finally burst through the haze.

"Paul, don't you remember me? What's happened to you? How did you get here?"

She couldn't name the expression on his face, but it was close to pity mixed with disappointment. The dread she'd felt earlier now returned full force, and she pressed the back of her hand against her mouth.

"I'm not Paul," he said in a voice spiced with a Southern accent.

"No, you're wrong." Her words came out sharp and uneven. "You just don't remember that you're Paul. Something happened, and you don't remember."

"I'm not Paul," he repeated, and that strange mixture of sympathy and disappointment disappeared to leave a hardness. "I'm his twin brother, Mitch. Who are you?"

She opened her mouth, but no sound emerged. Too many words wanted to crowd each other out. Her knees threatened to buckle again, and instinctively he reached out to steady her. The moment they touched, a frightening affinity assailed her, more powerful than anything she'd felt, even with Paul. She jerked away from his touch. He stared at his outstretched hand for a moment before letting it drop.

Not Paul, not Paul. His words echoed in her brain, and she remembered how his mouth had felt different from Paul's, and for that moment when he had kissed her back, how that kiss had been so different from Paul's. She put her hand over her mouth again.

"You kissed me back."

He shrugged, tucking his thumbs in the waistband of his shorts. "You kissed me first."

"But I thought you were someone else. You didn't."

"I kissed you back out of instinct. Who are you, anyway?"

Instinct! Her whole world had been lifted up and crushed in the space of a heartbeat, and he'd kissed her out of instinct. But he was right; she had kissed him first, had thrown herself at a virtual stranger. Paul's twin brother.

"My name . . ."—she took a deep breath, steadying herself—"is Jenna Elliot." Out of some instinct of her own, she held out her hand to him.

When their hands connected, she felt that jolt of affinity again, and of awareness. His hand was damp, yet he squeezed hers without apology. Their skin slid against each other before his fingers locked around her hand. Her chest hurt, but other sensations overrode the pain. Mingled with the anxiety over what Mitch's existence meant was an odd giddiness she'd never felt before, and a warmth that burned in the pit of her stomach.

She found her gaze on his mouth again, on the blond hairs that sprouted from around it. Several of the strands of hair that had escaped his ponytail stuck to the side of his neck. Beads of sweat slid down the contours of his collarbone . . . She blinked, bringing her gaze back to his face and pulling her hand free of his.

"Did you say your last name is Elliot?" he asked, eyes narrowed in interest.

"I was married to Paul." She soaked in the details of his face, so familiar and beloved, then met his eyes again. "Your twin brother." She let her gesturing hand linger in the air just in front of his face, then let it drop. "You look so much like him." Her voice had gone soft at that as she let herself take in the familiar curves of his face, the broad forehead and soft, sensual mouth. She found herself reaching out again, fingers hovering just beneath his chin. She'd loved Paul's chin, the way it dipped in beneath his lower lip.

"I'm not Paul," he said in a firm voice, startling her into dropping her hand.

"I know that . . . now." Or at least part of her did. There was still some crazy part that wanted to believe it was somehow Paul. "I'm sorry if I'm staring," she said, mortified to realize she had been, and that he'd been watching her do it. "It's just that you . . . you really look so much like him." She wished she could interpret the many things going on behind those deep brown eyes of his.

"You gonna play or make kissy-face?" one of the men called out in a deep, booming voice.

"Go on without me, Bob!" Mitch waved them back to business, not taking his eyes from her. And ignoring the remark that had Jenna flushing in embarrassment. The men slowly took up their game positions, but their gazes kept slinking back to Jenna and Mitch. She remembered Mitch's primal scream, seeing that it matched his voice and the power she saw in his eyes.

"What do you mean, you *were* married to him? Are you divorced? Or did he take off and disappear?" Mitch asked.

Jenna swallowed hard. "He died in a car accident. Nine months ago."

"No. He can't be dead."

"He is."

"Then why did you think I was him?"

She squeezed her eyes shut, rubbing her forehead. "I . . . wanted to believe it was somehow him, alive all this time. I know it sounds crazy, but for a few minutes . . ." She opened her eyes. "For a few minutes, it wasn't."

"He can't be dead," Mitch repeated, and Jenna knew well that disbelief.

"He hit a telephone pole. They said he probably didn't feel any pain, that he sustained head trauma immediately." She dipped her head. "You know, they tell you that, about the pain, as though it makes everything all right." She met his gaze. "It doesn't, does it?"

Now he scanned her face, and she saw the change on his expression when he realized she was telling the truth.

He closed his eyes, becoming still. Jenna felt the strongest urge to put her arms around him, to share the grief she felt as strongly as he did. Her body stirred at the thought, and she quelled the urge. It was only because he looked like Paul that her body came to life, she assured herself. The tickle in her stomach, the warmth flowing through her veins, all because of the similarity.

You never felt this way when you stood close to Paul, a voice whispered.

Don't be ridiculous! Of course I did.

Mitch opened his eyes at last. "Why did you wait so long to tell me?"

It was at that moment as she took in the accusation in Mitch's eyes that she realized the depth of Paul's betrayal. He had kept the knowledge of his twin brother from her. But why? "I . . . I didn't know about you."

His eyebrows furrowed. "How could you not know?"

"He never told me. He said his father died some years back in an airplane wreck, that his mother died from cancer before that, that he was raised in Philadelphia. He never said anything about you."

"Airplane . . . cancer? *Philadelphia?*" Mitch went pale for an instant, but color flooded back into his face as he moved closer. "It's all a lie. Everything he told you."

She moved back, pressing against the bark of the tree. "What?" The word came out as a whimper. But she knew. Hadn't she known the moment she'd felt at home here?

Mitch regarded her with an amount of suspicion she didn't understand. "He grew up here, right there in that house. But you already knew that."

"I . . ." He was confusing her, accusing her, yet he was right in a way she couldn't explain to him. "I wondered. When I got here, I wondered if . . ."

"You had to know. Why would you have come here if you didn't?"

That was the question she'd dreaded. "I found some things in his papers," she lied. "I came here to see what they meant."

He seemed to dismiss his suspicion for a moment, giving her an assessing once-over. "You were his wife." She nodded, feeling too aware of his eyes as they traveled over her body. For a moment, she wondered if he could see the scar that ran down the center of her chest, feeling that naked under his gaze. "Why did he lie to you?"

She couldn't help the cold shudder that rippled through her at the blunt question. "I don't know."

He stared off in the direction of the pasture and whispered, "Why didn't I feel it when he died?"

"Feel it?"

He turned back to her. "I would have felt it if he'd died."

"What do you mean?"

He looked past her. "When Paul and I were growing up . . . our whole lives, really, we had this connection thing between us. If one of us was hurt, angry, whatever, the other one would feel it."

Should she tell him that Paul's heart beat within her, that in a way he was still alive? No, she wasn't ready yet. "It's the truth. I have his death certificate with me."

"Tell me what happened."

She related the events of the car accident, even admitting Paul's reckless driving and lack of a seat belt. She let the words sink in for a moment before asking a question of her own. "Did you keep in touch with him?"

"He left here nine years ago. Just left, without telling anyone where he was going. No one ever heard from him again. I knew he was alive. . . ." He shook his head. "Thought he was alive. I figured one day he'd come back, when he was ready."

"Why did he leave?"

"It was after our parents died." His gaze drifted off again. "Where did he live? Where was he all these years? What did he do with himself?" His gaze took her in again. "Besides marry you?"

"We have a home in New Hampshire." She caught herself at the word "we." Her voice went softer. "We lived all over, buying old houses and renovating them."

"I can't believe he even left Texas."

"He loved it here," Jenna caught herself saying. When Mitch shot her a questioning stare, she amended, "I'll bet he loved it here. I can't imagine why anyone would leave a place like this." She took her gaze from his and scanned the property. It was as though she could feel Paul's ache at having to leave. *Why did you leave, Paul? You obviously loved it here.* Did she want to know? The man who had been her life had lied about who he was, or at least where he'd come from. What had driven him away from his home and his past, even his accent?

"Let's go inside," Mitch said, leading the way back through the trees.

He left her no choice but to follow him. Faced with his backside, she lost the sense of familiarity between Mitch and Paul. Mitch carried himself with sureness, shoulders straight and wide, stride confident. In contrast, Paul, she realized, walked slower, shoulders slumped. And even though Paul worked on houses for a living, he never had the muscles Mitch did. Through the thin jersey shorts, Jenna could see the contours of his behind, small and firm. Awareness tingled through her, and she quickened her step so she wouldn't have visual access anymore. But that didn't help the memory of his mouth on hers.

How could she feel like this after losing Paul? She'd sworn she would never feel this way about a man again. But Mitch wasn't just any man. He was Paul's twin.

Mitch glanced over at Jenna as she stepped up beside him. Pretty, fair, feminine. Dad would have approved of Paul's choice for a wife. For once, Paul might have made the man happy. Of course, that depended on Jenna's background. Dad was willing to overlook his own, but not that of a daughter-in-law.

One thing was certain: the woman passed in the kissing department. What was a guy supposed to do when a pretty woman threw herself into his arms and started working on his mouth? He hadn't missed the way she kept rubbing the back of her hand over her mouth either.

She's my brother's wife.

His brother, his twin who was dead. The knowledge was a lead weight inside him. Mitch led Jenna around the garage to the front entrance of the house. At times he'd thought the worst of Paul, but as they walked through the terrace, a hundred memories assailed him: playing hide-and-seek among the huge potted plants, climbing on the balcony over the front door (which they'd gotten walloped for), and many more in quick succession.

Paul had been his other half, the one person who understood him. Even though Paul hadn't shared Mitch's need to fit in with the other kids in town, he'd innately understood the reason why. Dad wanted his sons to live up to his status of being the big fish in the small pond of Ponee. He hadn't understood that neither twin wanted that. Mitch wanted to be a part of the population, and Paul just wanted to immerse himself in his schoolwork and fiction books. Even in their differences, they'd been united. Until that horrible day . . .

"Mitch?" she asked in that soft voice of hers, making him realize he'd stopped.

She had the most incredible almond-shaped eyes, gray and thickly lashed, with a haunted quality. And a small chin that begged to be gently pinched. That first moment he'd seen her, he'd been struck with the oddest sensation of knowing that this stranger would have the key to set him free of the past. He wasn't even sure how he'd become aware of her presence. Something had made him look up, though it had the worst timing. But the physical tramping had been nothing compared to the slam in the gut when he'd seen her. Or when she'd thrown herself into his arms.

Now he was staring at her. She had reason to stare at him, he supposed. He looked like the man she loved, the man she'd recently buried if she were telling the truth. He had no excuse other than general fascination. She had a great mouth, pink and tilted up at the corners. A woman with a mouth like that ought to be used to a man staring.

"Come on," he said a bit too gruffly as he moved past her and opened the front door.

Harvey rambled up the walkway, making big-dog panting noises. Jenna shrank away, eyes wide.

"Don't worry about Harvey; he thinks he's a cat."

"A cat?" She lifted an eyebrow.

"Yeah. He was raised by a mama cat and her two kittens. Come on, boy."

She paused in the foyer, taking in the staircase that curved upstairs, the marble floor and crystal chandelier, all with an appreciative fondness. What was she really here for? A piece of his spread? Money-grubbing females were lower than slugs.

Along with her awe, though, lingered the hurt of someone betrayed. "He never told me," she said, even softer than usual. Then her voice went flat. "Why didn't he tell me?"

Part of Mitch wanted to distrust her as he did most women. No matter who she was, though, she deserved common courtesy.

"Would you like something to drink, eat?"

She pressed a hand to her stomach. "I couldn't think of eating right now, but I'd love a glass of tea or water. And a place to freshen up."

He stepped back into the foyer and pushed open the door with his elbow. "Powder room's in here. I'm going to jump in the shower, but I'll be back down faster than a spooked horse'll run the quarter mile."

Another common courtesy: don't scare your guest away with your sweat. He raced through the routine, jumped into a pair of shorts and a shirt, and headed back down. She was just walking out of the powder room when he returned. Harvey hadn't followed Mitch as he usually did. Instead, he had sprawled out on the cool marble outside the powder room waiting for Jenna.

"Traitor," Mitch whispered to the dog. "I'll get you a

glass of that tea you mentioned earlier,'' he said to Jenna, nodding for her to follow.

She took in the house as she followed him to the kitchen, where he poured two glasses of tea over ice and handed her one. She seemed to take the glass carefully, as if trying to avoid physical contact with him. Or maybe it was his imagination.

He held out a chair at the table nestled in the circular breakfast nook. Self-consciously, she sat down, and as she did, their arms brushed together. She looked startled as she met his eyes, but quickly looked away. He hadn't given it away, but he'd felt something too, some inexplicable connection. He took a seat across from her, annoyed to find his loyal dog flopping down at Jenna's feet.

She had a sweet smell about her, and though she probably wouldn't have believed him, he could have told her she hadn't needed refreshing. She'd looked fresh and pretty, schoolteacherlike in her blouse buttoned all the way up to her chin. But behind those eyes he felt her apprehension.

What was she apprehensive about? And what she was after? He'd figure the latter out soon enough. She reached into her purse and produced a piece of paper. *Ah, now we're getting somewhere.*

''I . . . I wasn't sure what I'd find when I came to Ponee, but I brought these.'' She laid out Paul's death certificate and some photos. Her hands were shaking.

Mitch didn't touch the certificate at first, repositioning himself to read it. It looked real enough. Why hadn't he felt it? Even through the nine years of separation, he sometimes *felt* something from Paul. Mitch had always been sure that if some terrible thing had happened, he would have known. He glanced up at Jenna, who was also staring at the certificate. She met his eyes, then looked away. She was hiding something, or at least not telling him the whole story. He'd get it one way or the other.

''How long were you married?''

''Five years,'' she said in that silky soft voice of hers.

"Kids?"

Sorrow shadowed her eyes, and she shook her head. She looked out beyond the curved glass to the terrace and backyard. "Who is that?" she asked of the silver-haired woman turning ribs on the barbecue pit, stereo headphones on her head, bouncing to some country beat, no doubt.

"That's Betzi, my—the housekeeper. I always supply dinner to the Sunday football Bobs, and she makes the best ribs in the tricounty area." He found himself adding, "Sneaks in a pinch of jalapeño for a kick." He walked over to the counter and brought back a platter of brownies. "Also makes the best brownies, chock-full of walnuts." He pushed the plate toward her.

She stared wistfully at them, then took one. "Paul loved brownies with walnuts."

"We used to polish off a tray like this in an hour. That's if Betzi didn't catch us."

She stopped mid-bite, then continued. "I used to hate walnuts, or any kind of nut. But now . . ." She looked at the brownie contemplatively, then took another bite. "I like them."

Mitch got caught up in watching her mouth bite into the brownie and almost forgot to help himself to one.

Jenna's eyebrows furrowed. "What did you call those guys? Football Bobs?"

"Old joke. We used to go round calling each other Bob. Hey, Bob. Yeah, Bob. That kind of thing. It caught on."

She nodded, but obviously didn't get it.

"You and Paul renovated old houses," he said, hard-pressed to imagine his twin doing something so physical.

"Yes. It was something we both loved. He was checking out a house in Maine when he died."

"Maine?" Now why did that ring a bell in his head? There were a lot of bells ringing, all centered around this woman. Now she was looking at his mouth, and it was making his stomach feel as though he'd just downed three beers in a row. He rubbed his chin and realized he hadn't shaved. "How did you two meet?"

She smiled at the memory, looking out the window again. "I was being a dreamer, looking at this old home that had just gone on the market. Paul was the real estate agent who showed it to me. We hit it off instantly. Both our parents were gone, and we had no one else." Her face flushed, and she looked at him. "Or at least he said he had no one."

Mitch's expression hardened. Paul had wiped him right out of his life, his own twin. "He had me, and he had Betzi. Betzi's not family," he added at her questioning look, "but she might as well be. She practically raised us while our mom was busy with her trips to Dallas and her charities." He watched her face, watched the way each word made her expression change a little. She didn't know. No one could act that well, and he was good at picking out liars. But he could tell she wasn't parting with the whole story.

"He lived here his whole life?" she asked, seeming disconcerted to look up and find him watching her.

He didn't shift his gaze away, settling instead in a relaxed position to watch her more fully. He tapped out a beat on the edge of the table with his fingers. "We were born here, upstairs. We came without much warning," he added at her surprised expression.

She stared at her hands, spread out on the glass tabletop, not all painted up with long nails either. In fact, she had the hands of a woman who worked, with little flecks of paint in the creases of her nails. She looked back at him with those big, gray eyes of hers. "Why did Paul leave?"

Mitch decided not to tell her everything yet. If she were up to something, she might trip up if he didn't give too much away. "I was hoping you could tell me."

She shook her head. "Can I ask you something?"

"Anything," he said with a shrug.

"Why do you keep staring at me?"

Because you're the prettiest damn woman I ever did see. He leveled with her another way, though. He reached across the table and wrapped his fingers around her wrist. She started, pulling away her arm, looking like that spooked horse he'd thought about earlier.

"That's why I keep staring at you."

She kept her arms next to her body, wariness filling her features. "What are you talking about?"

"I know you feel it too. Whenever I've touched you, there's something weird between us, like static electricity, only stronger. It's not that I don't find you attractive, but this is different from sexual attraction."

He saw color flame into her cheeks, and she busied herself with taking a long draw from her tea. Without meeting his eyes, she stood and walked to the refrigerator where she'd seen him put the pitcher of tea. She poured a glass, than halted, staring at something inside. Pulling a jar of tamales from the fridge, she held it up to him. "You eat these too?"

He shrugged. "Bad midnight-snack habit, dipped in hot chili sauce. Paul used to eat them too, by the dozen. I take it he still did." How much had Paul changed over the years? Who had fought his battles for him, or had he just slunk away like he always had? Jenna didn't look like the kind of woman to cause him much trouble.

She put the jar back and closed the door, facing him. "There's something I haven't told you." Her fingers traced a line from her throat to her chest. "It might explain a few things, at least the . . . electricity you're talking about."

Three

Betzi Mulligan basted the ribs again, rocking her head to the beat of Billy Dean's "Billy the Kid." Pretty soon all the football Bobs would rush onto the back lawn hungry as a bunch of cowboys after a cattle run. If Mr. and Mrs. Elliot had ever seen such a sight, they would have fainted dead-out. No one from town had been allowed at the homestead unless they were buying a horse, were paid labor, or were a "somebody." She liked the Elliots well enough, but they were bigger snobs than the family her mother had worked for, and they'd had more money than the Elliots, God rest all their souls.

Mitch had always done what he could to bridge the gap his father had created between the Elliots and the rest of the folks. Truth to tell, Betzi didn't mind the fracas once a week; it broke up the routine. Could be worse things than being one woman around a bunch of sweaty, virile young men. Her mother, Harriet (Etta to her friends), had been brought up to serve in the finest of homes with all the pomp and circumstance high-society Texans required. Betzi had learned her craft from Etta, but had been grateful to escape Dallas city life and work for the Elliots and their coming twins out in the country land.

Betzi could hear the distant hollers of the young men playing that ruffian sport. After she closed the barbecue lid, she turned to flop back down in her lawn chair when movement in the breakfast nook caught her eye. The semicircular glass alcove stuck out from the rest of the house, farther

than the similar music alcove. She narrowed her eyes, trying to look past the reflection. No one was supposed to be
in the house right now.

With her spatula poised like a weapon in front of her,
she crept through the gathering room door, crossed the music alcove and the dining room to the kitchen. The sound
of a woman's voice was even more out of place. Her
mother's quarterly visit wasn't due for another week.

All right, so the spatula wasn't exactly a lethal weapon,
but Betzi wasn't exactly a frail flower either. She puffed
up her shoulders and moved stealthily toward the door
opening. With spatula raised, she took a big step into the
kitchen. "Hands up!" She looked from Mitch sitting at the
table to the young woman standing by the refrigerator.
"Oh."

Mitch covered his face for a moment, but his smile was
genuine and showed not the least bit of irritation. Well, it
wasn't as if she'd interrupted them at a vital moment; they
were nowhere near smooching.

"Mitch! What are you doing in here? I thought you were
out with the Bobs." Betzi looked at the woman. "Now, I
understand finding something better to do, but it sure gave
me a start seeing someone in the house when there
shouldn't have been."

"What were you gonna do, flip the intruder to death?"
Mitch stood and walked over. "Betzi, this is Jenna Elliot."
Betzi raised her eyebrow at the name. She'd never heard
of kin named Jenna. "Jenna, this is Betzi, the presiding
queen of Bluebonnet Manor."

Betzi shook the woman's hand, looking at Mitch for
further explanation. The boy could be as blunt as a board,
but sometimes he could hold back just enough information
to drive a person crazy.

Jenna's and Mitch's gazes met, and something odd
passed between them that Betzi couldn't understand. Just
as quickly, they turned away from each other. Betzi narrowed her eyes at Mitch. "You didn't go off and get married without telling me, did you?"

Jenna's face flushed, and she swore that Mitch's did too. He never blushed, not that she could remember.

Mitch's voice was low when he said, "Jenna is—was Paul's wife."

"Oh, my Lordy, you see why I never jump to conclusions? Never assume, that's what my mama always told me," Betzi said. "Makes an ass out of *u* and *me*. Spells out the word, get it?" She shook her head. "Paul . . . wait a minute. *Was*?"

Jenna nodded, a sad expression on her face. "He died in a car accident nine months ago."

Betzi's heart went cold. "Paul . . . dead? How? When?" She was angry with him for disappearing, but she'd held out hope that he'd come back and explain everything.

Jenna told her about the car accident, and Betzi could see the pain sharply outlined in her features.

"I can't believe it," Betzi muttered, turning away, needing to meet no one's eyes for a moment. It seemed impossible that he was gone, that he'd never come back. She'd imagined the scene so many times, Paul walking in, everyone dealing with the joy of his return, the anger at his departure. She pushed away the burning sensation inside her, wanting to deal with her own pain in private. "When did you say he died?"

"Nine months ago. It took me this long to . . . track down his family."

When the two traded that look again, Betzi got the distinct feeling there was more to it. Not that it was her business. Well, it was her business, but she didn't have rights to ask if it concerned personal family matters.

"Where do you come from, Jenna?" Betzi figured that was a safe enough question.

"A little coastal town in New Hampshire called Oceanside."

"All the way from up there?" She looked at Mitch. "You did invite her to stay in the guest room, didn't you?"

Mitch did, at least, have the decency to look chagrinned. "We didn't get that far yet."

Paul had sure picked a looker, he had, though there was something fragile about her, like she'd seen a lot of unhappiness in her life.

"I appreciate the offer, but I can stay in town. I passed a little motel on the way here I'm sure will do fine."

"Nonsense," Betzi said, waving away that stinker of a motel. "She'll stay right here, won't she?" she asked Mitch, though he wouldn't dare dispute her. She knew her place in the household, and if it had anything to do with manners and social graces, she was in charge.

Mitch, however, didn't look as though he were going to dispute her anyway. He braced a hand against the refrigerator and looked at Jenna. "Yeah, she's going to stay here. We have a lot of catching up to do, don't we?"

Jenna didn't look so sure about the situation, though. Betzi couldn't imagine why she wouldn't jump at the chance to stay there instead of the fleabag in town.

Still, Jenna smiled graciously. "Thank you. I . . . I wasn't actually planning to stay long—"

"Nonsense," Betzi said again. "You certainly didn't come all this way to turn around and go back home again. After the Bobs leave, I'll get the room all ready for you." She rubbed her palms down the front of the apron that read, "Don't piss off the cook." Mitch had bought it for her as a gag gift. "Do you need anything? A drink, snack?"

"I'm all taken care of, thank you."

"I'm glad you looked us up. We've been worried about Paul these years. I'll just be glad to know he was happy."

A shadow passed over Jenna's face. "He was happy," she said after the slightest of pauses. "But I'm sure he missed you all, and this place."

"We missed him. Sure would have liked for him to bring you around. Why did he stay away so long?"

Mitch answered for her in a hard tone of voice. "Seems he had better things to do than think about his home." Another look passed between the two. And then silence, that awkward kind where everyone's trading looks and no one's saying anything.

"Well, I'd better get back to the ribs. The Bobs are still coming for dinner, aren't they?" she asked Mitch.

He shrugged. "Can't turn 'em away now, can we?"

"Don't suppose so. We'd have a riot on our hands, what with them smelling the ribs all day. Nice to meet you, Jenna. Welcome home."

Betzi didn't know why she'd said that, but then sometimes things came out of her mouth for no apparent reason. She just went with it and turned to go back outside.

She might be off—hardly ever, mind you—but there was something strange between the two in the kitchen. Almost an electricity that reminded her of times past, love lost.

Could there be a spark between Paul's widow and his brother? Why, they were both good-looking and legally available. Betzi knew nothing would ever come of it, though. Mitch was a lot of things, some good, some bad. But the man was honorable, and a long-ago vow would keep him from acting on anything that might spark up between them.

"You were saying," Mitch prompted the second the door closed after Betzi.

He was standing far too close for Jenna's comfort, and he smelled far too good. Whatever he was wearing went straight to her senses, clouding them with essences of spice, lemon, and something sweet thrown in. His damp hair was loose around his shoulders, leaving wet patches on his white shirt. One side of his collar wasn't folded down, as though he'd dressed in a hurry.

The cool face of the stainless-steel refrigerator pressed against her back, leaving her with no place to move away from him. It was crazy to feel so . . . so caught up in him like this. It was wrong. She never wanted to feel this way about anybody, but especially not Paul's twin brother.

"The reason for this *thing* we have when we touch," he pushed. "Is because?"

She forced herself to look right into his face, so familiar, yet so foreign. "I have Paul's heart."

That set Mitch back. She saw him swallow, watched the muscles in his neck working. "You mean . . . for real?"

Her words came out in a rush. "For real. I was waiting for a donor, my heart wasn't living up to its end of the bargain. Paul was brain dead after the accident, but his heart was still working. He'd made arrangements, like a will, only he was leaving me his heart. He must have gotten tested to see if we matched, and we did." Her voice dropped to a whisper. "So I got it."

"They took your heart out—"

"And put his in," she finished quickly.

He ran his hand back through his hair, looking down for a moment. "Wow. Wow," he repeated, shaking his head. "I've heard of transplants, but . . ." He looked at the place where her heart beat within her. "Paul."

"I'm sorry."

"Why?"

His eyes held her fast, making her lose her train of thought for a second. That was another difference between Mitch and Paul. Paul had never looked at her as though he were probing her soul. "It's just that, I don't know, sometimes I feel . . . guilty. For getting his heart. I lived, he died." She knew guilt was common among transplant recipients, but she had more reason for feeling that way. If she hadn't been sick, if she'd been able to give him a baby, maybe they wouldn't have moved around so much, maybe he wouldn't have gone to Maine that day.

"You shouldn't feel guilty."

She was grateful that he didn't somehow hold Paul's death against her.

"But it does explain a lot," he continued, letting his gaze drop down and then back up to her face again. "I thought I might be going crazy, feeling . . . strange whenever I touched you. Because of the connection." He got an enlightened look on his face. "That's why I didn't feel him die. Because his heart was still beating . . . is still beating."

His voice lowered, and he stretched out his hand and held it only an inch from her chest. She swore she could feel the heat emanating from his palm. "Inside you." He let his hand drop.

Jenna realized she'd been holding her breath, waiting for him to touch her. She quietly released it, assuring herself she'd have pushed him away if he had.

"They took your heart out and put his in," Mitch was saying as she caught herself staring at his mouth again, caught herself wondering if the hairs around his mouth were soft or prickly. "Did they take out your heart before putting his in? Does it feel . . . different?"

The few people who knew she'd had a transplant asked her questions as though she were some kind of Frankenstein experiment. Some even wanted to see her scar. But Mitch's words didn't smack of that morbid curiosity. Still, talking about those few minutes when she'd had no heart were eerie. It gave a whole new meaning to the term "heartless."

"I can do most of the things anyone can do. But it feels different in a way maybe only you can understand. Paul led me here," she said, feeling sure enough to tell him now. "Now I know why." When Mitch gave her a questioning look, she added, "He wanted to make peace with you." Pinpricks of unease scampered across the back of her neck. That peace, that sense of doing the right thing . . . it would come at her expense, at the expense of the one thing that mattered most—her memories.

He narrowed his eyes, but not suspiciously. "You can feel him?" He looked at the place her heart resided.

She hadn't realized she'd put her hand over her heart. "I feel . . . things. Like the urge to come here, a place I'd never heard about before." She gave a nervous laugh. "Does that sound crazy?"

He shrugged. "I haven't decided yet. Do you get anything else?"

Jenna wasn't ready to tell him about the images she'd gotten from Paul's jewelry. And why was he so ready to believe her, to want more information? "Just feelings, nothing specific."

He walked over to the table where Paul's death certificate lay, stepping over the mound of solid black hair that was Harvey. The pedestal beneath the glass top was a fancy gold pillar of some kind. Fancy table, sculptured throw rug, Italian tiles, and what looked like a mutt. It was an odd combination. And where did Mitch fit into all of it?

The air where Mitch had been standing was filled with that spicy scent. Paul never wore any scent except the stale smell of the cigarettes he thought he was cleverly hiding from her. She walked up behind Mitch. Paul had worn his hair ultrashort. She caught herself reaching out to touch a strand of Mitch's hair and jerked her hand back.

What was wrong with her? She was mixed up, that's all. Paul had been ripped from her life so unexpectedly, and she'd lived with her precious memories of him and nothing more for the last nine months. And now, without any more warning than Paul's death, she'd found his twin brother. And this connection between them, because of Paul's heart. That was confusing things too.

Mitch turned around, obviously surprised to find her standing so close. He held the pictures of her and Paul in his hand. She'd brought their wedding photo and a few of Paul working on their homes.

Her heart lifted. "Do you have pictures of him I could look at?" She smiled at the mere thought of seeing his childhood pictures.

His gaze dropped to her smile, and he turned away and tossed the pictures on the table. "Sure, after dinner. Any minute now twenty guys are going to overtake the back yard, hungry for beer and ribs. We can eat and then I'll send them on their way."

She imagined all those men making grunting noises and jumping on one another. Years of conversing in awkward sign language with people who didn't speak her tongue had ill-prepared her for making small talk with one person, much less a bunch of men who called themselves Bob. "I don't know if I'm up to that kind of socializing."

He reached out and grazed her chin with his crooked finger. "Betzi'd have my ear if I didn't at least introduce our guest to the fellows. Besides, you look like you could use some fattening up. Come on, I'll get your things and show you to your room."

Fattening up? She wanted to dispute that fact, but she realized he was right. Not that *he* had any right to mention it to her. Maybe he should have met her when she was bloated from the steroids, before they'd cut down her dosage.

She followed him, glancing over at the family room the galley kitchen overlooked. Brown leather couch, nooks and crannies that held art objects, and thick cream carpet made the room feel warm. On each side of the huge stone fireplace were twenty-foot-high windows, and through one of those she could see her rental car.

Despite her desire to see Paul's pictures, the car made her eager for escape. Everything she learned about Paul made him feel further from the man she'd married. His family, his home, it all started to obliterate the tidy past Paul had created, the past that had been a part of who he'd been to her. Was there more? A dark secret foreshadowed by the worry gnawing at her? Maybe it was better to hold on to the familiar than to venture into a place where darkness could snatch away the only thing that mattered.

Mitch led her through a utility room and past a back set of stairs. A door opened to the parking area and her car. She pulled the keys out of her pocket, fingering the ignition key. She could leave. Thank Mitch for his hospitality, get the heck out of Dodge. She could return to New Hampshire and pretend this never existed, that this and Mitch were all a bizarre dream.

"Your keys."

Mitch's voice stirred her from thoughts of fleeing. His hand was held out, capable, work-worn hands with long fingers. "I need to get in your trunk for your bags," he said when she kept staring at his hand.

Reluctantly she handed them over, and he popped the trunk and took out one small bag. "This it?"

She merely nodded, still trying to find a way out.

"You pack light for a woman," he said, closing the trunk and heading back to the door. He had her keys. Now he had her bag, which contained her purse and return ticket. There was no escape. But she knew Paul wouldn't allow her to give up this quest. If she left, tomorrow night she'd no doubt find herself on the phone with the travel agent again. She slowly followed him to the door that led back inside.

Why are you doing this to me, Paul? Have you brought me here to make peace with your twin? I can do that right now and leave. But she couldn't leave yet, somehow she knew that. She would have to deal with Paul's past, his betrayal . . . and these shameful feelings she was having every time Mitch was close.

She followed him up the stairs, Harvey-the-mutt close behind. She reached down to pet his mop top, finding the hair silky soft. He looked up at her with adoring black eyes, tongue drooping out. She normally didn't touch animals, steering clear of germs because of her suppressed immune system. Well, she'd just wash her hands right away.

At the top of the stairs, she found herself at the end of a long hallway. She stopped before a gallery of photographs that were lit from above. Her hand went to her throat as she saw pictures of Paul as a youngster.

Paul had a few photos of his parents when they were young, or at least his supposed parents. But he'd explained that all of his childhood pictures had gone up in a fire. She'd never thought anything odd about that; after all, she had few pictures of her younger years herself. Her parents had been more concerned with saving lives and souls than documenting their daughter's life. Jenna had understood that; well, at least most of the time. With all of their moving about and primitive living conditions, there wasn't room for sentimental journeys anyway.

But here, as further proof of Paul's lies, was a wall of

his life, his real parents, real childhood home. Many pictures showed the twins together, driving miniature Jeeps or racing remote-control cars on an elaborate track. Even though they were dressed alike, Jenna could tell the difference between them immediately. Mitch had always been a bit bigger than Paul, more filled out and tan.

Paul had looked happy in an innocent way back then, perhaps free of the melancholia that haunted his life with her. In one picture he laughed, all gap-toothed, while opening presents at a birthday party, Mitch beside him and just as gap-toothed. The backyard was decorated with streamers and balloons and one of those inflatable bouncing tents. The adults in the photo were all dressed in elegant finery, champagne glasses in hand.

In another shot, Paul was studiously trying to lawn bowl, lower lip pulled between his teeth in concentration. How many times had she seen him do that? Mitch stood to the side, perhaps giving him instruction. Why hadn't he shared any of this with her? The ache inside was double: one for his betrayal, and the other for the loss of him. No matter what, she loved him.

She wiped her palm across her cheek, not even aware that she'd been crying. There was another ache inside her too. Seeing these photos reminded her of what their child might have looked like. These pictures represented the three ways she had lost, and in that moment grief overcame her. It had been a long time since she'd let herself cry, and she hated herself for giving in now.

She'd forgotten all about Mitch until he said, "I'm sorry."

She turned to him, his image blurry with her tears. For a moment she let herself think it was Paul, apologizing for leaving her, for putting her through this. She started to say something, but her words came out a soft whimper.

She heard him whisper, "Don't cry," and then he moved close, sliding his hand up into her hair and pulling her against him. Not Paul. He felt different. His arm held her close, pressing her cheek into the hardness of his shoulder. He brushed his jaw back and forth against the top of her head. She was enveloped by him, by his strength, and at the same time, his tenderness.

But the feelings that swept her into their fold were quite different, startling in their intensity. She desperately wanted to slide her arms around his waist and hold him close, to feel all of his body against hers. She craved his warmth, and the comfort he offered. She felt him inhale deeply, felt his exhale of air on her hair. This felt so right, so completely, totally—*wrong*!

Her eyes snapped open, and she stepped back. He looked away, running his hand through his hair. His lips parted, as though he were going to say something. When he looked up, she realized she was watching him. Instinctively she turned toward the pictures of her husband, the only man she loved, the only man she would ever love.

Her stomach trembled. What was happening to her? It was Paul's heart, binding her and Mitch in a way that couldn't be explained. Her body was responding to Mitch as though he were Paul, she was sure of it. It was another reason for her to flee this house.

Mitch picked up her bag from where he'd set it down and continued to the end of the hallway. Shakily, she followed, buying time to gather her wits by pausing to look to the right, where the wall became a balcony that overlooked an immense room below.

She looked up to see Mitch watching her warily from the open doorway. His wide jaws tensed, the muscles in his neck flexed. She pushed herself forward, concentrating on the doorway and not the man.

"Don't feel as though you have to . . . offer me comfort. I'm quite used to handling it myself."

"I'll keep that in mind," he said as she walked by him. He set her bag on a wooden chest at the foot of a beautiful swan bed. The carpet and window dressings were shades of mint-green.

"It's lovely," she said, glad that her voice was firm and

polite. "I'd like to take a shower and change before dinner."

"There's the bathroom, walk-in closet," he said, opening and closing doors.

She could feel his gaze on her as she studiously avoided meeting it. Instead, she looked around the room.

"There's something you should know," he said, making her turn to face him just by the hard tone in his voice. "If you're entertaining any ideas of cashing in on Paul's inheritance, forget it."

For a moment she couldn't say a word. And then, all she could do was stupidly repeat the word, "Inheritance?"

Mitch stood stock-still in the framed opening, arms at his side. "His half of all this." He made a gesture that she assumed included the entire estate. "It was set up that if Paul died before me, the balance goes to me unless he has an heir." The muscle in his jaw flexed again. "Just so you understand."

Jenna crossed her arms over her chest. "You think I have an ulterior motive to claim part of some estate I didn't even know about?"

"Dunno."

"In other words, you think I'm lying. That I knew about this, and that I came here to scrounge something out of Paul's family." He only blinked, nothing more. "When I married Paul, he had a thousand dollars in his bank account. That's all I know about his vast amount of wealth . . . his inheritance." She bit out the last word, narrowing her eyes at him. This felt much more comfortable, animosity instead of tenderness.

Mitch had an amazing capacity not to let anything show on his face, just as he had after holding her in the hallway. "You really didn't know anything about the inheritance?"

The money in the car. The thought came to mind and clicked into place like part of a jigsaw puzzle. "No, I didn't."

Mitch saw the flicker of knowledge in her eyes before her denial. He'd wanted to clear the air with her, but mostly he'd wanted to put some negative distance between them. What he'd felt in the hallway had jolted him no less than the time he'd stuck his finger in a socket when he was a kid. He'd held her against his body and felt . . . *felt* Paul's love for her. It overwhelmed him with a need to protect her, to keep her safe and warm and loved. Mitch had never felt anything like it before, never felt such a deep sense of love or need.

He shook away the thought, concentrating on the woman standing before him. She was lying to him. He'd let his judgment get clouded, especially when he'd held her in the hallway . . . a surge of heat swept through him at the memory of what he'd felt, but he pushed it away.

"You're lyin'."

She blinked at the bluntness of his statement. "I'm not lying. I never knew about any of this."

"You knew something, though."

She looked guiltily away, arms still tight around herself. "Did Paul ever take money from his inheritance?"

Her question threw him off. He was ready for sidestepping, or further denial. "Four times."

Her face went pale, annoying him with how fast it broke down his wall of reserve. The softness of her voice turned low and dull when she asked, "When was the last time?"

"Last November."

She looked away, pressing her lips together. "Was it four hundred thousand dollars?" she asked in a near-whisper.

"Yes."

"He had it in the car with him when he died. I . . . I didn't know where he'd gotten it, didn't want to know. I couldn't find any evidence that he'd taken a loan, and no one came looking for payment."

Her gray eyes looked straight into his as she'd said that, and he saw truth there. Could he trust himself, though? This woman had already knocked him off balance in more than one way. "What did you do with the money?"

"I . . . spent it."

Ah, just as the cynical side of him suspected. She'd probably fixed up the house, bought a new car. Before he could ask her on what, though, she answered him: "I paid medical bills with it. Our insurance company weaseled out of paying for some of the cost of my surgery."

She'd looked away, which was lucky for Mitch. He didn't know what had shown in his eyes.

"It's all gone," she admitted, "but I can repay you. I can . . . sell the house, buy something smaller."

Mitch knew he lacked in the area of perceptiveness and sensitivity, so why was it incredibly obvious to him that the prospect of selling her home broke her heart? "I'm sure we can work something out," Mitch found himself saying. Four hundred thousand wasn't worth putting this fragile-looking woman out of her home over. If she didn't ask for anything more, he'd let it go without a second thought. After all, Paul had taken it out to do as he wanted. "What'd he do with all that money?"

"I . . . I don't know."

He could see the pain of her admission. He steeled himself and said, "How could you not know what your husband did with eight hundred thousand dollars?"

She winced, making him regret the words. "I don't know. Maybe he put the money into the houses. He handled the financial end of everything."

She was lying again, or at least holding something back. "He take drugs?"

She threw her hands down, facing him squarely. "No!"

"Maybe you didn't know—"

"I would have known. He didn't take drugs, he didn't gamble. We were together . . ." Her chin trembled, and she turned away. "A lot."

What this woman did to his insides. Mitch shook his head. She was pale and delicate, like an angel, yet beneath that he saw strength.

"Maybe I should leave," she said, walking to her bag. "I don't see any point in—"

He met her at the bag, wrapping his fingers around one

small wrist, feeling that connection again. "Don't go." The urgency in his voice startled him. He let go of her and tempered his voice. "I need to know about Paul, about his life after he left here. You're the only one who can tell me." He saw reluctance in her eyes and pressed further. "I'm the only one who can tell you about his life before he left. Don't you want to know who your husband was?"

She swallowed hard, looking up at him as he stood too close. "I'm not sure if I want to know any more. I know too much already."

"That he lied to you." She nodded. "Don't you want to know why?"

"No."

How could she not want the truth? Mitch wanted to shake her, but he'd already overstepped the boundaries as far as touching her went. "Nothing is more important than the truth. You know just enough to haunt you, have just enough answers to spur a thousand questions." He knew that too well. For years Paul was the only one who could give him the truth, and now he was dead. But Mitch's initial feeling when he'd first seen Jenna had proven true: she could give him the answers that might free him from the past. Or bind him even tighter.

"I can live with the questions," she said. The trembling was gone, and she squared her shoulders and stood tall before him. "What I can't live without are my memories of Paul, of what we shared together. His past may have been a lie, but our life together was real and true." She swallowed again. "I don't want any part of his inheritance, not money or property. He left me his love and wonderful memories. But there is something he didn't leave me, something I want very badly."

If not money or assets, what could she mean? Her face had flushed a becoming pink, and he braced himself. He had a feeling it wasn't going to be simple. "What is it?"

"I wanted to have his baby. We couldn't try before because of my condition, and now he's gone." Her gaze had dipped for a second, but now swept across his face in such a tender manner, he actually felt touched by her. "You're his twin brother; you share his genetics, his looks. You are the closest thing I have to Paul, and in you I have one last chance to make a long-time dream come true. Maybe . . . maybe this is part of why Paul brought me here."

Mitch felt a tightness circle through his chest. His voice had gone low and hoarse when he asked, "What are you asking me?"

"I want you to give me Paul's baby."

Four

Jenna took her sweet time in the shower, anxious to put as much time as possible between her request and seeing Mitch again. She pulled out a white jumpsuit with a high collar so her scar wouldn't show. Her hand automatically pulled the brush through her hair as it dried, but she stared at nothing.

Was she crazy? Absolutely, positively. She'd had no intention of asking Mitch for something as outrageous as his sperm. But like the pieces of Paul's past that clicked together, so had her request. Even she hadn't realized where her words were going until they were out of her mouth. Paul knew how much she wanted a baby. Was the baby, or prospect of having one, her part of Paul's inheritance, the consolation for finding his lies?

The look on Mitch's face! Jenna's mouth quirked into a smile. With his accusations so easily spilling from his mouth earlier, her one request had rendered him speechless.

She'd gone on to say that she only wanted him to donate sperm to a fertility facility so that she could be impregnated with it, that she would sign papers disallowing any claim on him or Paul's estate on the child's behalf. His lips had been slightly parted, eyes wide with disbelief. A desire to walk closer to him, to touch him in her appeal, had overcome her, but touching Mitch was dangerous. She shivered with the memory of being in his arms, safe and protected . . . and something more. Not more, she amended. Different. And not safe.

It was her heart, she decided. She and Mitch shared a connection through Paul's heart. *Keep that in mind. Don't lose your head over it.*

When she couldn't linger any more, she finally stepped out into the hallway. Party sounds filtered in through the French doors of the two-story room across from her own. Through the upper windows, she could see men of various ages lounging around, laughing and eating. She couldn't see Mitch, not that she was particularly looking for him.

She shivered at the thought of going out there and trying to be polite, answering questions. The events of the day were wearing on her, so many people to deal with. And she wouldn't be able to meet Mitch's eyes without giving away the apprehension over her request. Her fingers curled over the wood railing on the balcony. Slowly she pushed herself away from it and walked down the hall. The collage of pictures caught her eye again, but instead of seeing the pictures, she saw Mitch pulling her into his arms. She continued on, down the back stairs that led to the kitchen.

Wasting time, she poured herself another iced tea, then took out the myriad bottles of pills she needed to take every evening. After piling them on a small plate, she put the bottles back in the flowered travel bag. Peering around the opening to the French doors leading outside, she spotted Mitch sitting off to the side in a chair. For an instant her pulse jumped, imagining it was Paul. Paul with long, honey-colored hair surrounded by friends. No, not Paul at all.

She could hear them talking. "Hey, Bob, pass me a beer, will ya?" "Sure, Bob." "Thanks, Bob." One man tossed a beer to Mitch. "Ya oughtta have a beer at your own party, Bob."

Mitch didn't even open the bottle. He was poured into a lounge chair, in the center of the men, yet in a way she innately understood, set apart from them too. He looked lost in thought. Was he thinking about her request? What would she do if he said yes? Just that thought made her pulse speed.

As he started to look in her direction, someone tossed a football in his lap. Jenna pulled back into the kitchen and busied herself with popping her pills. Inevitably, as though she had no control over it, her gaze sought Mitch again. He was sexy and beautiful in a way that Paul wasn't, and she tried to figure out why.

"Ah, that's where you're hiding."

Betzi set several tins on the long counter that separated the kitchen from the family room. Harvey, the black mop, followed her in, tongue lolling out of his mouth. When he saw Jenna, he seemed to find her more interesting.

Embarrassed at having been caught watching Mitch, Jenna moved away from the window and smiled sheepishly. "Hiding is right, I'm afraid." She nodded toward the noise, the sudden shriek of laughter outside. "I'm not up to that kind of socializing right now."

Betzi's vivid blue eyes smiled along with every muscle in the sharp angles of her face. "Seems strange to have a guest in the house and not introduce her around. But can't say as I blame you. Mitch just cut off their beer supply, and before long, I guarantee they'll all be gone." She lifted an elegantly arched, thin eyebrow. "Well, all except Mitch, of course."

"Of course."

"Would you like me to bring in some ribs for you?" At Jenna's apprehensive look, she added, "I won't even tell anyone you're in here."

"I'd appreciate that. They smell delicious."

Betzi winked. "It's my perfume. Works on the men every time."

Jenna felt herself giggle. How long had it been since she'd done something so simple and wonderful as giggle? Obviously much too long, because the action felt foreign to her.

"I can give you a supply to, you know, help in the romance department."

Jenna held up her hand. "I'm not shopping, but thanks anyway."

"Nonsense," Betzi said. "Everyone needs some romance in their life."

That image of Mitch holding Jenna upstairs rocketed into her mind. "That's the last thing I need right now, believe me."

Betzi acknowledged that statement with a smile and lift of her eyebrow that hinted at doubt as she headed back around the corner. She returned with a rack of the most sinfully delicious ribs Jenna had ever tasted. She sat on one of the stools at the long counter, out of sight of the commotion outside. The stools reflected the less gaudy aspects of the house's decor, made of metal with a galloping horse on the back support. The padded seat simulated the hide of a painted horse. They didn't go with the marble countertops or fancy tile floor at all.

"How did you and Mitch meet?"

Jenna blinked. "You mean Paul, don't you?"

"No, Mitch. You seemed to already know each other when you arrived here."

"No, we've never met before. I never even knew about him."

Betzi considered that, running her fingers down the close-cropped strands of silver. "You'll forgive my forwardness, but it comes with the territory of being the queen of Bluebonnet Manor." Those last words she spoke in an amused tone. "I know the ebb and flow of this place, and everyone in it. When I walked in earlier, when you and Mitch were in here, I felt the stirring of a storm. We don't get many twisters our way, but when a small one sweeps through, I've always felt it long before."

Betzi waited patiently for Jenna to put her thoughts together. What kind of storm had she detected? "I don't know if Mitch told you, but I have Paul's heart."

"He told me."

"Mitch said he and Paul had this connection between them. Because I now have Paul's heart, Mitch and I have the connection. That's all it is." At Betzi's skeptical expression, Jenna looked around and segued into a different subject. "Part of me wants to know why Paul left this behind, and part of me doesn't want to know too much."

"I suspect it had something to do with his parents' deaths." A shadow passed over Betzi's features. "But we don't know why he left."

"What happened to their parents?"

"That's something you'll have to take up with Mitch. Paul's leavetaking hit Mitch hard. Roams the house, unable to sleep through the night ever since. Unanswered questions are the worst."

"But sometimes the truth can wreak more havoc than the not-knowing."

Betzi leaned against the opposite side of the counter. "Nonsense. Truth's always better than hiding your head in manure."

Jenna had never been around people who spoke so bluntly, and she had no experience in the realm of arguing. "I'm not so sure about that," was as close as she got.

Betzi let that pass and thankfully changed the subject. "Anything you want to know about Paul and Mitch, just ask. I'd be glad to tell you, from their first diapers on."

"I know all I need to about Mitch," Jenna said with more vehemence than she'd intended. "I mean, I don't . . . I want to know about Paul. He told me such a different past. He didn't even have a Texas accent."

Betzi waved that off. "Their father tried to eradicate that. He wanted them to sound like city boys, uptight and sophisticated. Paul tried to please his father, he did. Mitch was always the rebel. Said he was born in East Texas and was proud to sound like it."

Jenna could clearly imagine him saying that. "Paul and Mitch are so different."

"Always were. Mitch was the protector, fighting Paul's fights, taking up his side no matter if he was wrong or right. Paul hated confrontation. Now don't get me wrong about Mitch, he didn't go round picking fights. But if there was some injustice, he'd do his best to make it right, especially if it involved Paul."

"Shame on you, talking about me behind my back," came Mitch's voice from the opening.

Mitch only looked slightly chagrinned, but it was with some curiosity in his eyes that he met her gaze. The sun slanted down through the skylight, lighting his hair to a golden shade of honey. Even those tiny hairs around his mouth were set off.

"Watch it or I'll tell her how long it took to potty-train you," Betzi said, straightening. "Are the Bobs gone?"

"Every last one of them. Everything's bagged up for Juan to take in the morning. Thanks, Betz." He leaned close and gave her a quick peck on the cheek.

"Always my pleasure. I'm off, then."

Jenna's throat tightened at the prospect of being alone with Mitch. Bad things happened when they were alone.

"Thank you for the company," Jenna said, giving Betzi a warm, genuine smile.

"It was a pleasure chatting with you, m'dear," Betzi said just as warmly. "I'm off tomorrow, but I hope to have another chance to talk."

"That would be nice. I'd like to hear more about Paul, his childhood." Jenna made a point to look at Mitch then, to make sure he understood it was Paul's life she was interested in, not Mitch's.

As soon as Betzi closed the door behind her, the tension in the room steadily rose. Jenna reached down to pet Harvey. "Paul had a dog like this for a while," she said, wanting to fill the silence. "He got hit by a car." Paul had taken care of the details, not telling her anything. He'd even tried to hide his tears from her.

Mitch leaned against the far end of the counter, but she could feel his presence as though he stood next to her. "Harvey was a stray. Don't know where he came from, but one day he just appeared out by the stables. He was kinda cute, so I decided to keep him. 'Sides, Norma Jean wouldn't have let me take him away anyway."

Jenna kept her gaze on the dog, trying to pick Paul's voice out in Mitch's. Not even close. So Paul hadn't ditched his accent as part of his lie. That made her feel a little better.

"Who's Norma Jean?"

"The mama cat who adopted him."

"Oh," she said, drawing the word out. "A black dog named after a big white rabbit."

"Yeah. How'd you know?"

She looked up at him then. "I was kidding, actually. You named him after *the* Harvey?" When she realized they were sharing a smile, she turned back to the dog.

"No one could see him for the first few weeks I started spotting him at the stables. Not that he was really invisible, just sneaky. My employees thought I was seeing things, so I named him Harvey."

Jenna smiled, but kept it aimed at the dog. "Now you're too big to be sneaky, huh fellow?" Then something he'd said made her look up. "Your employees?"

"I breed horses." He met her gaze, but kept his expression completely straight. "You know, selling the offspring, training the young horses . . . stud service." Those last two words hung in the air, which had become tense again.

Was that how he'd taken her request? "I didn't mean it like that."

"Is it so different?"

"Yes!" She came to her feet, moving closer before she could think better of it. "I'm not asking you to . . . well, it's not because I want champion bloodlines."

He leaned close, making her body tense. He smelled like mesquite smoke. "No, you want Paul's bloodline. Admit it: you want to pretend the baby is Paul's."

"Yes," she said on a breath, feeling warm all of a sudden. "I want to feel as though I have something of him. What's wrong with that? It doesn't hurt anyone."

Something shadowed his eyes, and he looked away for a moment. "Come on, let's go look at those pictures you wanted to see."

Without thinking, she reached out and grabbed his arm.

He stopped, pausing for a moment before turning to face her. She quickly let go, feeling that disturbing sensation pass between them.

"What about my request?"

"I can't."

He looked at her, and she tried hard not to let him know how his words affected her. With two words, he'd crushed her hopes and dreams. She blinked, trying to keep all emotion from her face. It was a crazy request, she knew that. Certainly out of the ordinary. But how could Mitch equate it with stud horses?

Mitch broke eye contact and walked through the doorway. She followed him through the long dining room with a shiny black table inlaid with stone. A matching china cabinet and buffet lined the wall facing her. On the opposite wall hung a gorgeous painting of an ocean wave that gradually transformed into running horses. Late afternoon sunlight filled the music alcove, where a magnificent piano gleamed black and shiny, complemented by a lapiz stone bench that matched the dining table.

She paused there, sliding her fingers across the surface. "Did Paul play?"

"Yeah. He was pretty good too, though he hated it." Mitch took a step toward her, head tilted. "Can you play?"

"I've never tried." Forced piano lessons were hardly part of her childhood. She didn't understand the interest in his eyes.

"What about now that you have Paul's heart? Can you play now?"

Something about the question set her on edge. "No, I'm sure I can't. Paul never even let on that he knew how to play."

"What about memories? Can you see or feel anything from his past?"

"No," she lied.

Suspicion clouded Mitch's eyes, but he turned and continued on. What was the big deal about playing piano? She followed him, wondering at the enigma he presented. Suspicious, cold, but with a streak of tenderness he probably hated.

The gathering room was two steps below the level of the rest of the house. Upstairs was the balcony and the door to her guest room, and on the wall facing her the largest television screen she'd ever seen. Flanking that were built-in speakers as tall as the ceiling. To the left of that was another fireplace made of carved marble. A teal-colored leather couch ran along the entire back wall.

Mitch nodded for her to take a seat, walking to a built-in bookcase that looked to house every electronic device known to man. He pulled out two large photo albums. Her body tensed as she realized they would probably be sitting side by side on the couch, looking over the pictures. Not even Harvey's presence made her feel better as he dropped down near the side of the couch. He started licking his leg, preening like a cat.

On the way back to the couch, Mitch pressed a button on a remote-control unit and aimed it back at the bookcase, waking up an impressive stereo setup. Rock music poured from everywhere, even the ceiling, though a softer variety than what she'd heard earlier. Behind Mitch, steps led up to a half-moon bar that had a lighted column of bubbling water behind it. With another press of a button, the lights above the couch came on, leaving the rest of the room lit only by the fading daylight.

The pool of light made her feel cozy, and that put her on edge even more. She focused on the bronze sculpture of galloping horses on the coffee table, and then beyond. The room was arranged in small gatherings of chairs and love seats, set up for multiple conversations. Even though she felt uncomfortable around crowds, what she wouldn't have given to have a few people scattered about. Instead of being alone here with Mitch.

Gold-and-crystal wall sconces were arranged all around the room, gaudy in their intricacy. The couch and chairs were simple elegance, but most everything else about the room screamed excess. She looked up as Mitch walked over, set the albums on the glass tabletop, and dropped down on the cushy sofa beside her.

Jenna found herself saying, "The couch is yours, isn't it? I mean, you chose it. But the sconces, the coffee tables, they're your parents'. Right?"

He didn't keep the surprise from his face. "How'd you know?"

How did she know? "I guess I finally figured out why the house's furnishings are so eclectic. Some of it belonged to your parents, but you've been putting in your touches here and there. Like the stools at the kitchen counter and the horse painting in the dining room."

He bent one knee as he sat facing her on the couch, his right arm resting along the top of the couch. "Very right. But you still haven't said how you figured that out."

It startled her to realize she felt, for that moment, as though she knew Mitch better than she knew Paul. "I handled the interior decoration of the houses we renovated. I have an eye for styles and the personality they reflect. Somehow I don't see you buying the coffee table with the golden cherubs holding the glass top."

His laugh was low as he looked at the coffee table at their feet. "I hate this stuff. But it's all I have of my parents." Abruptly he pulled one of the photo albums from the table and opened it. "I don't know what you're looking for exactly." He pushed the album toward her. "But look to your heart's content."

She thought for a moment that he was going to leave her to it, and for some odd reason that disappointed her. Instead, he leaned against the arm he'd propped up on the couch and watched her, making her wish he had left.

Mitch couldn't remember a time he'd felt so off balance. As he watched Jenna flip through the pages of his and Paul's lives, he tried to compare these feelings to anything else that had happened in his life, but this was something altogether different.

Her outrageous request for his sperm had sent a twister

through his psyche. He should have been insulted, shocked. But the reason behind her request stirred something he never felt: jealousy. Jenna was so devoted to Paul, loved him so much, that she was willing to make an unheard-of request of a virtual stranger. The fact that she readily admitted she would consider the baby Paul's stung even more. There was a time he'd have done anything for his twin, but not now. Not until he knew the truth.

Unbidden, a vivid image of him and Jenna making love flashed through his mind. Naked bodies, slick with sweat, and Jenna murmuring his name—not Paul's. He sucked in a breath, then coughed to cover it. He waved away her concern, ducking his head.

Despite his cover, his body had taken full notice of that image, and that was something Mitch couldn't pretend away. Cripes, he wasn't a teenager anymore. He was twenty-eight, a successful businessman and horse rancher, and most importantly, sitting next to his brother's wife.

No matter that Paul was dead, a vow was a vow. And that hot summer day when he and Paul had come to blows over a woman, they had vowed then and there never to get involved with a woman the other had feelings for. They both dumped the object of desire and made a blood promise. It was a turning point in their relationship. For the first time they realized how unique and special their bond was.

Having the "coughing fit" under control, Mitch leaned back and watched Jenna again. She smelled sweet and clean, she looked warm and soft. She was Paul's wife, the woman he'd loved. Hadn't Mitch felt that so strongly, and then when she'd grabbed his arm in the kitchen, something else: Mitch felt Paul's plea to protect her.

She'd said Paul's heart had led her here, and now Mitch believed her. He had to look past the bizarre attraction he felt for her, an attraction that would lead nowhere, and find the truth. If Jenna could "feel" Paul, maybe through that connection she could tell Mitch what had happened the night their parents died. He already knew that Jenna wasn't going to open that door readily, because that door could reveal an ugly truth that would rock their worlds.

Mitch wasn't afraid to face it. Jenna obviously was. The truth had more dire consequences for him, and not knowing haunted his days, kept him from opening his soul and letting anyone in. He had to know, and he wasn't willing to protect Jenna at the cost of that truth.

She looked at him then. "How old was Paul here?" She pointed at a picture of Paul sitting on Mickey Mouse's lap at Disney World.

"We were nine." Mitch knew she hadn't asked his age, but where he and Paul were concerned, they were . . . well, they simply were.

What did surprise him was she never confused him and Paul. She smiled faintly at a picture of the twins in tuxedos at the age of ten, attending a fancy party in Dallas. Her finger rested on Paul's image, making Mitch's stomach twist. Beyond her smile, though, he could see the hurt of Paul's betrayal. Like in the hallway, except that she wasn't crying this time. He was glad; he couldn't afford to hold her like that again.

Her faint smile disappeared when she got to the section of his and Paul's teenage years. High school dances, proms, and Mitch and Paul with their dates. He couldn't even remember the names of the girls in the photos. Paul hadn't dated much, had only gotten really serious about one woman. Mitch stiffened at the thought, catching Jenna looking over at the movement.

"Bad memories?" she said, looking back at a picture of Mitch kissing his date's cheek, hamming it up for the camera.

"Nah. Don't even remember her name." That wasn't the woman he'd thought about.

"You seem to have dated a lot more than Paul did."

"He was looking for something . . . deeper. I only went out for fun. Most of the girls in town were only interested in one thing." At her lifted eyebrow, he added, "Our money."

"Oh, that explains your distrust."

He narrowed his eyes. "There's more to it than that."

She backed down, turning the next page. It was her turn to stiffen at a picture of Paul among a group of people during a picnic. She pointed to the one particular woman Mitch had just been thinking about.

"Who is that?"

Her question was posed innocently, but he detected something tremulous beneath her voice. "Becky White. She's the one Paul got most serious about."

Jenna was blinking rapidly, though not in danger of crying. "When he left town . . . did she go with him?"

"No, he left her behind too. Why?"

"Just wondered," she said, lifting her shoulders. She didn't fool him for a second. She was lying again. "She's from here then?"

"Yeah, from, as my dad used to say, the white trash side of town. My parents couldn't stand her, thought she was a gold digger. I think she reminded my father of where he'd come from; he grew up in the same part of town she did." He focused on Jenna, curious about her reaction. She quickly turned the page, asking some question about another picture.

"You know her, don't you?"

She didn't meet his eyes. "How could I know her?" Another second or five of his relentless stare. "I don't know her."

She had a cute chin, slightly pointed, and he turned that chin toward him. "Why are you lying to me?"

"I'm not," she stated, moving away as though his fingers were on fire.

"Did she send you here?"

That question jarred her, and she slammed the album closed. "I have never met the woman."

"She's dead."

That didn't seem to surprise her any. Jenna stood, holding the album to her chest like a shield of armor. "I need to get some rest. It's been a long day."

The sunlight had long faded, leaving them in a dark

room but for the puddle of light on the couch. "Jenna, I want answers. It's not asking too much."

"Yes it is." She turned, setting the album down as she walked up the two steps and around the corner. "Just like my request was asking too much of you."

He heard her footsteps on the stairs, then watched her walk toward her room. Her head was bent low, shoulders stiff, as she disappeared into her room and quietly closed the door behind her. Mitch wanted to follow her, confront her. But his body stayed rooted to the floor as he realized what had set off the warning bell before.

Paul had died nine months ago in Maine.

And so had Becky White.

Five

Jenna's mind wouldn't shut down. Images and feelings bombarded her, refusing to let her flip the closed sign and turn off the lights.

On the other side of her door she could hear the television. Mitch kept the volume low, but the base rumbled right through the door. Betzi had said he couldn't sleep at night. Jenna pictured him sitting on the couch washed in the glow of the television. She sighed, turning over for the hundredth time. The man was impossible, insensitive and uncooperative. So why was she picturing him at all?

Guilt propelled her from bed, and she whispered an apology to Paul. *It's because of my heart, and your connection to him. That's the only reason I'm having these feelings. I don't want them, believe me! The guy's a jerk, nothing like you at all.*

Her traitorous body agreed with that last part, flushing with the heat of remembering the way he'd touched her in the hallway. She hadn't so much as had a thought about sex since her surgery. She was just now gaining back her weight, but the scar was still deep red, still looked like a zipper that Dr. Frankenstein had left behind to open her up again if need be. The only man she wanted to see her naked, to make love with, was Paul.

She wore silk pajamas, and even those she buttoned way up to her neck. For a moment she stood at the door, listening. Maybe Mitch had fallen asleep on the couch.

Jenna stepped out into the hallway. The television sent

crazy reflections across the walls, but downstairs the lights were out. Only the recessed hallway lights were still burning. Her intention was to keep close to the wall and walk down to the gallery again, but she found herself walking to the balcony.

Just as she'd pictured, Mitch sat in the undulating lights, arm extended as he aimed the remote control, feet up on the coffee table. He wore white cotton pants and no shirt, hair loose and wild-looking, as if he'd been running his fingers through it. She had given no indication that she was up there, yet he started to look in her direction.

She moved on down the hallway, not ready for another confrontation with him. Tomorrow morning she would leave. She could not let Paul keep her here any longer. Besides, she and Mitch had come to an impasse. He would not help her, and she could not help him. Learning the truth was too high a price for her memories. She knew that Mitch wasn't telling her the whole story, just as she was holding back. It was just as well.

There was another door on the right after she passed the foyer opening. It was closed, but she found herself pausing before it. She pushed herself on, stopping at her destination. The overwhelming grief didn't come this time, though she was enveloped in a bittersweet warmth as she studied each picture. She reached out, touching a young Paul on a tricycle. He looked so happy, and it made Jenna face the truth: those pictures back home weren't lying. Behind Paul's smiles lingered a shadow, and that shadow originated here, probably at the time he'd left. Probably because of the reason he'd left.

She'd hoped to take a picture or two home with her, but they would remind her of that shadow. Besides, she'd have to ask Mitch, and she didn't want to ask him for anything else. She'd be fine with never seeing him again.

Coward! her inner voice cried out.

Yes, she was a coward. Because she could still feel Mitch standing there pressing her cheek against his shoulder, could still feel the way his hard chest felt against her breasts . . . *Stop it!*

In keeping with her admitted cowardice, she decided to take herself back to bed before Mitch came up and found her there with a flush on her cheeks. She stayed close to the left wall, hoping that Mitch wouldn't see her walk by.

As she passed the door she'd noticed before, her body came to a halt.

That anxious feeling crept through her. She stared at the fancy brass door knob. Before she knew it, she had opened the door and stepped inside.

In the light from the hallway, she made out a bed and dresser. French doors led out onto a balcony, and faint moonlight spilled in through the square panes of glass.

It was Paul's room. She knew it, though nothing in particular gave her that impression. She tried to turn around, not wanting to go any farther. She didn't belong there, did not want to be there. Dread edged in on her, the same way it had when she'd approached this house.

Her feet took her to the bed anyway, and she found her hand hovering over the tufted surface of the bedspread. Carved bedposts adorned each corner of the bed, and she redirected her hand toward them. Like the pine tree earlier, she felt as though they could keep her from sitting on the bed, or going farther into the room.

The air conditioner kicked on, washing cold, fresh air down on her face and shoulders. Her fingers curled around the wood, and her body went stiff. Anguish, deep and complete, overtook her. Anguish, remorse, and the sound of Paul's muffled cries. The sensations crashed through her like cymbals, dizziness dropping her to her knees. Jenna thought nothing could be as terrible as what she'd felt upon hearing of Paul's death, but this was far, far worse.

What have you done? A woman's voice rang through Jenna's head, urgent words filled with shock. And again, Paul's anguish rocked her. She curled up into a ball, overwhelmed by his wracking sobs.

"What have you done?" It was her own voice now uttering the words over and over again.

"My God, what's wrong?"

Jenna lifted her head, finding Mitch at the doorway, chest heaving. All she could do was tell him, "I don't know," in a throaty voice that didn't even sound like her.

He dropped down beside her, checking her for perhaps some injury. "What happened?"

Before she could stop herself, she reached for him. Her arms went around his neck, and she buried her face against his bare chest. She couldn't stop crying; Paul's anguish still had her in its hold. It was only the feel of Mitch's arms sliding around her waist that started to quell the tears. She felt like a lost little girl, all curled up against him, unable to think of letting go. She couldn't think past the safe, warm way he made her feel. He held her tight, his cheek touching her forehead, one hand sliding up and down her back.

When the tears subsided at last, exhaustion crippled her. She didn't want to move, did not want to leave the warmth of Mitch's body. She wiped her eyes and nose on her sleeve.

He kept stroking her back as he softly said, "Jenna, tell me what happened."

She slowly lifted her head, finding herself looking at his mouth. He still hadn't shaved, but the hairs were long enough to be soft and not prickly. Her cheek brushed against those hairs, and she moved slowly back and forth. All of a sudden she wasn't tired anymore. She hadn't felt so alive since she could remember, body pressed against his, the feel of his soft hair twining between her fingers.

When she raised her eyes to his, he was watching her, pupils wide and dark. Their mouths were almost touching, so close her lower lip felt the hairs just below his. The anguish had left her in a daze, feeling needy and empty. But Mitch completed her, filled her. The hand he'd been stroking her back with slipped up into her hair, sending goose bumps over her neck. She closed her eyes, leaning forward the slightest bit, just enough to feel the softness of

his lips. He opened his mouth a little, moving his lower lip
along the bottom edge of her upper lip. She became aware
of his other hand, squeezing softly where he held her waist.

She let out a sigh as desire surged through her. Their
mouths were still grazing, testing. He'd been eating chocolate brownies, and that made her hungry in a way that had
nothing to do with food. Blood rushed to her every nerve
ending, making them ache to feel his touch. She felt the
heat emanating from his body, enveloping her in that spicy
sweet scent. She wanted to merge with him, to melt right
into him. His skin felt hot beneath her hands, soft skin,
hard beneath. Her fingers swam in the waves of his hair,
and even that seemed so intimate, so possessive.

She'd never felt anything like this before, this urgency,
this rush that enveloped all her senses. Her eyes opened
slightly, and in the dim light she saw that his eyes were
closed, lost as she, lost . . .

Way too lost. She scrambled to find her way back.
Wherever this was, this place of heat and desire and passion, was not where she belonged. It was a dangerous, foreign land. Somehow, through the mist, she knew this. But
her body screamed that she belonged right there, and nowhere else.

*No, I belong with Paul. Paul, my husband. This is
wrong.*

"Oh, my . . . oh, my," she mumbled, losing her balance
in her hurry to get away. She found her footing, but her
knees were so weak, she dropped down on the bed.

Mitch had pulled his knees up, rubbing his face with
both hands. He gave his head a shake and looked at her,
that sexy haze still in his eyes. "Now that you've got me
totally inside out and upside down, you wanna tell me what
that was all about?"

How could his voice sound so steady? She looked away
from him, shame reddening her face, but he drew her back
the same way Paul had drawn her into the room. She caught
her gaze drifting down to the mouth she'd almost kissed,
and to her horror, still wanted to. Why didn't it feel any-

thing like Paul's? Their mouths looked alike, but she'd never felt with Paul the way she had with Mitch.

She rubbed the palm of her hand across her mouth, hoping to erase the feel of his mouth on hers, and the tickle of tiny hairs. "I don't know what's happening to me. I think I must be going crazy."

"We're in sync so far."

At those words, she dared a look at him again. He was serious. Well, as serious as he could look with his bare chest and mussed hair, hair she had mussed. . . .

She looked away again. "I came in here. . . ." She wanted to make up some lie to cover what she'd felt, to make it all sound logical so he'd drop it. But she was so bad at lying.

"You just happened to pick Paul's old room."

That got her attention. "This *is* Paul's room, isn't it? It was like he led me in here, the same way he led me to you. I mean to your house," she added, flushing again. No way could she blame *that* on Paul!

When she hesitated, he asked, "Why were you crying? I mean, bawling like all your horses went up in a barn fire." He propped his chin on the arm that spanned his knees, waiting for her answer.

"I don't know." He wasn't buying it. His eyes narrowed, the way they had every time she lied to him. Lousy liar, she chastised. "I felt this—this anguish. And remorse. I could feel it when I touched the bedpost, Paul's feelings."

He seemed to digest this, his expression becoming more somber. "I heard you say, 'What have you done?' "

"I did?"

"Over and over, before I came in."

Before she'd nearly thrown herself at him. Jenna would never forgive herself for that. Sure, she'd enjoyed making love with Paul, but it wasn't an experience she couldn't live without. She sometimes daydreamed about making love with Paul again, but she didn't crave it. In Mitch's arms, she craved the feel of his skin against hers, the taste of his mouth, even the brush of those tiny hairs. She blinked, unnerved by the direction of her thoughts, cha-grined to find him studying her.

"I don't know what it meant. I don't," she repeated when he gave her that skeptical look again. She stood, hop-ing her knees would keep her upright this time. "I think I should be getting to bed now."

He was on his feet before she could even begin to move, hand curled around the bedpost, blocking her way. "Uh-uh. I want to know something, and I want the truth." He was standing close, muscles tense. She realized she was staring at his chest. Apparently he did too, because he lifted her chin with his finger, making her meet his eyes. "When you curled up in my lap . . ." He let the words drift off. They were hard enough for Jenna to hear, much less the rest of it. "Were you thinking I was Paul?"

"Yes." The word was automatic, born of guilt and not truth. His hand dropped from her chin. She had to think it over, and not with Mitch's eyes boring into her. Damn him and his truth!

Mitch blinked, then shifted his gaze away, fingers tight-ening around the post. He didn't want her to see the spear of disappointment that shot through him at that word, spo-ken so surely. He deadened his gaze to her, the woman who loved his twin so damned much she'd pretend Mitch was him. She'd pretend to have Paul's baby with Mitch's semen. Damn Paul for being so lucky, when it was his careless love for Becky that made Mitch so wary.

He took a step closer to Jenna, smelling the sweetness of her. He couldn't explain what had coursed through his body when she'd put her arms around him, slid her fingers up into his hair. When her mouth had grazed his. But he sure as hell hadn't wanted to offer the poor widow comfort. Hell, after that episode, he was the one who needed com-fort.

Mitch squared his shoulders, making her look up at him with uncertainty in those haunted gray eyes. Just to increase that uncertainty, he let his gaze drop to the mouth he'd almost kissed. That one innocent touch, though, had rocked him more than any hot lovemaking, more than *anything* he'd ever experienced. He waited for her to squirm before looking at her eyes again. This had to stop, whatever burned between them.

He moved close, hating the way he admired her for not backing off. "Jenna, I'm not going to be Paul's proxy. I may look like him, but inside I'm nothing like him. Get past it, because I'm sure as hell not going to play his part in your bed."

Her face paled, jaw tightened. "Get away from me."

He grabbed her arms, holding her to the spot before she could move. "You're connected to Paul in some way I can't understand. I don't need to understand. What I do know is you can tell me what happened the night our parents died. You hold the answers."

"Let me go."

He couldn't let her go yet. He had to impress upon her how important it was for the truth to be known. Mitch had too much at stake. "Our parents were butchered in their beds while they slept."

"My God." Her eyes shadowed. "What does that have to do with the truth? And me?"

"Paul might have been the one who killed them."

Those words stilled Jenna as though he'd produced the knife himself. Her eyes widened, jaw slackened. She overcame her shock quickly, though, shaking her head. "Paul didn't do anything. He was gentle, kind." Tears glittered in her eyes. "He cried when his dog was hit by a car. He bawled like a baby. He wouldn't do anything so horrible!"

"I don't know that he did it, Jenna. But I have to find out. Let me tell you what happened that night. You tell me if anything comes to mind." He took the breath he needed to push out the words. "Paul and I were eighteen that summer. He was involved with a girl our parents didn't approve of—Becky White." At those last words, he'd watched Jenna's face carefully. She'd washed away all expression. "He was stressed out about it, because he was *really* in love with the girl, and our parents were putting a lot of pressure on him to end it.''

''I don't want to hear any more,'' she said, trying to back away.

He held on to her, pulling her closer yet. ''You have to hear it, Jenna. Usually I took up his fights for him. He never was good at fighting. But I agreed with Dad on this. I figured Becky for a gold digger, but Paul wouldn't listen. He'd just walk away from me. He was set on marrying her.

''Paul and our dad had an all-out stampede of words the night my parents died. I tried to butt in, but Dad told me to go clean stalls if I was so interested in other people's sh—well, anyway, I went riding and when I got back, the storm was over. I could hear Becky crying in Paul's bedroom, and I figured Paul caved in and broke up with her. I went to sleep, and when I woke up, Betzi was screaming for help. She found my parents.''

Mitch shuddered, wishing he'd found them instead. ''Paul and I were the first to come under suspicion, of course, because we had the most to gain by . . . their deaths. Believe me, the sheriff wanted to nail us, but he didn't have any evidence. Paul even had an alibi. He had been at Becky's house all night, or so they claimed. Even her father corroborated the story, and they weren't exactly buddies.

''But that never made sense, not if Paul had broken up with her. I didn't tell anyone about that. Paul denied she'd been crying. He said they left after the argument, but I didn't hear them leave. I wanted to believe him, but it didn't feel right.'' Mitch reached out and wrapped his fingers around her arm. ''It felt like a lie. The last time I saw Paul, he tried to block me out. I reached out like this, and I hated what I felt: remorse and guilt. Probably the same thing you felt. And then he disappeared, which told me he was running from something.''

Mitch stared at the intricate carvings in the post, remembering. ''The window in my parents' suite had been jimmied open, and a bunch of their jewelry had been taken, so eventually the sheriff chalked it up to a burglary gone bad. I kept hoping Paul would come back with a good reason for taking off, but he didn't. He didn't write or call or anything. What was he running away from? Guilt?''

She shook her head again, sending her hair flying. "I know him. He wouldn't."

He hadn't let go of her arms, and now he could feel the blood pulsing through her veins. Blood pumped by Paul's heart. "Jenna, you didn't even know where he came from. He was a lie."

"Not with me, he wasn't."

Tears were flowing down her cheeks now, though her eyes were still red from her last crying jag. But these tears cut into him, because he'd caused them. But he had to know the truth. It would set him free, he hoped, and maybe it would set her free too.

She crumpled onto the bed, bending over her knees. "He protected me; he would never hurt me."

Like he was hurting her; Mitch heard the unspoken words. He felt the overpowering urge to protect her too, to take her in his arms and make it all go away. It was Paul, somehow communicating his love for Jenna to him. But Mitch couldn't love Jenna, and at the risk of the truth, he couldn't protect her either.

She surged to her feet swiping at her eyes. "I'm sorry that your parents were murdered. I'm sorry you have this overwhelming urge to find the truth. But the truth isn't going to help you. If Paul did kill your parents—and I know he didn't—what peace is that going to bring? He's dead. He can't go to prison. The truth only hurts. I'm not going to let it hurt me, do you understand? I've had enough heartache."

"If he was so good at protecting you, why did he bring you here? You said it was to make peace with me. Maybe he wanted to confess, through you."

"Maybe he just wanted to say goodbye. I'm saying it, for him and for me. Goodbye." She pushed by him and disappeared around the corner.

He wanted to tell her about the connection between

Becky's death and Paul's accident. The words died in his throat, though. He didn't trust himself to follow her. Now it was Mitch's turn to slump down onto the bed. She couldn't understand what peace the truth would bring, and he wasn't sure he could make her, by shaking her or by kissing her. She'd misunderstood the reason Mitch wanted to find out if Paul killed their parents. It wasn't to get some kind of justice. It went much deeper than that.

Jenna threw her things back into her bag, grabbed her purse and keys, and nearly ran down the main staircase. The foyer was lit only by the flashes of the television, but it was enough light to get the door unlocked. The alarm pad next to the door blinked, but she didn't care if the thing went off. All she wanted was to escape. As soon as she got inside her rental car, she locked the doors and started the engine.

Paul hadn't killed his parents! It was insanity to even think it. He hadn't brought her here for a confession. The anguish she'd felt was Paul's grief, not guilt.

She half expected Mitch to come racing out after her, but he didn't. She had never felt so relieved when she turned onto the highway and left Bluebonnet Manor behind in the darkness.

But another feeling hovered above her relief. It was the sense of having fled the house in the dark of night before in the same kind of panic.

As she drove through the hours of the night, two things would not be put to rest: the coincidence that Paul had dated Becky White, the woman who had died the same day Paul had and in the same area. Worse than that, something else haunted her. The feeling of being in Mitch's arms again, the way it made her body feel, the way she'd felt safe and loved. Apparently she'd become a better liar than she'd thought; Mitch had bought the biggest one yet. Unfortunately, she hadn't mastered lying to herself.

She knew exactly whose arms she'd been in, and whose mouth she'd wanted to kiss. And it wasn't Paul's.

"Oh, you are so messed up." She punched the buttons

on the radio, trying to find something to distract her. "But you're going to put it all behind you, aren't you, Jenna? Because there is no way on this earth you're going to see that man again or think about him. He's T-R-O-U-B-L-E all right," she said after hearing a country singer spell out the same word. "As long as you never see him again, you can forget all this happened, forget how he felt, and remember what you're supposed to be remembering: your husband, the man you loved. The only man you're ever going to love."

Mitch stood by the French doors in Paul's old room and watched her go. His muscles tensed as the battle waged— let her go, or bring her back?

In the end, he let her go. He'd worked with enough wild horses to know when one was spooked beyond reasoning. Holding her down by force wasn't going to get him anywhere with Jenna.

He hadn't even had enough time to sort through the jumble of thoughts and feelings before he heard Betzi's slippers snapping down that hallway. "In here," he said in a deadpan voice he hardly recognized as his own.

He blinked when Betzi turned on the light. "She left?" Betzi's eyes said, *You chased her away?*

"Yeah, I chased her away," he answered.

"What in blazes did you do that for? You don't really think she's here to try and wrangle money out of you, do you?"

Mitch stared at the place by the bed where they'd almost kissed. "No," he said, though he'd wanted to say yes, that's why he'd pushed her to leave. He leaned back against the door, feeling the mullions bite into his bare back. "No, she doesn't want money. She wants to have my baby."

Betzi's blue robe fell open as her arms dropped to her side, revealing her old-fashioned white gown. *"What?"*

"Let me rephrase that," he said, hating the other bite he felt, the bite of jealousy. "She wants me to donate sperm so she can pretend it's Paul's baby. No strings attached."

For the first time he could remember, Betzi was speechless. Her mouth worked, but nothing came out. Finally she said, "Is that what I felt between you two in the kitchen? The storm brewing?"

He shook his head. "She hadn't asked me yet. And there's nothing between us. Nothing."

The authority he'd wanted to strengthen his voice with failed him. Betzi merely gave him a shake of her head. Heaven help him, she'd slipped into her motherly mode.

"Don't you be fibbing, Mitchell James Elliot. Have I ever been wrong about a storm brewing?" He had to admit she hadn't, though grudgingly. "Let me tell you, there's a hell of a storm brewing between you two, though I'm not sure why."

"It's because she has Paul's heart. You remember how connected we were, like the time when I left the baseball game and raced home on my bike because I knew—felt— something had happened to Paul? He'd fallen down the stairs. That's all it is."

Betzi gave him a clearly skeptical look. "What are you going to do about her?"

His body knew what it wanted to do with her, but he stopped his thoughts from straying down that trail. "She's the closest thing I've had to finding out the truth. The connection, the fact that Paul led her here. . . ." He pushed away from the door. "She can tell me what happened that night. But she's not talking."

"She loved Paul, still does, I imagine. Would you want to know some sordid truth about the man you love?"

"Yes," he answered. "I loved Paul too. We were a part of each other. I can't go on without knowing if he was behind our parents' murders. I can't let Jenna go, not when I'm closer to finding the truth than I've ever been."

"That's why she left, isn't it?"

That was only part of it, but he simply nodded. He could still see the startled look on her face when she realized what she'd been doing with him. Hell, he'd probably looked just as startled. "Somehow I've got to get her to help me find the truth—"

"And not fall in love with her in the process," Betzi added, finishing his thought and knowing it.

"You know that's not going to happen."

She crossed her arms over her chest, bunching up the ruffles on her nightgown. "But Paul's dead."

"No, he's not," Mitch quickly said. "Part of him lives in her." He couldn't tell Betzi about the love he'd felt— Paul's love—when he'd touched Jenna. "He loved her, and she still loves him. Loving Jenna would be wrong, period. Besides," he found himself saying in a lower voice. "She'd always see Paul when she looked at me." He shook his head, wishing he could take those last words back. "All I want from her is the truth. And I'm going to get it, some-how, some way."

"Don't be a bully."

She didn't realize that being a bully was a lot easier than being gentle. Gentle led to the kind of thing that had hap-pened right there in Paul's old room and by the photo gal-lery. Striking a balance was going to be about as easy as convincing the mares to foal during the day instead of the middle of the night.

"I'll try." He walked past her into the hallway. "G'night, Betz."

She regarded him thoughtfully, but said nothing more than "Good night, Mitch."

He heard her walk downstairs and through the door that led to her apartment over the garage. The moment the door closed, emptiness descended on him. The television was still on, but he couldn't hear even a murmur. He started to head down the hall, but paused by the collage of photo-graphs.

"You didn't deserve her," he said to one of Paul's pho-tos. "But you knew that, didn't you?" He stood there for a few moments, awash in the memories the photographs depicted. All those years he'd had a friend and ally no matter what. "You brought her here. But why?"

Mitch dragged his feet as he went downstairs. Paul's death certificate was still lying on the table in the kitchen, along with the photographs Jenna had brought. He picked up the piece of paper that seemed to weigh as much as a horse. His throat went dry as he stared at Paul's name. It was as though he stared at his own death certificate, as though his name were typed there.

When he turned it over, he saw that the blank side was covered with a detailed sketch of interconnected flowers and lines. Jenna. He knew as his finger traced the lines that she had drawn this. This morning he hadn't known she even existed. Now she flowed through his veins as though she were a part of him. He closed his eyes, now awash in the forbidden memories of holding her. He punished himself with them, over and over again.

He should have pulled away from her, told her that she was confused. His body had wanted to pull her close, kiss that mouth so temptingly close to his.

Instead, he'd settled for somewhere in between, offering comfort, but taking it himself as he let her wake his senses.

He opened his eyes, balled up the death certificate and flung it so hard, he grunted with exertion. It landed without incident on the marble countertop. He looked at the pictures on the table, of Paul standing next to Jenna after they'd said their vows. They were a handsome couple, though Mitch's eyes were mostly on Jenna. He focused on Paul now, the first time he'd seen his twin since his abrupt departure nine years earlier.

Marrying a woman like Jenna should have made him the happiest man on earth, but Mitch could see something was missing. The spark, he realized. Paul had no spark, no life in his eyes. It was as if he'd lost his soul when he'd left Bluebonnet Manor. With a swipe of Mitch's hand, the photos flew several feet away.

The usual night restlessness galloped through him at hyper speed. What was he going to do about her? Betzi's question echoed through his mind as he got dressed and went over to the stables to take a late-night ride. Midnight Blue wasn't too happy about being roused for an impromptu run, but the stinker cooperated about as much as she always did.

Mitch took the long, winding trail that soon disappeared into a forest of pines. Midnight knew the way, and Mitch leaned close to the horse and relished the familiar rush of becoming one with the powerful animal.

By the time he returned to the stables, hot and damp from the humid night air, Mitch knew exactly what he was going to do about Jenna.

Six

"You think I'm loony-tunes, don't you?"

Jenna waited for Dr. Sharidon's reply, though he seemed too busy taking her blood pressure and checking his chart to have heard her. Or maybe he was trying to come up with a nice way to say, "Yes."

"You've been taking your medication?" he asked at last.

She let out an exasperated sigh, but answered in civil tones, "Religiously. I exercise every night, feel great, energetic."

When she had last asked the doctor about her strange cravings, she'd been willing to take his word about it being part of the mourning process. But not this time. After all she had gone through in the last week, she needed answers. A visit to the library had gleaned at least some information.

"You know, other transplant recipients have experienced strange sensations. What I'm feeling isn't entirely unusual. Claire Sylvia wrote a book about her experiences, how she got these cravings and dreamed about her donor without knowing a thing about him. She was right, even down to his name."

Dr. Sharidon gave her a patronizing smile, looking at her over the top of his horn-rimmed glasses. "Yes, I'm familiar with her. Recipients have reported . . . occurrences. You have a part of someone else's body inside you. Naturally a recipient is curious, and fantasizes about their donor."

Jenna slipped off the table and followed the doctor to the counter along the wall. "But she knew his name. And what he looked like. And that he liked chicken nuggets."

"Jenna—"

She didn't let him try to talk her out of this. "There was another guy who couldn't dance anymore after getting a transplant. And I found an article about a woman who, after getting a new heart, suddenly hated country music. She'd loved it before. When she was able to track down her donor's family, she discovered that he and his wife had been arguing about what station to listen to. She wanted country, he wanted rock and roll. They were fighting over the dial when he lost control of the car. He was killed in the accident. Even knowing all that, even wanting to love country music again, her heart wouldn't let her. You can't attribute all that to fantasizing."

He removed his glasses in a slow, deliberate way, his patience reminding her of Paul. "Why is this so important to you?"

"I need to hear that this isn't my imagination. I know it isn't, but I need to hear it from you. From someone who counts."

Several seconds ticked by before Dr. Sharidon spoke. He leaned against the counter, clipboard tucked against his chest. "There are many things in life that I can't explain. What I can explain is that the heart is a pump. It doesn't contain a soul, like romantic literature likes to imply. There are some who proclaim a thing called cellular memory, doctors even. I categorize them with the UFO and ghost believers." He actually smiled then. "Not that I tell them that. But there is someone—"

"Who?"

"I'm sure he'd be interested in speaking with you. Wait here for a moment and let me see if he's available."

He returned fifteen minutes later. "He's seeing a patient right now, but he has a few minutes if you don't mind waiting."

"I don't," she said so quickly, the words ran together.

"I didn't think so." His wry expression faded. "You listen to him, but I want you to keep one thing in mind: it's time for you to let the past go."

Those were words for Mitch, not her. "There's nothing wrong with holding on to memories." Especially if they were all you had. "I still love my husband."

"But you're angry with him too."

"I . . . I'm what?"

"You're angry. I see it whenever you talk about Paul dying. First for leaving you, and now for hiding his past from you. It's perfectly natural, Jenna, but it's not healthy. You've healed physically, but not emotionally. These . . . visions you're having are only manifestations of that anger. I'm pleased with your progress, but I have to tell you, if it weren't for the fact that Paul made arrangements, you probably wouldn't have been accepted as a recipient."

Her mouth dropped open. "But you said I was dying, that when you sent my old heart to pathology they said I would have only lived another two months, three tops."

He raised a hand. "Before Paul's death, you were the perfect recipient. But quite frankly, a woman whose husband has just died suddenly, and who has no one else to help her through the traumatic recovery process of both, isn't the best candidate. At the time I had reservations about giving you his heart. But you're a strong woman, and you've come through it. Now it's time to let go of the negative emotions you're harboring and get on with your life."

She wasn't taking advantage of her second chance. Didn't she always feel guilty about that? Whenever she saw people laughing together, playing, she longed to be like them. But she'd never been able to do that, even when Paul was alive.

"All right," she said. "I'll try my best." If only she could learn to lie better.

He nodded. "That's all I can ask of you. Dr. Wallen should be here shortly. Take care of yourself, Jenna." He dipped his head and walked out.

All right, maybe she'd offended Dr. Sharidon by not gobbling up his words like a hungry dog. Before her transplant, she might have. But she was tired of being at the mercy of doctors who decided how much she should know, tired of feeling helpless where her own body was concerned. She followed all the orders, but now it was time to take some control over her life.

Dr. Wallen took longer than shortly, but he eventually walked in after a short tap on the door. She realized she'd expected a guru perhaps, or at least some throwback to the hippie days who could talk about organs retaining parts of people's souls and little green men in the same conversation.

He had a small ponytail, but that's where his hippie similarities ended. He was well over six feet tall, with freckles on his face; he wore a deep purple shirt beneath his lab coat. He was carrying her chart, immersed in whatever he read there as he batted the door closed with his behind. He dropped the chart down against his thighs and gave her a warm smile.

"Jenna, I'm Dr. Andy Wallen. It's a pleasure to meet you." His hand was soft as he gave hers a squeeze. "Sit down, please. I see that you had a successful heart transplant nine months ago and that you are experiencing some rather interesting phenomena. Dr. Sharidon referred you to me because I'm conducting a special study on just this sort of thing. And I'm a heart-lung recipient myself."

Jenna felt her body relax. "You are?"

"Six years ago. Every year on my new birthday I celebrate with one beer." His smile disappeared. "But you don't exactly have every reason to celebrate your new chance. I'm sorry about your husband. It must have been hard going through recovery without him."

"Thank you." She didn't want pity, not from this man, and especially not after what Dr. Sharidon had said. "I had help." She cleared the knot out of her throat. "You've had these strange cravings too, then?"

"Nothing dramatic, not like what you've had. Cravings

for Italian food when I never cared for it before. I used to be a morning person, and now I'm a night owl. It was enough to get me asking around, and I found out that many recipients had some kind of change since the transplant. Tell me about your experience."

Jenna told her story again, and this time it didn't sound as loony. All Dr. Wallen could say afterward was, "Wow." She let it all sink in as he digested it, thankful that he didn't have that awful patronizing look Dr. Sharidon had.

"Some of what you've experienced is consistent with what I've found in others, even the sleepwalking. I had a case once where a patient, after his transplant, had a deep desire to go to the ocean. He lived in Michigan, had never left the state, and had no plans to. The desire became so overwhelming that he made reservations and took a trip to San Diego."

Jenna leaned forward. "And what happened once he got to the ocean?"

He shrugged. "He didn't. The plane crashed, and he died. But my point is, maybe a person's desires can remain in the cellular memory of the organ, and therefore transfer to the recipient. The woman you mentioned took on some of the traits of the young man whose heart and lungs she received.

"We don't know how much of a donor's memories stay in the organ or what might trigger them to manifest in the recipient. Some people report no changes at all. But perhaps because your heart belonged to your husband, and he knew you would get that heart, he held on to his wishes, his desires." Dr. Wallen fisted his hand at his chest. "Maybe he wanted you to carry out those wishes. Like the man who felt he had to see the ocean."

Jenna swallowed. "But he died because of those wishes."

"He did. But that's not the point. His death wasn't a direct correlation of carrying out the donor's wish. It was just a fluke of fate. You have to decide if carrying out Paul's wishes is worth the price you may have to pay."

He understood. She wanted to hug him, but she was sure

that wasn't appropriate. Instead she clasped his hand. "I can't tell you what it means to have someone understand what I'm going through."

His expression, however, remained troubled. "I understand some of what you're going through. I have to admit, though, that your case is somewhat extraordinary. I'd like to talk to you some more about it, record it for my project."

"Sure." She took the card he proffered. "Will this . . . these feelings . . . will they go away someday?" Particularly the ones about Mitch, she wanted to ask, but she hadn't told him about that part.

"Some of them, like the food cravings, become a part of who you are now. I still like Italian. And that man from Michigan, he might have still wanted to see the ocean even after he visited it once."

"But that's not the point," Jenna inserted with a smile.

He pointed his finger at her. "Exactly. Other things, like these memories of Paul's might fade over time. Or they might not, not until you act on his desires. But the point is, do you want them to go away?"

She started to say of course she did, but the words didn't come out that way. She let out a sigh instead. "I don't know."

Jenna pulled into her driveway after her appointment, pausing as she always did to take in the house. It was stark white against the blue sky, windows flanked with blue shutters, wraparound porch edged in decorative wooden railings. Just as clearly she could see the way it had looked when she and Paul had bought it: peeling paint, railing posts falling away. But through the house's age and neglect, she saw something else: home. She and Paul had stood at the edge of the yard, talking about what they would do to the outside.

Paul had looked over at the smile encompassing her face. "What are you thinking about?"

"There's something about this house, Paul. I felt it the

first time we saw it.'' She'd turned to him. "Don't you feel it?''

He shrugged. "I just see a good bargain and a lot of work. This is the biggest investment we've made yet, but I think it'll pay off.''

She sighed, turning back to the house. "Forget the investment for a minute. Imagine it painted white, fixed up pretty, even a white picket fence around the front. Maybe it reminds me of the house my family lived in before they sold everything to save souls. It says home to me.'' She watched his reaction.

"Jenna, you're not getting sentimental on me, are you?''

"No, of course not. Well, I don't think I am anyway. I just like this place. We talked about settling down somewhat when we have a baby.''

"Maybe. But we have a good thing going. Sometimes the best buy isn't where you want it to be. What does it matter where we live, when we have each other?''

She gave him a hug, squeezing him tight. "That's true. What would I do without you?''

It usually took him a moment to return her affection, but he always did. He wrapped his arms around her. "You'd be snapped up by another guy.''

"What a horrible thought.'' As her tired spells increased, she wondered if Paul would soon be the one left alone. The latest round of medication wasn't working. "You're the only one I want snapping me up.''

He chuckled. "Good.''

She wanted to give his bum a little squeeze, but Paul had been embarrassed the one time she'd tried it, so she turned to the house again. It looked neglected, as did most of the houses they bought. But this one reminded her of all those children she'd seen in the poverty-stricken villages. Desperate for restoration, for comfort and love. As a young girl, she'd delighted in making a sad, hopeless face smile, even if for a moment.

"It's only a house,'' Paul's voice echoed in her mind.

Jenna blinked, realizing she was still sitting in the car

with the engine running. She got out, grabbing the bag of groceries from the front seat.

On the fireplace mantel sat a picture of her and Paul taken during a whale-watching cruise last June. Jenna had been mesmerized by the beauty of the whales, and in the picture she fairly glowed. Paul was smiling too, but the shadow in his eyes was so obvious now. She looked into their brown depths searching for the reason. Was it guilt that tainted his smiles, guilt over an affair with Becky, or perhaps from his past? In those blue moods, was he haunted by the family he'd left behind?

She wouldn't let her thoughts go further than that. On the trip back to New Hampshire, she had tried to convince herself that the two days in Texas hadn't happened. No Mitch, no Ponee, nothing.

It wasn't working. Even though she wouldn't let herself think of any of it, she could feel the sweet memories of the past fading. She'd started questioning everything.

She was going to have to fight to keep those precious memories dear, despite what Dr. Sharidon had said about letting the past go. What new memories could possibly take their place? And dreams certainly weren't worth the imagination they were printed on.

After lunch, Jenna went to work. She pulled on her old jean shorts and T-shirt, already marred with dashes of paint. The mayor's wife had picked up her dresser the day before, raving and taking a handful of Jenna's business cards to hand out to her friends. The woman's check meant another few payments on the mortgage. Paul's insurance policy hadn't covered much more than his burial.

Next up were the finishing touches on a children's bedroom set. The furniture was already painted cream. Jenna had sketched a design of roses and tulips, which her client had loved so much, she'd commissioned Jenna to paint a border in the girl's room as well.

Being in the workshop with the windows thrown open to the ocean breeze and working on a paying project usually made Jenna happiest. Not today, not even when she forced a smile. Uneasiness rustled through her the way the breeze rustled through the leaves. She sat on her little stool in front of the dresser. The brush sailed over the faint pencil lines, but seemed to have a mind of its own as it added additional swirls and flourishes.

The breeze picked up, whispering at her ear. She found herself looking around, though she had no idea what she expected to find. Her fingers worked faster and faster, expanding on her sketches with more flowers and swirls. Adrenaline coursed through her, stepping up her heartbeat and making her mouth dry. The sound of a motorcycle coincided with a burst of wind, making her think of flying down a country road surrounded by the roar of the engine. She felt injected with the rush of the experience. Where was she getting these thoughts? She'd never even been on a motorcycle before.

She looked up, scanned the yard. Everything around her was peaceful. Her garden was dappled with late afternoon sunlight, the air alternately filled with the sound of a lawn-mower, of children playing on the beach beyond, and the wind washing it all away from time to time. Yet adrenaline screamed through her.

Jenna watched her hand dipping the brush into the paint, creating more flowers, back into the paint again. Her whole body tingled with anticipation. Painting was supposed to relax, not create uncomfortable energy. She shifted the stool over to the side and continued her painting frenzy. Every few minutes she felt compelled to look up, scan, then return to her work.

Had she taken the wrong pill this morning? Or too many of the right one? Her heart was palpitating, and she pressed her palm against it. Was she rejecting? The last time she felt like this was . . . when she'd been in Mitch's arms.

She jerked her head up and sucked in a breath. Blinked. No, this could not be. She blinked again, hoping the image would disappear.

He had paused by the corner of the house when she'd

looked up, but now advanced on her. Steadily. With confidence. As though he had every right to be there. Her hand was still pressed over her heart, but it wasn't helping. Mitch. She tried to conjure up the anger and humiliation she'd felt because of him, but nothing overrode the jolt of desire that shot through her.

He wore baggy blue jeans, a brown leather vest that opened to his bare chest, and in his hand he carried a helmet and a black jacket. She swallowed. The motorcycle she'd heard. She felt shaky, but realized that the sense of anticipation had eased away the moment she'd seen him. She brushed a strand of hair from her cheek as she stood.

He walked through patches of sunlight down the stone pathway that led right to her. His hair was pulled back in a ponytail, though a lock of it hung over his forehead. He was clean-shaven, but there was still a dangerous quality to him, a sense of rough-and-tumble and adventure all wrapped up in a delicious package that sent torrents of those forbidden feelings through her.

She felt an irresistible urge to run and throw herself at him like she had that first day she'd seen him. Just the thought of those arms wrapped around her sent her tipping forward before she realized what she was doing.

What his presence means is trouble, she told herself as he drew up in front of her. T-R-O-U-B-L-E. He smelled of fresh air, leather, and male. As his gaze swept over her, she became acutely aware of her shabby appearance. Her first thought was whether her scar showed, but she remembered that the T-shirt she wore covered it. And then, how long had it been since she'd last shaved her legs?

"You drove all the way here from Texas on a motorcycle?" she asked, forgetting all manner of politeness.

"I wanted time to think. Riding's great for thinking."

She waited, looking into eyes so like Paul's, yet so different. Mitch's eyes were full of spark and life. Finally she couldn't handle looking at him without saying something. "We don't have anything else to talk about."

He set down the helmet and jacket, then stepped closer to her. "Yes we do."

"And that is?" Her voice had gone soft on her.

"I think we can give each other what we want."

Her body reacted to those words before she could think better of it. She forced herself to look away for a moment. "I told you I didn't want anything."

"I'm not talking about money. I'm talking about the baby you want." He seemed to push out the words: "Paul's baby."

Her eyes widened as they met his. "You'll donate . . ." She couldn't even speak the words now.

"Yes, I'll donate. But I want you to help me find the truth. That's the deal."

Those words shattered the joy that was building inside her. The truth again. That horrible truth that could threaten to destroy her memories. She turned back to the workshop, staring at the little girl's dresser. Little girls, babies, all the tears she'd shed in her nursery. The images crashed into one another, pulling and twisting Jenna's insides like taffy.

"All right," she heard herself say. She was winning, but she was losing too.

Mitch released a breath. "I thought I'd have to . . . argue a little, convince you what knowing the truth means to me."

"The only thing I care about is what the truth means to me. Having a baby . . . that means more." She didn't say "having Paul's baby," remembering Mitch's talk of stud horses. "And how did you find me?"

"I did some checking."

"Why did you come all the way here in person?"

"It wasn't exactly the kind of thing I wanted to say via Ma Bell."

"Oh. Well, I suppose not."

She grabbed up a rag and wiped her hands with it, keeping her mind off her emotions. "Did you bring some kind of agreement? About the baby, the inheritance?"

He walked to the corner of her workshop, looking out

over the ocean. The breeze played with the loose lock of hair, making her want to brush it back from his forehead.

"I know you're going to pretend that the baby is Paul's." He swallowed. "You loved him, so I can't blame you for that. But I can't pretend that the baby you'll be carrying isn't mine, or that it doesn't exist. I want to set up some kind of trust for him—or her—and I want to be part of his life. As an uncle."

For that moment the arrogance in his posture disappeared, leaving behind something raw and vulnerable. She exhaled, looking away from him for a moment. She caught sight of two little girls on the beach running around their mother as they headed back to the car. One ran back and leaped into her father's arms, and he swung her up into the air.

"I never thought about what having a child might mean to you. I guess I imagined that it was only sperm, nothing more. You must think I'm pretty coldhearted."

"Not coldhearted. Single-minded, maybe."

She was grateful that he was being kind about it. She didn't deserve it. "But you should know that, well, there are risks."

His body stiffened. "For you? Because of your transplant?"

"It is because of the transplant, but most of the risk is the baby's. Recipients can have children, but there is a chance the baby won't survive."

"What about the reason you had to have a transplant to begin with? Is it hereditary?"

"My doctor doesn't know exactly why my heart walls started thickening. As far as I know, no one in my family had the problem. The doctor said it would be okay to try. Maybe it's wrong to take the chance; maybe I'm a bad person for risking it, but I want a baby, my own—"

He took the hands she gestured with in his, stilling her words. "Stop condemning yourself." He looked down at where their hands touched, then let go.

Too many things bombarded her at once. The affinity in

his touch, and his words. His presence alone. That *he* was being coldhearted by making her face the truth, but then had the nerve to show her this tenderness. Jenna rubbed her palms down the sides of her shorts, really looking at the dresser for the first time. "Oh-h-h, my gosh."

Mitch followed her gaze. "What's wrong?"

The dresser looked like something out of a bordello. She took in his profile as he tried to figure out what was wrong. He was going to be part of her life if she had a baby. When he turned to look at her, she quickly averted her gaze.

"Guess I was a little heavy on the flowers." She had felt Mitch's arrival. Not good. And now he was here in the serenity of her backyard, and it was her place to offer him a bed for the night. If ever she'd wished for a night to be over, it was this one. "I've got a guest room . . . you're welcome to stay in it."

If he picked up on the falter in her voice, he didn't indicate. "That'd be great, thanks."

Jenna nodded, then headed toward the back door. He picked up his jacket, helmet, and a duffel bag he'd left nearby and followed her into the house.

The sun catchers painted prisms across the kitchen. She wondered how Mitch would see her home, her and Paul's home. It wasn't big and fancy like his place, but she loved it all the same. When she turned around, she felt slightly off-kilter. It was like having Paul back home again, yet this Paul was more physical, more dangerous.

He was looking around the kitchen when he met her startled look. "I only look like him, Jenna. I'm nothing like him," he said in that Southern drawl.

She felt a warm flush cross her face. "I know. It's just . . . weird. I'm sorry." She knew well that Mitch and Paul were nothing alike, and looked different in the most important way: their eyes. "Come on, I'll show you the guest room."

He took everything in as they walked through the middle hallway and up the stairs. She'd offset all the dark wood in the house with light accents, but walking up those stairs with Mitch made her feel suffocated. She opened the door to the guest room and stepped back, not at all ready to be inside the room with him.

He walked past her and set his things on the bed, a four-poster like the one in Paul's room, she realized. Remembering what she and Mitch had done by that bed made her step back. He caught the movement.

"Jenna, don't look at me like I'm the big, bad wolf."

But he was, the very bad wolf. She wrapped her arms around herself. "It's the truth I'm afraid of." Well, not entirely. "Come on, I'll show you the house."

Mitch followed, feeling responsible for that fear in her eyes and the way she held herself protectively. But he had to find the truth, and besides, he'd promised to give her what she wanted.

He could see how thin she was. Thin and afraid, yet willing to face him and the truth to get what she wanted. The woman was a paradox of fragility and strength. He understood why Paul had tried to protect her.

But this is what you wanted, brother. You brought her to me, and now I'm finishing it.

"This is our—my bedroom," she said, leaning into the open doorway across the hall from his room.

Her slip cranked up that strange jealousy that had resided in him since her arrival at his house. It got even worse when he looked at Jenna and imagined that Paul had touched her everywhere, had loved her and made sounds issue from her throat when she came. He didn't meet her eyes, instead peering into the room where all that he'd just thought about happened.

A big bed covered in a blue and white bedspread, blue carpet, and a ceramic dog, the room she and Paul had shared. Large windows spanning the length of the house opened to the ocean, framed in flowered fabric he somehow knew Jenna had fashioned into spirals. Along the top edge of the wall was a painted border of seashells. In one corner sat a treadmill and a stair stepper.

She caught his gaze returning to that bed, and he looked

away. "Nice," he said, feeling far from that word at the moment. He had given a lot of thought to this whole situation, weighing the cost of finding the truth against hurting Jenna, and against starting something that could not end well for either one of them.

"That's the nursery," she said in that soft voice, nodding toward a closed door across the hall and starting to walk down the stairs.

"I'd like to see it, considering . . ." He wasn't even sure how much of a role he wanted to play in this child's life, but he realized he couldn't just walk away.

She stiffened, but slowly turned back and led him to the door. His boots sounded loud on the wooden boards beneath them. His senses were heightened around her, taking in the smells of polish and paint and even her deodorant; he could feel the heat from her body, the warm air coming in through the open window at the end of the hall; and mostly he could sense her hesitation at showing him the nursery.

She opened the door and stepped inside, like a mother ready to protect her cubs. She was not in that self-protective posture anymore, now with her feet apart and arms at her side. But her eyes gave away her vulnerability, and suddenly he felt like the big, bad wolf.

When he could tear his gaze away from Jenna, he looked around at the little piece of motherly heaven she'd created. The polished crib and mobile, a frilly bassinet (at least he thought that's what it was called) . . . and the beautiful border along the top of the wall filled with bears and balloons. He remembered the border she'd drawn on the back of Paul's death certificate, the roses she'd painted on the child's dresser and the seashells in her room.

He met her eyes, the woman who had created this haven and filled it with her love and dreams. "When did you do all this?" he asked, finding his voice reverently soft.

"When Paul and I moved in, after we'd renovated the interior. I . . . I couldn't try to have a baby until I had the transplant, but I always decorated one of the rooms as a nursery. I thought it might bring good luck.''

God, he wanted to pull her into his arms and hold her tight. He wanted to make her smile, laugh, and sigh contentedly. His voice sounded funny when he said, ''I'm sorry I used this to get the truth. It was all I had.''

Her fingers curled over the edge of the crib. ''It was enough,'' she said, a bitter edge in her voice.

He leaned against the door frame, pressing his cheek to the wood. ''Do you think I want Paul to be guilty? You think I want to find out my twin brother had the capacity to murder his own parents?''

''Then wouldn't it be better not to know?'' she asked. ''Can't you just go on and assume Paul is innocent? I can. Even with what I know, I can because I love him.''

He shook his head, feeling the edge of the frame biting into his cheek. ''I can't let it go. I can't . . .''

''Why?'' She walked closer, close enough for him to reach over and run his finger across the smear of pink paint on her cheek. She had broad cheekbones, creamy soft skin.

He let his hand drop when he realized what he was doing. ''Paul and I share the same genes, the same environmental influences. If he's a murderer . . . then I could be one too.''

Seven

Mitch's words echoed in Jenna's mind as she prepared dinner. She focused on those words, because dealing with all of it—Mitch's arrival, her agreement, having his baby—was too much at once.

That vulnerability she'd seen in his eyes when he'd spoken those words, oh, my, what it had done to her insides. Not that he'd intended to let her see it. Mitch wasn't the kind of man to use such a ploy, or to even think of it. And just where did she get off, *knowing* him so well?

Jenna looked down to realize she was mangling her beautiful tomatoes, banging her knife down on the same slice again and again. She stilled her hands, closing her eyes for a moment. Last week she had been comfortable, if lonely, in her little world, safe with her memories. Now she was a wreck.

The knife banged down on the cutting board, and she set it aside before she ended up chopping off a finger. Had she sold her soul to the devil by making this bargain with Mitch? It was sure looking that way. Wasn't the devil the source of these sinful feelings she felt whenever Mitch was near, and especially when he touched her?

The devil made me do it. Now she knew why people embraced that trite saying as an excuse for treachery. But that was the coward's way out.

She involuntarily rubbed the back of her hand across the place on her cheek he'd touched. After she'd given Mitch a brief tour of the downstairs, they both retired to their rooms to shower. When she'd walked into her bathroom and looked at her reflection, she'd experienced something so foreign to her, she had to lean back against the wall. Vanity. She'd seen the paint streaking her face, her disheveled hair, lack of any makeup, and had actually cringed. In fact, the only thing that looked good were her eyes, bright and shiny for the first time in a long while.

Even as she had piled her hair on her head and swiped some blush on her cheeks, she told herself she was doing this for her. She sighed. Still a lousy liar. *Where do you get off caring what he thinks about the way you look?*

And now Mitch was coming down the stairs. Each footfall stepped up the pace of her heart. She told herself not to look anywhere near the doorway, but Mitch didn't just walk into a room—he seemed to burst in, full of energy. She was looking at him before she could chide herself for doing so.

"Nothing like a cold shower to invigorate a man," he said, shaking his damp hair. He wore a white cotton button-up shirt and another pair of blue jeans.

"Sorry about that. I wasn't sure if the tank would handle two showers at once; Paul and I always made sure there was enough time in between our showers for the water to heat up."

He moved up next to her, taking in the sorry little puddles of tomato guts on the cutting board. "That could sure put a damper on taking a shower together." When she looked up at him, he added, "I mean, you and Paul."

She turned quickly back to the tomatoes, wishing she hadn't looked so shocked at his words. Of course he hadn't meant for *them* to take a shower together. Just the thought of it . . . oh, brother, just the thought of it. She didn't mention that she and Paul had never taken a shower together. An image of their bodies sliding together beneath the flow of cool water jumped to mind, and she had a terrible feeling the Elliot man in the image wasn't Paul.

"Can I help?" Mitch asked.

She wanted to send him far away from her. "I could

use another tomato." *I hear they're nice and ripe out in California this time of year.* That's what she wanted to say, anyway. "If you don't mind going out to the garden and picking one."

"Sure."

He was out the door in a flash, striding across the backyard as though he belonged there. No, he certainly did *not* belong there!

Her reprieve was brief as he came in tossing the tomato up and down, catching it with a soft smacking noise. He set it down on the board in front of her, looking at the pulpy mess. "Looks like the last one exploded."

"Spontaneous tomato combustion." She'd never felt so uncomfortable in her own kitchen before.

"Hate when that happens," he said with a chuckle.

"I'm just making a salad. I'm afraid I don't have a lot of meat around the house, but I do have a leftover grilled chicken breast I can add to the greens."

He grinned, a heart-stopping smile like she'd never seen before. "I brought some of Betzi's brownies for dessert."

"Great." She nodded, feeling awkward as they held each other's gaze. "I've got some tamales in the cabinet too," she said just to say *something*.

"Tabasco?"

"In the fridge next to the fire extinguisher."

He laughed, and it warmed her that he found her sorry attempts at humor amusing. He fished a tamale out of the jar, poured the hot sauce on the end and took a bite. "I can set the table if you point me to the silverware."

"Sure, that'd be great. In that drawer; dishes are over there."

He wasn't wearing shoes, she noticed, as he set the table by the window. Paul always wore shoes, even when he was just lounging around the house. Mitch had sexy feet, and she honestly couldn't remember what Paul's feet had looked like to compare. She supposed they were the same. So why hadn't she noticed? She finally finished the tomatoes and started chopping up the different kinds of lettuce.

When she couldn't put the task off any longer, she carried the bowl to the table.

Jenna poured two glasses of iced tea and reluctantly sat down across from Mitch, who was twirling one of her sun catchers with his fingers. A plastic case on the table held her array of prescription bottles, and one by one she laid out the more than dozen pills she had to take twice a day. If ever she had to do this in public, which was rare, she couldn't help noticing people gawking as though she were some addict.

Mitch watched with curiosity, but his attention seemed to be on her hands and not the pills themselves. "Your transplant?"

She nodded, feeling completely self-conscious as she started swallowing the pills two by two. "Every morning and every evening. They suppress my immune system so it doesn't think my new heart is some foreign object and attack it. That's called rejecting."

"How long do you have to take them?"

"Forever."

He lifted his eyebrows at that. "Tell me about the surgery. What was it like?"

"The surgery itself only took about three hours. It's actually simpler than some heart surgeries. Then I spent almost four weeks at the hospital, then another three months at a special apartment complex near the hospital. After that, I came back here."

He leaned forward, propping his chin up with his palm. "Do you have to be careful about what you do? Eating right, not straining yourself, that kind of thing?"

"Not any more than the average person. I have to go in for biopsies every year, exercise regularly, and I have to be careful about germs."

Mitch tilted his head, as though he found her words endlessly interesting. "Did you know it was Paul's heart . . . when they put it in you?"

Jenna finished taking her pills. "I didn't know until I reached the hospital. My doctor told me that Paul was in

Maine . . . brain dead. And that he'd arranged for me to
have his heart. His retrieval team was already there, waiting. I gave them permission to donate his other organs too.
I tried not to think about getting his heart." She started
pouring low-fat ranch dressing on her salad, wanting to put
an end to this conversation.

Mitch must have sensed this, because he gave the dove
sun catcher beside him another twirl and said, "I don't see
Paul living here."

She remembered her earlier realization that Paul hadn't
put his touch in any of the homes they shared. The lace
curtains, the fruit border she'd painted, the white tiles with
tiny designs in the corners, all hers. Mitch kept looking
around the kitchen, tapping on the edge of the table with
his fingers.

"We collected Toby mugs," she said, wondering why
such a lame thing had come out of her mouth.

Mitch lifted an eyebrow. "Toby mugs?"

She pointed to the shelf that ran along the wall behind
him where they kept their collection. "We used to give
each other mugs for birthdays, Christmas. We'd try to find
the rare ones, surprise each other." Her voice trailed off.
Mitch wouldn't understand the excitement of finding the
one mug Paul had wanted. Mitch wouldn't collect mugs;
he'd collect horses, women.

Women? Where'd that come from?

"And you paint them too," he said, nodding toward
the border on the opposite wall. From a distance, it
looked as though she had another shelf crammed with
Toby mugs.

"I had a lot of time on my hands, and, well, I can't
afford to splurge on the real thing anymore. I got the col-
lector's book out and painted the ones I wanted."

Mitch studied her painting for a moment, but brought
his attention back to the table. "I figured Paul would end
up being some hotshot at a bank, something cerebral. He
liked being indoors, didn't like physical work." The

rhythm of his fingers was getting more elaborate, and he'd added the plate to his "drum set."

"He loved working on our houses. He didn't do the heavy labor chores; we hired those jobs out. But he enjoyed the painting, sanding, especially the intricate work."

Mitch leaned forward, fingers now quietly splayed on the white tablecloth. "Tell me about him, Jenna. What was he like?"

She felt such affinity with Mitch, even though they hadn't touched. They both sought the answers that would connect the Paul that Mitch knew to the one she had married.

"He was . . ." She had to look away from Mitch; looking at him while thinking of Paul messed with her mind. "He was smart, good at business, ambitious. Very sensible, calm. And very loving," she felt compelled to add. "He was a good husband." *Except for the secrets.* "He didn't like to go out; he was very much a home-body, which was fine with me. I've never been comfortable in crowds."

Mitch took a bite of his salad, but he put down his fork. "He had this place, he had you. Why doesn't he look happy in the photographs you have all over the house?"

She winced, not only at the bluntness of his words, but his immediate perception of what she'd only recently discovered.

"I don't mean to imply you didn't make him happy," Mitch added, appearing chagrinned by his words.

She looked away for a moment, then back at him. Of course, she hadn't made him happy, not totally. "He had . . . blue moods." She'd called them blue because somehow that made them seem less serious. "Times when he sank so deep inside himself I couldn't reach him. He never said why he had them, and I never asked. Maybe I didn't want to know." She set down her own fork. "Was he . . . like that when he was younger?"

He shook his head. "Aw, he was quiet, always was a little into himself that way. But not a sad kind of quiet."

His eyes darkened. "Maybe he felt guilty about something."

"Or maybe he just missed his family and felt bad about lying to me." Her voice had risen in sharp tones, enough to make his eyebrows rise. "You say you don't want Paul to be guilty, but I think you've already convicted him."

"I've had a long time to think about whether Paul murdered our parents. Most of what I came up with didn't look good. That doesn't mean I want him to be guilty. But I'm willing to face the truth, whatever it is. Our parents were murdered. He has a shaky alibi, as far as I'm concerned. He felt guilty—"

"But you said he'd been fighting with your parents before they died. Maybe he felt guilty that he hadn't made amends."

"The fact that he'd been fighting with them is another piece that casts doubt on his innocence. What I felt from him wasn't just guilt either. It was remorse. Just like you felt in his bedroom. And he shut himself away from me. We were close once; he should have moved toward me, not away. And the biggest piece of the puzzle is that he ran away. He *ran,* Jenna."

"He was being a coward," she said, surprised that the word had even come out of her mouth in regard to her husband. "It's true. He shied away from anything he didn't want to hear, even the news."

"He was always a coward. He came to me to fight his fights for him. But this time he ran away from me. Why would he run away from the one person who could help him?"

"He didn't do it."

Mitch regarded her for a long moment. "I hope he knew what he had." He picked up his fork and took a healthy bite of his salad. "Don't let me keep you from eating. Seems to me you could use some nutrition."

She decided not to ask what he'd meant by that first sentence, focusing instead on the last part. "That's the second comment you've made about my weight.''

"A woman has to give her body what it needs, fill in those curves.''

She tried to ignore the way his accent had wrapped about the words "woman" and "curves,'' making them slither right down her spine. "You have no place lecturing me about my eating habits. Or my curves.''

Mitch leaned back in his chair. "Sure I do. I'm your brother-in-law. And the father of your baby-to-be.''

That sent a flush of heat to her cheeks. Her mouth dropped open, but before she could come up with something to say, he said, "Jus' eat and save your piss and vinegar for later.'' He picked up his fork again and stabbed one of the tamales. "I have a feeling you're gonna need it.''

Mitch had, surprisingly, helped clear the table, though Jenna would have preferred he go watch TV like Paul usually did. Finally she'd told him to clear out in pretense of being a good hostess, something she had no idea how to be.

He was her brother-in-law. She hadn't thought about that, hadn't thought to give their relationship a name. But that made it sound so innocent and normal, and what burned between them had nothing to do with either.

Jenna, stop thinking like that! It's just this connection between you. Get yourself under control, get through this, decide if you're really going to take him up on his end of the bargain, and get him the heck out of here.

She brewed fresh-ground coffee and prepared a tray to take into the office where they would start their journey into the past. Once everything was ready, she carried the tray into the office—and stopped in the doorway

Mitch sat at the huge desk, reminding her for that split second of Paul. But she couldn't linger on that impression for more than that second, because Mitch fit in the office . . . differently. Where Paul had almost been swallowed up by the desk, Mitch looked right behind it. And at home, she noted with a wrinkle of her nose. After a moment, he paused in his perusal of Paul's collection of Edgar Allan Poe's stories and looked up at her.

She put herself in gear and moved forward, hoping he hadn't noticed his effect on her. She had to recognize this strange . . . attraction, if she dared call it that, and put it in its place: out at the curb with the rest of her garbage.

Mitch had turned on only the desk lamp, creating a cozy glow around him. Jenna set the tray on the edge of the desk, backed up and turned on the overhead light with her elbow.

"So we can see," she said in wilting tones. She pulled up the chair she had always used before Paul's accident, keeping the corner of the desk between her and Mitch.

He upended a plastic bag onto the tray and dumped out what looked like cookie crumbs onto the silver platter. "Betzi's brownies didn't make the trip very well," he said with a shrug. He scooped up a handful and, tilting his head back, poured them into his mouth. "They're still good," he added when he saw her looking at the mound of chocolate and walnuts.

It wasn't their state that had her baffled; just that nine months before, she wouldn't even be thinking of scooping up anything containing walnuts and eating it. Now, she reached over and took one of the larger pieces. He watched her chew, making the usually involuntary procedure a study of concentration.

"Happy?" she asked, wiping her palms together.

He pondered that for a moment, leaving her in the unnerving position of looking into those eyes that weighed her simple and blithe question. "Nope," he said at last, turning back to the desk. "Fix your coffee, and we'll get down to it."

As she got up, she realized he had assumed the role of man of the house. "Do you always come into people's homes and order them about?" she asked.

He looked around, as though just realizing he'd taken over the desk. "Dunno. Don't think so."

"Then do you make a habit of ordering women around particularly?"

"Nope."

Finally she sat down and looked at him. He was sitting back in the chair, chin propped up by his hand, elbow on the armrest.

"You want to fight about it?" he asked, an amused fire in his eyes.

Jenna opened her mouth, but didn't know what to say. She had never dealt with someone like Mitch before, and she honestly didn't know what to do about him. "No, I don't want to fight."

"Might do you some good."

"No, thank you."

"You're holding it all in, just like my brother used to do. It's no good. Sometimes you got to let it all out."

She placed her fingers on the edge of the desk, staring at them for a moment. "I like being calm. That's the way I am. Paul and I were civil people."

He lowered his head just the slightest bit, meeting her eyes and sending a funny curling sensation through her stomach. "Sometimes it's good to go a little crazy."

"I wouldn't know."

"Speaking of that, you have a place where I can live up to my end of the bargain? You know, one of those fertility places, sperm banks, whatever."

"No. I hadn't thought about it after you turned me down." Not entirely true, but she hadn't gone as far as finding a facility that would handle the procedure. She didn't even know how much it would cost or where to start looking. Would "sperm" be a listing in the Yellow Pages? "I'll look into it tomorrow."

He nodded with a deep dip of his chin. "Just so you know, I'm owning up to my end. Are you ready to own up to yours?"

She lifted her chin, determined to get through this. "Yes." No.

Mitch leaned forward, meeting her gaze squarely.

"You're the key, Jenna. You're the one who's going to tell me what happened that night. When you were crying in Paul's room, when you said you'd felt his sadness, I knew you had some kind of connection with him."

"He didn't run away. He only needed time to sort things out."

"*Nine years?* Without a word to his family?"

Their faces were only a foot apart, and she could smell the brownie he'd eaten mixed with that lemony cologne. She turned to the line of pictures along the back of the desk, six Pauls looking at her with that shadow in his eyes. He wanted her to make things right, and he didn't care if the truth hurt her. But she still didn't believe he was a murderer.

"What do you need me to do?" she asked.

He smiled. "That's my girl."

"I'm not your girl." Her words came out in a rush, as though she were trying to convince herself more than him.

"I didn't mean it like that," he said in a soft voice.

"I'm Paul's girl. And I believe in him and his innocence. Maybe he did lie about his past, and maybe he was a coward, but he didn't murder anyone."

He sat back in the chair again, tapping a dull beat on the leather desk pad with his pen. "Do you think I like wondering if my own twin brother was a murderer? I never thought he'd be capable of murder, not my calm, sensible twin." He shot her a look, and his voice went louder. "He held it all in, his anger, his passion. It was all locked inside him, and I had to wonder if the capability of murder was locked in there too. Every day I hated myself for thinking that, for suspecting the one person I could always trust."

He stood and walked closer to her, and Jenna could feel the heat and energy he emitted. "I hate him and I love him, but I've got to know the truth. It's the only way I can stop this war going on inside me." He crouched down beside her. "I need your help, Jenna. I need you to be honest with me."

Jenna was frozen for a moment, though thawing quickly from his heat. Paul had had no passion locked inside him, she wanted to say. She'd thought that of herself as well. But Mitch's passionate plea touched something so deep inside her, she couldn't even name it. All she knew was a hunger grew from that place, a hunger to touch Mitch and draw some of that passion into herself.

"Tell me about Becky White," he said.

"I don't know much about her. I . . ." She reached for the drawer where the newspaper articles were, pushing the plastic bag farther back. "This is all I know."

Mitch read both articles, then looked up at her. "That's how you came to Ponee? From reading this?"

"No. That's what made me decide that I had to go there to get some answers, but it was Paul who told me to go. And then I read the article and knew why. Or thought I knew."

"You thought he was sending you to Becky's family."

"I wasn't sure. But I found myself going right to Blue-bonnet Manor, and then to you." She remembered that first moment all over again, Mitch standing there slick with sweat about to get tackled. Her tackling him. Would she ever live that down? "I thought . . . maybe, that Paul was seeing her."

"No." Mitch shook his head with certainty.

"How do you know?"

He leaned on the top edge of the chair, regarding her with a curious stare. "I know he loved you completely."

She came to her feet before she'd even realized it, hands crossed over her chest. "How?"

The clock on the bookcase ticked three times before Mitch answered. "I felt it." He looked away, then back at her. "That night in the hallway."

She sank back down into the chair. "But how?"

"Because you have Paul's heart, and maybe Paul and I still have this connection between us."

Was that why Mitch had held her so tenderly? She wanted to ask him, but stilled her tongue. No, she should be rejoicing that Paul loved her, that maybe he hadn't been seeing Becky. "Why do you suppose he's doing this?"

"I think he wants us to know the truth about that night."

But why this pull between us? she wanted to ask. Instead, she asked. "Do you still feel it?"

"Paul's love? No, not like that. I've felt . . . other things, but not that. All I know is, it was real. I've never felt anything like it before in my life. He loved you, Jenna. With all his heart, he loved you."

Jenna shot to her feet. "Don't say it anymore! I don't want to hear that from you, do you understand? You have no right to tell me that." He straightened, raising his hands, but she advanced on him. "Not until you can tell me this: if he loved me so damned much, why did he lie to me? Why did he die and leave me here all alone?" She sucked in a breath as she heard her words shouted out, underlined by threatening tears. Straightening, she faced him and calmed her voice. "What other things have you felt?"

He hesitated again, obviously regretting mentioning them. Another three ticks on the clock passed. "He wants me to protect you."

She laughed, a harsh sound she'd never heard before. "Oh, that's perfect. He makes me find you, you who want to know the truth at any cost, but he wants you to protect me too. Well, here's a word to both of you: I don't need your protection. I can take care of myself. I don't need anyone, got it? You're both stomping on everything in my life. Just do what you have to do and go. But don't think you can make it all better by putting your arms around me because Paul wants you to."

What had become of her? She inhaled deeply, unwilling for Mitch to see how surprised she was at her anger. "You didn't want me to lock in my feelings. Well, there you have them. And you know what? They're tiring. I just want to be alone for a while. I'd say make yourself at home, but you already have. Good night."

And she walked out, through the kitchen where she grabbed her sweater and headed toward her sanctuary in the gazebo.

Mitch stood there for a long time after Jenna left, listening to the ticking of the clock that seemed to get louder and louder. Her words seemed to bounce around the walls of the office, knocking his insides around. Yep, that's what he'd wanted, for her to express herself. He could see what burned in her eyes even as she proclaimed to be so calm. Maybe he shouldn't have told her what he'd felt. Hell, he didn't have the rules to this game. And he never thought about what he said, he just . . . said.

Jenna was angry. What he hated was that she was aiming it at him. Sure, he deserved it, for coming here and making her face the truth. But she was wrong about one thing: he hadn't held her because of Paul. No, Mitch couldn't get out of that so easily.

He walked into the darkened kitchen, saw the lights leading up the path to a gazebo. He could see her sitting out there staring at the black ocean beyond. There was something else, something she'd said that edged into his conscious. He pushed it back, sensing it was something he didn't want to know.

She had more fire than even she realized. "That's my girl," he whispered before turning and going back to the office. His girl. Why did that sound so right? He thought of her comment about his making himself at home and realized he had. Not because of arrogance, though admittedly he had plenty of that. No, because he felt as though he belonged here.

And that reason for belonging was Jenna.

If Mitch thought Paul had screwed up his life before, that was only the beginning. Maybe he would find out the truth about that night long ago, but Mitch was going to face a whole new agony. To Jenna, he was the jerk who was stomping her world and who also looked like the man she loved and lost. To Mitch, she was a woman with a delicate beauty and a fiery strength that left him wanting something he couldn't have.

He walked out the front door and got on his bike. Maybe the wind could blow away this mess in his head.

Eight

Jenna heard Mitch's motorcycle roar to life and hoped to God he was leaving. She picked her way over the rocks down to the beach, and in the dim moonlight made a smiley face far removed from the way she felt.

The way she felt. Wrapping her sweater tighter around herself, she looked back at her home. It was warmly lit, welcoming. And lonely. For so long she had successfully buried her feelings, but Mitch had brought them boiling to the surface. She'd never spoken to Paul as she had to Mitch, never let her feelings explode in such an outburst. In fact, she couldn't ever remember letting go of her emotions like that.

"Don't cry, Jenna. The world is a harsh place, and sad things happen." Her mother's voice echoed in her mind, and Jenna saw herself as a little girl unable to let go of the brown-skinned baby girl who had died in her arms.

"We gotta save her, Mama. She's not really gone. See, she's still warm. Feel her. She's not too far gone yet."

Her mother took the baby from her. "We have to go on and try to save the next one. Save your energy for that."

Her parents had never let her express her emotions, and they'd never expressed theirs either: Death and suffering were part of their daily lives, and they bore it all with stoicism. She used to think her parents were cold, but now she understood the delicate balance they'd maintained between caring and not caring too much.

Mitch had upset her precarious balance.

To prove that, her heart sped up when she heard his motorcycle return. She had to restore her serene facade, deal with the truth tomorrow, and try to piece her life back together afterward.

She gave him enough time to go upstairs before making her way back to the house. As she opened the kitchen door, she remembered something he'd said. *I hate him and I love him, but I've got to know the truth. It's the only way I can stop this war going on inside me.*

"You all right?"

His voice startled her, as did the sight of him leaning in the doorway. His hair was disheveled from his ride, face flushed.

"Fine."

He nodded, straightening. "Good night, then."

She opened her mouth to return the farewell, but something she'd never admitted before came out instead. "I feel the same way about him."

Mitch turned back to face her. "What?"

She removed her sweater and hung it up on the hook by the door. She found herself walking toward him, pausing in the doorway in front of him. "I lie in bed at night listening to the blood pulse in my ears, and I hate him with one beat and love him with the next." The guilt she expected to feel didn't come, and neither did recrimination shine in the eyes that held her gaze.

When he reached out and touched her chin, warmth washed away the chill inside her. "It's okay to hate the person you love sometimes. Hate, love, and joy make life worth living."

When his thumb ran along her lower lip, she felt that pulse she'd spoken of jump to life. No, no, not with Mitch! She shouldn't be feeling this way about him. She hated him for making her face the truth about her husband, hated him for making her feel warm and tingly every time he looked at her. She would—could never love him.

She moved away when she realized he wasn't releasing

her. Breaking away from his gaze, she turned and said, "Good night."

Long after she'd prepared for bed, she could still feel his touch on her chin and lower lip. He'd touched her like that several times, and Jenna could remember every second of each touch. As she got into her bed, she had a startling realization. Paul had been her husband, yet he'd never touched her like that. He held her when she needed a hug, yes, and whenever a touch seemed appropriate. But he'd never just reached out for no particular reason and connected with her.

She had seen other couples do it, those subconscious touches that spoke of intimacy hardly noticeable to others. But Jenna had noticed, and she'd always felt a peculiar emptiness or longing, perhaps. She'd never thought to question why, because she had a perfect marriage.

She shivered, pulling the covers up over her shoulders. One question haunted her as she tried to drift into sleep: if the surge of electricity between her and Mitch was because of the connection they had from Paul's heart, why did Mitch's touch affect her so much *more* than her own husband's had?

Mitch woke with a start, surprised to find daylight creeping through the lace drapes. When was the last time he'd slept through the night?

He put on jean shorts and a blue T-shirt, both a little wrinkled from having resided in the bottom of his duffel bag, and headed downstairs. The sounds of Jenna in the kitchen made him feel more at home than he did, well, in his own home. Betzi was usually puttering around in the kitchen in the mornings, but something about the knowledge that it was Jenna making those clinking noises sent a strange kind of warmth through him.

"Good morning," he said, helping himself to a cup of coffee.

She was standing by the sink, slathering butter on a bagel, wearing blue shorts and a white shirt. "If you say so."

She gathered up her coffee cup and plate and said, "I usually eat breakfast out at the gazebo. You . . . can join me if you want."

It wasn't really an invitation, but Mitch piled three bagels on a plate and followed her out to the gazebo. The air outside was cool and crisp, and the salty breeze toyed with her light hair as she sat watching the people on the beach.

Something in the distance made a smile curve her mouth. It was the first time he'd seen her features relaxed, her eyes lit with pleasure. He took a deep breath to get rid of the tightness inside him, then looked to see what could make this lady smile like that.

Three kids were squatted down on the beach studying a circular arrangement of stones. Someone had left a happy face there last night. When she realized he was standing there, that smile disappeared, chilling him at the thought that he could extinguish it with his presence alone.

"You were born to smile, you know that?"

She just looked at him for a moment, then turned away. "I don't have much reason for doing it anymore."

She let those words hang, and they did hang heavy around Mitch's neck. He cleared his throat. "You said your parents were gone."

She nodded, looking out over the pale blue ocean. "My parents were missionaries. When I was six, they got the calling, as they put it. We traveled all over Africa, helping the sick and poor." Her voice grew soft, and she smiled faintly. "There were times when I understood why they did what they did. All those people looking at you like you're the only hope they have. We were always the minority, and sometimes they thought we were godlike. And when we could save a sick baby . . .

"It was wonderful. We *were* godlike then. But all those other times, when we held them as they gasped their last breath." She shook her head. "I'm sorry, I don't know why I'm telling you all this. You were asking about my parents. Being the minority wasn't always a good thing. We were perceived as a threat to some. Like the group of rebels who gunned my parents down. My parents knew about the unrest that day, but they went into town anyway. Maybe they thought God would protect them." She looked over at him. " 'He giveth, and He taketh away.' "

She had seen so much, explaining the haunted look he sometimes saw in her eyes. Those gray eyes had seen tragedy so young. Whatever it was that had started to bother him last night returned to niggle at the edges of his mind.

"And He taketh away and He giveth," he said, referring to Paul and his heart. "You weren't with them when they were killed, were you?"

"I followed them," she said in that low, soft voice. "I was afraid. Maybe I thought I could keep them safe by being there. But I couldn't. I hid in the bushes until the rebels left, and then I ran back to the village like a coward."

"You weren't a coward," he said, imagining a young girl who must have been terrified. "How old were you?"

"Fourteen."

"What happened afterward? Where did you go?"

"I went to live with my grandmother in Haiti until she died. The church she was affiliated with scraped together some money, enough to get me back to the States. I got a job with a furniture restorer, paid the church back and met Paul and I don't want to talk about myself anymore," she finished in a stream of words.

His fingers curled over the arms of the chair. That shadow edged closer. "During your surgery . . . and afterward. Who was with you?"

"I told you, I don't want to talk—"

"Just tell me."

She shifted in her chair. "There were lots of people around. Doctors, nurses, all kinds of people. When I came home, I hired a nurse to stay with me here for a few months."

He shook his head, quick jerky motions. "I'm not talking about people who were paid to take care of you."

She looked away, but he caught sight of the tremble in

her chin. Her words came back to haunt him: *I can take care of myself. I don't need anyone, got it?* The realization hit him like a wrecking ball, right in the gut. He shot to his feet, leaning over the table toward her.

"You went through it alone, didn't you?"

She backed away from him, mouth tightening. "Yes, I went through it alone. I didn't have a choice. But I'm here. I survived. It's not the first time I've been alone."

He straightened, running his hand through his hair. "God, Jenna, you lost your husband and went through major surgery . . . alone."

This delicate woman had survived, but he could see at what price in her eyes. That son of a bitch abandoned her because he was driving recklessly, doing something he shouldn't have been doing. All he'd left her was this house and a string of lies. And now Mitch was being a bigger son of a bitch by making her face those lies.

"Dammit!" He slammed his palms down on the table surface, making her flinch. "Dammit." Then he turned and stalked back to the house before he went against his vow and took her in his arms and made her forget everything for a while. He wanted to erase every sad memory that tainted her eyes. Those times she'd cried, they were the times the fortress she kept around her had crumbled. He'd watched her quickly patch it and hold up that cute chin of hers as she did it.

Where was this rage coming from? The same place Paul's love and protectiveness had come from? Not from Paul, that much he knew. He stared at the pictures lined up along the edge of the desk in the office.

"If I see you in hell, I'm going to make you pay for what you did to her."

And then he sent those pictures flying across the room.

Jenna stared at the kitchen door for a long time, feeling overcome by Mitch's display. All that passion blazing in his eyes on her behalf had wrapped around her insides. No one had ever been angry for her, or even at her. It was strangely touching. After a short time, she picked up their uneaten bagels and returned to the house.

He was standing in the kitchen. "Let's go for a ride. Clear our heads before we start."

She had no choice but to follow him, or so it seemed. He grabbed his black leather jacket on the way to the front door. When they stepped outside, he headed to the shiny red and chrome motorcycle. It was a Harley Davidson, with storage compartments on the back and each side. The seat was long enough for a passenger.

"Why don't we take the car?" she asked.

"We don't have to talk on the bike. We just ride and feel the wind."

Not being closed up in the intimate space of the car was almost enough to give her the courage to ride the beast. Not that he was giving her a choice. He held up the jacket for her, and she slid into it. She was instantly enveloped in the sense of Mitch, as though he'd put his arms around her. He unhitched a helmet from the bike, walked over and placed it over her head, then put his on.

"I'll be careful," he said at her apprehension, straddling the seat and nodding for her to do the same.

She'd never ridden a motorcycle before, although she'd had a scooter in Haiti. She stepped over the seat behind Mitch.

With a lurch, he started the bike, and she cringed at the loud blast of sound so early in the morning. He turned around and said, "Hold on. Lean with me into the turns, okay? Don't try to fight me."

That's when she realized she'd have to put her arms around him. This was worse than talking! At least she didn't have to look him in the eyes, she thought, sliding her arms around his waist but trying to keep her upper body from touching his.

Within moments they were speeding down the winding road along the coast. As soon as he'd hit the gas, she had instinctually moved up against him. Holding on for dear life, she assured herself.

She watched familiar sights whiz by, swept up in the cool air blasting her, drunk on the speed. She could feel Mitch's muscles working as he maneuvered the bike around the curves. Beneath her splayed hands, his stomach moved in and out with his breathing.

For the first time since her transplant, she felt alive and free. Carefree. Exhilarated. She let all of her anxieties and doubts go, reveling in the powerful sound and vibrations of the bike.

Her body stirred at the revelation, combined with all the other sensations swirling through her. She was pressed intimately against Mitch, breasts crushed against his back, thighs pressed against his. Heat burned wherever they touched, a sensual dizzying heat she'd never felt before. She could feel her heart racing in tune with the engine, the adrenaline coursing through her the way it had just before Mitch arrived.

He pulled into one of the small beach parking lots and turned around. "You all right?"

She blinked, feeling a little too all right. "Fine," she shouted back over the engine, knowing that word didn't touch the way she felt.

He nodded and hit the gas. Mitch was everything this bike was: stimulating, fast, rumbling with energy. Dangerous to feel like this with him, dangerous to be pressed up against him like this and enjoying it.

Still, she felt an acute disappointment when he turned into her driveway. She jumped off the bike the moment he killed the engine, but all of the vibrations and heat still rocketed through her body.

He took the helmet from her, their fingers brushing casually but not without impact. "Now that we've cleared our heads . . ." he said, his mouth quirked in a way that indicated the ride had not, in fact, cleared his head.

She ran her fingers through her hair. "Yeah. It worked wonders."

*   *   *

Mitch had brought a list of the dates Paul had withdrawn money from his account. In the hours after her ride, Jenna had dug through the files looking for the bank statement that matched those dates, finding each one missing. She had requested that the bank fax her the missing statements.

Even though the big desk was cluttered with papers, she noticed that the pictures of her and Paul weren't sitting along the back edge of the desk anymore. Mitch had stacked them on the far corner.

When he noticed her looking at the stack, he said, "We needed the room."

Mitch took each page as it came off the fax and laid it on the desk. "Here's the first deposit," he said, pointing to a two-hundred-thousand-dollar entry. "Three days later he withdrew it."

Jenna could only stare at the numbers. Up until then, she had convinced herself that the missing statements were a coincidence. But now more evidence mounted against Paul.

"The second withdrawal matches another deposit and cash withdrawal made in December two years ago for one hundred thousand dollars."

"Maybe he put the money into the houses we were buying and didn't want me to know about it."

Mitch matched up another deposit/withdrawal. "Do the dates coincide?"

She willed them to match. In every case, like the last one, the transaction occurred some time before they'd sold their house and bought another one.

Mitch had a determined expression on his face, as though he'd become an auditor for the IRS. His eyes softened, however, when he looked up at her. "Do the dates coincide with those blue moods you were telling me about?"

"I . . . I don't know. I never kept track of them." She tried to remember what they'd been doing when each one hit. "Christmases. And . . . before he died. He was down in the dumps before he went house-hunting in Maine. Real edgy, restless, walked in his sleep more." There were times when Paul had seemed suddenly frantic to sell their current house and move on.

"So we don't know for sure if his moods centered around these withdrawals. None of them were made just before Christmas, but that's a tough time of the year for a lot of people." He looked at the calendar, but she had the feeling that statement was true of himself as well. "What did you do last Christmas, Jenna?"

"Started hating Christmas," she admitted. "I was living in that complex near the hospital. We set up a tree and decorated it, sang carols." She'd been so empty, singing words of joy and not feeling any of it. Feeling guilty over that. Not wanting Mitch to feel pity or worse, that passion on her behalf, she said, "How will we ever find out what Paul did with that money?"

"We might not. But if we put enough pieces together, we might be able to at least make a guess."

"How much money did he have access to?"

"We're allowed to withdraw four hundred thousand a year without question, plus expenses and upkeep on Blue-bonnet Manor." Mitch's expression grew grim. "Even after Dad died, he still wanted to control us. He stipulated that we have to go through our financial manager if we want to withdraw more than that amount. That's why I'm making my own money."

The wind chimes from the house next door tinkled pleasantly, adding to her building hope. "Yet over these last nine years he only took out eight hundred thousand." *Only!* "If he killed your parents for money, wouldn't he have taken advantage of that, and of living without expense at the manor?"

"I've hung my hopes on that too, but it doesn't mean anything. Maybe he couldn't deal with it once the deed was done. Maybe it was a crime of passion. He'd been having problems with my parents. Something could have snapped. Maybe after he realized what he'd done, he didn't want anything to do with the money."

"Maybe he just couldn't handle the horror of his parents' deaths. Somebody broke into his home and killed his parents. And then the police looked at you and him as suspects. Of course it was stressful. Who wouldn't want to get away from all that?"

His mouth tightened into a line. "I didn't."

"Well, you're a tough guy. Big, bad Mitch the bully." That got him to his feet, hands clenched at his sides. "Maybe we all can't be as tough as you," she continued, standing as well. "Paul wasn't a strong person, but that doesn't make him a murderer."

"I'm not a bully. I just want the truth, and I told you why."

She didn't want to think of his admission, spoken in a moment of vulnerability. "But you're already convinced Paul is a murderer. Why do you want to convict him?"

He moved closer, but she didn't back down. His voice was deadly low when he said, "Why are you protecting him? He lied to you. He got himself killed doing something you didn't know about. He hid money from you." Mitch grabbed one of the fax copies and wrinkled it up. "Everything about him was a lie. How can you stand there and defend him? How can you be willing to turn your back on the evidence and go on believing he was some damned *saint*?"

Her chest was hurting, and his closeness and anger made it hard to breathe. "Because I loved him!" she shouted back, feeling the strength in those words. She did love him, even now. She still had her memories to hold on to.

"He didn't deserve your love." Something dark laced his low voice. "He didn't deserve you."

To her horror, she felt her eyes watering. "You're right! He didn't deserve me. I was a hardship. We wanted children, and I couldn't give him any. He worried about me all the time, knowing I could die soon. We paid astronomical insurance premiums because of my condition. But he didn't care! He didn't run then. He stayed with me and loved me anyway." *You make me a good man.* No, no, he was already a good man. "He never complained about any of it! Not when I was too tired to work on the house, or fix dinner, or even make love!''

All the rage and anger roiled into a fierce storm, and the thunder in her head transformed into the beating of her fists against his chest. ''Don't tell me I didn't deserve him! It's you I don't deserve! I don't deserve you coming here and tormenting me!''

Her fists landed with dull thuds against his hard chest, not pushing him back an inch. But it felt so good to let out some of that pent-up anger, and directing it at Mitch was much safer than directing it at Paul.

After a few moments he grabbed her wrists and jerked her body against his. Still holding her arms, he leaned down and covered her mouth with his. She couldn't resist or push him away. Her body went slack against him, and he let go of her wrists to slide his arms over her shoulders. Her heart was pounding, first from her anger and then from his kiss. His mouth moved against hers, fingers sliding up into her hair and tilting her head for better access.

Why was she letting him do this? *Because it feels so right. No, no, it's wrong!* She couldn't hold on to any of those thoughts, though, as her body melded with his, crystallizing their mysterious connection until they felt like one person instead of two warring factions.

His tongue slid across the seam of her lips, and her mouth opened to him as though they'd been kissing for years. She heard strange noises and realized they were coming from her throat as she hungrily sought his tongue. Her body crackled with electricity, trembling under the onslaught of desire. His mouth was warm and alive and made her want more. Fingers of heat traveled from her core down her thighs and up to tingle at the tips of her breasts.

Not strong enough to move away, she tried to conjure up her and Paul's kisses, tried to tell herself they were more exciting than this. Just as her body could not lie about what Mitch was doing to it, neither could she lie to herself— Paul had never kissed her like this, had never ignited the kind of desire that swept her body.

She knew she had to stop, but she was beyond control. His mouth was soft and lush, and she wanted to kiss him until the clock on the bookcase stopped ticking altogether. She could feel his deepening breaths, each exhale pressing his chest against hers.

His movements became slower and slower, and she opened her eyes to find his closed tight. Her head was tilted back, though until that moment she hadn't noticed the strain on her muscles.

Slowly his eyes opened. She felt vulnerable, as though she'd been caught doing something bad. And she was! Very, very bad. Yet, she still couldn't tell her body to move, to get away from him. What was wrong with her? She'd lived without physical contact with a man for so long, and hadn't missed it until . . . well, until Mitch.

"We shouldn't be doing this," she said against his mouth. What she really wanted to do was get lost in that mouth again, feel what she had to admit she'd been missing with Paul.

"I know. I guess I should let you go," he said in a sexy, hoarse voice.

"Yes, you should."

Neither of them was actually willing to break contact. Finally he loosened his arms, and she took a wobbly step away from him. Thank goodness the chair was nearby, and she held on to the back of it. He leaned against the edge of the desk, bracing his hands on the surface.

She couldn't meet his eyes, though she knew he was looking at her. She covered her mouth with her other hand, hoping to still the warm, tingly sensation rippling across it. She had no idea what to say, what to do. She could slap him, she supposed, but she'd been much too willing a participant to blame him fully. If she were a flip person, she could say something sarcastic. Instead, she walked to where the pictures were stacked and placed them along the edge of the desk.

I'm sorry, Paul, she thought with each one she replaced. *It's you, and this connection I have with your brother. Isn't it? Maybe the combination is making everything more intense. He's sexy and passionate, and I'm responding on one level to that. But he's your image, and our hearts seem to speak to each other.*

She looked up at Mitch. His eyes were dark as they focused on the last picture she'd set upright. He drew his gaze from her fingers up her arm to her eyes.

"Do you want some lunch?" she asked, desperate to break up the weight of tension in the room.

"Lunch?"

She might as well have asked him if he wanted to go hunting for slugs. "Yes, lunch. Food. It's nearly noon. You keep saying how you want to put meat on my bones."

Fire flared in his eyes as he took in those bones. She swallowed. Perhaps that hadn't been exactly the right thing to say.

"I mean, you are hungry, aren't you?" She closed her eyes, searching for words that wouldn't trip her up. After a moment she opened them again and said, "I'm going to fix lunch."

"You've done it again. Put that wall around you."

"It's safer than having your arms around me." Where was this bluntness coming from?

He nodded, rubbing that indent beneath his mouth with the side of his finger. "You don't want to talk about what just happened?"

"Absolutely not."

She walked out of the office, giving him a wide berth in case he got an idea about grabbing her arm and pulling her back. He followed her into the kitchen where she started whacking on another innocent tomato.

"Don't you want to hit me or something?" he persisted. "Tell me off? You're getting pretty good at it."

She kept her concentration on the tomato, forcing herself to make nice, even slices. "I am, aren't I?"

"I guess it wouldn't be proper to say that you're awfully good at kissing, then." When she shot him a look, he was standing over by the window. "I could apologize."

She felt a pleasant warmth wash over her, and mangled the neat slice she'd been working on. Nobody had ever said she kissed good, not that she'd kissed many men. She decided to mangle the bread instead. "You could."

After a moment, she couldn't help giving him a sideways glance. He shrugged. "I could apologize, but I'm not really sure if I'm sorry." His voice lowered. "On a base level."

She turned her attention back to the bread, feeling all warm and prickly. "I'd rather pretend it didn't happen at all."

He nodded solemnly. "That might work."

"I've already forgotten. See? Everything's fine." Her voice, however, sounded unnaturally high.

"Would it help if I told you I had no intention of kissing you?"

He looked like an innocent little boy, although she knew better. "I'd rather forget it."

"Okay, fine." He sat down at the table, picked up the sugar spoon and tapped the porcelain sugar bowl with it. "Can I help?" he asked a moment later.

"No!" She cleared her throat. "No, thank you. Just stay there . . . relax, I mean."

"It's not going to happen again. If that's what you're worried about."

"You're guaranteeing that?"

He nodded, looking completely at home at her table. His legs were spread, fingers busily tapping away. "Paul and I made a promise to each other a long time ago that we would never . . . get involved with a woman whom the other had once loved."

Eager to change the course of the previous conversation, she asked, "And what prompted that?"

"A woman, naturally." That easy grin again, the one that made her stomach flip-flop. "Paul brought her out to the ranch one afternoon. Turned out she liked me better. I didn't know he liked her so much; to me, girls were fun to hang around with for a while, but Paul always did fall heavy. He caught us kissing behind the barn. He was so mad, he tried to hit me. He threatened to get plastic surgery so we wouldn't look alike. Instead, we made the promise, a vow sealed in our blood." He raised his hand, and she saw a tiny line that matched one Paul had had on his left palm.

She realized the conversation had, in fact, come full circle to the kiss they'd shared in the office. "I have some leftover salmon in the fridge. I can make up a salad with that."

He obviously recognized her change of subject for what it was and granted it to her. "Fine. But tonight, I'm fixing dinner."

Nine

Mitch kept forgetting why he'd come to New Hampshire. Oh, it would come to him, and then he'd look at Jenna and . . . forget. This thing that had been wrapped around his soul for ten years had vanished. What was he really doing there?

What he was doing was enjoying the way her arms felt around him, the fresh air washing over him, the sound of the engine between his legs, doing something so simple and ordinary as riding to the grocery store. He'd been surprised when she'd suggested taking the bike.

"We're only going to pick up a few things," she'd said in that soft voice that affected him as though he were being called to dinner.

Like he would have argued with her anyway, her looking a little shy, and him knowing she'd be putting her arms around him. He'd recognized that look of pure bliss on her face that morning, and remembered feeling the same way when he'd taken his first ride at twelve. Then his daddy had whipped him but good for hanging out with "the trash of Ponee." The very next night Mitch had snuck out just to prove to himself who was boss. That time he hadn't been caught.

He parked the bike, lifted himself off the seat and helped her. Just that nothing little touch he hadn't even thought about shivered through him. Their eyes met, and he told her that this physical contact didn't count, and she said it sure as hell did, but didn't reprimand him for it. All this was said without a word.

They seemed to realize this at the same moment, breaking eye contact and simultaneously busying themselves with removing their helmets. He felt like a teenager again, falling in lust for the first time. This was different, though, more intense. He was aware of every nuance about her, her proximity to him, even an ultra-awareness about his own body.

Shoot. This wasn't lust.

He opened the door for her, and she walked through. Even thin, she filled out her shorts just so. Her hips swayed, not exactly in a sexy way, but enough to fill him with a longing he hadn't felt in a long time. Maybe not ever.

What are you saying, Mitch? No way are you in love with this woman. Got that? She was married to your brother, and still loves him. If she's responding to you, it's only because you look like the bastard who loved her . . . and lied to her.

"Mitch?"

She said the word in that same way she'd said it at his house, when he'd drifted off in memories outside the front door. But that word on her tongue sent a different wave of warmth through him this time.

He blinked, realizing he was still standing there with his back holding the door open. "Coming."

Oceanside Mart wasn't what he'd call a grocery store. It was the kind of store you'd see in Mayberry with a little bit of everything and a friendly older lady behind the counter who probably knew everyone's business. The whole town was like a facade on a movie set, old and quaint marred only by the occasional tourist shop.

"So, what are we having, chef Elliot?" she asked, a wry smile on her face.

Damn, she looked beautiful when she smiled. She didn't do it nearly enough, not that he'd given her much reason. But they'd come to a sort of truce tonight after their kiss. Maybe they'd gotten each other out of their system.

Hardly. Maybe she'd gotten him out of her system.

"Good old-fashioned red beef to put some meat on these bones." As he walked by her, he gave her a pinch just under her rib cage. He was doing it again, like he couldn't keep his hands off this woman.

"You're not a quasivegetarian, are you?" he asked, perusing the meat selection.

"No, I just don't care for red meat. And no, it's not because I'm a transplantee."

"You knew I was gonna ask you that, didn't you?"

"Yup," she said again, suddenly finding the meat packages interesting. "I'm just like everyone else now, watching cholesterol and fat grams the same way everybody does."

"Would beef ribs be out of the question?"

She eyed the ribs he was pointing at. "I could handle it."

He picked up two packages and went off in search of corn. Disgust washed over him. Here he was, supposed to be finding out the truth, and he was picking out fixings for dinner and getting hot for his twin's widow. He'd held her in his arms and discovered how right she felt there.

One thing he was sure about: when he'd kissed her, when he'd had her body pressed up against his, Paul had nothing to do with the way he'd felt. It was all Mitch in there, getting lost in her mouth, wanting to feel all of her, reluctant to let her go. What made him feel even crummier about doing it in the first place was that she was probably dreaming it was Paul. Mitch deserved every ugly thought he was thinking about himself. And they were pretty ugly.

"I got some butter for the corn," she said, coming up beside him. "What's wrong?"

He'd been standing there holding the stupid package of corn like a zombie. "Just can't imagine eatin' any other corn but Texas corn," he said with a drawl.

That was another thing he'd noticed lately: his accent was getting stronger.

That's because Paul didn't have an accent, his conscience said.

With a grunt, he walked over to the beer section.

"And here I only thought it was the winters that made living in New England so wicked bad."

"Don't you be giving me a hard time, now. When you're born in Texas, you get used to the best." He found his gaze involuntarily dropping down over the white fabric of her shirt and the way it molded her breasts. He jerked it back up to meet her eyes. "The best of almost everything."

"Oh, my Lordy, my Lordy!"

They both turned at the woman's voice beside them, at the sound of her plastic basket hitting the floor and embarrassing old-lady things spilling out. She was itty-bitty, about seventy years old, and staring at him as if he were standing there naked as a plucked chicken.

"Millie!" Jenna rushed to the woman. "What's wrong?"

She pointed to Mitch, finger trembling. "It's . . . it's your husband. He's come back to life."

Jenna looked at him, then back to Millie. "Oh, no. No, it's not Paul."

Her voice dropped to a dramatic hush. "Not Paul exactly, but his . . . spirit. Oh my, yes, I've heard about these kinds of things. You loved him so much, you've brought him back. It's not good for you, dear. You have to get away from him right away."

Except for the spirit stuff, that probably wasn't bad advice.

Jenna took the old lady's hands in hers. "It's Paul's twin brother, Mitch. He's very human, believe me."

Something else Mitch could agree with.

Millie walked closer and stared up at him as though he were some Frankenstein creation Jenna had made.

"Pleased to meet ya," he said in his heaviest accent yet.

"This is Millie, the nurse who stayed with me after the surgery. She lives around the corner from me."

Millie only nodded, still struck with curiosity. "You said Paul had no family."

"He didn't."

"Then how do you explain him?"

"I mean, that's what Paul told me. But it wasn't true."

Millie snapped her fingers in front of Jenna's face. "Snap out of that dazed state you're in. You have to tell Paul's spirit to leave you to mourn in peace. It's no good, I tell you. I had a cousin, her husband died in a train accident. He haunted her for fifteen years afterward. Got to be she'd fix him meals every day. Wouldn't talk to anyone else *but* Bill. Went crazy, I say. Take my advice, girl. Get away from him." And then the woman scooted off, casting a backward glance at them before turning the corner.

"I never thought about running into someone I knew," Jenna said, obviously feeling bad for spooking the lady. "We didn't know that many people, didn't get out much."

"Why did Paul keep you hidden away?"

She turned back to Mitch, surprise in her face. "What do you mean?"

"Seems like he hid you away like his little treasure. Didn't take you out, moved all the time."

Her defensiveness pricked at him. "We didn't feel comfortable in crowds. I wasn't used to being around people much, and he didn't make me deal with it. He seemed to like being with just me, and I liked being with just him."

How real damned cozy. She headed toward the front of the store, shoulders straight. No matter what they found out, Jenna was going to keep loving Paul for what he was to her. Mitch followed her, trying to quash the awful jealousy with a paraphrase of words he'd heard in church often enough: *Thou shalt not covet thy twin's wife. Or her devotion.*

Jenna watched Mitch standing by the grill from the safe distance of the kitchen. He was wearing jeans and a white T-shirt, looking as delicious as those ribs smelled. She squeezed her eyes shut at the thought and forced herself to go upstairs and shower. She'd let Mitch take his shower first and gave the water heater enough time to warm the water again.

To her chagrin, she found herself putting on a pretty sundress (with a high neckline), then standing in front of the mirror brushing her hair just so, applying a little color to the mouth Mitch had said was born to smile. To the mouth he'd brought to life with his kisses. She stared at her image and sighed. What was wrong with her?

Paul had often told her how pretty she was, but with Mitch . . . well, she could see those words in his eyes, could feel his appreciation. Surely Paul had meant what he'd said. But he'd only complimented her when the occasion called for it, like the times she'd prettied herself up for dinner. He never glanced over at her during a quiet moment when she looked plain and told her that he saw beauty.

"This is crazy." She rubbed off the lip color with her palm and changed into a long T-shirt and leggings, turmoil twisting in her stomach. The turmoil turned to a snaking warmth that curled through her feminine regions. She wanted more of that kiss, and she wanted more than that kiss.

She pulled up her shirt and studied the scar that ran from the top of her collarbone to just below her ribs. The doctor had said it would fade over time, but she hadn't worried. She had been sure no one would see it but herself. What would Mitch think of it?

"No one's going to see it," she whispered. "Especially not him."

On the way downstairs, she found herself pausing outside the nursery door, as she often did. Something was different. She took inventory. Everything was still there. Then what?

It was her. She didn't feel the anguish of loss anymore. Was it because Mitch was offering her the hope of having a baby now? She felt more turmoil at the thought of going through with it. Having a baby meant keeping in touch with

Mitch, letting him get involved with their baby's life. *Their baby?*

No, she couldn't do it. When his quest for the truth was sated, she needed to cut ties. Once he was out of her life, she would forget all about him and go on. For the first time, she felt she could go on. Something was stronger inside her, as though she had faced the devil and walked away unscathed.

Without the bargain, you can stop this search into Paul's past, a familiar voice said inside her. The voice she'd lived with all her life, she realized. *Run, coward, run!*

She wasn't going to hide from the truth anymore. Paul wasn't a murderer, even if he was a liar. She was going to follow this through, because she knew he wouldn't allow her to let it go. Nor would Mitch. She was strong; she would find the truth and put it behind her and still keep her cherished memories. The truth wouldn't give her the strength to carry on. Only her memories would.

"Dinner's ready!" Mitch called from below.

How had he insinuated himself into her life and home so easily?

Just as she reached the bottom of the stairs, she caught a glimpse of something on the front porch. Jenna narrowed her eyes. Gray curly hair. Atop a tiny woman who leaned against the front window and peered in.

Millie.

Jenna pulled the front door open, startling the woman. "Millie, what are you doing?"

The lady was acting like a geriatric spy, peering behind Jenna, whispering, "Is he around?"

"Who, Mitch?"

She nodded emphatically, drawing Jenna out to the porch and closing the door behind her. "The spirit, whatever it is that you call him."

Jenna tried not to laugh. "He's not a spirit, Millie, but I apprec—"

Millie grabbed hold of her hand. "It's worse than I thought, Jenna. It might be that . . ."

She glanced around again and whispered, "I think Paul's come back to claim his heart. Maybe he can't rest until his body parts are buried with him. It happened, you know. Man went around killing everyone who got his organs so he could rest in peace."

"Oh, Millie, I think you've taken your love of the *X-Files* a little too seriously."

"Don't laugh my words off. I know Paul wanted you to have his heart, but maybe he changed his mind. Maybe a person can't go on without his body parts intact. We don't know, Jenna. We don't know how it works. But you've got to listen to me."

Jenna was sure she was going to have some lovely dreams that night. But she decided to humor Millie, if just to get her on her way. "Who should I call?" It was all she could do not to utter, "The Ghostbusters?"

"Here's what you got to do." Millie looked around again. "He's got you under his spell. It's understandable, you and Paul being so close and all. You have to break the spell."

That was the most sensible advice yet. "How?"

Millie shoved a brown paper bag at her. "There's a candle in there. The next time . . . he appears, I want you to burn this candle, and say the following verse three times: 'As I watch this candle burn, your peace my heart will yearn; / And when the flame dies down, our souls will no longer be bound.' Go on. Repeat it."

Jenna did.

"When you're finished saying it, extinguish the flame with your breath. Don't let him blow it out." Millie squeezed her hand. "Good luck." And then she was off, scurrying down the walkway and across the street. Jenna wasn't sure whether to laugh or shake her head. She did both as she headed back into the house.

When she walked into the kitchen, she was startled to find the table set, a pile of beef ribs smoking on the table, drinks, and her bottles of pills all lined up in front of her plate. He was standing next to the table setting the last bottle in place.

Mitch said nothing, holding her chair out and waiting for her to sit down. She pushed herself forward, catching that lemony, spicy cologne he wore.

He sat down across from her. ''What's that?'' he asked, nodding toward the crinkled bag she held.

''Mm. Well, it's a candle.''

''Candle?''

''To make you, er, go away.'' She pulled the peach candle from the glass holder and inserted the purple one. Then she lit it and repeated the vow, or at least as much as she could remember. Particularly, though, about their souls not being bound anymore. Mitch simply watched her, concentrating especially on her mouth as she pursed and blew out the candle. ''There.'' Then she looked up at him, tilting her head. ''It didn't work. You're still here. Maybe I said it wrong.'' At his perplexed look, she added, ''Millie stopped by a few minutes ago.''

''Ah, that explains it.''

''She thinks you're Paul's ghost, here to either comfort me or take my heart back. Remember, she has a cousin who fixed meals for her husband's ghost for fifteen years.'' She didn't mention the spell she was supposed to be under.

''Is that right? Well, did he fix meals for her too?'' He gestured toward the spread in front of them.

''Er, no.''

''And I didn't disappear when you blew the candle out. That only means one thing.''

''You're not a ghost?'' she ventured.

''That lady's elevator does not go all the way to the top floor. Can we eat now, or are you going to start spraying me with holy water?''

Jenna lifted an eyebrow at him. ''Don't tempt me.'' She reached for the smaller rack of ribs on the platter. He buttered his corn and covered it in salt and pepper. She watched those fingers that so easily reached out and touched her, then forced her attention to the pills she had to take. Mitch had touched each of these bottles, had placed them here for her. It was an odd gesture, one she didn't know how to interpret. No matter, it made her feel strange anyway, both giddy and uncertain and . . . touched. He didn't watch her as she took all those pills, instead busying himself with tearing the meat off the bone with his teeth.

Stop watching him, Jenna! She started working on the food in front of her. Using her fork and knife, she cut the meat away from the bone. The first bite was heaven. She was sure she hadn't eaten anything this good in years.

He grabbed the loaf of crusty bread and ripped off a piece of it, then tossed it to her. Surprised, she barely caught it.

"This is finger food, Jenna. The best way to enjoy it is to dig in with all your senses. Just pick it up and tear into it like the cavemen used to do." He demonstrated, making pleasurable noises that vibrated in her stomach.

"But it's messy to eat it that way."

"Your point?"

"It doesn't feel right to eat that way in front of . . . others."

"It's not like we're getting naked." He peeled a strip of meat off the bone by moving his whole head. "Did you eat with your fingers in front of Paul?"

"I . . . er, I don't know." She honestly couldn't remember ever eating anything like this with him.

"Try it."

She set down the hunk of bread and pulled one of the ribs free from the rest. As daintily as possible, she took a bite. Warm grease coated her lips, and she wiped her mouth with a napkin.

He shook his head. "You've got the heart of a Texan, remember? We love our meat. Just imagine you've been out riding horses all day, working up a sweat, and now you're eating your first big meal of the day. You're starving, tired and hot. All you want is to dig in. You don't care how it looks because no one else cares."

"Why are you doing this?"

"Because you don't look like you're really enjoying it. Eating satisfies one of your base needs, and you ought to be getting satisfaction from it. No wonder you're so thin." He leaned closer. "Eat like you haven't had anything for years."

Her body responded to his words, but food wasn't the base need it was craving. She picked up the rib and sank her teeth into the meat, tearing away a piece like Mitch had done. He looked pleased, only then taking up his own rib again.

His mouth was slick with grease, wet and soft-looking. When he reached for his corncob, she tossed her rib bone in the extra bowl and did the same. She didn't reach for her knife to cut the kernels off, instead slathering them with butter and sprinkling on salt. Peppered butter ran down between Mitch's fingers, and she soon felt the warm liquid sliding down hers.

The succulent kernels burst in her mouth as her teeth punctured them. Eating *could* be an experience, she realized, taking in the feel of the nubs against her lips, the smell of butter and the smoky ribs, the taste of the salt on her tongue.

He dropped the naked cob into the bowl and picked up the loaf of bread, breaking off a piece and dipping it into the puddle of butter and pepper the corn had left behind. The butter ran down his freshly shaved chin. She wanted to reach over and run her finger down the indent of his chin, wipe away the butter and lick it off her finger.

She found her finger running along her own buttery chin, found her tongue licking it off. He was watching her, a feral glaze in his brown eyes as he ripped away another piece of bread. She watched his mouth move, imagining how their mouths would slide against each other if she kissed him now.

The usual blue serenity she felt while eating in this kitchen was replaced by red, a hot red that flowed through her body and drugged her senses. Her movements were slow, heavy; her eyes felt full and liquid as she put the cob in the bowl and cut another rib from her rack.

Who knew eating could be so sensual? Who knew *she* could feel so sensual? What this man was doing to her she couldn't explain, and at the moment, didn't want to. Their eyes rarely left each other. Their movements picked up in speed. She felt an intense awareness of her body, where warmth pooled, where their legs barely touched beneath the table. She felt alive, more alive than she'd ever felt in her life, as though she were being reborn, coming into the world for the first time.

He threw a stripped rib bone into the bowl and sat back in his chair, head tilted. "The way you look at me, Jenna . . . do you see him? You still want him, don't you? Even after all he's done."

Jenna blinked, trying to push away the sensual haze around her. She hadn't been thinking of Paul, hadn't been wanting Paul when she'd been looking at Mitch. What had she been telling him with her eyes as she'd stared at him all hungry and hot? "Yes," she answered to all of Mitch's questions, guilt replacing those crazy things she'd been feeling moments before.

Mitch winced at the word, as though she'd slapped him. His eyes burned into hers. "I'm not Paul. I'm nothing like him."

"I know that." Her eyes were locked to his, unable to look away.

He wiped the back of his hand across his mouth, making her feel even guiltier by reminding her of her thoughts about kissing that mouth.

"If you keep lookin' at me like that, I'm gonna rip your clothes off and love you till you have no doubt which Elliot I am. And I'm gonna do it right here in the kitchen."

Her insides jumped at the words soaked in a rich Southern accent. She should be shocked at his nerve to say something like that to her. She could see him peeling off her T-shirt, stripping her out of her leggings, laying her down on the kitchen floor and—She covered her face. It wasn't

Paul she was seeing; it was Mitch. She was betraying Paul with his own twin.

She dropped her hands and steeled herself. "You're the one who came barging into my life and home, taking over like you live here . . ." She swallowed, pushing herself on. "Kissing me, telling me to get hot and bothered by eating—" She shook her head, thrashing herself for nearly admitting she *had* been hot and bothered. "I lost my husband only nine months ago, and I think you're taking advantage of that, especially the fact that you look like him. Maybe you think you have some point to make, that you can kiss me or . . . even more. Is that your way of getting even with Paul? Trying to seduce me? No matter what you say about Paul, I'll never stop loving him. And no matter what you try to do to me, you'll never make me forget him. Don't use me for some vendetta."

He stared out the window, eyes narrowed. Finally he looked at her, and his voice was low when he spoke. "I'm here for one reason only, and that's to find out if my brother killed our parents." He came to his feet, and before she could stand too, he boxed her in by putting one hand on the back of her chair and the other on the table in front of her. He lowered his face to hers. How she craved his kiss, and how she hated him for making her want one.

His mouth was only a half-inch from hers, voice low and grainy, when he said, "The reason I want you has nothing to do with Paul." His eyes took her in, and she saw that he also hated himself for the way he felt. "It has nothing to do with it being wrong. It only has to do with you and me, and none of that makes it right. I'm a shit for feeling this way, but I'll tell you this: I ain't trying to take his place. So don't look at me and think about him, because I will make that fire in your eyes burn for me."

He tilted her chin up and slid his thumb over the slickness of her lower lip. "Maybe it'd be better if you hated me. It'd be better for both of us if the only thing I see in your eyes when you look at me is hate. Just don't forget that hate and love are the strongest emotions; sometimes it's easy to confuse 'em.''

He stood and grabbed the bottle of beer he hadn't yet touched. ''I'll meet you in the office.'' And then he walked out.

She wanted to believe that he wanted her only for revenge, but she could see in his eyes that he spoke the truth: he wanted her, period. That revelation shivered up her spine, made her fingers tighten on the edge of the table. No, he only believed he wanted her. It was this connection between them, that was all.

Even as he told her to hate him, he touched her and made her want him instead. Love and hate . . . they *were* easy to confuse. They twined inside her, making her love and hate Paul, and . . . what about Mitch? She wanted to hate him, and she couldn't let herself love him.

Slowly she pushed herself up from the table and cleared away the dishes. Afterward she paused in the doorway of the kitchen, trying to conjure up the hate she needed. Her gaze locked on a picture of her and Paul on their honeymoon in Miami. That's where the anger came from, making her feel cold as stone.

You've done this to me. You brought your twin into my life, and now I'm so confused I don't know what I feel. I'm not going to let you hurt me any more by finding out you're a murderer. Or that you were seeing this Becky White. And I'm going to take all this anger I feel for you and aim it at your brother, because I don't want to feel guilty about him anymore.

And then she heard Paul's voice inside her. *Let your anger go. Let it go, Jenna, and live.*

She frowned. *I can't. It's all I have, and if I let it go, what will be left?*

For the next two hours, Jenna and Mitch went through piles of papers in the office. She'd dragged down boxes from the attic, representing all the years of her marriage, now reduced to paper.

She sat at one end of the desk, and Mitch sat at the other. His hair fell down over his forehead as he leaned over a file. He looked wholly consumed by his task, studiously keeping his gaze from meeting hers. That was easy earlier on when a stack of folders in the center of the desk separated them; except for the one time they'd both reached for the same folder. Now the stack was low enough for her to see him try to blow the lock of hair out of his face and toss the folder on the floor.

Mitch had shut himself off, as though their earlier conversation had never happened. She found herself replaying his words in her mind just to make sure they had been spoken. *Let them go, Jenna. He obviously has.* But that bothered her, and she found herself wanting to discuss it again. Things had been so much easier with Paul. He was always even, always just . . . there. She'd seen Mitch suspicious, angry, passionate, wolfish, and tender.

I've seen more sides to Mitch than I ever saw of Paul. Mitch chose that moment to glance up and catch her with goodness-knows-what expression on her face. She tightened her mouth and kept looking through the files.

Mitch had said he could feel Paul's love for her, yet he swore that was not the reason he wanted her. Maybe he just didn't realize that Paul was reaching out to Jenna through Mitch. Was she falling in love with Mitch because of that connection?

Was she falling in love? No, this was all wrong! But her heart confirmed her worst fear. Well, this was ending here and now.

Jenna redirected her thoughts to the folder in front of her. She had insisted on trying to find out where Paul had put the money he'd taken out of his account, but not a penny could be accounted for. Through their tax papers, though, she could account for the entire eight hundred thousand dollars. It had come into their account, and gone right back out again. They'd paid taxes on it. And it had virtually disappeared.

Mitch finally tossed the last folder on the floor and said,

"He didn't put the money into your houses. Anyplace else you want to check?"

She stared at the empty place where the folders had been. "No," she said at last. "I can't think of anywhere he would have put the money."

"You're sure he didn't gamble or have any other vices?"

"I'm sure. He could hide his past, but he couldn't hide his present. We were together all the time."

"Did he buy you any jewelry that could be worth more than you thought?"

Jenna shook her head, unable to remember any jewelry besides her wedding ring. She looked at the simple gold band. He hadn't even been able to afford an engagement ring. "No, nothing I can think of."

Mitch stared at that ring for a moment before turning away. "Then we're left with one other option."

Jenna shot to her feet, not willing to hear it. "There has to be something we're not thinking of."

"And that is?"

She chewed on her knuckle. "I don't know! There has to be something, though."

"Jenna, look at these dates again."

She pulled herself to the desk and stared at the list of dates representing Paul's withdrawals from his account. "What about them?"

"I know you say that you and Paul were never apart, but he left you the day he went to Maine. Were there other times around these dates when he took off for a while?"

She found herself staring at his finger and not the dates it was pointing at. She blinked, focusing on the numbers. The date before the last withdrawal was almost Christmas two years before. "I think he took off one afternoon to go Christmas shopping. We lived in New York, and he said he was going into the city to find something special. But not two hundred thousand dollars' worth of special." Her voice sounded thready, flat. "I can't remember way back to nineteen ninety-three, and the first one was right around the time we met.''

''We're going to need to find out if Becky was out of town during these dates. The only person I know to ask is her father. They have an awfully nice spread on the east end of town for a trucker's salary. Seems to me that the write-up in the paper about her death said she'd still lived with him, but it didn't say what she did for a living. Oh, I think her dad said something about her writing articles for magazines or something.''

Jenna had gone still at the mention of Becky. ''He wasn't seeing her. You even said so yourself. He didn't have time to carry on an affair with her.''

She saw Mitch's expression soften for the first time since she'd walked into the office. ''I'm not saying he was doing her. But we can't ignore the fact that they were from the same place, and died near the same place years later.''

''Maybe it's a coincidence.''

''Like you coming to Ponee and finding me.''

''Could it be that Paul had gotten her pregnant, way back when? Maybe he was supporting the child?'' She couldn't believe she hadn't thought of it earlier.

Mitch was shaking his head. ''She didn't have any children.''

Like that day when all this had started, Jenna reached for the drawer that held the extra supplies and pulled out the plastic bag. Mitch couldn't see what she held in her hands, but perhaps he felt the significance the way she did; he sat back in the chair and waited, drumming his fingers on the arms of the chair.

Finally she unrolled the bag and let the jewelry fall out on her lap. She picked up the mysterious wedding band.

Jenna sucked in a breath as the image wrapped around her, sweeping her into that pitch-black sky and brisk, salty air, into Paul's anger. She kept holding on, feeling stronger than she had last time.

Jenna saw the ring lying in the palm of Paul's hand, felt the anger this ring represented. And then she saw the woman—Becky White. Becky looked smug, arms crossed over her chest. Paul moved closer, calling her names Jenna had never heard him use. Becky's expression turned to concern and rapidly to fear as he advanced, closer, closer, reaching out for her.

Becky screamed and ran backward, losing her balance on some loose rocks and falling back into that abyss of blackness. Past the yellow sign warning of the danger of the sheer drop. All Jenna could hear was the pounding of the surf far below and of Paul's heart as he stared down into that blackness. She felt his fear and disbelief. Jenna swayed, opening her eyes to find Mitch shaking her shoulders.

"Jenna! My God, Jenna, are you all right?"

She blinked, stunned by the fear in his eyes. "I . . . I think so."

"Your heart was racing. You went limp, and you had no color, and you wouldn't answer me." He ran his fingers back through his hair. "Cripes, you gave me a scare. I thought you were—what'd you call it? Rejecting. I was about to give you CPR."

She hadn't thought how her flashbacks of Paul's life would look to an outsider. For a moment she felt warmed by Mitch's intent to save her. But no one could save her from the truth now, and she had no one to protect her from its aftermath.

Her hand was closed tight, but slowly she opened it and lifted it to Mitch. His gaze moved from her face to what lay in her uplifted hand, and his eyes widened in recognition.

He took it, holding it up so that the diamonds sparkled in the light. "My dad's ring. Where'd you get this?"

Her heartbeat was still pounding from the image, but she felt it slowing as if under a great weight. "Paul was wearing it the night of his accident. It was too big for his fingers, so he'd wedged it on his thumb. I had never seen it before."

"My God." He was staring at it as though it were the truth he sought. "Remember when I told you that whoever killed my parents made it look like a burglary?'' He looked at her. ''This was one of the missing pieces.''

Her eyes were locked to Mitch's as the truth dawned. ''I saw it.''

''Saw what?''

''Becky's death.'' Her voice was so soft, she could hardly hear it herself. ''Paul was there. She gave him the ring, and he was angry. She fell off the cliff trying to get away from him. He must have panicked, and that's . . . that's why he was driving so recklessly that night.''

''What do you mean, you *saw* it happen?''

''Some organ recipients get food cravings from their donors. Some sleepwalk, some can't dance anymore, some hate country music. One man had to go see the ocean, but he died before he ever got there. But that's not the point,'' she said, shaking her head. ''The point is, I got some of those things, and something else, something no one else ever has. When I touch certain items belonging to Paul, I see things. Like a dream, only I'm not asleep. I experienced the car accident through him, and I felt that sense of doing the right thing I told you about earlier. When I first touched this ring, I felt his anger and saw the cliff that Becky fell from.''

''And you didn't tell me?''

She was staring at the sleeve of his shirt, at the muscles bunched up in aggravation. ''I didn't think you'd believe me. And . . . maybe I wasn't ready to tell you then.'' She looked at the ring he still held in his fingers. ''But I can't hide from the truth anymore. Paul did it. Why else would he and this woman have had the jewelry?'' She squeezed her eyes shut, but it didn't keep the tidal wave of pain from crashing down on her. ''He and Becky probably did it together. And all these years, he's been seeing her, giving her blood money. But she did something to make him mad, and he inadvertently killed her too.''

''Jenna—'' He reached out to touch her arm, but she pushed him away and got to her feet.

''Don't touch me! Haven't you done enough?'' Her face

felt hot, eyes stinging. "You got what you wanted. You have the truth, and all I have are the lies. Are you happy now?"

"No."

She wanted him to be feeling the anguish that rocked her. "Well, you ought to be. I want you to leave. We have no more business to discuss." Her voice was broken, rising in pitch.

"What about the baby?"

She let out an anguished sound she'd never heard before and pushed at his chest. He took a step back, but his arms were still out to steady her.

"I don't want Paul's baby, and I don't want your baby! Here, take his watch and ring, pack up your things and get out of here. I want you gone when I get back. I never want to . . . see . . . you again!"

Now the tears were coming, clogging her throat with emotion. She twisted off her wedding ring and threw it across the room. It hit the window with a sharp sound. She pushed past Mitch and ran through the kitchen and out into the cool night air. Her heart was pounding in her ears, as though a great monster chased her. She glanced back, but saw no one coming after her.

Quickly she climbed over the rocks down to the beach, stumbling on the path she knew so well. Her bare feet slid across the damp rocks, but she didn't care. She had to make it far away from her house, from the lie that was her life.

The coarse sand was cold and damp, the water rushing in as though it intended to grab her and pull her out to sea. She walked to the water's edge, and a frigid wave washed in over her ankles. It slowed her heartbeat, *Paul's heartbeat,* she thought with disgust. She had the heart of a killer! She'd wanted the baby of a killer.

A sob wrenched from her throat, and she took a step farther into the water. Her feet began to feel hot, her ankles stiffened. The wind buffeted her, as if trying to send her back to shore, but the waves kept pulling her forward. She took another step, water now licking at her knees. The spray dampened her leggings like a hundred icy pinpricks. She welcomed the numbness. If she submerged herself, would that numbness settle into her body and take away this shattering pain?

Ten

Mitch stared at the ring, then at the doorway Jenna had run through. He wanted to give her time to cool down so she wouldn't beat her small fists against his chest, so he wouldn't have to restrain her and end up kissing her again. But something stronger urged him to follow her.

He walked outside, expecting to find her in the gazebo. It was dark and empty. He listened, but could only hear the sound of waves crashing in against the rocks. She wasn't anywhere in the yard; he was sure of this, yet he couldn't see every dark corner. His hand went to his chest, where his heart was thudding like a bass drum in a rock-and-roll song. He looked out over the ocean, where a shimmering sliver of moonlight pointed right at him. She was down there.

He maneuvered over the rocks in the darkness, his bare feet slipping against the cold, slick surfaces. The beach wasn't far away, but the trek seemed like miles. He barely felt the gritty sand and pebbles when he reached the beach, only aware of the pull that led him forward.

And then he saw her, standing in the water looking out to sea. She didn't see him and wouldn't hear him. What the hell was she doing? Whatever it was, he wasn't going to let it happen. She looked small and frail standing there with all of God's fury washing in around her, hair blowing around her face. Damn her for scaring him like this!

The frigid water bit at his ankles as he sloshed through the water behind her. In one movement, he grabbed her around the waist, twisted her, and slung her over his shoulder.

She screamed at first, caught off guard no doubt. "Stop it! Put me down!"

He gritted his teeth and kept walking toward the house, trying to remember the path he'd taken. Her legs felt like ice against his arms. She wriggled, but her fight wasn't hard. Her fists banged against his back as she murmured over and over, "Put me down. Please, put me down."

He steeled himself against her pleas and kept trudging onward, up over the rocks. She was smart enough not to struggle as he balanced himself all the way up to her backyard, but the moment he hit terra firma, she started in again. Her motions couldn't cover the fact that she was shivering.

Are you happy, you son of a bitch? He hoped Paul was watching from wherever his soul was condemned. Or maybe he'd been talking to himself.

Mitch carried her inside the house and upstairs to her bedroom. He knelt before her bed and dropped her down onto the blue spread. The light from her bathroom spilled in over the bed, washing her stricken expression in a pink glow. She didn't move, and he wondered if she was in shock. Her body was trembling, hands clutching the spread.

God, she looked so lost. He climbed up on the bed, legs straddling hers as he wrestled with the soaked leggings. She wasn't fighting him anymore. He wasn't sure if that was good or not, but he didn't care about anything but getting her warm. He jerked the bedspread down from beneath her and got her legs underneath it. They were both breathing hard, staring at each other.

"Don't you dare do that again," he said, lowering his head.

"I wasn't—" Her teeth were chattering, and she clamped her mouth shut.

Through the spread, he started rubbing her legs. All he wanted to do was get her circulation going again, make sure her state of mind was stable before he went to his room. No way was he leaving this house tonight, not with her like this. He concentrated on his task, but something made him look up at her. She was watching his hands, and he saw that spark of life return to her eyes. But he could still see the despair too.

"He wasn't seeing her," he said. "I promise you he wasn't. I would have felt it."

Her mouth opened, but it took her a second to say, "But he killed them."

He took her hands in his, finding them just as cold as her legs. She was a porcelain doll, soft and limp, beautiful. "We don't know that for sure. But we're going to find out."

"No, I don't want to find out any more."

"It can't get worse than what we already think. Come back to Bluebonnet with me, touch something in his room." He still wanted to find out that Paul wasn't guilty. Now the reason was for her, only for her. "We'll find out what really happened."

She met his gaze, eyes dry, hair damp and salty. "All right."

He smiled, filled with something he couldn't define. "That's my girl." *My girl.* Had he ever said those words to anyone before? His hands involuntarily tightened on hers. She squeezed back. She felt like she belonged to him, like she'd taken up a space inside him. It hurt and it felt wonderful at the same time. "That's my girl," he said again, softly.

With closed eyes, she pulled their linked hands toward her, kissing his knuckles with her cool lips. His body trembled at that simple act. He felt himself sliding toward a place of forbidden beauty, a dangerous paradise. Even through the blanket between them, he could feel the warmth of her thighs pressed against his.

"Jenna," he said in a hoarse, broken voice. It was a word of warning, of question. He couldn't tell which anymore. He had to leave right now, before this went too far.

She opened her eyes, and that despair he'd seen was gone. Her eyes were dilated, eyelids heavy. She lowered his hands and maneuvered herself from beneath the covers. He started to move back, to get off the bed and put some distance between them. She was on her knees now, and all she had to do to stop him was reach out. He stilled, not sure what she was going to do, almost hoping she would slap him.

Instead, she placed her hands on either side of his face, tilting her head and studying him. Her hands felt warmer now. *What are you looking for, Jenna? Paul's not in here.* He wanted to say the words, but nothing would come.

Her hands slid from his cheeks back through his hair. He felt the shiver shimmer through his body, making him tremble, making his head rock back with the impact of her touch. He heard her sigh, a soft sound he felt against his throat.

Her hands journeyed down his neck, over his shoulders and down the front of his shirt, then across his stomach. He pulled his head forward, sweeping his hands up into her hair and looking at her. Was she seeing Paul in those dazed eyes? God help him, but he'd sell his soul to make love to this woman no matter who she saw. He knew it was wrong, knew it would only hurt in the end, but he didn't care.

"Jenna—" He leaned forward and kissed her, the way a starving man would embrace a feast. Her lips responded to his the way they had earlier, melding with his, moving with his. He pulled her up against him, and her arms slid around his waist. And they were lost. He knew the moment she pulled him even closer that he couldn't look back now. Face the reaper in the morning, but for the price of heaven.

Her breasts were crushed against his chest. He wanted to feel her, all of her. He broke the kiss long enough to pull at the bottom hem of her shirt. Midway, she put her hand up, and he thought the dream was over already. But the look in her eyes wasn't to stop him, but something else he couldn't define.

"I . . . I have a scar," she whispered.

He kissed her softly, then tugged her shirt over her head. Then he unsnapped her bra and tossed both aside. She had started to cover herself with her hands, but let them drop to her sides. He slid his splayed hand down the front of her chest, where a scar ran from the hollow of her throat to just beneath her rib cage. It marred her creamy skin, and yet, it was as though he'd seen it a thousand times, as though he had accepted it long ago. Following his hand was his mouth, kissing every inch of that scar.

She belonged to him, and so did that scar, like it was a part of him. His hands traced the curves of her breasts. Her body relaxed as she seemed to sense his acceptance, and then she tugged his shirt from the waistband of his jeans. He helped by pulling it over his head, but stopped moving before he could drop his arms again. She was looking at his chest, running her hands over the surface as though he were some precious object. Her fingers lightly traced the fine line of hair that ran down the center of his stomach, then unsnapped his jeans.

He didn't need any more encouragement to get out of those damp jeans, and he dumped both those and his briefs on the floor. Then he slid her white panties over her hips and long legs, kissing the top of her toe, her ankle, and all the way up to her stomach. Her ribs showed through her skin, and he vowed to put some flesh on her bones. He wanted to possess her, take care of her so completely she would want for nothing. It wasn't Paul's protectiveness Mitch felt anymore; all the desire and warmth came from him now, only him.

She slid down beneath him, and he covered her with his body. Skin against skin, mouth to mouth, he absorbed her. And she let herself be absorbed, moving closer still, rubbing against him as though she couldn't get enough. He wanted to give her enough and more. He ran his tongue down her jawline, nibbled at her neck, cradling her rib cage with his hands and watching her arch into his touch. Her fingers curled in his hair as he worked one breast over, then the other. She wrapped her legs around his sides and ran her feet up and down the backs of his thighs.

Her face was flushed, eyes closed when he lifted himself

to look at her. She was a precious gift, his to love for this time until reality reared its ugly head. He had to keep those thoughts away, and he dipped down to kiss them right out of his head. Her mouth was hungry against his, turned up into a soft smile.

"You are so beautiful, Jenna," he said, taking her into his memory. He ran the tip of his finger down that scar, including that in his words.

She sighed. Her hands slid up over his chest and settled on his shoulders. "So are you."

He closed his eyes, not wanting to think about her saying those words to Paul. He kissed her again, reaching down to stroke her thigh and tease that slick place between her legs until her breathing quickened and she made that sound he'd imagined when he first saw this bed. Her body convulsed, tightened against his. He was about to explode with every touch as his hardness brushed against her belly. And then she reached down and wrapped her fingers around him, making him choke back a sound.

"Oh, Jenna, you don't want to do that," he managed to say.

"Then how about this?" she said in a whispery voice, angling him toward her until the tip of him nestled against her wet flesh.

He braced himself over her, looking into her eyes. He didn't ask, wouldn't ask, who she was seeing when she looked at him like she loved him.

Her legs tightened around him as he buried his face in her hair and buried himself in her. She let out a yelp, but wouldn't let him move back to see if she was all right. Instead she held on tight and moved with him like no woman had ever done. She felt like no other woman he'd ever been with, wet and warm and wonderful and so . . . right. She felt so damned right, and that's all he wanted to think about just then.

Her breathing came in jagged rasps, and she made an incredible little noise that made him picture her mouth all round like an O. Her body shuddered as she clung to him.

And then she cried, "Oh . . . Mitch."

His name washed over him in a more powerful wave than the orgasm that followed right after. At that moment, she was truly his, body and soul. He held her so tight, he was afraid he'd hurt her. But she held on just as tight. And kept holding on until her heartbeat settled down to a reasonable rate. Her legs relaxed, lying against his.

Finally he couldn't crush her any longer. He wanted to see her, ready to face the aftermath of what had happened. She would hate him for taking advantage of her grief, just as she'd accused him of doing. And he had. Dammit, he had. She couldn't hate him more than he already did. He was more than willing to take full responsibility for this whole episode. He rolled over, pulling out of her with the action. All their shared heat seemed to seep out of him.

She seemed to feel the same, because she pulled the sheet up over herself and curled onto her side. Her eyes were closed, but he could see them moving beneath her lids. Her lashes fluttered with the movements. He reached over and settled the tips of his fingers on her forehead, then drew them down over her face. Her eyes opened, and her gaze flickered over the naked length of him before darting back to his face. He was deluding himself, of course, but he saw hunger in those eyes. Then she covered her face, stabbing him in the gut with her action.

He got up and put his jeans on, then sat back down on the bed. "Don't shut me out, Jenna."

Her hands dropped away from her face. Her broad cheekbones were tinted pink, mouth red from his kisses. He couldn't read anything in her eyes, couldn't feel anything from her. That scared him in a way he'd never been scared before. This woman who was not his hated him, and he deserved every bit of it. She belonged to his brother, and Mitch had just pissed on that sacred vow they'd made to each other. He was lying on his brother's bed with his brother's wife.

"I'm sorry, Jenna."

She sat up, still holding the sheet over her breasts. "Sorry?"

"Sorry that this . . ."—he gestured vaguely at the bed—"is so wrong. Not sorry it happened."

He wanted to reach over and push away a strand of hair that grazed her cheek. He wanted her to move into his arms and hold on to him the way she had in Paul's old bedroom. He wanted her again. A dull, thudding sensation moved through his body, deep down in the core of him. But this time he only wanted to hold her. To keep himself from doing any of that, he stretched out on his side.

He'd never made love to a woman before.

Oh, he'd had sex with women, hot, panting, playful sex with women who knew how to take a man to the edge and kick him right over it. He came away from it sated. This . . . thing that had happened with Jenna hadn't sated him at all. It left him hungry for more, but it also left him with a knot in his gut. He couldn't have any more, never again.

Jenna badly needed time to assimilate all the feelings bombarding her, but as usual, Mitch wasn't going to let her turn away from the truth. She didn't even know what the truth was. All she knew was that this man lying on his side on her bed wearing only jeans and with tousled hair had rocked her body and soul in a way she had never known.

She would never forget the way he'd looked at her scar, with utter tenderness. She had searched his eyes for repulsion, sure he couldn't hide that from her. All she'd seen was total and complete acceptance.

Even if she had not uttered his name, she couldn't lie about believing him to be Paul. He was not Paul, oh, no. She had never looked at Paul's naked body and been stirred right down to the center of her being. Even now, knowing how wrong it was to want him, she did. She wanted to wrap herself around him again and just be held by him. Never had she craved Paul's touch the way she did Mitch's.

She cleared her throat. "Maybe it's something we had to get out of our system."

His gaze dropped down over her sheet-clad body, then

pinned hers with sultry frankness. "Did it work?"

"It's this connection we have, this synchronicity because of our hearts."

"That may be so, but I can tell you this: I never felt like stripping my twin naked and loving him thoroughly."

She felt her face flush, ducking down to press her forehead against her knees. She felt naked in more ways than one; she felt naked inside, vulnerable. She was sure if Mitch said one wrong word, she would shatter.

Had Mitch experienced the world shatter into pieces when they'd made love? Her body still felt all warm and mushy inside, her skin still tingled where it had touched his skin. Maybe he *had* gotten her out of his system and wanted to see if she had too. She rocked her head from side to side. Had she ever felt more confused in her life?

And then she realized it: all the anger that had consumed her earlier was gone. Oh, traces of it were still there, but the most powerful, most painful part was no longer engulfing her. That's why she felt so vulnerable! She needed Mitch's touch, his comfort.

No, she couldn't need anyone, especially not him. She couldn't forget that Mitch was the one who had brought her to this desolate point in her life.

The searing disappointment she felt when Mitch left the bed was proof enough of the mess she'd gotten herself into. She lifted her head to find him standing at the foot of her bed, the rest of his clothes in his hand.

"What do we do now?" she heard herself ask in a small voice.

He leaned against one of the posts on the bed, a resigned look on his face. "I guess you can go on hating me. And I'll go on hating me. But this isn't over." She felt a strange glimmer of hope until he continued. "We're going to find the whole truth. If we don't, we'll never get past this. Get some sleep, Jenna."

And then he was gone, and a chasm of emptiness descended upon her. Feeling naked and vulnerable, she retrieved her nightgown and slid it over her head, then got back into bed. Once they got past this, what then? She looked at the rumpled sheets and smelled the scent of their lovemaking. Paul had driven her to this. He'd left her, and then, through Mitch, had taken everything she had left. And now Mitch had taken one more thing he had no right to: her heart.

Damn both of them! She slammed her fist down on the pillow next to her, Paul's old pillow, and then threw it across the room. Yes, this was much better. The anger rushed through her veins like a narcotic, numbing, soothing. Jenna curled up in a tight ball. Anger was the only thing that would keep her safe.

From a far distance, Jenna heard a pounding noise. It seemed muffled as though through layers of gauze. And then, clearer, Mitch's voice.

"Jenna. Wake up."

What was he doing in her bedroom? Oh, right, they'd made love. She snuggled back into the cocoon of sleep, reliving those sensual moments.

"Jenna!"

His hands curled over her shoulders, shaking her out of that wonderful, gauzy state to find herself sitting in the parlor on the wood floor. She jerked around, blinking at the overhead light. Mitch crouched beside her, hair tousled and eyes still holding the misty hue of sleep. Then she became aware of the heavy weight in her hand.

"What's happening?" she said, dropping the hammer with a loud thud.

Mitch reached over and ran his finger along the cracked edge of the cabinet in front of her. "I heard you pounding away at something down here. You said you walked in your sleep, but I didn't realize you also wielded potentially dangerous tools. Were you dreaming about bashing my head in?"

He was still wearing only his jeans. "Maybe." She almost smiled at the worried look that stole over his handsome, sleepy features. She averted her thoughts to safer subjects, like what *had* she been dreaming about? "I don't remember. Whenever I've walked in my sleep, since Paul's death, I never remember what I was dreaming about. Like when I made the arrangements to go to Ponee. I woke up on the phone with a travel agency. It was like Paul had orchestrated my movements, even my voice."

They both looked at the cabinet, and Mitch picked up the hammer. "He wanted you to tear open this cabinet."

"No, he wouldn't want that. He made this for me." She remembered how he'd kept it hidden while he'd constructed it, telling her it was a surprise. She grabbed the hammer from Mitch's hand and slammed the head into the cabinet. Wood splintered, reminding her of her life these past few days. *This is for your lies! This is for your black heart that I got!*

"Whoa, baby, you're gonna hurt yourself." He took the hammer from her. "I know I told you to let out that anger, but I'd rather it not be while you're holding a weapon."

The word "baby" slid through her like that warm butter melting over the kernels of corn. "I'm not your baby."

He slammed the hammer into the wood even harder than she had. "I know that. Believe me, I know."

She felt disappointed that he'd given up so easily. *What did you want, Jenna, a fight? You know where fighting has gotten you with Mitch. Is that what you want?*

No!

"Give me that hammer!" She wrenched it out of his grip. "It's my dream, my hammer, and my cabinet." She smashed the front edge of the cabinet again, and a piece of wood broke free. There was a compartment between the bottom of the cabinet and the inside. Her throat went dry. "You said it could only get better from here." She reached in and pulled out a heavy cloth bag. "Can you guarantee that?"

"Nope. All I can guarantee is that whatever it is, we're going to handle it together." He held her gaze, punctuating his words. "Open it."

She pulled her eyes from his and set the bag down. It

was a tartan material, innocuous enough. Her hands were steady as she unzipped it and upended the bag. Jewelry spilled out onto the floor, rings, watches, lots of glittering diamonds and emeralds.

She knew before she even said, "It's their jewelry, isn't it? Your parents'."

Mitch's butt hit the floor, but his gaze hadn't left the jewelry. He picked up a huge diamond ring, bigger than Jenna had ever seen before. "My mom's wedding ring. Her watch. Dad's bracelet. They used to put it all in a dish on the nightstand when they went to bed." His voice went soft. "They never worried about getting robbed, not in Ponee."

"He murdered them."

Mitch reached into the hidden compartment, patting the sides and back. "Where's the knife?"

"What knife?"

"If he kept all this incriminating evidence, why didn't he keep the knife?"

"It's probably hidden under our bed," she bit out, feeling the comfort of her anger wrap around her like an old coat.

"Is Paul telling you it's there?"

"No. I don't feel anything but tired. I hate him." She looked up at Mitch. "I hate him so much."

He didn't move, didn't blink. In his eyes she saw him wage a battle, but she didn't know what the stakes were. Then he abruptly stood and walked toward the hallway. When he reached the doorway, he turned back to her. "I came here looking for the truth, and I didn't care who it hurt. I thought the truth would set me free." His smile was grim as he shook his head. "I was wrong. But now I want the truth to set you free. Tomorrow we're heading back to Ponee."

She stood up, hands pressed to her chest. "What if it doesn't set me free either?"

"It'll only possess you if you let it."

He turned again and headed up the stairs. Why did she

feel as though he were talking about him possessing her and not the truth at all?

No, she was imagining things, letting his soft voice play tricks on her mind. He meant to set her free from the spell their hearts and this connection had on them. Who would they be then?

She turned around to find Paul smiling at her from the photo on the mantel. She looked so happy, arms around his shoulders, blissfully ignorant of the truth. ''Idiot!'' She swiped the picture from its place, then turned to the one hanging on the wall, their wedding picture. ''Fool!'' In every room of the house she went, plucking any picture with Paul in it. She'd had a damned shrine to the man in here!

In the office, she remembered how Mitch had stacked them up. ''Stupid!'' she said, picturing herself stacking them back up again, ever the faithful wife. ''Well, I'm not faithful anymore.''

She found her wedding ring sitting on the desk where Mitch must have placed it. There was a white band on her ring finger, and she looked at that band for a long minute. Then she opened the shallow middle drawer and set the ring inside.

The pictures across the back of the desk mocked her. She removed each one and set it on the stack she'd brought in with her. She stared at Paul's face in the last picture. ''There's something else you deceived me about, Paul Elliot. You never showed me what really, truly being made love to felt like.''

Now she knew. But it was with the wrong man.

Mitch wore a vest and blue jeans, and his duffel bag sat at his feet. His hair was tied back, muscles in his arms flexed. He was leaning in the kitchen doorway, arms crossed, staring out the kitchen window. If he'd noticed the absence of Paul's pictures in the house, he hadn't commented on it. Or on the fact that the ring wasn't on the desk nor was it on her finger. Jenna wondered if he was thinking about Paul and the jewelry they'd found. Or their lovemaking. Whatever it was, it put a grim expression on his face, tightened his mouth, and instilled a distant haze in his eyes.

Jenna had taken her pills and packed the bottles in her bag. "I need to make a call before we leave." He nodded, and she walked over to the phone and dialed. "Hi, Millie, it's Jenna. I'm fine. Yes, I burned the candle. Yes, I said the phrase. Three times." She slid a glance to Mitch. "It worked. Paul's spirit will no longer be haunting me. Listen, I'm going away for a few days, to visit friends. I didn't want you to be worried. Thanks, Millie. You take care too. Bye." She turned to the door. "Okay, now I'm ready."

He picked up both their bags and headed to the front door. The foyer was always dark, with rich paneling and only a fan window in the door. That was one of the things she'd wanted to change. Dim morning light seeped in over Mitch's hair and shoulders. His fingers were wrapped around the doorknob as he waited for her.

She paused in front of him. "I'm going to sell the house and pay you back the money Paul took out of his inheritance. It doesn't seem right to keep it, not when he'd intended to pay off his . . . cohort."

She thought Mitch was going to open the door, and only realized he hadn't moved when she came up face to face with him.

"You're not going to sell the house. Keep the money."

She couldn't meet his eyes anymore, and turned back toward the interior. "I'll probably sell it anyway. It doesn't mean anything to me anymore." She wasn't sure if that was true, at least not yet.

He startled her by saying, "Sure it does. But no matter what you do, the money is yours."

She turned to Mitch again. "Why would you do that?"

He took his time answering, as though he were running through several different reasons. "You're my brother's wife." Simple words, yet laden with textures she couldn't decipher.

And then he opened the door and walked outside. "Damn. I forgot about my bike."

She was still weighing his previous words. Was that how he saw her, as only Paul's wife? Jenna walked outside and saw the bike, all shiny and inviting in her driveway. They'd made reservations at the airport early that morning, but neither had thought about his bike being there.

"I suppose I could fly back here and then ride the Harley back to Texas," he said, walking down the front steps.

Something tickled her insides. "Or we could take the bike."

He turned at that, lifting an eyebrow. "For a two day ride?" Maybe more, depending on the weather.

That tickle became the feeling of liberation, of adventure and freedom. "It would clear our heads."

He made a sound that contradicted her words. "I doubt that." He seemed to assess her, but she kept her eyes on the bike, imagining hours of riding in the wind. When would she ever get a chance to ride on the back of a bike . . . arms wrapped around Mitch, her inner voice added. This was the new Jenna, the one who wanted to embrace her new life.

"You sure?" he asked.

"Let me cancel the airline reservations," she said, turning back to the house.

Riding on the open highways was everything Jenna thought it would be. Okay, her rear was getting a little numb, but all she had to do was give the word and Mitch would pull over. They'd already stopped once, and he'd asked her if she needed a break two other times.

She was determined, though, to be an easy rider. No complaints about her butt, the noise, or the rock and roll pounding from the radio. She wore Mitch's jacket again, and her arms were wrapped around his waist, body pressed against his hard back. It was innocent touching, after all, perfectly harmless.

Yeah, right.

Yes, there was something illicit about enjoying that part of it, and maybe it was that illicitness that had spoken to her when she'd seen the bike sitting in the driveway. Images of the night before drifted through her thoughts, stepping up the awareness of her body. She rocked her head back and let out a sigh no one could hear but her. Sensuality rippled through her, a new and wondrous sensation. For these hours on the bike, she didn't have to face anyone or think about the future, or the past. For these precious hours, she could just let go and feel whatever came to her.

Only once in a while did she remind herself that to truly let go, she had to put Paul and Mitch in her past and go on without any reminders of that part of her life.

A pack of Harleys caught up to them, leather-clad biker dudes just like the ones on television. Biker chicks hung on to their men just like Jenna hung on to Mitch. Some even rode their own bikes. Mitch waved, they waved, Jenna even waved. She felt part of them, and for several miles they all rode together like that. And she felt a part of life for the first time in a long, long time. Maybe ever.

That night they found a small, clean hotel just off the highway. What if they only have one room? she found herself wondering. The thought didn't bother her, and in fact, when Mitch walked out with two keys, she could have sworn disappointment niggled at her.

Ridiculous! The last thing she needed was to fall into bed with Mitch again. And by the distant look in his eyes, he wasn't too keen on the idea either. The nice part about riding on a bike, he'd said before, was that you didn't have to talk to one another. But Jenna found herself wanting to talk.

"We'll get cleaned up and grab a bite to eat," he said, heading straight to his room.

She was about to comment on how exhilarating the ride had been, how neat that those bikers rode with them, but she simply nodded.

Their rooms were next to each other, and while she took

a shower, she could hear the water running in his room too. It was easy enough to picture him naked beneath the water, all those muscles and that tanned skin. Nothing like Paul.

"What are you doing, Jenna? Just what do you think you're doing?"

Well, she knew what her body was doing, getting all tingly and warm just thinking about Mitch. How much of Paul was wrapped up in her feelings toward Mitch? How much was because of their hearts?

"He probably doesn't even want you anymore," she told her mottled reflection in the mirror as she dried off. "You're lousy in bed, you know." Though he certainly hadn't looked bored. "You're skinny, and you have this ugly scar. . . ." She ran her finger down the scar, remembering how Mitch had kissed it. Even *she* saw something dark in her eyes when she looked at it, but she'd seen nothing dark in his eyes, nothing but desire. She relived the moments when he'd pulled off her shirt and looked at her body so lovingly. "Stop it. Get some food into you, that's all you need."

Yeah, right.

Mitch's knock on her door a few minutes later had her rushing to get dressed. "Be right there!"

He was kneeling next to the bike when she opened the door a few minutes later. "Something wrong?" she asked.

"Just checking her over."

He didn't even look up at her, and that produced a strange pang in her chest. He was back in jeans and a T-shirt, and though his jeans were a little baggy, they still looked sexy on him. She wore shorts and the usual top that buttoned right up to her neck. For the first time, though, she'd actually wanted to wear something that went lower. For the first time, she had an awareness about her body, the way it moved and looked, the way Mitch would see it.

"We passed a place down the road, said they had the best steak this side of cattle country," Mitch said, straddling the bike.

She slid up behind him. "That little red dive that looked like it used to be a house?"

"Or we could find a Denny's or something if we go into town. If there is a town."

Her mouth quirked as she put on her helmet. "The dive sounds perfect."

He glanced at her, tilting his head. Then he turned back and started the bike.

The Red Spur did, in fact, have great beef, and Jenna ordered a T-bone before Mitch could tell her she needed more meat on her bones. She remembered the meal they'd shared, and watched him dive into his juicy steak with gusto. She put a piece in her mouth and savored the taste of it.

See, Paul, you didn't trample me. I'm still here, still strong. I was your wife for five years, but I didn't know who you were. You were a lie, so I must have been too. Now I'm going to learn who Jenna is.

She caught Mitch staring at the place where her ring used to be, but he quickly averted his gaze. She opened her mouth to explain, but closed it again. How could she tell him that she needed a break from being Paul's faithful wife, that she needed time to find out who Jenna was, and who Paul had been.

It wasn't until Jenna went to the rest room after dinner that she realized the music she'd heard in an adjacent room wasn't a jukebox but a live band. She'd never liked country music much, but as she leaned against the railing, she found her body moving to the beat. There were a few people on the dance floor, lined up and dancing in unison. Line dancing, she thought it was called. She smiled, watching a skinny woman in a cowboy hat try to learn the dance. Instead of being embarrassed by her awkward moves, the woman was giggling. The man with her was laughing too, shaking his head and patiently starting over.

Jenna leaned against the rough-hewn post next to her and wondered how she'd thought her life was so complete while life was going on out here in the world. She was only living such a tiny part of it all.

"Thought you'd up and run off on me," a low voice said.

She turned to find Mitch standing right behind her. He leaned against the same post, arm behind her head.

"I've never danced before," she said, *meaning* to say that she was watching the dancing. She quickly turned back to the dancers. "I just got caught up in the dancing."

"I've never line-danced either. Never been into country music."

"Paul only liked to listen to classical, and I got hooked on that." Mitch's face darkened at the mention of his brother. "I've never even been in a bar before." She took in the cluster of tables by the dance floor, the dark corners that offered a place for a sultry kiss. Her gaze took it all in, ending with Mitch. "I like it."

"You really haven't danced before?" he asked. "Ever?"

"Never. Paul wasn't much into dancing, and for a while, I couldn't muster the energy for dancing anyway. My parents thought it was sinful." She turned back to the dance floor. "It doesn't look awfully sinful to me."

The song turned slow, and the people out on the floor moved into tight groups of two.

Mitch chuckled. "It's only as sinful as you want it to be." He kept watching the couples moving to a song about missing the dance . . . the dance of life. Then he looked at her. "Wanna give it a try?"

Her heartbeat jumped. "Are you . . . asking me to dance with you?"

One side of his mouth went up in a smile. "Yeah, I guess I am."

"Should we?"

He took her hand, twining his fingers with hers and leading her down the steps to the dance floor. "No body contact." He swung her in front of him, keeping one hand twined with hers, the other hand going around her waist.

Her free hand rested upon his shoulder. They started to move, eyes locked, bodies in perfect unison.

She wanted to cry. The tingling behind her eyes, the lump in her throat, all threatened to turn into gushy tears. He was dancing for her, because she'd wanted to dance. He was doing this for her. Paul had done a lot of sweet things for her over the years, but this was . . . different. It meant more, this simple thing that felt innocent and sensual at the same time.

Their small circle widened as they became more confident in their moves. They turned, knees brushing, turned again. Her palms were hot and moist, but she didn't want to let go of him to wipe them off. As though he knew her thoughts, his fingers tightened on hers. Their bodies had started out at the maximum distance, but now they were only inches away from touching. She could feel his hand tighten on her back, as though he wanted to pull her closer but was fighting it.

She wanted to move closer, to feel the length of his body against hers the way the other couples were dancing. She wanted to press close enough to feel him grow hard against her stomach, to hear him make that sound he'd made last night. She wondered what it would be like to dance naked.

Her parents were right. Dancing was sinful.

Mitch cleared his throat. ''Jenna, we'd better stop dancing.'' He said it in the same way he'd spoken when she had, beyond her thoughts, wrapped her fingers around that very male part of him. What had gotten into her? It was as though Mitch sparked the base part of her.

''Why?''

''Because the song ended a minute ago.''

She blinked, looking at the line dancers maneuvering around them. It was that song she'd heard on the radio when she'd left Bluebonnet Manor, ''T-R-O-U-B-L-E.''

They'd stopped moving, but were still linked together. Mitch mouthed the letters, then led her away from the dance floor.

"I thought you didn't do country music," Jenna said.

"I don't. But I know trouble when I hear it."

To Mitch, the sound of the motorcycle engine seemed to explode against the walls of the hotel as they pulled into the parking lot. It was late, dark and quiet. He should be exhausted from riding all day in the hot sun, but restlessness ran through his body like a drug. He cut the engine, and Jenna jumped off the bike. She rode as though she'd been born to ride on the back of his bike. Born to dance in his arms.

Damn, this wasn't any good at all. He took his time getting off the bike, removing his helmet and shaking his head. The Red Spur had sold him a six-pack of beer to go, and he pulled that from the storage compartment. Maybe a few of those would kill his restlessness, along with a few other things.

He removed one of the bottles, opened it and held it out to her. She shook her head, and he took a slug.

"Thanks for dancing with me." Her soft voice reached out and snagged him around the throat.

He cleared the feeling away and said, "You looked like a woman who wanted to dance." Hell, with that look on her face, if she'd wanted to jump off the roof with him, he would have accommodated her.

She nodded, a faint smile on her face. "I did." She looked shyly downward. "I liked it."

"Well, maybe the next guy you, well, end up with . . ." He hated the words, but he had to say them for his own sake. "Maybe he'll like to dance. But even if he doesn't, don't let that stop you."

She looked up a little too quickly, and that shyness evaporated. "There won't be a next guy." Her shoulders stiffened. "I'll never let another man hold me back. I don't ever want to be in a position to put my whole life in anyone's hands again. It hurts too much when they drop you. And don't you dare feel sorry for me. Because you know what? I'm going to be just fine." She fished her hotel key from her pocket. "Just fine." And then she turned and went inside her room.

Mitch stared at her door for a long time, wanting to knock and knowing he shouldn't. Finally he won the war and went to his own room with his six-pack. Did Paul even know what kind of woman he'd married? Did he appreciate all her layers, the way she glowed when she found pleasure in something? The tilt of her mouth. He dropped back on the bed, legs spread, hand holding his beer bottle upright. *Had* she ever made those noises when she'd made love with Paul?

He lifted his head and took another slug of beer, trying to push those memories away. Jenna was a strong woman, stronger than probably she even knew. But that strength came from anger, and that wasn't going to give her pleasure in life, that was certain.

"Neither one of us deserves her, Paul. You lied to her, and I took away her happy memories. Worse, I look like you, and once, I hated thinking that every time she looked at me, she thought about her love for you. Now I know better: every time she looks at me, she feels her anger at you."

But she'd said his name. Mitch couldn't get past that, could not put it away like he should. He'd made love to his brother's wife, and it made him soar that she'd said his name. "We're both bastards, cut from the same genes and blood. I just hope to hell you're not the murderer it's sure looking like you are."

He took another drink, set the bottle on the nightstand, and reached for the phone. Betzi's sleepy voice answered. "Hey Betz, it's me. Sorry for calling so late. I wanted to let you know we're coming in tomorrow, probably toward evening. That's if we keep making good time."

Betzi yawned long and loud, right in his ear. "We?"

"Me and Jenna." He even liked the sound of her name on his tongue. Cripes, he was in it.

"You're not dragging that poor girl back with you, are you?"

He chuckled. "She may look dainty and fragile, but let me tell you, the woman has teeth."

"Mm, sounds like you've been bitten."

Mitch could well imagine that smug little grin on Betzi's face. He rubbed his finger down the bridge of his nose. "You could say that. The lady is something else."

"Mm."

He didn't like the sound of that "mm," but he had no defense. "We'll see you tomorrow sometime."

"Wait a minute. What are you doing about your bike?"

"We're on it."

Now he imagined Betzi's eyebrows jumping up the way they did when she was riled. "You mean to tell me you made her ride from New Hampshire to Texas on the back of your bike?"

"No such thing, ma'am. She wanted to take the bike. Couldn't have said no even if I wanted to."

"Mm. I think I like her even more than I did before. I'll get the guest room ready. Not that she used it much before you chased her away last time."

Yeah, he'd heard all about that, up one side and down the other. "Our girl's not going to run away anymore. When she leaves, she's going to turn her back and walk without ever looking back."

Eleven

Jenna felt that strong sense of homecoming as soon as they crossed Ponee's city limit, and it grew stronger as they neared Bluebonnet Manor. Even Harvey, the big black dog, ran to greet them from his place near the stables. The sun had just set, spraying the bowl of a sky with pink rays. It was hard to believe that a few weeks ago she'd been living in blissful, lonely ignorance. Since then she'd had her memories shattered, she'd made love with her husband's brother, grown stronger, and ridden halfway across the country on a motorcycle glued to a man she had no business wanting.

No matter how many times she told herself she should hate him, or at the least, not like him very much, something deeper told her to let herself go and love him. Paul? No, that connection again. Everything was so tangled up inside her.

Not that it mattered. She didn't want to fall in love with anyone, especially not Mitch. And he didn't want to fall in love with her either. Hadn't he said that he hoped *the next guy* liked to dance? How much clearer could it be? Maybe he was just as confused by the feelings their connection inspired.

She looked up at the house as they turned onto the driveway. Certainly she had enough to face without getting mixed up with Mitch.

He punched a button on his bike, and the garage door opened. She was glad to get on her feet again, to get away from Mitch at last. When she returned home, she would fly. She already envisioned that flight as a symbol of her freedom, of leaving the past far behind. She just didn't know what she was going to do with her life once she landed.

Always, landing was the scariest part.

Mitch alighted from the bike and removed his helmet. A lock of hair had escaped his ponytail, curling over his forehead. Harvey barreled into the garage, panting and dripping and full of exuberance. "Hi, there, fella," Mitch said, kneeling down and scrubbing the dog with his fingers. When Mitch rose, Harvey ran over to Jenna, giving her the same kind of enthusiastic welcome. Despite the fact that dogs carried a troop of dirt and germs, and Jenna's immune system was suppressed due to the drugs she took, she knelt down and petted him too. She felt so welcome here, so comfortable.

"Oh, brother, Etta's here," he said, looking at the Cobra parked in the far spot.

Jenna turned to follow his gaze. "Etta?" Girlfriend? A spike of jealousy lanced her.

"Betzi's mom. She worked for a family in Dallas for who-knows-how-long, and when they passed away, they left her a nice little booty. She travels all over, but we get the pleasure of her company every few months. Great, just what I need. More chaos."

He hung up their helmets on hooks evidently made for that purpose, grabbed up their bags and led the way inside. At the door, he stopped and blocked Harvey's way inside. "Sorry, fella, but you know how Etta gets around dogs. You'd better stay outside."

"She doesn't like them?"

He raised an eyebrow. "She'll start playing with him, get him so riled up he's tearing around the house like a black tornado."

He'd put on the country music station for the last couple of hours of the ride, and the music inside the house was a continuation. Luckily it wasn't a slow song that would remind her of the dance she and Mitch had shared. Nope, she didn't want to think about that at all.

"War!" a woman's voice boomed out, followed by a cackle. "Let's see what you got, girlie."

Mitch dropped the bags by the back stairs and walked into the kitchen and family-room area. Betzi was filling ceramic cups with chopped tomatoes and lettuce, and an older, small woman with eye-popping red hair was seated at the far end of the counter hovering over a deck of cards.

"Mitch!" Betzi rushed forward and gave him a hug. Then, to Jenna's surprise, she gave her a hug too. "Good to have you back." She shot Mitch a sly look, then said to Jenna in a lower voice, "You just keep biting him, you hear."

Jenna's mouth dropped open, but before she could ask just what Betzi had meant by that remark, the other woman walked over and inspected her. "So you're Paul's wife, eh? Well, he could've done a lot worse, a *lot* worse." She gave Jenna a nod of approval. "Welcome to the family. I'm Etta, Betzi's mama."

Jenna shook Etta's outstretched hand, fighting the urge to cringe in pain. The woman had the grip of the Hulk. "Uh, thank you." *I think.* "Nice to meet you. I'm Jenna."

Etta had Betzi's bright blue eyes and a smooth complexion for a woman who must be at least sixty. She wore a pink and black polka-dot sleeveless blouse, and her biceps were nearly as big as Mitch's.

"That comes from bench-pressing one hundred pounds," Etta said, obviously catching Jenna's stare. "I'm the top contender in the over-sixty-five division in the American Body Builders Association." She reached over and pinched Jenna's arm. "Could use a little muscle yourself, girlie. Want to borrow my *Iron Biceps* tape? It's almost as good as the *Iron Buns* tape."

"Er, thanks, but no thanks."

Mitch, who was busy checking out those ceramic cups Betzi had been filling, looked up. "Don't pick on her, Etta.

She just had a heart transplant nine months ago." He popped a piece of tomato in his mouth.

Before Jenna could warm under his defense, Etta said, "My boyfriend, Howard, had a heart-lung transplant, and he was playing tennis three months after the operation. Best way to treat that heart is to get it pumping, and there are some great ways to do that, if ya know what I mean." She bobbed her matching red eyebrows up and down. Jenna flushed as red as Etta's hair. "Don't get embarrassed, girlie. Sex ain't nothing to be ashamed of. Healthiest thing a body can do."

Jenna couldn't help but look at Mitch, but quickly turned back to Etta. "Is . . . that so?"

"Certainly. A good, old-fashioned orgasm gets your blood flowing, works your heart, burns calories, is even good for your complexion. Don't mourn for too long. Six months is plenty long to boo-hoo before getting back in the swing of things. I've outlasted three husbands, and though I loved each and every one of them, bless their hearts, not a one was worth giving up my life for more than six months." She looked over at Mitch, who was getting out a couple of plates. "Maybe Mitch can help you."

Jenna's mouth dropped open. Just the mention of an orgasm in the same stream of conversation as Mitch knocked her off balance. "What—?"

"Sure. Don't you know some virile young men you could fix up Jenna here with? What about Dave? He's a hunkeroonie, good with the horses; bet he'd get her engine revving." She made revving noises, *vroom, vroom.*

Mitch did not look amused. "She doesn't need my help, believe me." He nodded for her to join him, that lock of hair bouncing with the movement. "Nice hair, Etta. What color is it this time? Cheeky Cherry? Colossal Copper?"

Etta sat down in front of the two decks of cards. "Rah Rah Red." She tilted her head coyly. "You like?"

"It's astounding."

"C'mon, Betz, finish the war. We both put down kings."

Betzi rolled her eyes and headed over. "When they said I'd probably be taking care of my mother in her old age, I never imagined—"

"You just watch your mouth there, girlie! I'm younger than you are. Inside where it counts." Etta picked up her next card with long fingernails painted to match her hair. "You'll never beat this card."

"What are these?" Jenna asked as Mitch handed her a flat tortilla.

"Tacos. You've never had tacos before?"

"Not like this." She watched Mitch pile shredded beef, salsa, little green peppers, and tomatoes on his tortilla and followed suit. After her first bite, she was grasping for the glass of iced tea, chugging half of it down without even adding sugar. "Hot, hot," she said, rapidly sucking in air.

"Oops, should have warned you about the hot peppers," Mitch said with a sheepish shrug. "The meat's spicy too."

"After Miguel, life was nothing without spices," Betzi said.

"Who's Miguel?" all three asked simultaneously.

Betzi gave them a sly smile, laying down an ace to win the last round. "I met him when I was living in Dallas. He was a master chef at one of the best Mexican restaurants in the city. We dated," she said with a coyly innocent look. "He taught me a lot about spicy hot."

"Betz, you've been holding out on me!" Etta said, tossing her cards at her daughter.

Mitch and Jenna laughed, their eyes meeting over their tacos. Their laughter faded, and both looked away, clearing their throats. When Jenna saw that Betzi was watching them, she said, "The tacos are great, minus the peppers."

"Too bad we don't keep a fire extinguisher next to the peppers," Mitch said, referring to her earlier comment.

Betzi refilled Jenna's tea. "I figured tacos would be nice and light after a long drive, and they'd keep in the fridge until you got here. And Mitch, really, you could take the food to the table so your guest can sit down and eat."

Jenna waved that away. "I've been sitting on the back

of a bike for days, Betzi. The last thing I want to do is sit down. But thanks, anyway.''

"He could have offered," she said. "*If* he were a gentleman.''

"When did you ever think I was a gentleman?'' he asked, looking at Jenna for confirmation.

"He's a safe driver,'' was all she could say. She had a flash of him carrying her into the house, rubbing her legs to get her warm again. Everything had happened in such a haze that night, as though it were a dream. But now she remembered: *she* had reached for him, pulled him closer, kissed his hands. She found herself looking at those hands, covered with taco-meat juice. "And he's a perfect gentleman.''

He lifted an eyebrow at that, but wisely didn't comment, instead licking the drops she'd just been looking at. Betzi regarded them both thoughtfully, and Jenna made sure not to look at Mitch. What would her eyes reveal if she did? Jenna shook her head, chasing away the thoughts. She was just tired from a long trip, from the prospect, too, of facing what was ahead.

Etta slapped both halves of the deck of cards together. "I've got to do my *Iron Abs* workout tape before bedtime. You want to join me, Betz?''

"I can work up a sweat just watching you. No, I think I hear a good book calling me. Good night, kids.''

"Jenna,'' Etta said. "You come find me in the morning, and I'll introduce you to Dave. I think he'll snap the life right into you.''

"Er, no thanks, Etta. I'm not interested in meeting anyone right now.''

"Nonsense!'' she said in the same way Betzi said it. "You've got to stop mourning, girlie. Get on with your life.''

Jenna set her taco down. "I'm not mourning anymore. I just have no use for men at this point in my life. They're nothing but trouble.'' She shot Mitch a sideways glance. "But thanks for your concern.''

Etta merely waved her off. "Nonsense! Can't imagine having no use for a man. Can *always* find use for a man. Good night, kids."

They walked down the hall toward the garage, disappearing around the corner. Mitch shook his head, but he wasn't smiling. He packed up the leftover food while Jenna rinsed the plates and put them in the dishwasher.

"Who's this Dave?" she asked, more for the sake of conversation than curiosity.

"He's my head horse trainer, and I consider him my best friend. We've known each other since we played football together in high school." She detected an undertone beneath each word, or maybe she was imagining that what he was really saying was, *Don't even think about getting involved with him.* "Come on, I'll take your bag up to your room."

"How many people work here?" she asked, following him up the stairs.

"About fifteen, including some part-timers. Dave and I work on training the horses, I buy them, Tawny heads up our breeding program, Burt's the property manager, and a whole assortment of others."

She passed the collage of pictures, but none of that sadness lingered. Instead she saw Mitch holding her, the very beginnings of all the strange feelings she had for him. He saw her pause before them, but continued on to the room where she'd asked Mitch for his sperm. What a mess their relationship was, all the way from the beginning.

"Make yourself at home," he said, remaining in the doorway. "I've got to go out and check on my horses, make sure everything's hunky-dory." He hesitated, then pushed himself away from the door frame and started to go.

She felt gritty, longed for a shower, but found herself saying. "Can I come with you?"

He stopped and turned around, jamming his hands in his front pockets. "Are you sure you want to prolong your exposure to trouble?"

"Hmm," she said, walking toward him. "Like a few more minutes would matter."

"All it takes is a few seconds to go from zero to sixty, babe," he said, purposely not looking in her direction.

Or from kissing his hands to being in his arms. "I'll try to control myself . . . *babe*."

He shot her a sly smile, leading the way down the stairs. Babe. Had she and Paul exchanged endearments? Her life with him seemed to be rapidly receding into the past, even though she never forgot whose heart was beating within her.

They walked side by side through the thicket of pines toward the large barn structure. Harvey followed, always their shadow. Strategically placed lights shed enough light for them to see the way, and lit the structure bright white. Lights burned in some of the upstairs windows of the upper part of the T, but the long structure was dark.

"Are people still working?" she asked, not sure she wanted to meet anyone yet.

"People live up there."

"Really?" She looked up to see curtains adorning the windows, one with a sun catcher in it.

"I set up some apartments for visitors, but for the time being one of my employees needed a place to stay for a bit. And Dave's staying here until his house is finished."

One of the curtains shifted, and Jenna saw someone peer out. Mitch pulled out a set of keys and opened the door.

"Wow, what kind of barn is this?" she asked, taking in the plush lobby, the hallway beyond and the staircase leading upstairs.

"We put our horses to work around here. One answers the phones and greets guests."

She laughed at the mental picture that created. "I want to see one take that circular staircase."

He chuckled. "You wouldn't want to see it from too close an angle, I can tell you that." He checked a chart on the desk, flipped through a pile of message slips, then nodded for her to follow through another door. The floor was rough bricks leading to a large door at the opposite end. Flanking them were rows of horse stalls. She could smell the beasts, their manure and hay and other sweet smells. As soon as the door closed, more than a dozen heads popped out of their stalls to see who was visiting.

"Hi ya, fellas," Mitch called out.

Jenna felt an odd nervousness, even though the horses were obviously penned in. Mitch kept walking, his shoes making soft thudding noises on the bricks. Harvey walked down to the end of the stalls, obviously interested in something down there. Mitch walked over to the first inquisitive horse and rubbed its cheek, murmuring something soft to it.

Jenna cleared her throat. "Was Paul, by chance . . . afraid of horses?"

Mitch nodded, continuing to stroke the horse. "Much to the mortification of our father. You too?"

"Well, I don't think I used to be. I mean, I've never been around horses, but I have no reason to fear them. Yet I feel afraid."

"Paul had no reason either, but he was terrified of them. Dad bought a couple of show horses when we were teenagers. He was even talking about buying some racehorses, getting involved in the whole scene at Manor Downs in Austin." He tickled the horse beneath its chin. "For me it was love at first sight. But Paul, he didn't go for them. Dad was a bit of a bully, and he tried to force Paul to like 'em. Lot of fights over that," he said, nodding and obviously remembering those fights well. "He never came around."

Jenna moved closer. The plaque on the stall read "Led Zeppelin," and Led certainly looked harmless enough. "Did your father build this place, then?"

"No, he was only getting into horses when he was killed." He cleared his throat. "Paul and I were supposed to go to Rice University, but with the whole murder investigation, and afterward . . . well, that never happened. But I already knew what I wanted to do, so I got a B.S. in animal science, and everything else I learned along the way. Come here.''

Those words, spoken so softly, shivered through her. She walked closer, and he took her hand in his, guiding it to the horse's cheek. The hair was coarse and smooth, and the horse didn't seem to mind awfully much that she was touching it. She grinned, tickling Led beneath the chin like Mitch had done. Led returned the favor, twitching his lips and tickling her arm with his whiskers.

''Led here's a show jumper, with lots of ribbons to his credit. Smile for the lady.''

And Led did, baring his teeth. Jenna laughed. Now her nervousness was due to her proximity to Mitch, not the horse.

''Well, it's about time you decided to come back home,'' a female voice said from the vicinity of the doorway.

''Yeah, well, I needed a vacation. Tawny, this is Jenna Elliot. Jenna, this is Tawny Ayres, our breeding specialist.''

Tawny fit her name well, long and lean, with waist-length, straight brown hair. Jenna found herself smoothing down her hair in some ingrained female instinct. Tawny shook Jenna's hand, another hardy handshake. The girl's smile didn't cover her assessment, like a cat checking out an intruder. ''Elliot?'' She looked at Mitch. ''Didn't run off and marry someone on me, did you?''

Jenna picked up on that second territorial clue. She glanced over at Mitch, answering for him. ''No, I was married to Paul.''

Tawny's eyes widened. ''Really now? So where is the little stinker, anyway?''

''Dead.'' Jenna thought it interesting that Mitch hadn't told Tawny about everything. Of course, he'd probably left for New Hampshire soon after Jenna had. ''He died in a car accident last year.''

''Oh.'' Her pretty face fell for a moment.

''Did you know him?'' Jenna asked.

''Yeah, sure. It might sound, I don't know, kinda mean,

but it feels like he's been dead anyway, being gone so long." She shrugged off her words. "It's nice that you could come visit us." An out-and-out lie, Jenna could tell. Tawny looked at Mitch. "Everyone here missed you." Clearly including her. "Midnight was a real stinker, speaking of. Nipped Dave today, stepped on my foot."

"Midnight Blue's my personal horse," he said to Jenna.

She could only nod, her throat curiously dry. Tawny caught him up on some of the happenings during the week, and Jenna was left to stand there and try to act as though she knew what they were talking about. She felt grubby and wished she'd just stayed in the house, taken a bubble bath and gotten some sleep.

"Mitch!" A little boy of about three nearly flew from the doorway and into Mitch's arms. He scooped him up as though he'd done it a hundred times before, tilting him this way and that and eliciting squeals and giggles from the boy. "Put me on your shoulders! Where you been, Mitch? We missed you."

"Scotty, you're supposed to be in bed," Tawny said, though she didn't seem terribly upset.

Mitch set Scotty on his shoulders. "I had to take care of some business, buckeroo. Did you learn anything new while I was gone?"

"I trotted on my pony."

"Awright! Give me five, little man." Mitch held out his palm, and Scotty leaned forward and slapped it with his tiny palm.

Then Scotty added, "Mama was with me, so it doesn't really count."

"You were holding the reins, weren't you?" Mitch asked.

"Yep."

"Then it sure does count."

Scotty looked just like Tawny, though his face wasn't lean yet. Jenna watched Mitch's easy way with the boy and suddenly wondered if he were Scotty's father. Maybe he and Tawny were married. No, he'd said something about not getting married or deeply involved with anyone. But they'd never talked about whether he was seeing someone, or if he'd produced any children. Not that it mattered, of course.

Jenna swallowed a lump in her throat. It mattered. She didn't want to explore why, but it did.

"Scotty, this is Jenna. She's visiting for a spell."

"Hi, Jenna," the little boy said shyly, giving her a cute little wave with just his fingers. She felt her heart open right up to him. He ducked down, trying to hide behind Mitch's head and not very successfully.

"Hi, Scotty." Another lump. Damn. He was adorable, and she felt an overwhelming urge to touch him. He smelled of baby powder and something sweet, and all at once that yearning for a child burst upon her again.

"Do you have any kids?" Tawny asked.

"No." Jenna tried to say the word as though it meant nothing. And then she realized something: she and Mitch hadn't used anything when they'd made love. What if she were pregnant right now?

"Are you all right?" Tawny asked. "Didn't mean to pry or anything."

"No, it's . . . fine." But she could feel her face pale as Mitch turned to see what was wrong. Not that she could tell him. The prospect made a smile bloom on her face, color return. "I want to have a child. Paul and I . . . never did."

Tawny obviously knew Mitch well, felt comfortable with him, and was attracted to him. Could Tawny see that last part in Jenna's face as well?

"We'd better get you back to bed, young man," Tawny said, easing up close to Mitch to take her son down. She remained there a moment longer than necessary, shooting Jenna a meaningful look before moving back. "If you want to catch up, I'll be awake until eleven. Otherwise, I'll see you in the morning. Nice to meet you, Jenna. Scotty, give Mitch a kiss good-night."

Mitch bent over, and Scotty planted a kiss on his cheek.

He held on to the boy's little shoulder and whispered something to him. Scotty nodded, then walked up to Jenna and pursed his lips. Touched beyond belief, she bent down and pressed her cheek against his moist lips. He giggled and ran back through the doorway.

Tawny was obviously territorial about both her men, because she hesitated before smiling. She swung her long hair over one shoulder and said to Mitch alone, "Good night." Then she turned and walked back into the office building.

"She must live upstairs," Jenna said, remembering the person peering out through the curtains.

Mitch nodded, not watching Tawny's retreat but scanning the horse stalls. "Yeah, I hear you, Midnight." He walked toward the back where a horse was whinnying and stamping his hoof.

"Cute kid," Jenna said, following him. "Looks just like his mother. I presume that's his mother."

"Sure is. Hey, Midnight. See, I didn't up and run off on you."

Jenna realized she'd been searching Scotty's face for signs of Mitch. He did have brown eyes, but so did Tawny. His hair was straight and brown, nothing like Mitch's. She wanted to ask, but felt out of place doing so. She reached out and touched the black horse's mushy nose.

"Why do you call him Midnight Blue? Does he look blue in the sunlight?"

"No, I named him after a Lou Graham song. I name all my horses after rock and roll. Midnight's sire is Foreigner, and Lou used to be in that group." At her blank look, he added, "You don't know Foreigner? They haven't done much in recent years, but they were huge back in the eighties. Rock and roll has gone down the tubes lately, hasn't it, Midnight? No more songs about fast cars, fast women, and good ol'-fashioned sex. Everything is about nothing, blue cars and blue buildings and suicide. Give me some Led Zeppelin, AC/DC, Damn Yankees."

Her mouth was just starting to open and say, "Who?"

"Tawny said you were back," a male voice said. A tall,

blond man strode toward them. "That stinker is going with you next time you decide to up and disappear." He grinned. "But you brought back a souvenir. I'm Dave Hammond."

She shook his outstretched hand, not sure whether to be offended by being referred to as a souvenir or not. "Jenna Elliot."

"Paul's wife. Tawny just told me. I saw you the day you first came here. I was playing football," he added at her questioning look. "I'm sorry to hear about Paul."

"Thank you."

Dave filled Mitch in on a few things, shook her hand, and headed up to watch *Walker, Texas Ranger.*

Mitch said, "I think he wants to be a Ranger when he grows up. Come on, let's go back to the house. Looks like you're fading fast."

When they walked back into the office, Tawny's voice rang out, "Scotty, get back up here!"

All Jenna saw was a blur as the child streaked buck naked down the hall to wave at them from the balcony upstairs. "Bye, Mitch! Bye, lady!" He turned to see his mother racing after him, and darted around her back to their apartment.

She rolled her eyes, then chased after him. Even frazzled, the woman looked under control. Mitch chuckled as he locked up the office door behind them, but Jenna sank into silence. Had she ever felt so many feelings at once? Envy, longing, anger, heartache . . . she glanced over at Mitch as he rubbed Harvey's head . . . love? No, not love. *Go back and focus on the anger. It's simple, easy, powerful.* She remembered Mitch's words: love and hate are the most powerful of emotions. How true, how true.

The night was warm and humid, nothing like a New England summer night. And not at all like that desert Texas she'd imagined before she first arrived here. Crickets sang out, and the moon had come out to light up the pasture. Jenna couldn't help but turn back; just as she suspected, someone was watching them from behind the curtain again.

The uneasiness returned, churning her stomach. Was

it . . . could it be . . . jealousy? She might have dismissed it out of hand, but it was such a curious feeling, one she'd never really had before, that she wanted to examine it.

"Now you can tell Etta that you met the wondrous Dave," Mitch said, stuffing his hands in his pockets as they headed through the pine stand.

"I'll be sure to mention it."

She looked over at Mitch's silhouette next to her, lock of hair bouncing with his steps, shirt rumpled over his broad shoulders. Her mouth quirked, not quite a smile, but almost. Did he feel it too? Dave was good-looking in a rugged sort of way, tall and lean, complexion red from the sun. But he didn't stir her insides the way Mitch did. And this jealousy thing . . . how very curious. In an odd way, she felt *attached* to Mitch. As though she belonged to him, or with him maybe. Because of this connection they shared, she assured herself.

"Is Tawny married?" She just couldn't let it go, could she?

"Divorced."

"That's too bad. For Scotty, I mean. You seem like a good father figure for him."

Mitch pulled the band out of his hair and ran his fingers through it. "He's a good kid. His dad's a real son of a bitch. That's why they're staying here, to give him time to sober up and learn to behave himself."

"Oh." Well, that answered that question, anyway. But what about his involvement with Tawny?

They walked into the house and up the stairs. "Do you need anything?" he asked when they reached the top.

"Peace of mind, answers, or perhaps a handy case of amnesia."

He chuckled, a soft, low sound that shivered right up her spine. "Maybe I can help with the answers part, but I'm afraid I'm out of the other two."

She nodded, feeling at a loss for words. Finally, she looked down at the duffel bag he'd left by his bedroom door. "Do you have the jewelry?"

"In here." He tapped the bag with his foot.

"What are you going to do with it?"

"Dunno. Let's see what we find out."

"All right. Well, good night then."

"Good night."

Jenna sank into a tub full of hot water ten minutes later, head cushioned by an inflatable pillow she'd found in one of the cabinets. Instead of relaxing, however, she found herself crying. And for the first time, she didn't know why.

Forty minutes later, Jenna eased herself from the tub, feeling achy and tired. And oddly cleansed. Up until then, tears had proved useless, a sign of her own helplessness. She pressed her hand over her heart. Not this time.

She slid into her short silk nightshirt, brushed her teeth, and walked into the bedroom. Music filtered through the door, not loud, but definitely that rock and roll he'd talked about earlier. Then she picked up on another sound, this not part of the music. She eased the door open and found a pile of thick green towels in front of her door. Who had left them there?

Then she heard the sound of glass shattering. She stepped out into the hallway and looked out over the gathering room. The stereo was on, lights twinkling in sync with the music, but no one was there. She walked down the hall and peered into the open doorway of Mitch's room. It was dark, but for the moonlight spilling in from the French doors facing east.

More glass shattered.

She took the stairs quickly and turned the corner to find Mitch staring at the fireplace. His hair was damp, and he wore nothing but blue jeans. His muscles were bunched up in tension, fingers working the air. Then he picked up a framed photograph and, using a pitcher's stance, sent it flying into the fireplace. The glass shattered against the bricks in the back. No fire burned, and she could see remnants of other pictures in there as well.

"Son of a bitch," he said, picking up another picture and sending it off.

"Mitch, what are you doing?"

His shoulders tensed, but he didn't look at her. "Jenna, go back to bed."

She walked closer instead, even though danger radiated from him. He had a stack of family photographs on the table behind him, most of him and Paul alone. She walked around the table and tried to draw him away from whatever possessed him. "What music group is this?"

"Metallica. Now go to bed."

He had a wonderful back, all muscles and tension, one drop of water sliding down the indent of his spine. She felt so well acquainted with that back, after being pressed against it for two days.

"I don't think I should leave you alone," she said, pulling her attention back to the matter at hand.

"I'm having a little one-to-one with my brother." He picked up another picture, both twins in a Jeep. "Leave us alone."

He still hadn't looked at her, but she could see the cords in his neck tense as though he were fighting the urge to turn to her. She glanced down at her dark green nightshirt, not too revealing although the top part of her scar showed above the neckline. Her hand went automatically to cover it. She didn't know why, but she asked, "You heard me crying, didn't you?"

He threw the picture, harder this time. It hit the side, sending shards of glass over the flat stones in front of the fireplace. His voice was low, ominous when he said, "I need some time alone with my demons. Leave."

She should have gone. She even leaned away, but her feet wouldn't take a step. Her body wanted to take her over to him, and she found herself standing just behind him. She reached out, pressing her palms against his back. He swung around on her so fast, she didn't have a chance to even make a sound. He pushed her backward, several feet, until she felt the wall against her back. He pinned her wrists to the wall, and his mouth came down on hers.

She sucked in a breath through her nose, making her breasts press up against his chest. Her mouth opened to his, and his tongue ravaged hers, taking until she couldn't even think. Just as abruptly, he let her go. Anger burned in his eyes, but she couldn't tell if it was aimed at her, Paul, or himself.

"You gonna leave now?" he growled. "Or you gonna stick around and hate me even more for ripping your clothes off and taking you on that couch?"

His dark words spurred excitement within her, not fear. Her body came alive, just as it had the last time they'd made love. He looked wild, hair uncombed, chest bare, danger burning in his eyes. She wanted to inhale that fire into herself. She didn't move.

He was warring with himself; she saw it, felt it, responded to it. It was like the waves washing in around her all over again, and the exhilaration of Mitch throwing her over his shoulder and taking her to bed. This was a whole new part of her, a part she'd never even guessed existed. Her hands were still above her head, where he'd left them. She let them drop and tilted her head.

His voice cracked when he said, "God, Jenna, do you want me to hate myself more than I already do?" He reached out and ran his thumb down her cheek, then turned and walked away.

Her lips still burned from his assault, knees weak at the prospect of feeling his body against hers again. She heard his footsteps pounding across the floor, then the slam of the exterior door. Her heart was pounding, but that sensual beat was becoming overwhelmed by a different kind of warmth. He wanted her, and he hated himself for it. He wanted her.

Jenna saw something move out of the corner of her eye. Betzi peered around the corner, a startled look on her face. Jenna put her hand over her mouth, stifling the "Oh, my," that wanted to escape. Betzi must have heard everything, or at least the worst of it.

"Are you all right?" she asked, coming into the room now, assessing the damage.

Not by a long shot. "I . . . I'm fine."

Betzi walked into the kitchen and pulled out a pan, then poured in two cups of milk. "I heard a commotion and came down to see what was going on." Those words hung in the air, and Jenna felt embarrassment creeping up over her features. "Want to talk about it?"

Jenna wanted to run from the room and bury herself under her covers, but instead, she found herself saying, "Yes."

Twelve

Mitch walked toward the stables, blood pounding in his ears. Why hadn't she moved when he'd told her to leave? She'd just stood there looking at him with . . . something, something he couldn't figure out shining in her eyes. As though she were daring him to follow through on his threat, which he'd been damned close to doing. Too damned close, he noted, aware of his body's reaction.

He inhaled, letting the pine-scented air fill his lungs. Nothing, it seemed, was going to calm him down, nothing except turning around and going back to the house and taking her up on her dare. The first time he'd loved her, it wasn't planned; it just happened. From here on out, he would have to take full responsibility for his actions.

"Cripes, it's your brother's wife. No matter what, she was married to him, loved him . . . wanted to have his baby." That familiar spike of pain shot through him as he remembered the way she'd asked him to give her Paul's baby.

And when she looked at him now . . . when she had looked at him just a few minutes ago, whom had she seen?

The pine trees had a two-dimensional quality to them, and he felt the rough bark scratch his bare shoulder as he misjudged distance in the moonlight.

When he and Paul were kids, some wacky doctor had said Paul was a shadow twin. Mitch thought it was ridiculous, still did. Looking back, though, Paul had sometimes seemed like a shadow, never able to live up to Mitch's abilities, always wanting to fill his shoes. Now Mitch wanted to fill something of Paul's, and it wasn't his damned shoes.

He had reached the stables, and stopped to press his forehead against the door. It was the shadow thing that made Mitch vow never to take anything from Paul. Even when they were kids, Paul didn't have the guts to fight for what was his, to take what he deserved. Their father gave them nothing they didn't ask for, didn't earn. Paul never learned to ask or to fight, so Mitch did it for him. Mitch had come into the world five minutes before Paul and he'd easily stepped into the big brother role. Look how easily he'd stepped on their scared vow.

The truth would have to make him complete. Wasn't that what was missing in his life, the truth? He'd told himself that for years, if only he had the answers he sought, he could go on with his life and feel whole. Then why, when he looked at Jenna, was he sure that only she could complete his life? Of all the women he'd met over the years, why did that woman have to be his brother's wife?

Energy rumbled through him once more, and he found the hidden key behind the sign and went inside. The lights in the gym were blindingly bright. He turned them off again, led only by the dim light from the hallway. He knew the machines by heart anyway, and he set the weights by feel. He worked quietly, never letting the metal weights slam together.

"Mitch? Is that you?"

At first he imagined the soft, female voice to be Jenna's. But he knew it wasn't her, and something inside him wilted at the realization. He saw Tawny's lithe silhouette outlined in the doorway.

He let the weights slowly drop. "Yeah. Did I wake you up?"

"No, I couldn't sleep. Then I heard someone down here." She walked closer, leaning against the leg press machine Mitch was on. "Couldn't sleep either?"

"Haven't even tried. Haven't slept a whole night

through in years.'' Except for those nights at Jenna's house, where, miraculously he slept all the way through. When she wasn't tearing up furniture in her sleep, that was.

''But you've never come out here this time of night and started a workout.'' Tawny smelled clean and soapy, something like the flowers in the spring that sprang up all over the pasture. He could barely make out her features, but he sensed a difference about her. She leaned a bit closer. ''You want to talk about it?''

He let out something that sounded like a sigh. ''Yeah.''

She pushed away from the machine. ''Come on up, I've got a Lone Star or five.''

His body felt leaden as he climbed off and followed her through the doorway and up the stairs. She wore a cute boxer set, hair loose and swinging with her steps. He didn't want to talk. Everything tangled up inside him was too complicated to discuss with anyone. So what was he going to Tawny's room for? To exorcise his demons a different way? To prove to himself that any woman could make him feel whole, and not just Jenna?

Jenna stirred the marshmallows in her cup of cocoa with her cinnamon stick, watching the clouds go round and round. The house was quiet, Betzi having turned off the music. The silence made it that much more obvious that Mitch hadn't returned.

''Sometimes he takes walks at night,'' Betzi said, obviously catching Jenna watching the hallway. They sat at the long island in the kitchen on the horse stools Mitch had picked out.

Jenna nodded, unable to even deny she was waiting for him. ''Where does he go?''

Betzi shrugged. ''Don't follow him, of course, but sometimes I see him go out to the stables. Or he just walks around the house.''

Out to Tawny's? she wanted to ask. That strange jealous feeling swirled through her at the thought of them together.

"I don't know what to say about what you overhead. I . . . I'm afraid I don't understand it myself."

Betzi shook her head, running her fingers through her strands of silver. "I've never heard him like that before."

Jenna had actually been talking about her actions, not Mitch's. "He's so different from Paul."

"They always were different, though their father tried to make them into the quintessential identical twins. Mr. Elliot was thrilled they were having twins. It was something else that made him special. He was a good man, but he wanted to be better and set apart from everyone else. He made Paul learn piano and Mitch the violin, and he'd take them to the city and make them perform at his friends' parties. Paul hated the attention, hated being in the spotlight. Mitch pretended he couldn't play well, purposely botching up notes. All they wanted was their own identity, but Mr. Elliot wouldn't hear of it."

"It's amazing how different they are, personality-wise." Jenna's gaze went to the wall where Mitch had pinned her. Paul would never have done such a thing, would never have kissed her like that. "Paul was always so quiet, laid back. Mitch is so . . . full of life."

"He's full of it, alright." Betzi stretched out her legs, crossing her feet at the ankles. "They were always different, even as babies. Mitch was the first to break out of the crib and explore the house, the first to get lost on the property, first to talk and walk. Paul always gave up easily, no matter what the fight was about. Mitch pursued an argument to the bitter end."

"Paul did give up easily. You know, I never realized that about him, but now that you say it, I can see that. If a project got too complicated, he'd call in the professionals. I can't tell you how many puzzles I had to finish because he got confuzzled and walked away." But Paul wasn't giving up on Jenna finding the truth, that much was evident.

"Maybe that wacko doctor was right."

"Wacko doctor?"

Betzi shook her head. "Mr. Elliot was so frustrated because the boys didn't fit his image of what twins should be, he took them to this twin expert in Dallas. Sometimes one twin will absorb the other one in the womb; a woman might not ever know she was going to have twins. This expert had done umpteen studies on twins, and one of his theories was that if that process didn't quite complete, one twin would live in the shadow of the other. And he suggested that the shadow twin wasn't as whole as the other.

"It was ridiculous, of course, but Mr. Elliot thought it might be true. He explained it to the boys in hopes of spurring Paul to break out of his brother's shadow. What it did was make Mitch more protective of Paul, but it didn't help him break out, so to speak. What was he like? With you, I mean."

Jenna thought back over their marriage, from the houses they'd restored together to their lovemaking. "I think the doctor was right. Looking back, Paul seems so shallow. At the time, I had little to compare him with." She gave Betzi a brief history of her life. "He fulfilled my need to be loved and protected. I didn't even know I had needs he wasn't meeting."

Betzi's thin mouth quirked. "Like being ravaged on the couch?"

Jenna flushed hot, but she nodded. "I should have left when he told me to, but I didn't. I don't know why."

"Maybe you're in love with him."

Jenna blinked. "I can't be."

"Why not? I sensed something between you two that first day you came here."

"But I haven't known him that long; he's my husband's twin. He doesn't want to get involved with me."

"I wouldn't be so sure about that, Jenna. I was here, remember?"

Jenna ducked her head. "I remember. But I mean on a permanent basis."

"Because of the vow." Betzi took a sip. "But Paul's dead. And from the look in your eyes when you watch

Mitch, I'd say you're ready to go on with your life. Convincing Mitch, well . . . he's stubborn, but he's only a man. If you stay here much longer, he's going to see it's time to put that vow aside.''

Jenna glanced at the hallway again, wondering what her eyes were giving away. ''I am ready to go on with my life. How can I continue to mourn a man I didn't even know? All I feel for him is anger. There is something between Mitch and me, but I don't know how much of it has to do with my having Paul's heart. We have the same connection that he and Paul used to have. Okay, not the same exactly,'' she added at Betzi's skeptical look. ''But how much of it is the connection?''

''There's only one way to find out.''

Jenna rolled her eyes. ''That only made things more confusing.''

Betzi's blue eyes twinkled. ''What I meant was, let yourself go. Let your feelings take you where they may.''

''I can't. After what Paul did to me, I don't want to need anyone like that again. What Mitch cares most about is the truth, even at my expense. What Paul cared most about was hiding the truth, at my expense. You see the parallel? How can I let my feelings take me to a place I'm not sure I want to go? What will happen after we find the truth? Did Paul murder his parents? You see, it's all so tangled up, me, Paul and Mitch, the truth.'' She dropped her forehead into her hands, kneading away the tension. ''It's easier just to hate all of them, including myself for getting into this mess.''

Betzi stood and rinsed out her mug. ''All I can tell you is, follow your heart.''

Jenna let out a long breath. ''That's what got me into all this in the first place!''

''Think about this, m'dear: why did Paul bring you here?''

''To find the truth.''

''Why?''

"To make peace with Mitch, peace between him and Paul."

"Why?"

Jenna blinked. "What more?"

"Think about it. I'm getting some sleep. Good night, m'dear."

Jenna walked over to the broken picture frames they'd stacked after cleaning up the glass. She picked one up, being careful not to cut herself on the shards, and sat down on the couch. Mitch must have had these in his room, and now he must believe that Paul had killed their parents. But he wouldn't admit that to her, because he didn't want it to be true. Now it was she he was trying to save, though, not himself.

Paul and Mitch, so alike on the outside, so different inside. Was Paul a shadow twin? Maybe Mitch *had* gotten most of the personality, the passion. She stared at a picture of Mitch teasing Paul at what looked like a picnic.

"Paul, why did you bring me to Mitch? It couldn't have been to make peace, because everything we've found so far has brought nothing close to peace. He thinks you're a murderer, and me . . . I'm not sure anymore. So what was the real reason?"

She waited, turned to her inner self, to her heart. And then the words came, from somewhere deep inside her. *To heal each other.*

She wanted to laugh, but the sound that emerged sounded more like a sob. "In case you haven't noticed, we've caused each other more damage than healing so far."

Find the truth, Jenna. Find the truth.

She thought of the jewelry Paul had hidden away, and led her to find. "Haven't we already found it, Paul?"

Find the truth. The truth will free us all.

She rested her forehead against the top edge of the frame. "I'm not too fond of the truth these days. But we'll keep looking. I want to be free, Paul. I want to be free."

*   *   *

"A little more to the left," Tawny said in a soft, low voice. "Just a bit more, yeah, right there. Perfect. Drive it in, Mitch. You are just too good to me. And so well hung."

Mitch ignored the innuendo and drove the nail into the wall, then hung up the picture he'd spotted leaning against the living room wall. He took a step back. "I hope it was as good for me as it was for you."

"Hah, hah, hah. All right, you've fixed the window, unjammed my toaster, and now hung my picture. But that's not what you came up here for."

The apartments over the stable offices were small, only one bedroom and one bath. At the moment, the living room seemed more like a closet to Mitch, and getting smaller with each passing minute. Tawny, still wearing her boxer set, sprawled out on the sofa, and he dropped down in the chair adjacent. Scotty was tucked away in his little racing-car bed in the bedroom, leaving the adults to do as they pleased.

"You're right," he acknowledged, taking a sip of beer. He wasn't going to admit that he was buying time. "I've been thinking about that guy who's coming in Thursday to look at Pink Floyd. I want you to do a background on him, make sure his story checks out."

Restlessness coursed through his body, making him want to jump out of the chair and fix something else. But he couldn't see anything else that needed fixing, so he reined it in, drumming his fingers instead.

What was he doing here? He and Tawny had been friends for years, the sexual undercurrent mostly ignored on his part. One of his rules was never to get sexually involved with an employee, but here he was in her apartment alone on a Friday night.

Tawny pulled her leggy frame from the couch and walked over to him. Her brown hair spilled over her shoulders as she leaned down in front of him. "Why are you here, Mitch? It's not to talk about the guy looking at Pink Floyd."

"Dunno." He was running away, just like he'd accused

Jenna of doing. But it was for their own good. If he was going to break one of his rules, the employee one was the better one to break.

She slid onto the chair with him, straddling his hips with her legs, hands on his arms. "Can I make a suggestion?"

Then she leaned forward and kissed him. Her lips were warm and soft, just the way he remembered them from many years before. He kissed her back, nudging her mouth open and plunging his tongue inside. Her thighs contracted, pinning him tighter. Her hands slid across his chest as she deepened the kiss.

The lesser of two evils, he thought. If he had sex with Tawny, could he kill the wanting inside? If he put his arms around Tawny, would he think only of her and not the way Jenna felt in that same place? Tomorrow would he look at Jenna and not want to love her into oblivion anymore?

Love her. The words shivered through his body, making his fingers tighten on the arms of the chair. He'd used those words before in relation to Jenna. Not have sex, but love her. He'd never used that expression with any of the women he'd been to bed with. *Because you've never loved a woman before.*

"Damn it," he said, coming to his feet and bringing Tawny up onto hers. He set her apart from him.

"What's wrong?" she asked, arms crossed in front of her.

"Dunno."

"You don't know. You come up here half-naked and sit there looking incredibly sexy with that sultry expression on your face, and when it comes to performing, you back off. It's that stupid rule of yours, isn't it? Let that go. You're letting something wonderful slip right through your fingers because of your rule."

Those words swirled through his insides. He walked to the window and looked out. Through the trees he could see light coming from the family room where he'd pinned Jenna to the wall. "It's more than just the rule," he said, thinking not of Tawny at all but of Jenna, his brother's wife.

"Why'd you come up here tonight?" she asked, walking up beside him. "It's her, isn't it? Paul's wife. She shows up and leaves, you go halfway across the country to bring her back, and suddenly you're working out in the middle of the night. You've got it for your brother's widow, don't you?"

"You don't know anything."

"You want her and it's killing you. So you came up here hoping I'd help chase away your demons." She pulled at his shoulder, trying to make him face her. "Isn't that right?"

He turned and gave her what she wanted. "Yeah, that's right. But my demons are too big for you to exorcise." He started walking to the door. "Good night, Tawny."

"You're a bastard!"

He paused at the door, then turned back to her. "You got that right too."

Facing the truth was a pain in the butt. He walked down the stairs and out into the night air. He'd been ready to deal with the ramifications of finding out Paul was a murderer. He knew he could handle that, even if it meant that he could have those genes too. He'd been ready for that for nine years.

But he'd never counted on Jenna.

Mitch had always tried to do the right thing, but he was a sinner six ways and counting. He tried and convicted himself before anyone else could do it for him. God help him, but he was in love with his brother's wife.

Other women had come and gone in his life, and he hadn't missed them. But the thought of Jenna slipping through his fingers slammed him in the gut.

He walked quietly into the house, ready to clean up the mess he'd made. She was right; he'd heard her crying when he'd brought some extra towels to her room. It hit him then, what he and Paul had done to this woman, this delicate woman who had weathered so much pain in her life. Paul was a murderer, and Mitch had forced Jenna to face that fact. Both twins were slime. He'd gone to his room and taken the pictures kept in the dresser drawer, seeing not two smiling, identical faces but two men who had hurt an undeserving woman. Then he'd sent them flying into the fireplace.

And when he'd seen her standing there, what had he done? Not apologized, but thrown her against the wall and kissed her . . . threatened her! Bastard, bastard, bastard, he chanted, walking into the family room. The fireplace was clean. Great. She'd even cleaned up the mess for him. Like she was cleaning up his brother's mess. *Just stick the knife in a little deeper, Elliot. Good. Now twist it.*

He didn't know what made him turn around, but he did . . . to find her lying there on the couch, one of the pictures sitting on her stomach. She was asleep, arms crossed over the broken frame, ash-blond hair spread out on the cushion. He couldn't move, couldn't even breathe. He was the devil, and she was an angel, looking beautiful and innocent on his couch.

When he could finally reason himself to leave, he stopped and leaned down over her. She smelled so much better than Tawny, looked so much sexier sprawled out here in that short nightgown that bared her long legs. His curse to fall in love with the wrong woman. He reached out and pushed a strand of her hair from her cheek, letting his finger trace the line of her jaw.

"That's my girl," he whispered, so softly his words broke.

His girl, he thought, shaking his head at the words that came so naturally from his mouth. She wasn't his girl. Could he hate himself any more than he already did?

Jenna woke to the sound of soft-spoken words coming from the kitchen. She opened her eyes and blinked, getting oriented. Sunlight spilled in from the windows on either side of the fireplace. It was still early in the morning, and a misty layer of fog hovered just above the ground outside.

The smell of coffee filled the air, making Jenna long for a bagel. Was Mitch back? She looked down to find the picture on the couch with her.

Jenna recognized Etta's voice. ''I'm just saying that she makes a lovely picture lying there with her husband's picture, but she's too pretty to waste her life away wishing for things that can't be.''

''You just keep your fingers out of that girl's life,'' Betzi said. ''You don't know nothing about nothing.''

''What are you talking about? I know how to fix up things, you notwithstanding.''

''Leave my life out of this. Don't you need to pump iron or something?''

''Hmph.''

Jenna sat up, not awake enough to quell the disappointment that Mitch wasn't there. ''Good morning,'' she called out, getting to her feet. ''Coffee smells great.''

Betzi got a cup for her, shooting a warning look to her mother. ''Morning, m'dear. What was it, couch night?''

Jenna fixed her coffee with lots of sugar, then nibbled on a muffin from the platter. ''What do you mean?''

''Mitch spent the night on the couch in the gathering room. Not that it's the first time he's done that, but it was just funny coming in and finding you both on the couch. Different couches,'' she amended quickly.

''I didn't know he'd even come back. I mean, I don't know when he came in.'' But he had come back. Had he seen her on the couch? Probably not, though she'd had that strange dream that he'd touched her cheek. ''Is he up yet?''

''Up and out to the stables,'' Etta said, running her fingers through her Rah Rah Red hair. Or was it Cheeky Cherry? ''You want me to take you out there? Bet you could meet Dave and all the others.''

''I already met Dave,'' she said, taking her coffee in hand. ''You know, I got the impression he likes older women. Much older women. Well, got to get dressed.''

''Older women?'' Etta said, puffing up her hair again. ''I never knew that. Did you know that, Betz?''

Jenna couldn't help her grin as she headed up to her room. The last thing she needed was someone trying to set her up. She didn't want to belong to any man.

That's my girl.

Mitch's words halted her steps for a moment, but she pushed herself to continue on. Especially she didn't want to belong to him. So why had his words popped into her mind so clearly?

"Hmph," she muttered, opening her bedroom door.

An hour later she walked out to the stables. There was a lot of activity, with several cars parked in the lot beyond. Two men she'd never seen before were working with a horse in a field set up with jumping gates. On the far side of the stables, Dave and Mitch were working with three teenagers each sitting on a horse. Mitch wore one of his vests and had his hair tied back. Jenna felt as though she'd walked out there a hundred times to see him, as though this were her Saturday-morning routine. He was giving a black boy instructions on posture and hadn't seen her yet.

Tawny and Scotty were standing outside the ring watching, and the look Tawny shot Jenna made the eighty degrees feel more like twenty. Maybe last year or even last month she would have retreated, but Jenna had dealt with a lot more than an unfriendly woman who probably considered her competition.

"Good morning," Jenna said, leaning against the fence.

"Hi," Scotty said, wiggling his little fingers.

Jenna grinned, wiggling her fingers back at him. "Hi. How come you're not out there on a horse?"

" 'Cause Mommy says I'm not old enough to learn." He turned to Tawny. "Am I old enough now? It's been a long time since I asked you."

"It's only been since this morning." She met Jenna's gaze. "Don't give him any ideas."

"Sorry." She looked up to find Mitch watching her. He acknowledged her with a nod and went back to instructing. "I didn't know you taught people how to ride here."

"We don't." When Jenna waited for more of an answer, Tawny seemed reluctant to say, "Mitch does it for free for some of the kids in town. The ones who can't afford instruction. If they show promise, he sponsors them to go to a riding school north of here."

"How nice." She watched Mitch with a whole new appreciation of his warmth.

"Yeah, he's a swell guy," Tawny said sardonically. "How long you going to be around, Janine?"

"It's Jenna, and I don't know yet. A few days."

"What is it, exactly, that you're doing here? I mean, you never came here with Paul, so you don't have any ties here."

The sun felt warm against Jenna's face, and she closed her eyes to it. "I came here looking for answers."

"Do those answers have something to do with Mitch?"

Jenna looked at Tawny. "They have everything to do with Mitch."

Tawny nodded, eyes narrowing. "Is it because he looks like Paul? He's nothing like Paul, you know, if you're looking for a replacement. They never were alike."

"I know and I'm not looking for Paul's replacement."

"You know, then, about the vow he made not to get involved with anyone Paul dated? Or married."

"Yes, I know."

Tawny kicked the fence post with her boot. "I'm the one who started the vow." When Jenna gave her a surprised look, Tawny said, "I dated Paul for a few months. When he brought me out here, I got to know Mitch. There was this instant thing between us. I told Mitch that Paul and I weren't really dating. One minute we were talking, the next, making out. Then Paul caught us, and the next thing I knew, I was out of both their lives. You might want to keep that in mind."

Jenna caught herself smiling. "I will."

Tension radiated from Tawny.

"Are you the demon Mitch came to me trying to exorcise last night?"

Tawny's words sunk deep in Jenna's stomach with claws outstretched. It was Mitch's voice that interrupted. "Hey." When he looked at Tawny, something passed between them. Whatever it was, though, wasn't pleasant. Then he looked at Jenna, and the icky feeling in her stomach melted away. "When I'm done with the kids, we'll take a ride." Then he purposely shot Tawny a look that warned . . . of what? He returned to the kids as they rode round and round the ring.

Tawny turned and stalked toward the stables. From somewhere below, a disgruntled voice said, "I wish I could ride on one of those horses."

Jenna looked down to see Scotty with his arms crossed in front of his chest, staring intently at the horses in the ring. "Well, I can't help you there, but if you'd like, you can sit on the top of the fence here in front of me."

He considered that, then nodded. "I can perr-tend I'm on a horse. Only little kids call them horsees, you know."

"Well, you're not a little kid. Someday you'll be able to ride just like those kids."

She helped him up and balanced him while he swayed to and fro, making horse sounds. "Someday I wanna own a bunch like Mitch."

Every time Scotty leaned back against her, she caught the little-boy smells of baby powder and something sweet. She wondered what kind of father Mitch would make and shifted her thoughts out of that territory.

A little while later, the parents took their kids home, and Mitch walked over to where she and Scotty were. "Hey, little man, you ridin' a horse?" He tweaked Scotty's nose.

Scotty giggled. "Yep, sure am, and he's twenty hands high."

"Wow, that's pretty big, bigger than any of my horses." Mitch lifted the boy up and swung him around, then set him down. "Go find your mama. We've got to head on out, and I don't want you out here by yourself."

"Can I come wid you?" he asked, tilting his head and making Jenna want to scoop him up into her arms.

"Sorry, but we're taking the steel horse. You know how your mama feels about that thing. Go on, now."

The steel horse. Jenna's heartbeat stepped up a pace, or was it because Mitch was standing rather close, or that they were alone?

He met her gaze and said, "If you want to slap me for last night, can you at least wait until we're in the privacy of the garage?"

"What makes you think I want to slap you?"

"You should slap me. I was out of line."

"But you warned me to leave. And I didn't."

He let those words hang for a few seconds before saying, "No, you didn't." Then he headed off toward the house, leaving her to follow. "So what were you and Tawny talking about?"

"Apparently you had some demons to exorcise last night," she said, feeling that odd jealousy swirl through her again.

He nodded, giving her a wry look. "A couple."

"And did . . . she help?" She hated the way the words sounded to her own ears.

Mitch stopped in the middle of the patch of trees. The sunlight filtered across his face. "I'm beyond help, Jenna. It'd be best to remember that."

She nodded. "I'll keep that in mind." When he started walking forward again, she reached out and touched his arm. He went instantly still. Through their skin she could feel his energy and turmoil. "Paul wants us to find the whole truth."

He turned back to her, and she dropped her hand. "What do you mean?"

"I asked him why he'd sent me here . . . to you. In the beginning he'd told me it was to make peace, but we've hardly had that."

He ran his fingers through his hair, looking over at the house for a moment before meeting her eyes again. "Ain't that the truth. So you think there's more to find?"

"I'm not sure. He seems to have thought so. But that's

not why he sent me here. He wants us to heal each other.''

He leaned back against the tree as though his knees had given way. ''Heal each other? Did he tell you how he proposed for us to do that?''

''No.''

Mitch tilted his chin up, leaving her to look at that long throat. He rocked his head back and forth a little, then finally looked back at her. ''He'd better enlighten us real quick, because what we do for each other has nothing to do with healing. Come on.'' He grabbed her hand and started leading her toward the house, but let go a few seconds later. It was such a natural move, she'd hardly thought it was inappropriate.

''We can take the Bronco if you want,'' he said, walking up to the open garage. Etta's Cobra was gone.

''The steel horse is fine,'' she said, liking the sound of the words. ''Where are we going?''

''To pay a visit to Becky's father. I want to ask him some questions about that night. I thought you might be able to pick up some vibes. Later, we'll go into my parents' room and do the same.''

After he eased the helmet over her head and put on his own, he backed up the bike and started it. She climbed on, used to the feel of the engine, the seat, and of Mitch's body as she slid her arms around his waist.

It was easier to be angry at herself than Mitch, especially when she was snuggled up against his back and enjoying it far too much. She focused on their destination. Maybe finding the truth was the way they were supposed to heal. Certainly Paul didn't intend for her to fall for his twin. She closed her eyes.

Yes, she'd fallen all right. For all the wrong reasons, but she'd fallen hard. What had been in Paul's heart when he headed for that telephone pole? Had he thought to bring together the two people he loved, knowing they would connect? Her eyes popped open. Was this how he wanted them to heal, by falling in love?

Mitch took a left turn and rode toward town. She realized she'd increased the pressure of her hold on him and eased up. She couldn't believe that Paul would want such a thing. He just wanted them to clear his name, if he wasn't guilty. Or maybe find out the real reason he had killed his parents.

People waved at Mitch as they passed through the cluster of stores, but their gazes lingered on the two of them much longer than the greeting. Who was that woman beneath the helmet? they were probably wondering. Heck, even she didn't know anymore.

Sometimes she felt like that little girl living in a desolate village holding a dying baby and feeling helpless. But she saw glimpses of a woman standing tall and strong, turning away from that sad past and walking forward. What she couldn't see anymore was the woman who had been married to Paul, who had loved him with everything she was.

Mitch took one of the side roads and headed south for several miles before pulling into a long driveway with stone bunkers on either side. Not as impressive as Bluebonnet Manor, but the property stretched out for quite a while. The house was a simple two-story, and both it and the yard looked neglected. Weeds sprouted from around the porch, and the house needed a coat of paint. Jenna had seen houses that looked far worse, but their spirit still showed. This house, however, spoke sadness to her.

Mitch stopped and let her get off, then put down the kickstand and joined her. "His rig's not here, but I'll see if anyone else is around. He's probably on a road trip." A dusty Ford truck was the only vehicle in sight.

No one answered, and they headed back to the bike. "Do you get anything from Paul's heart? Becky didn't live here back then; they lived in an old trailer. The trailer park isn't even there anymore."

"I don't get anything. What is it you hope to find out from him?"

"I want to know if Becky was out of town during the times Paul took money from the account. I want to know if they were in touch over the years. I want to shake him up a bit.''

That prospect of Becky and Paul being in touch didn't hurt the way it had before. Maybe she couldn't hurt any more when it came to Paul.

Or maybe your heart is otherwise occupied.

She didn't know where those words came from. But she did realize that the inner voice had said her heart. Hers, not Paul's. She looked up to find Mitch watching her.

''I still don't think he was cheating on you. Not the way he felt about you.''

''You know what? I can handle it if he was. I might be mad at him, but I already am anyway.'' She looked up at the house, then back at Mitch. ''Do you still feel his feelings?''

''No. Just those few times.'' His gaze dropped to her mouth for a second. ''I never kissed you for Paul, and I never loved you for Paul. I'd like to use that as an excuse, but I can't. He had nothing to do with it.''

He walked over to the bike and put his helmet back on. She did the same, settling once again behind him on the seat. While Paul had wrapped her in a cloak of lies, Mitch was brutally honest. He was beating himself up over their kisses, over their lovemaking. He said he'd never loved her for Paul. Did he love her? Did she know what love really was?

All she knew was that everyone she thought she loved died. Her parents had said they loved her once in a while, but they'd robbed her of her childhood. Her grandmother was as driven to save lost souls as her parents, and she had died too. And Paul often said he loved her, but he'd been a lie. Mitch was the worst prospect yet for loving her. He'd dragged her into facing the truth, regretting it only when it was too late. He'd made her lose her precious memories, made her question what she'd had with Paul.

But he made her feel. Now she wondered if she'd ever really *felt* before. And without Mitch, would she again?

Thirteen

One of the Bluebonnet Manor traditions was a huge Mexican feast on Saturday nights. Everyone who worked at the
stables was invited, and Betzi covered the kitchen island
with colorful ceramic plates and bowls of everything from
tamales (not the kind in jars) to enchilada casserole, her
own creation. Etta sat next to Dave, spending a lot of time
regaling him with stories of her weight-lifting victories.
Tawny provided the animosity while Scotty provided the
entertainment to offset it.

Mitch provided prickles of self-awareness, but Jenna
was also superaware of him. The way the deep blue of his
shirt set off his blond hair, the way his white pants hugged
his derriere, the grace of his hands despite the calluses.
Even the way that one lock of hair had a mind of its own,
separating from the rest and curling over his forehead. She
doubted Mitch would be embarrassed if his woman grabbed
that derriere. With Mitch it would probably be the start of
something sexy and fun.

When he glanced up at her, she realized she'd been staring at him and turned to listen to Scotty, who was telling
Mitch he wanted to be a cowboy and gather in the cows
every night. He'd make sure none got away, he assured
Mitch with an earnest nod of his head.

"You'll be the best cowboy anyone ever saw, little
man."

"Maybe I should be a cowman, then, huh?"

Jenna had never been comfortable in crowds of people,

even small crowds. But except for Tawny, everyone made her feel a part of the group. They asked her safe questions about what she did for a living and New England, and she told them about watching whales and the historic gardens in Oceanside. No one asked much about Paul, though she was pretty sure no one but Betzi and Mitch knew she'd received Paul's heart or that she was even a transplantee. She was a normal woman without peculiarities, at least on the surface.

Feeling warm and accepted, she excused herself to freshen up. She remembered the powder room by the foyer and found herself primping her hair, checking her teeth. She squared her shoulders and looked at her reflection. She was smiling, really smiling. All those years living with just Paul, she thought she'd been happy. Paul had stolen her twenties the same way her parents had stolen her childhood. Her smile faltered. Anger was familiar, more comfortable than any of the new experiences she'd encountered. Even the charm of family traditions.

She stared for a long time at the woman in the mirror, wondering just who she was.

The strange pull started when she left the powder room. She found herself turning left instead of right, walking through the lounge that opened onto the gathering room. Mitch seemed to find the family room more comfortable for his gatherings, so the room was quiet and empty of the conversation that drifted from beyond. And that's where she wanted to go, but Paul's heart, it seemed, had other ideas.

The door to the master suite was hidden around the corner from the bar, but Jenna went right to it. The door was closed, but she didn't hesitate as she turned the knob and pushed it open. The room was immense, with a marble fireplace and a column-flanked alcove that looked out to the backyard. This beautiful room was filled with discarded furniture, boxes, and other items, used only for storage, tainted by murder.

Mitch had intended to bring her in here earlier, but when

they'd returned to the house, Dave asked him to look over an injured horse. She hadn't even known where this room was, but Paul had.

She leaned on the wall by the door, resting her cheek against the cool surface, fingers grazing the gold-plated switch plate. The image flashed before her eyes without warning—a man and woman lying in a gilded sleigh bed, covered in blood, lying oh-so-still. And that agony racked her body, shaking her to her core. Her knees buckled and she grabbed for something to keep her from falling.

That something turned out to be Mitch, who caught her from behind. His arms slipped around her waist, and he held her against him.

"What happened? What are you doing in here?"

She blinked, tried to gain her balance. His hands were still holding her shoulders, and she felt brave enough to look where the bed had been. Nothing but the gaudiest pool table she'd ever seen, adorned with carved ram's heads at each leg and coated in gold. "I saw them." Her voice was a harsh whisper. She turned toward Mitch, her cheek brushing his jaw. "Your parents."

His body stiffened. "Where? How?"

"Paul. He was in here. It felt the same way it did when I felt his anguish in his old bedroom. But this time I was in here."

"What were they wearing?"

"There was so much blood, it was hard to tell. I think she was wearing a pink nightgown. It was shiny, with tiny straps. He—your father—was wearing maybe a white T-shirt, but he had the sheets pulled up to his stomach. They looked like they were sleeping, but they . . . weren't." Her voice hiccuped as she remembered again.

He pulled her close until her cheek was pressed against his chest. "That's what they were wearing. But Paul wouldn't have seen them. By the time he returned from Becky's, the police wouldn't let anyone in here. Why did you come in here by yourself?"

"Paul led me here, the same way he led me to his bedroom the first time I was here. Why is he doing this? Everything we find out is more incriminating.''

She felt warm and safe in Mitch's arms, too warm and safe. One of his hands stroked down her back, up and down, up and down.

"Stop looking." He moved back and tilted her chin. "I don't want you hurt anymore."

"There isn't anything left inside me to be hurt."

"Oh, Jenna." He pulled her closer and rested his chin atop her head. She could feel Mitch's pain radiating right into her. "I wish I could make it go away."

He had done this, she reminded herself. Don't feel bad for him! He's the one who brought you to this place. She moved out of his embrace. "Paul wants us to find the whole truth. There must be something we're missing. I got the image when I touched the wall, here. He must have done the same thing, leaned against the wall."

He put his hand on her shoulder. "Jenna, you don't have to do this anymore."

"What do you mean?"

"I mean, we can stop. We can leave it alone, just like you wanted to do."

She searched his face, finding nothing but seriousness. "You'd give up your search for the truth? The very thing you've lived for all these years?" He nodded. "Why?"

"Maybe I'm afraid of finding anything else."

"You're not afraid of anything."

He paused a moment before answering, but she saw the muscles in his jaw twitch. "How can you be so sure about that?"

Regret shadowed his eyes. He wasn't afraid of finding the truth, that she knew. He was afraid for her, of what the truth was doing to her.

"I have to know. Not only for Paul, but for myself." And she placed her palm against the wall. The image flashed through her mind again, the blood and Paul's agony. *What did you do, Paul? Show me what happened.*

Show me the missing piece of this puzzle. You owe me the answers.

Paul took a step into the room, then another. But as he continued to walk closer to the gilded bed, something blocked her from going forward with him. Almost like an opaque curtain had dropped before her. She tried to push past it, but it was bigger than she was.

She opened her eyes, finding Mitch hovering over her.

"God, Jenna, I hate when you do that. I keep thinking you're going to . . . die."

"Don't you want to know what I saw this time?" Maybe it was mean, but she rather liked the concern on his features.

After a hesitation, he asked, "What did you see?"

"Nothing more. But that's not the point. It's like he doesn't want me to see any more. His room. I felt his agony in there before."

She walked around the corner and up the central staircase, and Mitch followed. The first memory that assailed her was the kiss she and Mitch shared there by the bed. She sat down on the bed, holding on to the post for support. He stood beside her, hand on the post just above hers, body tense.

She closed her eyes and concentrated. The agony swept over her again, and the woman's words—Becky's words—*Paul, what have you done?* Jenna felt dizzy again, and the taste of liquor permeated her mouth. Her head swam with the effects until she pulled herself from the image. She covered her face with her hands.

Mitch knelt down beside her. "What'd you see?"

"He was drunk." She lifted her face to his. "The truth isn't helping. Everything we find out just looks worse and worse." He started to touch her arm, but she shrugged him off. "I need to be alone for a while."

"All right, I'll leave you alone. But after everyone leaves, I'm coming up to get you. I'm going to show you an activity you'll find very therapeutic. Be prepared to sweat."

*   *   *

Jenna's body had been on edge since Mitch had dropped those provocative words. She'd changed into shorts and stared at her reflection in the bathroom mirror. For all those years when she'd lived without mirrors, without bathrooms even, she seemed to be making up for lost time. For the first time, she appraised herself as a woman. Was she pretty?

She fluffed her blond hair, caught the glint of a few silver strands. She tilted her chin up, turned her face. Passable, she decided. Around Mitch, she had become aware of her body, and of the feminine currents that coursed through her.

With Paul, she'd never found herself daydreaming about their lovemaking. She'd never looked at him and felt the stir of longing. Mitch awakened all these disturbing, delicious feelings inside, and all it took were a few words to heat them to a boiling point. What had Paul seen when he'd looked at her? Someone to protect, to shield from the world's woes. To hide away from the world. Maybe even to pity.

What did Mitch see? More than that, but how much more? She sighed, pulling down the collar of her shirt to reveal the top of her scar. Did it mirror the one on the inside, the one that ran the length of her soul? She touched the marred skin, wondering if either scar would really fade over time.

Never would she forget Mitch's acceptance of the ugliest part of her. If he could accept it, then she could too. Wearing low-cut shirts, however, would take some time. She released the collar and patted the wrinkles she'd created. Then she walked downstairs where the last few people were finishing up the remaining tidbits from dinner.

Mitch was watching Scotty chase Harvey around the living room, trying to ride him. Was that a wistful expression on his face?

Scotty's laughter filled the room like the singing of angels. Jenna wanted to bottle the sound and wear it all the time. "Come on, horsee Harvey. I mean, horse Harvey. Giddy up!" The big black dog ducked and escaped capture once again.

Mitch looked up at her, obviously surprised she'd come back down so soon. He was leaning against the kitchen counter, leg jiggling with nervous energy.

"Arrggh!" Etta's voice charged through the room where she was elbow deep in an arm-wrestling contest with Dave. "Come on, young thing, show me what you got."

Dave stared hard at their joined hands, the muscles in his arms bulging, veins popping. Both Etta's and Dave's faces were red, teeth bared. Jenna took the stool next to Mitch and watched Etta push, push, and finally bring Dave down.

"Two out of three," he challenged.

Etta, wearing a bright purple tank top which showed her own impressive display of muscles, tilted her head. "Consider playing a match of strip arm wrestling?"

Jenna watched Dave's face go an even deeper shade of red, if that were possible. "Ah, I don't think so."

Etta grinned, obviously enjoying having the upper hand, so to speak. "Lesser men have taken the challenge. *Older* men have taken the challenge."

Dave got to his feet and hitched up his faded blue jeans. "Well, truth of the matter is, you'd have an unfair advantage. See, I'm not wearing any underwear." Etta's mouth actually dropped open, and her gaze jumped to the seat of his jeans. "Gotcha," he said, walking to the counter. "But I'm curious: how many times you win?"

Etta stood, hands on her hips. "I've got more men's clothes than I'll bet you do." Her eyebrow, finely lined in black, rose. "Might be you're afraid to take the challenge?"

He dipped his chin. "Very afraid, ma'am." With a wry grin, he winked at the audience he now had. "Anyone up for riding into town and catching a movie?"

"I will, I will!" Scotty chimed in, coming up short when

he saw Jenna for the first time. He gave her that little wave of his, then ran over to Dave. "Can I go?"

Tawny shrugged, looking at Mitch. "You want to?"

"Nah, I'll pass tonight." He shot Jenna a look that said he had more interesting things to do, then pushed away from the counter. "Go on, kids. Have fun."

Betzi, who was wiping down the counter, gave Jenna a warm smile that hinted of mischief. Hadn't Betzi once said she could sense a tornado coming from miles away? Jenna's body went on edge again.

"Come on, Etta," Betzi said, hanging up her towel. "Let's do the town."

"Whoopee-do. That's about as exciting as making a log cabin with lollipop sticks," Etta mumbled. " 'Course, that may be the only way I'll see action 'round this place." She looked at Jenna. "You coming with us, girlie?"

Did everyone look at her, or was she paranoid? "Er, no thanks."

Etta nodded her head indiscreetly toward Dave. "Well, one of us ought to get some action. You sure you don't want to come?"

Tawny's expression was rigid when she said, "Maybe she wants a different kind of action. The kind she can get around here." She glanced at Mitch, then turned and walked toward the door.

"We're goin' to a movie, we're goin' to a movie," Scotty chanted, skipping to the door, charmingly oblivious to all the undercurrents. "We're going to see an *action* movie."

Jenna envied him his innocence. "I wish I were three again," she said when everyone had gone.

"Would you do it all over again? Or would you live life differently, if you could?"

His question took her back. "I don't know. I thought about life—and death—a lot when I learned about my heart problem. But I never wished for a different life."

"Wishing never changed anything, did it?"

"No. I wished I didn't have the heart disease, wished

I'd had a better, happier childhood, wished Paul hadn't died. It never made a difference.''

''Maybe it's better to wish for something in the future, instead of wishing to change the past. Come on, let's go sweat.''

She was already sweating, the blood rushing through her veins at supersonic speed. They walked through a moonlit night filled with the smells of earth, grass, and pine. Harvey panted behind them, though he looked like a dark blur. Mitch's white pants stood out against the grainy night, captivating her with the swing of his gait.

She cleared her mind of such thoughts. ''We're not going for a horseback ride, are we?''

''Nope.''

They walked to the stable offices, and he unlocked the door and stepped aside for her to enter first. He walked down the hallway and opened the third door. Half the lights came on when he flicked the switch.

''A gym?'' She felt faintly disappointed, but didn't want to explore what she'd really expected. ''Wow, I've never seen a setup like this, except maybe in the movies.''

The walls were mirrored all way round, reflecting the myriad chrome machines as well as her and Mitch into infinity. ''It's here for everyone to use. Be warned if Etta asks you to spot her,'' he said, nodding toward the free weight area. ''She grunts a lot. And cusses.''

''I'll keep that in mind. If I keep eating like I have been, I'll need to start working out on more than my treadmill. I know, I know, I need some meat on my bones.'' She pinched her stomach. ''I'm getting meatier, believe me.''

For a moment, Mitch looked at her with a hungry expression, as though she were a juicy steak for his taking. No, it was probably her imagination. Had to be. This whole sweat thing had sent her brain—or more precisely, her libido—into warp drive.

Their eyes met, and her body responded to something it saw, some secret communication it failed to notify her of. This was crazy. She'd had a steady sex life once, and hadn't had these mystifying feelings. And she hadn't missed that sex life.

But Paul wasn't Mitch.

Paul hadn't looked at her the way Mitch did, hadn't touched her in those unconscious ways that loved in more ways than any words could.

Well, not love, not from Mitch. Couldn't be love.

Mitch walked over to some strange contraption and held up a pair of boxing gloves. "I know you'll find this hard to believe, but sometimes I get full of piss and vinegar and need to work off some of that anger." He laid his hand against the black leather cylinder. "This is for whatever's pissing you off. For me it's been Paul or the horse that won't break for us or the mare we tried to save but couldn't."

He walked closer and fit the bulky red gloves over first one of her hands, then the other. He laced them up tight, bracing her gloved hand against his chest. "It's a computerized punching bag. It doesn't grunt, or hit back, or pour guilt on you. It just lets you take out all your anger until you don't have any left. For you, the bag can be Paul, or it can even be me."

Jenna stared at the bag. It was taller than she was, attached to a heavy base. "So this is the Bluebonnet Manor therapist?"

"Better than your average shrink," he said in a Yogi Bear voice, making her grin despite herself. He walked over and turned on the stereo built into the wall. The rock and roll he favored filled the room, bounced off the walls and surrounded her. "All right, think about whatever it is that's on your mind when those beautiful gray eyes of yours frost over."

Beautiful? She shifted her gaze to the bag and what Mitch had said prior to the "beautiful gray eyes" thing. She remembered Dr. Sharidon talking about her anger. "I think I have plenty to be angry over, don't you?"

"Sure. Not long ago you were safe in your little world, living with your memories of your wonderful husband. But he dragged you out of that safe place and brought you here. You found out he had lied about who he was, where he came from. Forgot to mention that little detail about having a twin brother. And was I understanding? No, I forced you to look even deeper, because maybe that wonderful husband of yours wasn't just a liar; maybe he was a murderer.''

She could feel the frost shuttering her expression, just as he'd said. "I don't like this." Her hands were prisoners in the padded gloves.

Mitch moved closer, his face intent, reminding her of those times he spoke of. "And when I chased you down in New England, you still defended him. You wanted to forget everything and curl up with memories that were nothing but lies. Go on, hit the bag. Hit it, Jenna.''

She slammed him in the chest instead, catching him off guard. With an "Oof," he took a step back.

"Why are you doing this to me?" she asked.

"Because I've been where you are." His voice was low, and she had to strain to hear him through the music. "After my parents' murders, the sheriff and his deputies swarmed around trying to pin it on Paul, me, or both of us. Not only did I have to deal with the murders, but I was a suspect. People looked at us like we were already convicted.

"I know anger, Jenna. Before I was smart enough to get this thing, I went out and picked fights. With guys a lot bigger and meaner than me. I know where you're coming from. Sometimes the anger's so twisted up inside, you don't even know who you are anymore. It becomes a part of you, an ugly part that darkens everything in your life. Let it go. I want to see who the woman is behind the anger.''

Before she could even respond to those words, he turned her to face the bag. "Like a boxer. Fists up, body loose. Go to it.''

She felt ridiculous, standing there like some runt boxer facing the black bag. Anger, anger, anger, twisting inside her, taking over her body. She didn't know where it left off and her real self took up. She felt small and weak, the victim of life. A little girl standing in front of her mother, head lowered as her mother spoke.

Don't be selfish, Jenna. We can't leave all these people who need us just so you can go back home. Think of others. You're one life, and they are many. We can make a difference, and so can you. Those kids back in the States are learning hopscotch while you're learning about hope.

She'd wanted to learn hopscotch and jump rope. She wanted her parents to take care of her sometimes too. She wanted to be selfish.

Jenna punched the bag. Her glove landed with a dull thud, hardly moving the bag at all. Even so, something loosened inside her, breaking free like a chunk of a glacier. She swallowed, feeling her eyes sting. Wasn't it a glacier that sank the *Titanic*?

"That's my girl," Mitch said, his words distant.

The sound of a baby crying echoed in her mind, the memory that haunted her most. That tiny, emaciated baby lying in a little girl's lap looking for that hope Jenna's mother had spoken of. The baby's mother had died two days before, and there wasn't any food for the baby. It reached out to her, suckling on her finger. Where was the hope? The food and supplies were weeks late, and even Jenna and her parents had eaten nothing but rice for days. The baby's crying faded by degrees, its flailing arms ceased their reaching.

"What do you see, Jenna?"

"A baby. It's dying."

"What baby?"

She punched the bag, this time making it rock back on the spring-loaded pole. "Just a baby, hungry and alone like all the other babies." Her voice had taken on a childlike lilt. "And I'm too young to do anything. I can't help her."

The baby girl closed her eyes. Jenna jostled her, squeezing and trying to get her to suckle again. The baby's ribs rippled beneath her skin, rising and falling, and then no longer. Jenna had carried the baby to her mother, held her out. *Please, Momma, help her!* She could hardly talk through the sobs that racked her. Her mother took the baby from her and set it in a basket near the bed of the woman she was attending. *Don't cry, Jenna.*

"Put it behind you," she said, hitting the bag again. "Don't cry."

Another piece of the glacier broke loose, and she felt bare to the icy waters.

"Who said that?" Mitch asked in a low voice.

"My mother." She punched the bag again, and this time it rocked farther back.

"God, Jenna." She focused on the bag, the memories.

And then the sound of the helicopter filled the air. Her mother and everyone who could move ran out to the hope they'd been waiting for. Jenna stood by the baby in the basket. Hope had come too late.

You make a good man of me. Paul's face now floated in front of the bag.

"Why? So you could repent? Did taking care of your sickly wife make up for killing your parents?" She jabbed the bag, once, twice. It struck her as so true, it took her breath away. He'd been stoic, so glad to accommodate her illness. And before that, so willing to protect her from her wretched childhood. His penance. That's what she'd been, his penance.

She attacked the bag, beating it the way she'd beaten on Mitch's chest back in New Hampshire. With a last, fierce punch, she sent the bag rocking back, only to have it rebound and knock her backward . . . into Mitch. They both went sprawling onto the floor, but she wasn't sure if landing on Mitch's hard body had saved her much discomfort. With her awkward gloved hands, she tried to right herself. He placed his hands around her waist and set her on the floor next to him.

"I thought you said it didn't hit back," she said, trying to gather both her dignity and her senses.

"You pounded on it but good. Feel better?"

Another piece of the glacier broke away, and all at once she felt raw and exposed. She couldn't meet his eyes, ashamed of what she'd revealed. She wrapped her arms around her legs, gloves bumping each other. "Yeah, sure."

He shook his head. "You're doing it again, that frost thing."

The anger settled comfortably around her shoulders. The ice had re-formed its protective shelter around her soul. "Sorry."

"Don't be sorry to me. Be sorry for yourself. Jenna, you had it. I could see it in your eyes, you were letting go."

The current song was softer, and Jenna heard, "For all tomorrow's lies." She listened to the words, about having someone to love through the storms, for tomorrow's lies. She nodded, meeting his eyes at last. "I know. I could feel it breaking away." She wiped one glove across her cheek, surprised not to find wetness there. "I was afraid," she admitted in a whisper.

"Of what?"

"Of what would be left once the anger went away. You're right. It is part of me, and maybe it's always been part of me. It feels comfortable, like an old friend. Maybe there won't be anything left of me once the anger's gone."

He reached out and cupped her chin, thumb stroking back and forth below her mouth. "Take a chance. It's better to deal with whatever you're feeling than to hide from it. Then you can put it behind you."

She batted his hand away with her bulky glove. "I'll bet you've never hidden from anything in your life."

He chuckled softly. "Not since my dad stopped whallopping us with the ruler."

"Will you take these off, please?"

He braced her hand between his thighs and untied the laces. When her hands were free, she wiggled her fingers and rubbed the moisture off on her shorts. He bounced one leg with a restless energy she could feel, drumming his fingers on the carpet.

"I'm not ready," she said, sensing that he was waiting for an answer of some kind. "When I'm ready, I have to do it alone." If she was going to feel that vulnerable, she didn't want Mitch there, didn't want to feel the need to reach out to him.

He got to his feet and extended a hand to her. "It's all right to reach out for help."

She eyed him, wondering if he knew how he'd read her mind. Reluctantly she linked fingers with him and let him pull her to her feet. "That's easy for you to say. You've got people here who care about you, who will stand by you no matter what."

He hadn't let go of her hand yet, instead squeezing her fingers. "So do you, Jenna."

His words squeezed her heart the same way his fingers squeezed hers. She thought of Betzi, Etta, Dave, and Scotty, all a part of Mitch's family whether they were related or not. Of course, Tawny *wanted* to be related, but Jenna couldn't blame the woman for wanting this, wanting Mitch.

"You were right about the strongest emotions being love and hate," she said, pulling her hand free because it felt too good entwined with his. "But it's a lot easier to hate, believe me. You risk nothing by hating someone. You risk everything by loving them."

With his finger, he pushed away a strand of hair from her cheek. "It's a lot like the difference between having sex and making love. There's a hell of a lot more at stake."

And then he walked past her toward the door. He stopped in the doorway, still finding her standing there with his words knocking her system for a one-two punch. "Are you coming? Or having second thoughts about pounding me into the Christmas season?"

Making love, making love . . . the words echoed through her mind during the walk back to the house. Was he talking about what they'd experienced? He had used the word "love" in regard to getting physical, but what did he really mean by it?

If only she could sort out Paul's part in all this. She had his heart, and that heart still had a connection to Mitch. Mitch had even felt Paul's love, so how much of that influenced what he now felt for her, whatever that was?

They were walking through the pine trees now, back into night air that was so different from what she was used to, yet felt so familiar somehow. Mitch walked beside her, quiet but for the sound of his footsteps on the pine-needle-covered ground.

Harvey's fur brushed her bare leg as he waltzed by, making her jump. She patted the place over her heart, that treacherous, mysterious heart, and said, "Scared me. I'd forgotten he was there."

"Lost in thought, are we?"

"Lost . . ." She paused, wondering when her heartbeat would at last resume its normal rhythm. "Lost in a vast mining-tunnel system without a light." She could feel his questioning gaze even in the dim moonlight that filtered down through the trees. "Lost in a foreign land without a translation book or a map. Lost like a blind person dropped into the center of New York City. All around me I know the colors are brilliant, yellows, reds, pinks, but it's like I'm color-blind. They're there, but I can't see them."

He stood in front of her, warm and solid and real, one of those colors she couldn't see. "I don't know how to help you, Jenna. But I can bring you a light in the tunnels. I can give you a map if you tell me where you want to go. I can lead you out of the city if you hold on to me." He shook his head. "But the colors . . . I don't know how to show you the colors."

"You've shown me the colors. When I've let you, you've shown me. But mostly I'm afraid to see them." The air was heavy and still around them. He would show her the way, give her the light, lead her from the darkness, if only she would let him. Slowly she reached out until she felt his skin. Her fingers wrapped around his arm, felt his muscles tighten, then relax. "You said if I deal with my emotions, I can put them behind me. If I deal with the way I feel about you, will I get past that too?"

"How do you feel about me?"

She opened her mouth, but the words wouldn't come right away. Finally she said, "I don't know. I don't know how I should feel about you. I told you I was lost."

He leaned forward and kissed her, a warm, languorous kiss that instantly deepened when she opened her mouth to his. Now her heart was pounding like crazy from this, the first kiss that had come from something deeper than passion. He took a step closer, threading his fingers across her temples and into her hair, tilting her head back. Her arms went around his waist, pulling him closer until their bodies flattened against each other. She could feel the length of him press into her stomach. His legs straddled hers, as though he couldn't bring her close enough.

He finished the kiss, touching his lips to hers a few times, then opening her mouth once again to his. This felt so right, and in his arms she didn't feel lost anymore. She wanted him to dispel the doubt in her heart—about her heart. But he couldn't do that; only she could. Maybe he would lead her to the truth.

She heard him sigh, then realized the long, soft sound had come from her. He followed that with another sound that came from deep in his throat. He tilted her head back and kissed down her jawline. She was swept into a dazzling oblivion, sending her heart into overdrive.

We'll get caught out here.

Paul's voice, echoing through her mind and heart as his brother made her crazy with his kisses.

No, we won't. We'll be quiet.

Becky's voice, whispered in the dark. Jenna could see them out here in the patch of pines, Becky pulling Paul up against her as she leaned on the tree. "Stop being such a worrywart and kiss me, you fool." She gave his derriere a squeeze, and he didn't seem the least bit embarrassed about it.

In fact, Paul covered Becky's body with his, smothering her mouth and making gusty noises despite his worries. "I want you so bad," he whispered between kisses, working on the buttons of her blouse. "I've got protection."

"We don't have to use it," she said. "I trust you."

"My dad would kill me if you got pregnant." He pulled

her blouse apart, exposing creamy, full breasts in the moon-light spilling through the trees. His mouth worked down the side of her neck, over her collarbone to nuzzle first one breast, then the other. His saliva left slick patches.

"Paul, Paul, oh, Paul," she uttered, burrowing her fingers in his hair.

He undid the zipper on her shorts, still licking and nibbling at her breasts. He pushed her shorts down, then stripped to nothing. With a snap of his arm, he tugged her down to the mat of pine needles.

"Do me, Paul. Do me this instant."

Jenna felt herself in the flashback, felt her keen desire to get out before she saw any more. It was Mitch's voice that brought her back, though.

"Jenna, for God's sake, what's happening?"

She blinked, finding him shaking her the way he had at the house in New Hampshire. "I'm here," she said, putting her hand to her pounding heart.

"You did it again, didn't you? Went off on some . . . journey in Paul's head."

She nodded, feeling weird and dirty and oddly aroused at the same time. "He and Becky—"

He dropped his hands and turned. "Jenna, do you know what I think when you do that? That you're dying. Your pulse is racing, your eyes are blank, and I can't get you to respond to me. I thought your heart was rejecting like you said it could do." He exhaled loudly. "What did you see this time?"

She ran her hand over her stomach. "They were making love. Right here." She'd never seen Paul like that. Of course, she'd never seen him with another woman, but he'd never even been that way with her.

Mitch shook his head, and even in the dim light, she could see frustration in his face. "Why did he pick this particular moment?"

"I don't know. Maybe because they'd been kissing here against this tree." The beautiful moment was shattered, and she longed to call it back and forget Paul making love to Becky.

"I know Paul and I made a vow, and I tried real hard to keep it." He ran his hand through his hair. "Okay, not hard enough, but I tried, and I beat myself up every time I violated that vow with you. Even when I thought about violating that vow. But just now, when I kissed you, it was like I was released from it. I thought, hell, I'm alive and he's dead, and he doesn't deserve your love anyway and, well, it just didn't make sense anymore." His mouth tightened. "So, did you kiss me back because you saw him and Becky?"

"No! Of course not. That happened after I'd kissed you back. Did you kiss me because you were feeling something from him?"

He took a step away, then turned back to her. "I told you I don't feel anything from him anymore. I'm not the one having his thoughts while we're kissing. You are."

She shrank back from him. "It wasn't as if I were thinking about him on purpose, or pretending I was kissing him."

"Maybe not, but Jenna, I'll never know with you. I don't do anything halfway, especially not kissing a woman. Or loving her. But you've got all this other crap going on in your heart, and it's messing with my head big-time."

Did he love her? Her throat went tight at those words, and though she should be responding to his other words, she couldn't get past the question in her mind. Did he mean loving her or making love to her, or were they the same to him?

"Come on," he said before she could gather her words together. "Let's go back to the house before I do something rash."

"Like what?"

"Jenna," he growled, "don't push me right now."

She didn't want to leave things like this. Something inside her desperately wanted to make things right, but she didn't know how. Everything he'd said was true.

As they reached the door leading into the house, she said, "I told you I was lost."

That stopped him, stiffening his body like a board. He slowly turned around. His voice was low and somber. "Maybe I don't have a map or a light. Maybe I can't help you after all."

He walked inside, leaving the door open for her to follow. She closed it, needing one of the nightly walks she used to take back home. First she walked around the massive house, realizing she was looking for Mitch in the kitchen. This wasn't working; she needed him *out* of her mind, before she went that way herself. *Too late!* an inner voice taunted. Not Paul's but her own.

Mitch's bedroom light burned now, and she stood beneath the balcony feeling her body pull her toward the exterior spiral staircase that led upstairs. She slowly wiped the back of her hand across her mouth, longing to feel his lips there instead.

What a mess she'd made of her life, this new chance. She turned and walked back to the stables, listening to the crickets' song and the shuffling noises of the horses in their stalls. She leaned against the outer fence of the ring where Mitch taught underprivileged kids to ride. And he had room to talk, messing with his mind big-time! The man was a bundle of contradictions, tender and hard, passionate and cool.

She kicked at the fence with the tip of her sneaker, her mind sliding back to their kiss in the woods. The man could kiss, that was certain. And he was right; he did it one hundred percent. She felt that stirring in her body, the longing and the fear. She let out a long sigh and pressed her forehead against the post.

"How could you let this happen?"

She didn't even know if she was addressing herself or Paul. She stepped through the gap in the fence and looked at the ring. Then she started dragging her foot through the dirt, making a large half-circle around the outer edge. Then two eyes, big round ones with pupils. And a nose. She didn't know if it looked like a happy face, since she couldn't see anything clearly in the moonlight.

When she stepped back out of the ring, she felt lighter. The clouds skittered across the slate-gray sky, making the moon wink at her. She leaned against the post again, and stared at the pocked complexion, clear at this cycle.

Whatever Mitch had meant by loving her, she knew one thing: she loved him. But he only deserved one hundred percent, and she wasn't sure if she could give him that.

She looked over at the ghostly happy face in the ring. "How can I give anyone that when I'm not a hundred percent myself?"

Mitch sat on the balcony, feet propped up on the railing, cold Lone Star beer in his hand. He'd watched Jenna walk out to the stables, and just to make sure she returned safely, he waited until she walked back to the house. He didn't know what she was doing over there for so long. He'd had to quell the desire to find out for himself in the name of making sure she wasn't in trouble. He couldn't shake the memory of her standing in the water looking out to sea as waves crashed in all around her. He now knew that Jenna would never throw away her life like that, but she was sure good at tempting fate. He laughed, chugging down another swallow of beer.

Fate was tempted.

For the first time in a while, he was spoiling for a fight. Not with some stupid punching bag either. But hell, what would that accomplish? Same thing it accomplished way back when, a whole lot of nothing. Guarantee he'd still be just as frustrated with Jenna when he got back all black and blue. He took another swig of his beer.

She was right: it was easier to hate than to love, but he wasn't an expert in the latter category. He'd always chided Paul for falling hard. In truth, the thought of being consumed by a woman worried him, and if Becky had talked Paul into killing their parents for money, Mitch had good reason to worry. But here he was, consumed from the inside out. And he *would* kill for her, but only to protect her.

She was wrong when she'd said he wasn't afraid of anything. Spooked horses, wicked windstorms, none of that bothered him. What ripped through him when he held Jenna in his arms, now that was spooky.

He rubbed the churning in his gut, leaning his head back against the chair. The sky was mottled with clouds lit up by the moon. A romantic evening one might call it, if one were so inclined. Romantic enough for a kiss in the woods. He let out a long breath and trained his gaze toward the east again.

Years ago that shrink had said Paul was the shadow twin. But when Jenna had stiffened and told him about "seeing" Paul, Mitch had felt like Paul's shadow. Jenna might not still love Paul—he didn't know. But the heart that brought her to him also stood between them.

Maybe he was being insensitive. Sure he was, an insensitive wife-stealing bastard, especially when she'd looked so innocent and vulnerable and told him again that she was lost. He pounded the arm of the chair with his fist, feeling his stomach twist the way it had then. He'd walked away from her, and then she'd walked away from him.

Mitch didn't hear her or see her . . . he sensed her. She walked out of the woods and across the small parking area, arms around herself. He waited until she was almost beneath his balcony before saying, "Punch out any bags?"

She stopped and looked up through the railing. The bars of light filtered down over her face. "I didn't even try to go inside. And I didn't see any eligible men to exorcise my demons with."

He came to his feet and leaned on the railing. "Ah hell, I didn't exorcise anything with Tawny."

"Why should I care if you did?"

But she did. He could hear it in her voice, in the way she tried hard to make it sound neutral. Jealous women, now they weren't anything new. But from Jenna, it touched something deep inside him. He trained his own voice to sound emotionless. "Don't suppose you should."

"I don't."

"Well, now that we have that settled . . ." He let the words drift off. Now what? The urge to apologize was strong, but he didn't know what to be sorry for. Most likely there were too many things if he put his mind to it. "You gonna come to church with us tomorrow?"

"Church?"

"What, you don't think they let in sinners like me?" He was feeling particularly wicked, the mood much more comfortable than the raw words he'd said to her earlier. "Maybe I should get some more sinning in, you know, get my money's worth."

"Screw you, Mitch." She covered her mouth as though she were shocked she'd said such a thing.

He gave her a cocky grin. "Well now, that's a darned good idea. Stairs are right there, honey."

Her shoulders hunched up, but she let them drop. "What's gotten into you?"

"Didn't I just say I never did exorcise my demons?"

He could see her swallow hard. She had the prettiest throat, long and slender, creamy white. "You're serious about church?"

"Ponee tradition. Preacher was the one who came out after our parents' murders and told me and Paul he knew we hadn't killed 'em. Said he'd stick by us, and he did. He's fire and brimstone, all the way. Scare the sin right out of you."

She tilted her head. "Good. I'll go. And I'll pray for you."

He dropped back in his chair and took another swig of beer. "You do that, honey. Pray for my soul."

Because the truth was, while Jenna had Paul's heart, she had Mitch's soul.

Fourteen

"*What in the* world are you talking about? All right, we're coming." Betzi hung up the phone and looked at Mitch, who was finishing up what had been more food than Jenna had ever seen one man eat at a breakfast. "Tawny says we have to go out to the stables right away."

Jenna downed the last of her pills and the last bite of her *frittata*. Maybe it was the Texas air, or maybe it was Mitch, but she'd never eaten so much, nor enjoyed her food so much. At home, the ritual of taking her medication seemed such a large part of her day, simply because there wasn't much else to fill it. But here, with so many distractions, the ritual became a small part, like brushing her teeth. Except, of course, that brushing her teeth didn't keep her alive.

Mitch slammed a glass of orange juice down on the counter and wiped the back of his hand across his mouth. "Is it one of the horses? Is Boy George about to pop her foal?"

If he hadn't been such a jerk the night before, Jenna might have noticed how handsome he looked, dressed in gray slacks and a white button-down shirt. And how nice he smelled and the way his hair curled over his collar and the one lock that curled over his forehead. But that was out of the question now. She did notice, however, that his eyes were a bit red and wondered how many beers he'd had last night.

"*Boy* George is a female horse?" Jenna asked, aiming the question at Betzi and not *him*.

Mitch took a tortilla from the refrigerator and tore off a piece. "Boy George, pop star of the eighties, of questionable gender. Jenna, where have you been all these years, under a rock? Ready?" This he addressed to Betzi, who gave him a stern look that nearly made Jenna grin despite herself.

"You better be praying for redemption of that attitude of yours, Mitchell James Elliot." Betzi gave her lace collar a righteous tug.

He nodded solemnly "Jenna here's going to pray for my soul. Or maybe between you both you can have me vaporized." And then he simply walked out.

Betzi turned a questioning look to Jenna, a twinkle in those blue eyes of hers. "Apparently we missed the real action movie here last night."

Jenna and Betzi walked outside into the warm, sunny morning. Mitch was already walking through the patch of pines.

"It's better this way, believe me," Jenna said.

Betzi touched her shoulder, halting Jenna in the square of shade beneath Mitch's balcony. "I don't know what's going on between you two, and it's really none of my business. But I like you; you're kind of like the daughter I never had. And Mitch, well, he's the son I never had. Oh my, that means if you two got together, it'd almost be incestuous!" She placed the tips of her fingers to her mouth, then shook her head. "Nonsense! Whatever am I thinking? Anyway, I think you should know that you possess something no other woman has ever possessed, at least to my knowledge."

"Severe doubt? Insanity? Insecurity?"

Betzi chuckled. "Well, we all have a degree of that. No, m'dear, nothing like that. I'm talking about that man's heart."

Jenna's throat constricted. "And here I thought it was something so simple as wearing out my welcome."

"Nonsense." Betzi nodded for Jenna to continue walking with her to the stables. "Thing is, I really do like you. No matter what happens between you and Mitch, you're always welcome here. That's from the queen of Bluebonnet Manor, so don't you doubt it."

Jenna's heart warmed, and she reached out and gave Betzi's arm a squeeze. "Thank you. I haven't had family in a long time, and I've never had a real home. But this place . . ." —her gaze swept the green pastures and grazing horses and the butterflies alighting on patches of wild flowers—"feels like home to me, and you, almost everyone, feel like family."

Betzi grinned. "Tawny'll get over it. Mitch would've never gone for her anyway, and Lord knows she's been trying long enough."

Jenna shook her head. "You do know everything that goes on around here, don't you?"

"I know enough. I've known Mitch for so long—that would be all his life—I know his moods, his temperament." She nodded toward where Mitch had joined a small group by the ring. "I've never seen him touch a woman the way he touches you. I mean those small, unconscious touches. You've got his heart, but he ain't too pleased about it."

"It's my fault. I'm too doubtful, insecure . . . insane, maybe. Sometimes I hear Paul's voice, and sometimes I feel as though he's here with me. It kind of freaks Mitch out. Not that I blame him. It doesn't make me feel very stable either. I don't know how to get Paul out of here." She tapped her chest. "Or how to tell how much of what Mitch and I feel for each other is Paul."

"You're not the first woman to have two mens' hearts, though not quite in this way. It's not your typical lovebird problem, I'll admit. I know what I'll be praying about this morning." She gave Jenna a wink.

Prayer. Jenna had almost given up on God, especially in those days after Paul's death. God had taken Paul away, but He'd given her life and the strength to deal with it all. He'd never made any guarantees, after all. So she'd decided to ask if He'd take her back, remembering from her childhood Bible readings that He never turned anyone away who sought Him.

"Elves came! Elves came!" Scotty came racing at them, leaping at Betzi. She scooped him up with a grunt and gave him a bear hug before setting him down again. He looked shyly at Jenna and gave her that little wiggly-fingered wave. "Hi."

She grinned, returning his wave. "Hi." The boy's hair was glossy in the sunshine, and Jenna fought the urge to ruffle it the way the wind ruffled it.

"What is this you're talking about? Show us the elves," Betzi said, letting Scotty drag her by the arm to the ring.

And then Jenna remembered.

"Elves made a happy face for us!" Scotty climbed up onto the railing and pointed at the huge smile in the ring.

"Did you do that?" Betzi asked, giving him a feigned suspicious look.

"No! It was the elves, I swear."

"You can't swear on God's day," Betzi admonished.

"But I, um . . ." Jenna could see his three-year-old mind trying to sort through the difference between swearing and just saying the word "swear." He tilted his head. "Saying swear doesn't count," he finally decided with a dip of his chin that reminded her of Mitch.

Betzi grinned. "Oh, I guess you're right."

Jenna eased up to the fence and pretended to be surprised. Scotty reverently reached out and touched the inside of the ridge that made the smile. "Elves, magic elves," he said in an awed voice. "No one rides in here. We got to save it for forever."

Jenna had watched the kids on the beach marvel at the happy faces from a distance, but to experience it firsthand was more delight than she could have imagined. She knelt down next to him. "We can't save it, but maybe the elves will come back again and leave another one for you."

Even Harvey seemed fascinated, his head stuck between the rails, nose twitching. Scotty clapped his hands, utter anticipation on his cute features. "Will they?"

"Could be." When she looked up, she saw Mitch watching her. He knew. If it was anyone else but Mitch, she would have winked: *keep my secret.* But he wasn't giving anything away, except something warm in his eyes.

"Etta, did you do this before your morning walk?" Tawny asked.

"Not me, girlie. I don't have time to play in the dirt. I have muscles to work, sweat to, er, sweat." She puffed up her shoulders, showing even in her Sunday church dress—a vivid yellow with large purple swirls. "Didn't even notice it. Jenna!"

Jenna started at her name, thinking it was some kind of accusation. Etta waved her over. "Did you meet Dave?"

"Yes, twice. Remember, we all ate together last night."

"Maybe you should meet him again, just to be sure."

Jenna rolled her eyes, but Dave played along by shaking her hand. "Nice to meet you again, just to be sure."

His hand was rough, like Mitch's, but touching Dave didn't feel the way touching Mitch did. "Likewise."

They chuckled, Etta beamed and winked at Jenna, who tried not to roll her eyes. Scotty said, "Jenna said the elves might come back tonight!" Dave grinned. And the big blue Texas sky capped the moment, making Jenna feel so warm and complete, she wanted to laugh out loud.

And Mitch, he stirred other parts of her and made them feel alive too. For the time being, she put away the turmoil he caused and prepared herself to sing the loudest in church. And thank God the hardest.

Jenna lived up to her promise, and got everyone's attention with her lousy singing. She'd forgotten she couldn't sing. How long had it been since she'd belted out a hymn, or any song? Too long, apparently. It worked out all right, though, because the Bluebonnet clan simply raised their voices to cover.

Although people were curious about her, Jenna sensed that because she was with Mitch, she was accepted. People admired Mitch, coming up to him after the service and shaking his hand or sharing a joke. One man thanked him for working with his son on the riding program.

Afterward most of their group packed back into Mitch's Bronco. Tawny rode with Dave, but Scotty wanted to ride in Mitch's truck. Etta sat in the back humming one of the hymns they'd sung earlier. She'd done her darnedest to get Jenna to ride with Dave, but Betzi intervened and managed to get her in the front seat. Jenna wasn't sure which was worse.

"Did you pray for my soul?" Mitch asked under his breath as he snapped on the radio.

"Twice."

"God was probably still covering his ears from your singing."

She wrinkled her nose. "God loves me anyway."

Scotty leaned forward, or as forward as his seat belt would allow, and said in his most adult voice, "You shouldn't fight, 'specially on God's day."

Mitch did have the decency to look chagrined. "Sorry, little man. You're right. But since He's probably still covering his ears, I reckon I'm safe." In the rearview mirror he looked at Betzi, who sat behind him. "Making brownies today?"

"I don't know." She looked at Scotty. "Think Mitch deserves brownies?"

Both he and Jenna shook their heads and said, "No!," simultaneously.

"But I do!" Scotty quickly added. "I didn't fight with nobody."

"This is mutiny!" Mitch declared. "Mutiny, I say!"

Scotty giggled. "What's mootie?"

"A worse sin than fighting, let me tell you, little man." Mitch nodded solemnly. "Especially when it involves women."

"Huh?"

"I'll give you the lowdown when you're older."

Scotty tilted his head. "You can tell me next week. I'll be older then. Mitch, you gonna play foo-ball today?"

"Yep. You gonna be our quarterback?"

"Nah, Mama won't let me be a foo-ball Bob. She says I'm too little, but I'm big. Bigger than Toby Jones," he said, referring to a toddler he'd seen at church.

Jenna settled back in her seat. She still couldn't get over Betzi's revelation. It only added to that odd feeling she'd had for a while, that she somehow belonged to Mitch, that he belonged to her. Despite his crankiness. Maybe he'd revealed too much of himself last night and was now re-grouping.

Jenna didn't know how to read men. Paul had never revealed too much, never been cranky or kissed her when a kiss was unexpected. All she'd learned about men through him was leaving him alone when he was in a blue mood.

But Mitch didn't get blue. He just got cranky, apparently.

Jenna was glad she'd brought one nice dress, a simple white cotton with the usual high collar. Since she'd rolled it up in her duffel bag, she'd had to iron the heck out of it. Earlier she'd caught Mitch's gaze taking in the way it hugged her waist and swirled around her knees, and every second of ironing had suddenly become worthwhile. So while everyone else changed into casual clothes, she stayed in the dress.

Betzi was assembling the ingredients for her homemade brownies, and Jenna was chopping the walnuts, marveling at how good they tasted, at how she could have disliked them before. Mitch blew into the kitchen wearing jersey shorts and that cut-off T-shirt she'd seen him in that first day. He had great legs, dusted with golden hair, and the kind of stomach worthy of those Calvin Klein brief ads. He laced up his sneakers, then abruptly looked up and caught her watching him.

She directed her attention to the walnut she'd been chopping, a walnut that had suffered the same fate as those beautiful tomatoes of hers. It was mush, and she discreetly shoveled it to the corner of the cutting board. The man was really annoying.

"Hey! Get your finger out of there!"

Betzi's admonition came too late. Mitch had already dipped his finger into the chocolate batter and sucked it clean with a great deal of noise. He licked a spot of chocolate off his lip, and she remembered all too well how that tongue tasted. She cleared her throat and sent another pile of walnut dust off to the corner.

For a moment she let herself think of what it would be like between her and Mitch without the doubts, without Paul's heart between them. Warmth rushed through her, stilling her body as she imagined days filled with the kind of joy she'd felt earlier, and nights filled with the kind of passion she'd experienced last night. It was easy to imagine, too easy.

Mitch wasn't an easy man to love with his bruskness and drive to find the truth at any cost. And then he was too easy to love, for the same reasons, for the fire in his eyes and the way he made her feel so alive.

She was staring at his mouth, full sensual lips that kissed too well for her own good. She blinked, refocusing on her task. Easy to love. The words echoed in her mind, and she wondered if she'd ever be able to trust her feelings when it came to Mitch.

"I'm off to kick some butt," he said. "You gonna come watch, Jenna?"

"Er, I think I'll stay here and help Betzi. Have fun."

He let his gaze linger one moment too long for her comfort before turning to head out.

"I'll come watch," Etta said, walking in and rubbing her hands together. "Nothing like watching nubile, sweaty young men to get the blood pumping to all the outer regions." She wore shiny Lycra shorts and a tank top, and Jenna was sure she'd never seen a woman over sixty look quite that good. Jenna couldn't imagine wearing such an outfit, even before her surgery. Maybe . . . well, maybe when her scar faded she'd give it a try.

"May I escort you to the field, Mrs. Mulligan?" Mitch crooked his arm, and Etta slid her arm through his.

"Be my pleasure. You coming, girlie?" she asked Jenna, that same mischievous twinkle in her eyes that Betzi often had. Jenna shook her head. "You ain't afraid of overloading your new ticker, are you?"

Jenna instinctively put her hand over her heart. "Oh, it can take a lot, believe me." Her eyes just as instinctively went to Mitch, but she quickly averted them.

Mitch and Etta left arm in arm, and Jenna was able to go back to chopping nuts again. She found that if she stood in just the right place, she could see the men converging on the field to the right of the pine trees.

"You know, of course, that you don't have to stay and help me, don't you?" Betzi said, scraping the pile of chopped nuts into her chocolate batter. "I get paid to do this."

"I know."

"Thought so. But now the brownies are ready for the oven, and the ribs don't take much effort at all, and the way you keep looking out that window, you might as well just go on out."

Jenna flushed, ducking her head. "You're sure there's nothing else I can help with?"

"Well, you could mop the floors and wipe down the windows, and the gutters need cleaning. But I think you ought to go up and change, grab a chair from the garage, and situate yourself so you can watch those nubile, sweaty young men beat themselves up in the name of the sport."

Jenna grinned. "If you insist." She started to head upstairs, then stopped. "I need to wash some of my clothes. I couldn't exactly bring my suitcase on the bike, so I didn't bring much."

"Just leave them outside your room, and I'll take care of them."

"I can do them myself. I don't want to put you out."

"Nonsense! I—"

"Get paid for it, I know," Jenna said, finding herself liking Betzi more and more. "I wish I'd had someone like you around when I was growing up."

"Well, you got me now." Betzi leaned against the counter. "Since the, well, the murders, Mitch has made me feel like more than a housekeeper. His parents were formal as far as the help was concerned, but Mitch insisted I eat dinner with him, play my music, whatever I wanted. He's the one who called me the queen of the manor. But I'm not really the queen. I'd be glad to step aside for someone more worthy of that title." She winked, then waved Jenna off. "Go, watch the football Bobs and come back ready to eat the best ribs in East Texas."

Jenna paused, finding her soul becoming more and more entrenched in this place. "Thanks, Betz."

Jenna changed and found a lawn chair in the garage. She threaded her way through the pines, feeling déjà vu wrap around her. A sunny Sunday, the rock and roll, men shouting and laughing. It was that day last week—was it only a week ago?—all over again. There was that sound again, Mitch's primal yell as he weaved through the guys who tried to stop him. But his victory wasn't joyful, because as soon as he'd passed the white chalk line, he ordered the guys to get right back into position. His hair was loose, gray shirt damp over his chest.

Jenna emerged from the trees the way she had last week, just as the guy in front of Mitch hiked the ball. Mitch looked up, the way he had last week, as though he'd sensed she was there. Their eyes connected, she stopped breathing . . . and Mitch got tackled.

"Focus, Bob, focus!" one of his teammates said to Mitch after looking over at her. "You're falling apart, man!"

Mitch gave his head a shake. "You don't know the half of it, Bob."

Jenna forced her gaze away and headed over to where Tawny, Scotty, and Etta had set up their chairs a short distance from the playing field. She chose to sit next to Etta, but wasn't too sure about the decision when Etta raised her fist and yelled, "Okay, shirtless boys, time to come back! Get those cute little buns of yours in gear!" She turned to Jenna. "I always root for the ones that show the most skin."

Scotty gave her that wiggly-fingered wave of his, and then set off after Harvey, who was running back and forth on the sidelines. A minute later, Scotty came up behind Jenna's chair, peering around the back. "The smiley face is still there! I went and checked after church."

"I'll bet the elves will come back and make a new one tonight," Jenna said, catching Tawny's curious glance. "Be sure to check in the morning."

Jenna reached out and tweaked Scotty's tummy, and his laughter made her feel more high than any drug ever could. She wanted to hear that kind of laughter all the time, wanted to experience it herself. It was too easy to picture a little boy with gray eyes and dark blond hair with one errant lock hanging over his forehead. Her heart had given her a new life; had Mitch done the same?

The ball went sailing through the air, and Harvey followed Mitch as he ran back to catch it. Scotty followed Harvey, barking just like the dog.

"You drew the face in the sand?" Tawny asked.

"Yeah."

They both watched Scotty run over to the ring and peer through the railing, as though he suspected the face would disappear the same way it appeared.

Tawny shook her head. "It's all he's talked about." She gave Jenna a begrudging smile. "Who would have figured something so simple would take his mind off his daddy. He was supposed to come visit yesterday."

"I'm sorry." Scotty had run around to the far side of the ring. "Sometimes magic comes from the most unexpected places," Jenna said, finding her gaze sliding to Mitch, who was throwing the ball to another player with enough force to send it halfway across the state. The guy caught it in the chest with a loud "Oof!" and went tumbling backward.

"Hell, Bob, what're you tryin' to prove?" he grumbled when Mitch lent him a hand.

"I'm into the game, that's all. If you had been too, you'd have caught that ball and got us the point."

A couple of the guys in the vicinity gave Mitch a questioning look, but he stalked back into position. They looked at each other, then shrugged. Mitch reeked of impatience and intensity. Wherever the ball was, so was he. He tackled whoever had the ball with ferocity and pushed anyone in his way out of it.

It wasn't long before the scent of ribs floated their way. Jenna couldn't help but grin at the way the Bobs lifted their noses to the air, just like Harvey was doing. Mitch, however, ordered them back to the game. Some of the men grumbled, others glanced her way. She fought the urge to shrug apologetically for causing Mitch's behavior.

Etta shook her head and, with a sigh, said, "I hope I never get too old to appreciate men."

Jenna followed her hungry gaze to the playing field, where Mitch was bent and poised to catch the ball. His skin gleamed with sweat, muscles flexed with his movements. Unfortunately, she remembered all too well what that body looked like naked, what it felt like against hers. Her fingers tightened on the arms of the chair and her insides stirred at the memory. She felt Etta's sexual hunger too, but only for one man.

All those years with Paul, she thought she'd been satisfied sexually. He'd done the right things, the required things. But he'd never lit her on fire, never made heat pool in her lower belly and at the tips of her breasts. Since the transplant, she'd felt guilty about not taking her second chance at life with gusto. Well, now she wanted to do just that, wanted to wrap her legs around his waist and pull his body down close to hers. . . .

He chose that moment to look over at her, and Jenna sank low into her chair, feeling warmth bathe her face.

Could he sense her thoughts? Perhaps, because he caught the ball and let out that primal scream that sent shivers down her body as he barreled through his friends. Two of them grabbed him and sent him to the ground.

"Half time!" Dave shouted, taking the shirt tucked into his waistband and wiping his forehead with it.

Etta walked over to the water cooler and started dispensing cups of cold water. Tawny got up and stretched with a catlike grace that made Jenna feel awkward.

"You'd better do something about him," Tawny said, nodding toward where Mitch still lay sprawled out on the grass. "Before he kills someone." Then she wandered over to the cooler where the men clustered.

"He wouldn't kill anyone," Jenna said, though she didn't know if Tawny heard. Was it that obvious, the electricity between her and Mitch, the current that threatened to short-circuit them? Her chest grew tighter as she watched him push himself off the ground and saunter over, looking all kinds of dangerous with that gleam in his eye.

She remembered the punching bag and how he used that to eradicate his anger. He stopped in front of her chair, and she met his eyes. "What do *you* have left after the anger goes away?" she asked.

He leaned down, bracing his hands next to hers on the arms of the chair, and kissed her. Just like that, without any warning, preamble, or thought to who might see them, he assaulted her mouth, opening it and plunging his tongue inside. It only lasted a few seconds, though the sensations rocked her thoroughly.

"Besides an aching body? Something a lot scarier than the anger, babe, believe me."

And then he pushed off and sauntered over to the cooler. Jenna didn't—couldn't—bring herself to even look over to see everyone's reaction. She heard low whistles and murmurs from the men, but couldn't concentrate on anything but Mitch's words. What was scarier than the anger? For her, the monster that waited behind her anger was loneliness, emptiness. But Mitch couldn't possibly feel that, not with all his friends surrounding him.

Her heart, that heart that had generated both pain and hope and now confusion, thrummed inside her chest, making her fingers tighten. There *was* something scarier than even the loneliness: love. She didn't want to need a man again, didn't want to open herself up for the kind of pain Paul's lies had caused. Paul had demanded nothing from her; Mitch wanted it all. Worse, she wanted to give him all, more than she'd given Paul, more than she'd even known was inside her.

But how much of it was real? How much was her physical heart versus her inner heart?

"Girlie, you've been holding out on me!" Etta dropped down into her chair and gave Jenna a pointed look. "Here I been trying to hook you up with Dave, and you're already long gone for Mitch."

"Well, not long gone . . ."

Etta snorted, shaking her head. "I know long gone when I see it. I just thought it was aimed at the wrong guy."

Jenna blew out a breath. "I'm still not sure that it isn't."

"Girlie, you could do a lot worse, a *lot* worse, let me tell you."

The Bobs reassembled on the field, and for the first few minutes, Jenna felt as though every one of them assessed her. She found herself brushing her finger against her lips, back and forth as she remembered the way Mitch's mouth felt on hers. Tawny didn't even look her way when she returned. Mitch looked more relaxed now, apparently not bothered by the reaction his kissing her produced. He didn't barrel down even one guy during the first play.

On the second play, however, one of the Bobs twisted his ankle and went down. Mitch and Dave helped him up, but he couldn't put his weight on the ankle.

"It's only sprained. I can move my toes, but I'm out of the game." He limped over to where the women sat and dropped gingerly down on the grass. "Anyone want to take my place?" he asked kiddingly.

"I will!" Etta said, jumping to her feet. "I'll take on any amount of testosterone!"

"I can play," Tawny said, also getting up. "I could stand to knock some heads around."

Jenna guessed exactly whose heads she meant.

Some of the guys grumbled. "We can't play with women. We'll have to be . . . gentle." As though that were the equivalent of putting on a dress.

"Why not?" another guy said. "We can play the second half for fun. Besides, Mitch has run us ragged; I could use some easy play."

"If you both play, then we'll have uneven teams," Dave said.

"Jenna here can play too," Etta said, pulling her to her feet. In a low tone, she said, "You can play, can't you? With your heart, I mean."

Jenna stared at the men waiting to hear what she'd say. Play football? With a bunch of guys? Well, she wanted to experience life, didn't she? "Sure, I can play. Just tell me what the rules are."

"No tackling the gals," Mitch said. "Put your hands on their waist like this . . ." He demonstrated on Jenna, placing his hands on either side of her waist. "And they're considered tackled. Watch your hands, boys." In a lower voice, he asked her, "Sure you want to do this?"

"This might work better than a punching bag." But at the moment, she didn't feel that anger, only an increase in her heartbeat at doing something she'd never done before.

"No tackling?" Etta yelled. "Why, where's the fun in that?"

"We'll take Jenna and Etta," Dave said.

One burly-looking guy asked, "Are our new teammates going to take off their shirts too?" He was giving her a sly look, making her face flush with the realization that he was talking specifically about her! Goodness, why would anyone want to see her without her shirt, scar notwithstanding?

"Stuff it, Carl," Mitch said in a growling voice that

made Jenna smile. He walked over to the boom box and put in a new CD. "All right, let's play!"

"What group is this?" Jenna asked as he walked by, determined to learn about these rock-and-roll bands.

"Queen." His gaze lingered on hers for just a moment before he joined his team.

Queen. Betzi's words came back to her, about stepping aside for a new queen. Jenna shook her head and walked over to where Dave was giving his team, and particularly Etta, instructions. Mitch was moving his head to the song, a song Jenna had a suspicion was called, "Fat Bottom Girls." She thought of her own bottom, definitely not fat or even nicely rounded.

"Jenna, you got that?" She focused on Dave, embarrassed at having drifted. "Try to get the ball if you can, and run that way. Cross the line, and we get a point."

"Got it," she said. "Let's show the Bobs what the Betties have, Etta."

The only team Jenna had ever been part of was with Paul, working on old homes together. This was something entirely different, and within a few minutes, she felt the rush of working with her teammates, passing the ball, completing the play, and the disappointment of getting "tackled" by one of Mitch's teammates.

They huddled, conferred, planned their strategy. She hadn't done anything so physically exerting in years, hadn't felt the sweat gushing from her pores, hadn't felt the high of breathing hard after running. Last year taking a shower was exhausting. Now she was playing football of all things, using her body in a way she'd never used it before. Reaching new heights, using her potential.

Realizing how out of shape she was.

Neither Tawny nor Etta were hardly breaking a sweat, but Jenna had to brace her arms on her thighs and bend over to catch her breath. An hour on the treadmill every day obviously wasn't enough.

"You all right?" Mitch said as everyone regrouped.

"Great," she huffed, then smiled at the concern in his

face. "Really. I haven't given my new heart such a workout since . . ." Her face flushed, because the last time she'd felt so *alive* with her heart and blood racing was when she'd made love with Mitch. "In a while. I need to build up my stamina, that's for sure."

"There are ways to do that," he said, leaving the options wide open.

She watched him walk back toward his team and was struck anew by his grace and the confidence of his stride. Snapping out of it, she got ready for the next play.

An hour later, they were planning their last play. Dave looked over at Jenna: "I'm going to throw you the ball, and I want you to run with it. We're tied, and this is the final play of the game. Etta, cover her. Bob, you too. Okay, let's get 'em!"

Within seconds, the ball was in play and headed right for her. She wanted to win for the team. Her legs were achy, arms tired, but she wanted to win. She grabbed the ball and ran for it. Etta nudged Tawny out of the way, which was probably good since the woman had a wicked gleam in her eye as she'd headed right at Jenna. Etta ended up landing on top of Tawny. Another guy shoved her protective Bob out of the way, but she kept her eye on the chalk line not far away.

And then Mitch jumped out in front of her. She tried to dodge him, but he lunged forward and caught her around the waist . . . and lifted her right up on his shoulder, the way he'd done back in New Hampshire. He ran with her, light dancey steps that made her cling to his damp skin. He twirled her around, crossed her own touchdown line, and set her down on the grass.

"You win," he said, leaning over her and panting.

"But you tackled me."

"But I carried you over the line. Guess we'll just call the game even."

"Mitch." She exhaled, feeling crazy and light-headed and confused as she looked up at him. She loved him. No matter that he was sweaty with grass clinging to his cheek, no matter that he had stripped her defenses and left her wanting him, needing him. Damn the man. Did she have to let down all her safe barriers to feel alive? Would she have to cut out her heart to know whether what she felt was because of Paul?

His eyes shadowed, maybe seeing the doubt clouding her own. He pushed up, then helped her to her feet. "I hear ribs and Lone Stars calling our names," he said, letting go of her hand and cupping his ear.

Cheers went up all around. Some of the men walked toward the stables and washed themselves down with hoses. Tawny and Scotty went inside, and the rest of the guys started heading over toward the house. She and Mitch walked with them, surrounded by talk and laughter and Etta critiquing some of the plays.

"Later we'll see if Becky's dad is back," Mitch said, not looking her way.

"We can wait until tomorrow."

"No, I want to see him as soon as possible. I need to put it behind me, whatever we find."

"All right, we'll go after we eat."

Jenna walked beside Mitch, but he felt far away. She'd gotten a glimpse of joy, of love, and happiness. They edged into her soul, brighter than she'd ever felt. But reaching out for them, pulling them close, meant dropping the protective cloak that kept the hurt away. It meant risking her heart in a way she'd never risked it before, like when it had been taken out of her chest for those few minutes before the doctors had put in Paul's heart. First she had to find out how much of her heart really belonged to her, and how much belonged to Paul. Because Mitch would demand it all, without any doubts.

Fifteen

Mitch hated the upside-down feeling in his head and his stomach, hated that he'd impulsively kissed her in front of everybody, hated that she read him so well, hated enjoying the way her body pressed up against his and the easy way her arms slid around his waist. Eased up behind him on the back of the bike, she felt like his woman. His girl. For those miles they'd ridden with the group of bikers, she'd been his biker chick.

He'd started this journey looking for the truth, and he'd found a lot more than he'd bargained for. He'd found places inside him he didn't know existed. Now he needed to end this journey by refocusing on the truth. All the answers lay there. He knew this the same way he knew Jenna would free him the moment he'd seen her. Thus far, she sure as hell hadn't done that.

They pulled down the White driveway, and his fingers tightened when he saw the shiny semi sitting next to the house, parked next to the dusty Ford. Alan was back.

Mitch expected the man to hear his bike and come out, but he didn't. As they walked up to the door, he said, "Stay close to me, all right? I remember the man having a temper."

When Alan answered the door, his hair was wet, as though he'd just come out of the shower. The man was in his fifties, but he looked a lot older. He stared at Mitch, eyes suspicious.

"I'm Mitch Elliot," he said. It had been a long time

since he'd had to clarify who he was; Mitch, not Paul. Then he looked over at Jenna. Maybe not that long after all. "This is Jenna Elliot. Can we talk?"

Mitch pushed forward, and Alan stepped aside, seemingly surprised and taken off guard by their visit. The house was large inside, but messy. Alan obviously camped out in his worn easy chair; it was surrounded by newspapers, cartons of food, beer cans. He dropped down into it and lit a cigarette without indicating that they should sit also. It didn't appear that Alan had many visitors; the couch looked dusty. Mitch led Jenna over to it and sat down on the edge.

"We came to talk about Becky."

"Becky's dead," Alan said in a deadpan voice.

"I know, and I'm sorry." He turned to Jenna. "Jenna was Paul's wife." Alan's expression grew hard at the mention of his brother. "Paul died in a car accident. In Maine. Nine months ago."

He watched Alan put those facts together, eyes growing a harder shade of blue with every second. "So?"

"Don't you think it odd that both he and Becky died in the same place, and around the same time. In fact, they died fifteen minutes apart, twenty miles from each other." He'd checked the maps and times at Jenna's. "It's not a coincidence, is it?"

The man's beefy fingers tightened on the worn arms of the chair. "I don't know what you're talking about. Why're you comin' here bothering me?"

"We need to know what happened ten years ago, the night my parents were killed."

Alan's face shuttered. "Sheriff already asked me . . . ten years ago."

It was Jenna who asked the next question. "Had Becky been in contact with Paul recently?"

"No. Jerk left her, after all she done for him."

"What did she do for him?" Jenna asked.

Alan hesitated, then said, "Standing by him after the murders and all."

"Did she lie about him being here that night?" Mitch asked.

"No. He was here, just like we said."

"What was Becky doing in Maine?"

"She traveled. Wrote articles about places."

The man was lying; Mitch could feel it. He was still protecting his daughter. "You don't need to lie for her anymore. She's gone."

"I know she's gone!" Alan stubbed out his cigarette, jumped to his feet, then seemed to get hold of himself. He sat back down and lit another cigarette. "I know she's gone," he repeated in a low, even voice.

Jenna was staring at the silver lighter case with the turquoise stones. Even when Mitch asked, "Can we see some of her travel articles?" Jenna hadn't taken her eyes from the case.

"I don't have anything. I threw them away when she died."

Mitch looked around the room, finding more than two dozen pictures of Becky during her growing years. Her mother had died young, Mitch remembered. It had only been her and her dad for a long time. It wasn't too hard to believe that her dad had lied to protect her and her lover. It was harder to believe that Alan would have thrown away the articles when he'd kept all of her pictures.

"All right," he said, not willing to call the man a liar just yet. He listed off the dates and locations when Paul had taken money from his account and wherever he and Jenna had lived at the time. "Was Becky traveling during those dates?"

"I don't remember. That was a long time ago. Listen, I don't know what you're after, but you ain't gonna find it here. My girl didn't do anything. She didn't deserve to die." His voice had grown thick. "She was a good girl."

Mitch actually checked himself before pushing Alan. Jenna had done that to him, made him think about what he said, about being too brusque. But Alan sure as hell wasn't Jenna, and he didn't deserve any kindness if he'd lied to protect his daughter. "But my parents didn't think she was good enough."

Alan again shot to his feet. "I want you to leave now."

Mitch and Jenna got to their feet too. She was still looking at the lighter Alan held, his thick fingers rubbing the stones.

Mitch led Jenna to the door, standing between her and Alan. "My parents were trying to break them up. Maybe Becky and Paul decided to get them out of the way. Then they'd be rich, and free to love each other. Is that what happened? Maybe Becky convinced Paul to do it, and then convinced you to give them an alibi."

"Get out of here!"

"The only thing I can't figure out is why Paul left Becky behind. He must have felt bad about it. He gave her money to keep their secret."

Alan advanced toward them, his face flame-red. Mitch opened the door and nudged Jenna outside without taking his eyes off Alan. The man reeked of rage and guilt. Mitch was convinced he knew the truth, and he wasn't afraid of pushing to get at it.

"That where you got the money for this place, Alan? Hush money? Blood money?"

"Get out of my house!" he roared, pushing Mitch back a step.

He didn't want to get into a physical altercation with the man, not with Jenna there. "The truth needs to come out, Alan. Paul and Becky are gone; they can't go to jail now, can't pay for their sins. The truth needs to come out."

Alan shut the door in his face. Mitch turned to walk with Jenna back to the bike.

"Good thing you're not a cop," she said. "Subtle you're not."

She'd put the white dress back on after her shower, and she looked incredibly feminine and soft. Her blond hair curled beneath her chin and grazed her bare shoulders. He focused on the door that had been closed in his face instead, muscles bunching up. "I just want the truth. I hate liars, and the man's lying through his gap teeth." He turned back to Jenna. "Did Paul . . . talk to you? Did you sense anything? You kept staring at Alan's lighter."

She nodded. "Well, he looked familiar, but not necessarily in a Paul kind of way. I know I've seen his face before."

"Where?"

"I don't know exactly."

"Could he have gone with Becky when Paul gave her money? Maybe you saw him once."

"I don't think so. Maybe I'm wrong. But the lighter . . ." She shook her head, making her hair shine in the sun. "Something about it bothered me. *That* felt like it came from Paul."

He was still in her heart, or in her head. Mitch pushed away that thought, focusing on the truth. The truth would set him free, had to set him free. "What bothered you?"

"I don't know. When I first saw it, my heart started pumping faster. It was like . . ." Her eyes glazed over as she stared at a patch of dirt. Then she shook her head. "Do you know if Becky did travel a lot? Or if she did write travel articles?"

"Dunno. Becky wasn't someone I wanted to know better. I didn't trust her, especially after the murders. After Paul took off, she came over and asked if I'd heard from him. She looked pretty broken up about it, but all I could wonder was if she had anything to do with my parents' murders, and did she use Paul's love to convince him to kill them?

"A year later, she came by asking again. I'd heard that Alan was sick, but I didn't know what was wrong with him. Even if I'd heard from Paul, I wouldn't have told her. I couldn't get it out of my head. My parents were pretty mean to her, trying to scare her away. She had reason enough to hate them." He glanced back at the two-story house. "Let's blow." He could see Alan standing at the living room window watching them. The man was on edge enough to come out and brand a shotgun.

* * *

When Jenna and Mitch returned to Bluebonnet Manor, she discovered a startling truth: Betzi had Sunday nights and Mondays off, and she and Etta had driven to Fort Worth for a couple of days. Which meant Jenna and Mitch would be alone in the house. Perfectly, totally alone.

The thought sent ripples through her body. She wanted to be alone with him; she didn't want to be alone with him. He wanted too much . . . no, demanded too much. But he gave as much as he took, that much was true.

While Mitch had gone to check on the horses, particularly the very pregnant Boy George, Jenna had gone on to the house. She'd gone into Mitch's parents' room by herself. Now she was in control. She didn't want Paul to lead her around anymore.

And hadn't she told Mitch she wanted to face the truth alone? To face shedding her anger by herself? She'd survived Paul's death and her transplant by herself. She could handle the truth too. She placed her palm against the wall and closed her eyes.

The images came again, as vividly as before. She saw his parents in their bed, felt Paul's agony and shock, smelled the blood. But as he stepped forward, she felt that curtain again. The image faded, and she leaned against the wall as her knees went weak. She turned to the doorway, almost expecting Mitch to come in. Hadn't he always found her, here before and in Paul's room? Hadn't he been there when she needed him?

Did she need him? Oh, my, she did. She wanted him to appear and take her into his arms, to assure her without words that everything would be all right. She pressed her hand over her heart; this was her need, not Paul's.

"Jenna?"

Mitch's voice in the distance melted over her like warm honey. She left the room and walked to the kitchen. "I'm here."

When she turned the corner and saw him, he looked relieved. He smiled. "You all right?"

"Yeah, why?"

He shrugged. "Dunno. Just had this feeling . . ." He turned away and picked a brownie off the pile on the crystal plate. "Want a brownie?"

"No, thanks." Had Paul told Mitch she needed him? Mitch had said he didn't feel Paul's feelings anymore, but how much of what Mitch felt for her was real?

"Boy George is getting closer. She keeps lying down and getting up again, moving around a lot. I told Tawny to keep an eye on her and get everyone ready to mobilize. What's wrong?" Mitch bit off the corner of his brownie, but he was looking at her.

She leaned on the counter, rubbing her temples. "I wish I could get another heart. No, that's not right. That would mean someone else dying. That was one of the worst parts about needing a new heart; knowing that someone had to die so you could get it. You hoped you got one soon, but then wasn't that hoping someone would die?"

Mitch set down his brownie and walked over to where she stood. "Why do you want another heart?"

She couldn't meet his eyes, instead staring at the place where his black shirt tucked into his blue jeans. "I want to know who I am."

"And how much is Paul?"

She nodded. "And how much of you . . . us is Paul."

He pointed to his chest. "Me? There isn't any Paul in me."

"But you once felt things from him. Maybe you still are and don't know it."

He tilted his head. "Is that what you think?"

"I don't know what I think anymore." She stood up straight and walked around the end of the counter, fighting the need to pull close to him, to beg him to prove that what he felt wasn't Paul. But she couldn't give him that same assurance.

"If you'd gotten another person's heart, you wouldn't have found us. Is that what you really wish? That you hadn't come?"

She walked over to a picture in the family room, one she hadn't noticed before. "There was a time when I would have said yes. But now . . ." She shook her head. "I've lost my memories with Paul, but I've grown." She smiled "I've played football."

She focused on the picture, the whole Elliot family leaning and sitting along one of the short brick walls in the backyard. The twins were teenagers, standing together with Mitch's arm slung over Paul's shoulder. They were dressed alike, but Mitch had untucked his shirt. "You look like a happy family."

He came up behind her, surrounding her with that sweet, spicy scent she would always associate with him alone. "We had to. Just before that picture was taken, Dad ordered us to smile, and . . ." His voice went lower. " 'Look happy, dammit. You have everything you want. You owe it to me to be happy.' " His voice went back to normal. "We were the Elliots, the royalty of Ponee. We were supposed to stand out, to be different. Paul hated being the center of attention, and I just wanted to be normal. My dad didn't care if I was the fastest runner at school, the best football player, or the top hitter on the baseball team. I wasn't like him, and that's all that mattered. Paul and I were disappointments to him in the long run."

"Just because you weren't snobs?" Jenna turned, finding him too close behind her.

"Yep. 'You want people to respect you, to envy and revere you,' he'd say. Sure, people respected and envied us, but what was the point? Jealous kids are mean kids. I didn't want to be different or revered. I wanted to be respected, yes, but mostly I wanted to be liked. Being revered is lonely business."

"Is that why you work with those kids? Training them to ride, I mean?"

He gave her a one-shouldered shrug. "Actually, I started that because it felt good to give something back. My dad likened himself to Lyndon B. Johnson. The President. Heck, my dad wasn't modest. L. B. J. was born poor Texas, and he made it all the way to the White House. But my dad didn't give anything back when he was sitting pretty. He just kept taking.''

He started to reach for the picture, and she put her palm against it. ''No more throwing pictures!''

He gave her a sheepish grin. ''I was going to straighten it.''

''Oh.'' She let go and turned around. ''If you didn't like your dad's snobbery, why do you keep so much of your parents' gaudy furniture? It's not you.''

He looked around at the gilt coffee table, the dinette set. ''Something wouldn't let me give it away.''

''Maybe you thought you'd be letting your dad down again if you got rid of it all.''

''Are you analyzing?''

She laughed. ''I'm the worst person to analyze, aren't I? I don't even know what's going on inside my own head.''

He looked at the top of her hair, sliding his fingers back through it for a moment. ''Maybe you're right. Maybe it's time to make this place a home.''

She felt her heart tighten at those words. Home, the thing she'd wanted for so long.

When can we go home, Mommy?

We don't have a home anymore, honey. These people are our home now. Wherever we're needed, that's where we live.

He placed a palm against the wall next to her head. She tried to blink away what she knew must show in her eyes: need. But she was tired, so tired of fighting everything inside her. She reached out, threading her fingers around his neck beneath the softness of his hair. Her mouth opened, but the words wouldn't come.

Finally she pushed them out. ''Mitch, I need you to love me. I mean, to make love to me. I need you,'' she said simply.

He laced his fingers through hers, then lifted her hand

to his mouth. ''Jenna, I don't want to share you with him. Not for a kiss, not for anything.''

Her body was trembling, shaking from the inside out. ''It's just me, just you.''

He looked into her eyes, and she hoped he saw the truth in them. Whatever it was that he saw made him lean forward and cover her mouth with his. The kiss was long and sweet, but he broke away and led her upstairs. He snapped on the light beneath his ceiling fan.

His bedroom spoke of Mitch, from the simple, dark wood furnishings to the parquet floor and enlarged, framed photographs of what must be his own horses. There were clothes strewn over one chair, and a fireplace split the French doors leading to the balcony.

She took all this in within an instant, but her attention stopped at the huge unmade bed. His bed where he slept every night. She started reaching over to turn the light back off, but he halted her midway. ''Lights on,'' he said. ''Won't be the first time.'' He let go of that hand, trailing his fingers down where her scar was hidden beneath her dress.

She dropped her hand. There was no need to hide from Mitch. Their hands were still linked, and as soon as they reached the bed, he pulled her into his arms and into another long kiss, this one not so sweet. She felt herself fall into a deep chasm, far from the safety of her strength and anger. For tonight, she could reach out to him; tonight she would let herself need him.

''You're shaking,'' he said. ''Cold?''

She shook her head. ''I don't know why I'm shaking.''

He ducked his head, threading his fingers across her collarbone. ''Are you afraid?''

·   Only of the deep, dark places inside her, the places she needed a light to see into. ''No, no, I'm not afraid. Just hold me.''

He pulled her close, and she melted against his body. Reaching out wasn't so hard. All those months she'd stood alone seemed like some faraway, cold place. Mitch made it all go away, just by holding her, by running his hands up and down her back. He gave her strength and warmth, and all she'd had to do was ask. She would have never thought to ask Paul for something so simple as to be held by him. She closed her eyes and pressed her cheek against his chest. *Mitch, Mitch, Mitch.* She didn't want to think about Paul now, not ever. She wanted to lose herself in Mitch.

"Jenna," he whispered next to her ear. "I want to love you . . . God, do I want to love you, but if all you want is this, that's okay too."

She moved back, only far enough to see his face. He was serious. Her hands tightened their hold on his waist. "Would you believe me if I said I loved you?"

His mouth slackened. "Do you believe it?"

"Right now I do. Right now I don't even know who Paul was. I was married to him, but I know you better than I ever knew him. I've only known you for, what, a week, and I knew him for over five years. It's crazy, it's—"

He kissed her quiet, hand bracing her chin, tilting her head all the better to devour her with. Thank God he'd stopped her babbling. She'd already told him too much, but the words had come bursting out of their own volition. Her own, not Paul's.

He tasted like chocolate, sweet and decadent. Decadent . . . had she ever felt like that before? She pressed her body up against his, feeling exactly how much he did want to love her. She perched herself up on her tiptoes and rubbed her pelvis back and forth against that evidence, reveling in the sound of pleasure (or was that agony?) that issued from his throat. His hands dropped from her face to slide down her throat and then over her breasts. His thumbs circled her peaks, sending electrical shocks straight to her lower region.

Her body was still trembling, but it was ripples of pleasure and anticipation. Like the way she'd felt watching Mitch play football, only one hundred times as much. She leaned close to his face, but when he tried to kiss her, she nipped his lower lip. He gave her a wicked look, then lunged forward and ran his tongue over her lips. She nibbled his chin, feeling the slight brush of his stubble. He pulled her lower lip into his mouth, making incredible sucking noises. She opened her mouth and started to kiss him, capturing his tongue and moving her mouth back and forth over the length of it. His eyes rolled shut, and he pulled her flush against his body with a growl.

A tiger unfurled inside her, unleashing every naughty thought she'd ever had, every sexual fantasy. She would never again settle for rote lovemaking. She'd tasted passion and she wanted more. She pushed him back on the bed, then climbed up and tugged his shirt out of his jeans. His bare, tan stomach moved with his breathing, and she couldn't resist running her palm over the hard ridges. She leaned down and kissed his belly button, then ran her tongue over the soft hairs that led downward. She straddled his pelvis, unbuttoning his shirt.

"You've been hiding the wild side of yourself," he said, lying back with his arms spread, perfectly comfortable with being the object of her attention and admiration.

"From myself." She fished the last button through its hole and flung his shirt open. "I want to see the colors again." She leaned forward and kissed first one nipple, then the other. Well, now everything on his body was hard, everything except that fiery gleam in his brown eyes. That was liquid heat.

She ran her hands over his chest, marveling at the beauty of the male body. Perfectly sculpted, tan, skin soft, rib cage deep. She nipped his stomach, or what skin she could get to, then tried to pull his top snap open with her teeth. It took a few seconds, but she managed, then unzipped his jeans. He had to help get out of those, shimmying out of jeans and briefs at once. He started to lean forward and undress her, but she pushed him back again.

"Down, boy," she said in a playful, tough voice.

He saluted her, falling back on the bed. Paul had been shy about his body. Mitch was a different story altogether, as usual. It wasn't conceivable that a man should be this gorgeous, this perfect. That he should want her was even more preposterous. She took him in, every inch of him including the part of the male anatomy she'd never particularly found attractive anyway. But on Mitch . . . she shook her head, running her fingers over the hairs on his legs, feeling his muscles tighten in response.

When she trickled her fingers down the length of him, his entire body went rigid at once. She caressed the velvety tip of him, slippery with his essence. His hands splayed against the bed as she continued discovering him, every edge and ridge until he lunged up and twisted her around.

Suddenly she was the one lying beneath him. He didn't take nearly so long to remove her clothing, but he did take his [ohmygodi'mgoingto*die*ifhedoesn'tstopthisinstant] time being more tortuous than she had been. Using his mouth and his hands, he had her body arched and rigid, toes curled. And then she let herself go, completely, totally, riding-down-the-rainbow gone.

He hardly gave her time to catch her breath before starting again, sliding his finger through her wetness, bringing the shattering sensation back all over, and again, she was gone.

"How can that happen *twice*?" she whispered when she came back down, finding him watching her.

He slid up beside her, lying on his side, a cat-who-ate-the-canary grin on his face. "Dunno, but we could have a lot of fun trying to find out."

"Ooh." The thought of that shuddered right through her.

He rolled onto his back and pulled her on top of him. "You want to drive?"

"Me? On top?" Of course she'd heard about women "being on top," but she'd never tried it. "Yeah, I want to drive."

The first time he'd slid inside her, she'd been tight. Now he fit perfectly, sliding into her wet warmth. They moved together, but she controlled the rhythm. He touched a place deep inside her, a place that felt sharp, though not painful. It felt strange, but wonderfully strange, and she arched her back and lost herself in that feeling.

He twined his hands with hers. "Jenna, say my name."

Her eyes felt glazed, but she focused on his face, that gorgeous face, and said, "Mitch."

"That's my girl," he said in a tight voice.

And that glorious sensation exploded inside her body, and she kept saying his name over and over. She was his girl. Every fiber screamed it, every blood cell, every skin follicle. As her body pulsed around him, she felt him explode too, felt him fill her with him. His growl equaled what she felt inside, and he arched, pushing farther into her. His head was rocked back, throat exposed. Then his body went slack, and he let out a long, satisfied sound. His face was flushed, cheeks even pinker. He met her gaze, and his eyes looked as glassy as hers felt.

She smiled, feeling drunk and giddy. "I like driving."

"You can drive anytime, babe."

Those words hung in the air. Anytime, every time, one time, from here to eternity . . . what did they have? Before he could see the doubt creeping in, she carefully maneuvered herself so that she was lying on top of him, their bodies still connected intimately. She remembered how empty she'd felt when he had disengaged last time, though she couldn't blame him. It seemed forever ago.

His chest was warm and damp where her cheek pressed against it. Their breathing was in sync, bodies bonded together. His arm was slung over her back, fingers brushing up and down the base of her spine.

She wanted to tell him that Paul hadn't invaded her thoughts the way he had when Mitch kissed her the night before. She wanted to tell him that she was a little more sure she loved him, but she couldn't tell him that until she was one hundred percent sure. That's what he wanted, what he deserved. As much as she wanted to put Paul from her mind, she knew he had the answers. All of the answers.

Was he affecting Mitch's feelings toward her? Lying

there naked across his body, she felt devastated by the thought that Mitch really didn't feel this way about her. What if this was all Paul?

She pressed her cheek harder against Mitch's chest. No, she didn't want to think it. That thought scared her more than her doubts about her own feelings. Maybe Mitch truly didn't know that Paul was guiding his heart. If she gave her heart and soul to Mitch, and the connection between them someday withered away, would she be able to stand the heartbreak when Mitch came to his senses?

He pulled the sheet up over her shoulders, and she realized she was shaking again. "You're thinking too much," he said. "I thought we were just going to be."

She nodded, tightening her hold on him. She employed her new power of reaching out and asked, "Will you just hold me like this for a while?"

His other arm slid around her, and he held her tight.

"Mitch!" The female voice from outside the French doors startled both of them. She knocked on the glass. "Mitch, open up! It's important."

"Cripes. It's Tawny," he said, covering Jenna and grabbing another sheet to wrap around his waist as he went to the door and opened it. "What's wrong?"

Tawny took in his "attire," then her gaze slid behind him to where Jenna lay in the tangle of sheets feeling quite conspicuous. She turned back to Mitch, face tighter than it already was. "It's Boy George. She's about to foal."

"I'll be right there." He closed the door and turned back to Jenna, who was already slipping into her dress. "Dammit." He stepped into his discarded jeans. "You don't have to come."

"I want to."

"It's going to be messy. We might lose the foal, or even the mare. There'll be lots of blood." He said this while putting on his shoes.

"Are you protecting me, Mitch?" *Like Paul, shielding me from the world.*

He paused, looking at her, tilting his head. "Maybe I am."

"I've gone from seeing tragedy everywhere to being shielded from it completely. I want that middle ground, joy and pain." She glanced down at her dress, wrinkled as though it had been tossed off in a moment of passion. *Ahem. Speaking of joy and pain.* "I'll meet you at the stables. I'm going to change."

Sixteen

"I can't believe you slept with her!"

Tawny had been waiting for Mitch by the garage, apparently suspecting he might shirk his duties in favor of staying in bed with Jenna. Tempting though it was, a foaling mare was nothing to mess around with.

"Fine, don't believe it."

"Mitch, what happened to your holy vow? You've thrown it in my face enough times. I wasn't even married to Paul, I just dated him."

"That's between me, Paul, and Jenna," he said tightly. He'd worked through all that, but he wasn't about to explain himself to Tawny.

"Can't you see what she's doing? She's trying to continue her marriage by using you."

Her words prickled through him. "Tawny, butt out. It's none of your business."

"I guess loving you for eight years doesn't make it my business, then. Yeah, that's right. Before I married Chuck. It started that day you kissed me behind the stables, when Paul walked around the corner and caught us." She wasn't looking at him. "I know, it's no big surprise how I feel. You've been using excuses to keep me at bay for years. First the vow with Paul, and later, you hired me and then said you don't date your employees. But think about it: any woman who marries you is going to be involved in this place. That's what you want, anyway. What's the deal, Mitch?"

They'd walked out of the pine forest, and the overhead lights bathed them in an orange glow. He looked at the lean, attractive woman who now waited for an answer.

"You've known me for a long time," he said, pausing at the office door. "You know I don't do anything halfway. Have I thought about taking up with you, being the kind of dad Scotty deserves? Sure. But not one hundred percent. What I feel toward the woman I'll marry has got to be overpowering, all-consuming. I won't settle for less, and I won't give less."

"Is that what you feel for Jenna?"

Had he said . . . marry? "Closest thing to. Come on. Let's go have ourselves a foal."

Foaling was a household event, and Mitch knew Betzi would be bummed to have missed out. Dave, Scotty, and two other employees were there to assist, and Tawny's assistant, Sara, had just arrived.

"I just moved her to the foaling stall," Sara said, rubbing her hands together in anticipation. She already had the necessary supplies tucked in her pockets, like scissors, iodine, and packages of gloves. "She's just about ready to go."

"Lemme see, lemme see!" Scotty yelled out, following just behind Mitch.

"Stay back, little man. You can watch, but don't go inside the stall. You might get kicked. Besides, she doesn't want a lot of company right now."

Boy George, a gorgeous paint bred for her colors, had just dropped down onto the floor when he reached the large stall reserved for foaling. Tawny stepped into the stall with Sara following just behind, both women looking capable and ready. Mitch turned to see Jenna walk into the doorway area. Even with his mind trained on his horse's welfare, something altogether unrelated stirred in him at the sight of her. *Now* he felt complete, ready to go ahead with the foaling.

Scotty gave her a wiggly-fingered wave, and in his most authoritative voice said, "You can watch, but you can't go inside there with the horse. She might kick you." He punctuated that with a nod and looked over at Mitch.

Mitch nodded in approval, then turned back to the horse. When he'd hired Tawny, he'd found it difficult to let go and allow her to do her job. Now, he stood by with ease, ready to help with anything physical, if necessary. Fortunately, his days of sticking his hands into a horse's vulva were long over.

That job now fell to Tawny, who donned her shoulder-length glove as soon as the mare's water broke, lubricated it, and reached in to locate the foal's hooves and muzzle. Normally this was done quickly, to determine that the foal was in the correct position. Then the mare would be left alone to do her thing. Mitch watched as Tawny's studious expression turned to worry.

"The foal's backward," Tawny said, face now tight. "I can feel its tail."

Mitch let out an expletive, then apologized when Scotty made a sound of surprise. He knew nature wasn't always kind, but because he bred the horses, he felt responsible for putting their lives in danger. "Dave, call the vet!"

When he looked back at Boy George, he saw that Scotty had inched his way into the stall trying to get a better look. Just as Mitch opened his mouth to tell him to get back, Boy George rolled over, hooves flying right toward the child. Tawny and Sara were too busy getting out of the way, but Tawny's eyes widened in horror when she saw Scotty in the stall.

Before Mitch could even begin to grab for the boy, Jenna had lunged forward and yanked him backward. The mare's rear hoof caught her in the cheek, sending her sprawling backward onto the floor.

"Scotty!" Tawny yelled, running around the mare toward the stall door.

"Jenna!" Mitch screamed, scooping her up and getting her out of the way in case Boy George got another cramp and rolled back over.

Scotty had gotten to his feet, his lower lip pouted out.

"I did bad, didn't I? I just wanted to see the backward foal, that's all."

Mitch helped Jenna to her feet. "You all right?" She had a nasty red stain on her left cheek. "Can you tell if the bone's broken or chipped?"

She pressed her finger to the red area, wincing. "I don't think so. Feels more like a bad bruise."

"Scotty, you know better than to do that!" Tawny scolded, glancing back in the stall where Sara was trying to soothe the mare. Tawny hugged Scotty to her, but her gaze was on Jenna. "Are you okay? I can't believe he did that. If he'd have been kicked . . ." She shook her head. "You could have saved his life. Are you sure you're all right?"

Jenna nodded. "I didn't think about what I was doing. I just . . . grabbed for him."

Tawny swallowed hard, looking pale as she probably imagined what could have happened. "Thank you." To Scotty, she said, "Go upstairs. Now."

Scotty only took two steps toward the door, looking almost as frightened as his mother.

Mitch inspected Jenna's cheek. "Let's go back to the house and put some ice on it." It was already swelling, and the thought of her pain made him wince for her.

"You stay here," Jenna said, nodding toward the mare. "She needs you more than I do. I'll take Scotty to the house with me." She held her hand out to the little boy.

"You're not mad at me?"

"No, I'm not mad at you. Come on, you can help put ice on my cheek."

He took her hand. "I can make it better."

Mitch and Tawny watched them walk toward the door leading into the offices. "I know you can," Jenna said, glancing back at Mitch and letting him know with just a slight nod that she was all right. Then she and Scotty disappeared inside.

Tawny moved back into the stall, muttering, "I take back every bad thought I've had about her. Sara, let's try to get Boy George up and postpone her delivery until the vet gets here. I know what to do if we have to, but I'd rather leave it to the pro if possible.''

She turned back to Mitch, who had walked into the stall to help guide the mare to her feet. ''Most women would have played that to the hilt, taking you from where you're needed so you could play doctor. I almost think she was more concerned with making Scotty feel better than getting appreciation or sympathy.''

That thing inside Mitch that had started when Jenna arrived in the stables grew larger, brighter, almost overwhelming. He felt hot and high and full of the feeling that he could conquer the world. *She'd* done that to him. And he knew in that instant that he loved her. Not because she was Paul's wife, not because of her strength or beauty, and not because she had Paul's heart inside her. It was her spiritual heart that had captured him.

Now that he was sure, now that he'd gone and admitted it to himself . . . what was he going to do about it?

''Come on, Boy George,'' he said, pulling her to her feet almost single-handedly. ''We're going to have this foal, backward or not, and you're both going to be just fine.''

''I'm sorry,'' Scotty said for the fiftieth time.

''It's okay, sweetie. See, I'm not bleeding or anything.''

Jenna chose the chipped-ice option in the refrigerator door and filled a sandwich bag with it. In truth, she felt shaken, and her cheek felt as if it had swollen to engulf her entire face. It ached with a throbbing kind of pain, hurting even more when she'd bent down to change the shorts she'd dirtied on the stable floor. ''Come on, let's go watch some television.''

The first light switch in the gathering room didn't illuminate the room at all. When she followed the dim blue glow, she found that the entire east wall was covered with a magnificent plaster mural of running horses. Recessed light cans lit the textures and the darker shades of the horses. Then she realized it was a replica of the gorgeous painting in the dining room, of the horses running in from the surf, or rather, the surf becoming the horses.

It breathed of Mitch, of his spirit and his desire to break free of the gaudy constraints of his parents' tastes.

What she'd told Mitch earlier was true; he seemed more real to her than Paul had ever been. *Who were you, Paul?* And she felt the corresponding ache, Paul's ache to be more of a person, more of a husband. Was he so mired in guilt over murdering his parents that he couldn't break out? Find the truth, he'd asked of her. What more could there be?

Paul, let me go. Let me discover if what I feel for Mitch is real . . . one hundred percent real. That's the truth I seek. I am totally, completely in love with Mitch Elliot for no reason connected to Paul Elliot. But in my heart, I'm not sure.

"What are we gonna watch, Jenna?" Scotty asked, breaking her out of her thoughts.

She settled onto the couch where that first night she and Mitch had looked through photo albums. Even then, she'd been drawn to Mitch's image more than Paul's. Scotty settled next to her, and she slid her hand over his tiny chest and marveled at what the affection of a little boy could do to her soul.

Could a baby be growing inside her now? The thought scared her, but more than that, it filled her with a hope that overrode the hope she'd had even when she'd been married to Paul. She wanted Mitch's baby, wanted to give him a child he would love and teach to ride. She felt shame at remembering how she'd asked him to donate sperm so she could have "Paul's" baby. What a fool she'd been.

The thought of going through a pregnancy alone now terrified her. She needed Mitch to comfort her, hold her hand and tell her everything was going to be all right. Once she'd been so determined not to need someone again, particularly not a man. Needing Mitch, however, didn't frighten her or make her feel insecure. It made her feel human. If only she knew her heart.

"I can hear your heart pumping," Scotty said, pressing his cheek against her chest. "It's loud."

"That's because it likes having you so close." She gave him a hug, then pulled a remote-control unit the size of a laptop computer from the coffee table. "Let's see what's on TV."

A couple of hours later, Scotty was sound asleep. She wanted to go out and see how the mare was doing, but didn't want the boy to wake up alone in the house. Gently, she slipped from beneath him and walked to the windows in the family room. The lights around the stables burned bright through the trees, but she couldn't see anything beyond that. When she returned to the gathering room, she paused by the bookcase that held the photo albums. Removing one of them, she settled back on the couch beside Scotty and thumbed through the pages.

Looking at the gangly, teenaged Paul, she felt anger rise inside her. It was a comfortable feeling, more so than what Mitch's pictures elicited. At least with the anger, she didn't feel torn by doubt. She was *definitely* angry at Paul, no doubt about that. All those memories she'd fought so hard to keep—fought Mitch to keep—were now ashes of an empty life. She'd felt more, experienced more of life, with Mitch in a week than in the five years she'd been with Paul.

Jenna focused on the album again, flipping backward through time, wondering if it was Mitch's mother who kept such a faithful record of their lives together. More likely Betzi. Not a perfect family, but still a family.

Some pictures were at other homes throughout the years, making her wonder if they had second and third homes. There were pictures of Mitch's mother hugely pregnant and looking immensely happy about it. Wedding pictures of a flashy young man marrying his debutante at a huge ceremony. There were childhood pictures of that debutante, a princess with everything a little girl could ask for.

Jenna found it difficult to reconcile that kind of childhood with her own. But the anger she'd always felt toward her parents was only an ember now, and Jenna let it fade away again before going into a section of black and white pictures of Tom's—Mitch's father—past. There weren't many, as though he wanted to erase the blight of his poor childhood. Her gaze went to the picture below that.

A teenaged Tom stood in front of a souped-up car with several of his buddies, holding a trophy in victory. She couldn't tell what the trophy was for, but that wasn't what caught her interest. It was one of the guys who stood beside him, arm slung comfortably around Tom's shoulders—Alan.

Of course, many years had passed between that photo and the Alan she'd met that day, but she was sure it was him. She started to get up, eager to ask Mitch what it might mean, when Scotty murmured in his sleep and snuggled closer to her. Most likely Mitch wouldn't be in a position to discuss it with her anyway, so she set the album on the floor, propped her cheek against the now melted bag of ice, and closed her eyes.

Exhaustion crept into every muscle in Mitch's body. He'd convinced Tawny to let Scotty continue sleeping at the house with a promise of bringing him home in the morning. He knew she'd be up early to check on the foal's progress anyway, and getting Scotty up and ready would be one less task for an already exhausted mother.

"Ain't that right, Harvey?" he asked his shadow. Harvey woofed softly in return.

As he cleared the woods, the sight of lights on in the house stopped him momentarily. Jenna was in there waiting for him. The realization hit him hard, a new and wondrous feeling of the warmth that came with knowing the woman he loved was home waiting for his return.

When he found her in the gathering room, another new sensation hit him. She was curled up on the couch with Scotty, looking serene and content, even with the big red cherry on her cheek. The blue lights from overhead washed her in a surreal glow. His angel, with her long lashes, and lips that, even in sleep, turned up at the corners.

· His throat felt tight and dry. Maybe it was seeing her
with Scotty, or maybe it was helping Boy George get
through her difficult delivery, but something clicked in his
brain. He and Jenna had made love twice without any protection. It was the only time he'd done such a thing, but
stopping and throwing on a condom just hadn't been that
important considering she wanted a baby anyway and she'd
only been with Paul.

He didn't want to think about that, so he went upstairs
to take a quick shower and change into clean clothes. When
he returned, he sat on the coffee table and looked at her
and wondered what he would feel if she told him she was
pregnant with his child. His throat went even tighter as he
pictured her belly distended, face rosy the way Pam's had
been at church that morning. There was something magical
about a woman growing a child inside her, especially when
that child was his.

The only thing that would rob that magic was Paul's
presence lingering between them.

Scotty opened his eyes and looked at Mitch. He put his
finger over his mouth, and Scotty nodded and closed his
eyes again, falling back to sleep. Mitch saw Harvey settle
down on the floor next to a photo album, making Mitch
wonder what she'd been looking for. Would he and Jenna
ever be able to put aside their doubts and find the kind of
love he hadn't even known existed until now?

Jenna woke when she felt Scotty stirring. It took her a minute to remember why she was asleep on the couch with
him, and then another minute to realize Mitch was sleeping
in one of the chairs across from them. Harvey, who'd been
lying at his feet, perked up at her movement. She put her
finger over her mouth when Scotty started to say something, then pointed to Mitch. Even in sleep, his body looked
strong and muscular. His hair was tousled, clothes wrinkled, but he looked gorgeous. If Boy George hadn't decided

to have her baby last night, would Jenna be lying in Mitch's bed still, their bodies naked and entwined?

Scotty pulled her out of those thoughts, yanking on her arm and leading her to the kitchen. "Where's my mommy?"

"She's probably asleep. Let's get you fed, and then we'll take you home, okay?"

"Do you have Choco Crisps?"

"Hm, I doubt it." She eyed the plate of brownies on the counter. Brownies in milk? Nah, probably not. "Why don't I make up a real, old-fashioned breakfast? Eggs, bacon, the works?"

Scotty rubbed his belly. "Mmmm. I gotta peepee, but can I help after?"

"Sure." She watched the boy amble toward the bathroom in the foyer, his features still tinged with sleep. She couldn't help smiling, and then wondering how the mare's baby was. Taking the opportunity, she went upstairs and washed her face, startled by the purple and red bruise on her cheek. "It's only a bruise," she told her reflection. "It would have been most of Scotty's face if you hadn't intervened." She didn't think she'd saved his life, but she knew he'd have been hurt a lot worse than she was.

Mitch, looking as cute and sleepy as Scotty, ambled into the kitchen at the first aroma of bacon and coffee a short while later. "You look good in here," he said to Jenna, sniffing appreciatively over the eggs Scotty was stirring.

He might as well have said, "You just won a million dollars," for the way those words made her feel. Or maybe, "You just won the title of Queen of Bluebonnet Manor."

She didn't know what to say, so she simply smiled and pretended the bacon needed her immediate attention. Mitch walked closer, and she couldn't help but look up at him.

He reached out and grazed the edge of her cheek with his finger. "Our girl's got a doozie, doesn't she?" he asked Scotty. "You sure you don't want to see a doctor?"

Jenna was too caught up in the "our girl" to feel anything but warm fuzzies swirling about in her stomach. That sense of belonging to Mitch grew brighter still, edging away the dark shadow of her doubts.

"I did bad, didn't I, Mitch?" the boy asked. "Jenna got kicked because of me."

"Yes, you did, and yes, she did. But you learned something, didn't you, little man?"

Scotty nodded vigorously. "I'm not big enough to go in the stalls yet."

"That's right."

But he still pouted, looking for all the world as though he'd lost cartoon-watching rights until his forty-first birthday. Mitch knelt down in front of him. "What's wrong?"

Scotty looked down, lower lip trembling. "The elves won't come no more and leave a happy face 'cause I did bad."

Mitch and Jenna shared a look and an unspoken communication that smacked of the kind of intimacy she had always wanted with Paul. She hadn't known she wanted it at the time, but it explained the ache that had lingered within her throughout their marriage.

Jenna knelt down beside Mitch. "I'm sure the elves didn't come last night because there was too much commotion. But you watch: they'll be back tonight."

Scotty's face went from the depths of melancholy to as bright as the sun. "Ya think?"

"Yeah, I think." She looked over at Mitch, who was giving her that same look he'd given her when he'd figured out she'd left the smiley face in the ring. She ruffled Scotty's hair, then went back to her task. "And speaking of elves who stay up all night, how did it go with Boy George?" She picked the bacon strips out of the puddle of hot grease.

Mitch poured out three glasses of orange juice. "We tried to get her to hold off on delivery by walking her around until the vet arrived, but she didn't go for that idea. She dropped down in the ring and went into delivery. The biggest worry in a backward delivery is the foal pinching off the umbilical cord. We don't have much time to get the little guy out of there. We performed CPR and got him up and going pretty easily. The vet made sure nothing inside her was damaged. And then we all waited around for the first couple hours to make sure the colt passed his meconium—his first bowel movement—which is an event that is only exciting to those involved and not necessarily on-lookers.''

"Or those contemplating breakfast,'' she added with a smile.

"Sorry. You'd be surprised what passes for dinner conversation around here.''

"I suppose I could get used to it.'' Realizing what she'd said, she felt her face flush and added quickly, "Mom and baby are doing fine then?''

"Perfect.'' His gaze slid down her body. "As soon as we eat, we'll go check on them. Everybody takes shifts to watch the foal, make sure no abnormalities show up later.''

Jenna took all her pills, explaining to Scotty what they were for, before they ate breakfast together, just like a family.

"You need a sun catcher right there,'' Jenna said, pointing to the middle of the rounded windows.

There was more than sympathy in Mitch's eyes when he reached over and gently touched the edge of her bruise. "I need a lot of things in this house.''

She had trouble swallowing the bite of scrambled eggs she'd just taken. "Mm-hm,'' was all she could say. What did he mean, exactly?

"Let's go see the horsees—er, horses!'' Scotty said after shoving his last bite of bacon into his mouth.

"All right, buckeroo. Why don't you get washed up first?'' Mitch scooped the rest of the food on both his and Scotty's plates into a bowl that Harvey devoured in two seconds flat.

"Mitch, I want to show you something.'' She led him into the gathering room and opened the photo album. He looked a little wary until she turned the page to the photo and asked, "Is this Alan?''

His eyebrows knitted together. "Yeah, I believe it is. I didn't know my dad hung around with him. He never mentioned it."

"He left his past behind when he made his money. Maybe he left his friends behind too."

"I'm ready!" Scotty held up his hands, still wet. "Let's go see the horses now."

"Hold on a second, little man." He studied the picture more carefully. "I don't know some of the other guys, but the one on the end is Butch Thornapple. That's Reverend Thornapple to you and me." He went into the kitchen and dialed the portable phone. "Hello, Reverend Thornapple, this is Mitch Elliot. Fine, thanks. Sorry to bother you so early on a Monday morning, but I have a question I need an answer to. You knew my father when you were kids, didn't you? Drag racing? You?" Mitch chuckled, and Jenna got so caught up in the warm sound and the way it cascaded down her body, she almost forgot to continue listening. "Ah, I see. Well, can you tell me this: were he and Alan White friends? Best buddies, huh? Yeah. Mmm. I know it was a long time ago. Just curious. All right, thanks for the information. Bye now."

"What did he say?"

"They were best friends in high school. When my dad got his little inheritance at eighteen and turned it into a big lot of money, he left his old friends behind. Alan was pretty bent out of shape over it."

"Enough to kill him and your mother?" she asked.

"I can't imagine he'd wait all that time, over twenty years, to get revenge. But it gives him motive enough to cover for his daughter." His voice went lower. "And her boyfriend. I don't think Alan would lie for Paul, but he'd lie for Becky."

"Can we go now?" Scotty asked, forehead furrowed from impatience.

"Sure, we can go."

*　　*　　*

Tawny looked even more tired than Mitch, but the moment she saw them walk into the stable area, she raced forward and caught Scotty in her arms. "Missed you, big fella." She planted a big, wet kiss on his cheek, and he scrambled to be let down. Tawny walked over and nodded a greeting to Mitch, then smiled at Jenna. "Thanks again for what you did." She took a close look at the bruise on her cheek and grimaced. "Let me get you some ointment."

"It's okay. And you're welcome."

Tawny was already headed to the office door, but she turned and said, "As far as I'm concerned, you saved my boy. No matter what else . . ." She shot Mitch a meaningful look, then shifted her gaze back to Jenna. "You saved my son." She paused, as though she wanted to say more, then turned and went through the doorway.

"Dare I ask what the 'what else' part is?" Jenna asked.

Mitch leaned closer, paused, and said, "No."

They walked through the stables and out the back door. Boy George and her colt were standing in a small penned-off area. "What's the colt's name?" she asked as they neared the fence.

"Karma Chamcleon."

"Let me guess: one of Boy George's songs?"

"You got it. You catch on fast."

"I'm trying."

He smiled, and with the sun slanting across his face and lighting up his eyes, she knew she'd never forget it. She could feel it all the way deep inside. He reached out and touched her chin, one of those involuntary touches that stunned her with its impact.

"When you first came here, I was suspicious that you'd come looking for a piece of this place. Now it seems like you've been here forever. Like you belong here."

Was that because Paul had been born here? She wanted so badly to believe that those words came from Mitch's heart, that her response came from her own spiritual heart.

Tawny cleared her throat as she approached, Scotty in

tow. "Here you go," she said, handing her a small tin of ointment. "It'll help the color go down."

"Wow, look at the baby horse!" Scotty's shrill voice made the mare skitter to the farthest corner of the pasture, little Karma following close behind. "I keep doing the wrong thing," he said with a pout.

Jenna leaned down to his level and tweaked his chin. "And you know what? It happens even when you grow up. We're still confused about things, still don't know what we want to be when we grow up. We just stop having fun while we're at it sometimes."

Scotty pondered this. "Then I don't want to grow up."

Tawny ruffled his hair. "If you're anything like most men, you won't have to work very hard at that."

"Hey, hey, hey," Mitch said, looking indignant. "I resemble that remark." To Scotty, Mitch lifted his hand for a high five and said, "Let's never grow up." And then he proceeded to horse around with the boy, taking him for a ride around the stables. Scotty's laughter floated up into the air as the two disappeared around the corner.

"I want to grow down," Jenna said, wishing she could let loose like that. "I'm not sure how, but I've got a lot of years to make up for."

"You must have loved Paul very much," Tawny said.

"I did once. But I wish I'd met Mitch first."

Tawny sighed. "Me too. But for you, it doesn't matter. He's obviously in love with you."

Jenna looked at the lean, beautiful woman who stood beside her. "Why do you say that?"

"He broke a vow for you. Mitch is nothing if not honorable, even if he is stubbornly so. He wouldn't do that for just anyone."

Jenna let out a sigh of her own. If only she knew *why*. His heart? Paul's heart? Would she ever know for sure?

Mitch rounded the corner, Scotty riding his shoulders. The boy was in full giggle mode when they reached Tawny and Jenna. Scotty had almost forgotten about the horses until Mitch set him down. "I wanna ride the baby horse," he said, entranced once again with Karma.

"Not for a while, little man. But I'll tell you what: when you turn eight, I'll buy you a pony."

"You will? Really?" Then he frowned. "But that's a long time from now."

"Yep. But you can look forward to it all the time in between. No matter what, the pony's yours."

"Wow! I get a pony, I get a pony," he chanted, jumping up and down in time to his words.

Mitch answered Tawny's questioning look with a reassuring smile. Then she smiled a thank-you. He turned to the horses who had moved to the feeding trough not far away. Boy George, however, had lifted her head to assess if Scotty's ranting should warrant another retreat. Deciding no danger was imminent, she went back to the business of eating.

"What did the vet say?" Mitch asked Tawny.

They settled into a rather technical conversation that made Jenna glad she hadn't stayed for the whole birthing process. She walked over to Scotty and said, "Let's see if we can walk a little closer. Be quiet, okay?"

"Okay," he whispered loudly.

They walked to the corner of the fence, and although mother and colt watched them warily, they didn't seem to mind the audience. The colt was beautiful, almost white with a couple of brown patches on his side. It was one of the most enchanting scenes she had ever seen.

"You're not mad at Boy George for kicking you, are you?" Scotty asked in that loud whisper of his.

"No, I'm not mad at anyone." Her cheek was still tender when she smiled, but the motion was worth any amount of pain. She couldn't remember smiling so much in her life. "Aren't they precious?"

"Yeah, preshish," he agreed with a nod.

Several horses in the nearby pasture were watching the new mother and baby as well. Dave was in the ring with a horse, speaking in a coaxing voice. The morning sky was a huge blue bowl, big and bright. She loved her home in New Hampshire, but this was where her heart was. Not Paul's heart, though surely the feeling of home had started there. Now it was her spiritual heart that bubbled over as she took it all in.

From across the fence she met Mitch's gaze, and her physical heart fluttered. Unfortunately, where he was concerned, she couldn't tell the difference. Before she could really call this place home, she had to know for sure. And, of course, Mitch had to ask her. Not in the sly way he'd done this morning, but really ask.

Through the morning, Mitch and Tawny worked with the colt, and the vet stopped by to check on his new patient. Mitch went inside with him, and Tawny took Scotty to their apartment for a nap. Jenna walked around, talking a bit to Dave, chatting with Sara. The girl was abuzz with enthusiasm, telling Jenna in detail what had happened the night before and using terms Jenna had never heard of.

When Sara excitedly told her about Karma passing his meconium, Jenna could at least nod in understanding, though why it was so exciting still baffled her. She spoke so highly of Mitch, Jenna wondered if Sara didn't have a crush on him.

When Jenna realized that forty-five minutes had passed since Mitch and the vet had gone inside, she decided to venture into the offices to find out what was going on. She was feeling her energy level sag, gravity pulling her down. She passed one employee who pointed her toward the office. When she opened the back office door and stepped inside, she stopped. Mitch was asleep, sitting in the chair with his head on the desk. No matter that the overhead light was glaring down, that sunshine spilled in from the window.

The office was large and cluttered, bookcases crammed with tomes on horses. In one chair several days' worth of *The Wall Street Journal* were stacked up, and the in-box was full of mail. She saw several envelopes from investment firms and realized how much money Mitch must have. His watch bore some fancy Italian name, sure, but he wore no other jewelry. He had his toys, but she liked the fact that he didn't act rich.

Jenna made a sign that read Do Not Disturb and taped it to the door, then turned off the light and flipped the shutters. Dim light filtered through, bathing Mitch in soft pink. Except for the occasional conversation outside, all she could hear was Mitch's even breathing. He looked like a little boy, cheek flattened on the desk's surface, one hand in front of him.

After a few minutes of watching him sleep, she pulled up a chair on the opposite side of the desk and laid her head down near his, pillowing her good cheek with her hands and closing her eyes. Just a few minutes, she told herself. A catnap to refresh them both.

Jenna's eyes snapped open, and her heart beat like a drum inside her. Blackness pulsed around her, thrumming to the beat of her heart, adding to the panic that beset her senses as she tried to figure out where she was. This had happened in the hospital a few times, and in the apartment she'd stayed in afterward. She woke up, alone and afraid, trying to piece her life together.

But this time she wasn't alone. Mitch was stirring across from her, making coming-awake noises. Or at least she hoped it was Mitch. She remembered coming in, closing the shutters . . . she squinted at the place she guessed the window to be. Tiny slits of moonlight shone beyond.

She felt him come awake suddenly, sitting up without preamble, sucking in a surprised breath. "Mitch?"

"Jenna?"

She felt for his hand, gave it a squeeze. "We're in your office."

Silence for a moment. "But it's dark out."

"Well, we took a little catnap."

"That was in the middle of the afternoon!"

She chuckled. "Yeah, I know. I came in here to find out

what was keeping you, and you were out. I thought I'd grab a snooze with you, and . . . well, here we are. Let me turn on the light.''

He grabbed her hand as she started to get up, pulled her back. ''No, leave it off.'' His voice sounded soft and hoarse, and along with those words, it sent pinpricks of desire through her body. She started to sit back down again, but she felt him come around the desk and stand in front of her. He still held her hand, and he used that to pull her close enough to feel his body heat wrap around her.

His mouth covered hers, hungrily kissing her until she melted against him. Their thighs brushed together, and her breasts pressed against his chest. He threaded his fingers up into her hair, deepening the kiss, swallowing her whole. Because of the darkness, all her senses were intensified. She could feel the pad of every finger on her scalp, the tip of his tongue as it ran over the ridges on the roof of her mouth, could smell faded soap and his own scent, could feel the muscles in his back move beneath her hands.

He finished the kiss, sliding his thumb back and forth across her moist mouth. ''That's what I thought.''

She could hardly catch her breath. ''What are you talking about? *Why* are you talking?''

He chuckled softly, but the sound faded into silence for a moment before he spoke again. ''I wanted to find out if kissing you in the dark would be better than kissing you in the light. When I kiss you, whenever I look at you, I see this doubt in your eyes.'' He paused. ''Do you still see Paul when you look at me?''

''No,'' she said, unable to even comprehend that he would think that. ''I haven't seen Paul in a long time. Not even . . . not even when you held me in the hall that first time, or when we kissed in Paul's bedroom. I just told you that because I felt ashamed. I didn't know why I was so drawn to you.''

''What are you doubting, Jenna?''

''Why I'm so drawn to you,'' she said simply.

She could feel him nod. After a few moments, he said,

"I wish I could take away all the hurt in your life, but unlike Paul, I don't believe in running from the truth. I have my own truth that would better be put aside and ignored, but I can't do that. I'm going to lay it out for you, Jenna, and I'm not letting you turn away from it either."

His hands came up and cupped her face. "I can't take away the pain or the past, but I can love you enough to override it. I'll do better than protect you; I'll stand by you and give you the strength to overcome it. And you'll give me strength too."

She felt emotion rising up inside her, threatening to spill over. "Mitch . . ."

He placed a finger over her mouth. "Don't talk. Just listen, because I need to say this before the words get all jumbled up in my head. You've done that to me, Jenna. You've made me crazy, and a whole bunch of things I don't even want to get into right now. Not yet. I want to laugh with you, cry with you, and have children with you. I want you to make this place a home. When I look at you, I see my whole future. But you have to come to me without any doubts. That's all I'll accept. That's all I'll give you too."

Jenna could only stare at the place she knew him to be, that shadowy silhouette that was the man she loved. His words swam together, but what stood out most were the words "home" and "love." And "children." She held on to them, clutching them to her heart.

"Mitch, I'm so mixed up right now. But I want all those things you just said. And I want them with you. I know you deserve one hundred percent, and I hate thinking that Paul has anything to do with what we feel. And I think there's a way to find out, to get it straight."

"Not the way we handled it last night. That just made me crazier."

She couldn't help but smile, just for a moment, at thinking of their lovemaking. "Me too. No, this has nothing to do with your bedroom. In fact, it has to do with your parents' bedroom. Come on."

Seventeen

Jenna's heart was pumping loudly in her ears as she and Mitch walked through the pine trees. She looked inside that heart and found that it was she, not Paul, who led her back to the master bedroom. She was in control now. Unfortunately that brought her no comfort tonight; she was throwing her bets on a hunch, a vague feeling that the answers lay in that room and that horrid scene of murder. If Paul led her there, it meant he knew she'd find the truth. Jenna didn't have as much confidence in her own hunches, but it was all she had.

She couldn't lose Mitch.

The prospect sent her heartbeat skidding. Suddenly she realized that losing Mitch would be much more painful than losing Paul had been. If only she could pretend the doubt wasn't there . . . but she knew Mitch would see it. She could hide nothing from him, not with this connection between them.

When they walked into the master bedroom, she said, "I know the key to the past is in this room. Paul was in here, and I think Becky was too." She looked over at Mitch, whose expression was rigid. "Maybe Becky killed your parents and Paul covered for her."

"Then why was he giving her money?"

She looked around the room, trying to imagine it with a bed, dressers . . . the way it had been before the murders. Then she turned to the wall and started to press her hand against it.

Mitch wrapped his fingers around her wrist, halting her. "What if you see the murders? I don't want you to go through that, Jenna. Isn't there some way I can see it?" He placed his hand against the wall and closed his eyes. His other hand was still around her wrist. After a moment, he opened his eyes.

"I have to do it, don't I?" she asked.

He nodded.

"Remember, you said you wouldn't protect me from the past, you'd give me strength to face it. I'm ready."

She pulled her hand free, rubbed both hands together, and placed them against the wall. She drew in a deep breath as the room she'd earlier tried to imagine came into focus. From the corner of her eye she could see Paul's hand as he used the wall for support. She felt Paul's nausea rise up in her stomach, felt his dizziness swirl through her.

Don't get sick on me, Paul! We have a lot of work to do. Becky walked into view, in control, shaking Paul's shoulders. *We've got to make it look like a burglary.*

Paul took a step closer to the bed, gaze transfixed on the bloody figures lying there. *Our last words were arguing.* She heard Paul's thoughts whisper through her mind. *I'd agreed to break up with Becky, but I told them I hated them for it. I hated them. That was the last thing I said to them. But I never meant to kill them.*

Jenna felt her anger at those words swell up inside her. So it was true. He'd killed his parents, and led her here to expose the truth. But for what reason? Why had he put her through this?

The block was there again, that opaque mist that obliterated Jenna's view. Go past it, she ordered herself, but her eyes opened instead. She blinked, finding Mitch standing beside her waiting, that worried look on his face. She realized this was hard on him too, watching her go through this.

"You were right. Paul had broken up with Becky. And he felt bad because his last words with his parents were that he hated them. He didn't mean to kill them."

Mitch pounded on the wall. "Why does he keep holding on to you if all he shows you is more evidence against him?"

"He wants me to find the whole truth. He can't believe he killed them. I didn't see the murders. But I can't get past this block. I know there's something behind it, but I keep getting stuck."

Mitch laced his fingers through hers, pressing her against the wall.

"Mitch, this really isn't the time—"

He shook his head. "I'm not trying to get fresh, Jenna. I want you to try something. What were you thinking about when you ran into the block?"

"I . . . I wondered why he'd put me through this when all we keep finding, just like you said, is more evidence that he killed them."

"You got angry, didn't you?"

"Well, yes. I guess I did."

"I could see it, the way your forehead crinkled. Remember the punching bag, when you let go of the anger you had toward your parents?" She nodded, remembering also how she'd told him too much. "But you didn't want to let go of the anger you had toward Paul. You felt comfortable with it, you said. You were afraid to find out what was behind that anger, isn't that right?"

"You listen too well, you know that?" She twisted her mouth in thought, then said, "Yeah, that's what I said."

"I want you to let it go now. No matter what you find on the other side, I'm going to be here. Last night you reached out to me. Do it again, Jenna." He tightened his hold on her hands. "I'm right here with you."

She saw the strength in his eyes, felt it run from his hands into hers. What if she let go of her anger, but still had her doubts? How long would Mitch stand beside her when he could see that doubt in her eyes? *Be strong, Jenna.* She heard the echoes of her parents' voices, meshing with the voices of the townsfolk who hid her away after her parents' murders. *Be brave, little girl.*

With the intensity in his eyes, with his body close and fingers laced through hers, she believed that he'd be her strength. She had to take this chance, to shed that comfortable cloak of anger and find out what was behind it. If Paul was indeed a murderer, she and Mitch would deal with that. She could be his strength then, convincing him that he didn't have the murderous genes of his twin.

"I'm ready," she said on a whisper, her chest tight. In response, his hands squeezed hers. *I'm here* the action said without words.

She inhaled, imagining the red anger filling her lungs, gathering it into one tight ball and expelling it from her mouth. Her eyes drifted shut, and she spun back into Paul's soul again. He walked in a daze toward the bed, staring down at his parents.

We don't have time for regrets now, Becky said, picking up the jewelry on the nightstand, the very pieces Paul had hidden in the cabinet.

But Jenna felt no anger now. And as she turned to face Becky, she saw no opaque wall. Becky grabbed a pillowcase from the linen closet in the bathroom and threw the jewelry inside. She thrust it at Paul, who numbly took the bag with shaking hands.

Why don't I remember doing it? he asked in a lost voice.

You're blocking it out. Come on, Paul, work with me here! I'm trying to save your butt. We'll make it look like a burglary, go to my house and my dad will say we were there all night.

What if he doesn't?

He will! Come on, move it.

Paul walked over and took off his father's wedding ring, wrenching it from his finger. He stared at it for a moment, then dropped it in the bag. When he looked over at Becky, she was staring at something lying on the carpet by the door. She snatched it up and stuck it in her pocket, then went to work wiping fingerprints off the doorknob and other surfaces.

Paul hadn't taken much notice of that object. Through

his eyes, Jenna saw him numbly take the watch lying on the nightstand and put it in the bag. But Jenna had seen it. She opened her eyes and found Mitch still standing in front of her, still holding her hands.

"Paul did it, didn't he?" he asked, his face so close to hers that their noses touched.

She shook her head. "Paul *thought* he killed them. That's why he felt guilty. As usual, he'd given up too easily. But something had registered in his subconscious, and that something is why he brought me here to find the truth. Maybe it became clear when he saw his life flash before his eyes."

"He was covering for Becky, then. She killed them, and the son of a bitch loved her so much he covered for her. And gave her their money."

"Did Becky smoke?"

"What?"

"Did she smoke?"

Mitch looked up, remembering. "No, she didn't smoke."

"Mitch, we have to call the sheriff. It wasn't Paul and it wasn't Becky. It was Alan."

"What?"

"I saw the lighter. The silver-and-turquoise lighter he was using at the house. Becky found it when she was making it look like a burglary. She was surprised to see it, and she quickly hid it. Paul had seen it, but he was too much in shock to register it."

"So Becky wasn't covering for Paul, and Paul wasn't covering for Becky. She was covering for her father."

"I think so." Her heart felt lighter than it ever had, as though she could feel Paul's relief in finally discovering the truth.

"You can still feel Paul, can't you?"

"I can. He's happy. Relieved."

Mitch nodded, eyes wide. "He didn't kill our parents. He didn't kill them." For a moment his body relaxed, as though hundreds of pounds had been lifted from his shoulders. Then his muscles tensed again. "But why did Alan kill them? My dad had snubbed him so long ago."

"Only Alan can tell us. That's the final piece of the puzzle. That and why Paul was giving Becky money."

Mitch pulled her from the wall, gave her a quick kiss, and led her from the room. "We need to talk to Alan. I'll get the—" He glanced at Jenna. "I'll get him to confess. And since he used his daughter to cover for him, I'm going to use her to uncover the truth."

"I know you had your hopes of pinning my butt for my parents' murders," Mitch said, "but at least you can finally close the case."

Sheriff Kruger, naturally, had his doubts after hearing the story that evening. He'd handled the murder investigation, and Mitch was sure the man still harbored doubts as to Mitch's innocence. The arrogant son of the richest man in town was a good suspect, and the sheriff had clearly been disappointed in not making the case stick.

"You know I can't arrest the man because the lady here had some kind of vision about his lighter. I got nothing, not even enough to question him about it."

Mitch stood, jamming his hands in his jeans pockets. "That's why I'm going to get him to confess, and you're going to hear it."

"Wait a minute. You can't go in there accusing him. For one thing, it's not your job."

"I'm not going to accuse him. I'm going to accuse his daughter."

Kruger rubbed his forehead, looking at Jenna for help. When she didn't comply, he said, "I thought you said Alan probably killed them."

Mitch smiled. "I think he did. But his daughter covered for him, and probably died because of him. If he thinks she's going to be accused of the murders, he might either slip up or come forward."

"And if he doesn't?"

"He will. The question is, do you want to be there when

he does? Because I'm going to do it anyway."

Kruger obviously hated being pushed, but he finally acquiesced. "All right, I'll let you give it a try. But if he doesn't give us anything, I want you to back off."

"Wire me up." Mitch lifted his arms.

Kruger narrowed his eyes. "What do you think we have here, some kind of New York City crime unit? The biggest crime I got to contend with is when Booger Jones hauls off and smacks his wife when he's had too much to drink. And then she kicks him in the nuts, and I come over and haul the both of them in for the night."

Mitch leaned forward, hands spread on the desk. "Do you want to solve this case, or let it keep hanging over your head? The biggest crime in the county, still unsolved after ten years. The failure of the sheriff's department, the blotch on your clean reputation—"

"Of course I want to solve it!" He closed his mouth, getting control over his anger.

Mitch smiled, crossing his arms over his chest. "See, I can get Alan to blow just like I got you to. Getting him to spill is the only way we're going to nail him. I want the first chance to get him to blow. We already unsettled him on our first visit. I'm not a cop. I can bluff him and I don't have to play by the rules. You owe me the chance to do this, Kruger."

Kruger's face went red for a moment, then he slammed his hand down on the desk. "You're still as arrogant as your father! Think just because you got money you can go around the law, do what you want."

"This has nothing to do with my money. This has to do with the truth, the long-overdue truth. I'll do whatever it takes to get it." He glanced over at Jenna, who knew that too well. "I'll push whoever I need to." But he'd never push Jenna again. She'd taught him that, to watch where he trod with his heavy boots. But Kruger, he was a different story.

"All right. Let me call an old friend who's on the force in Fort Worth. He'll get us what we need."

* * *

By mid-morning Tuesday, Mitch was wired in more ways than one. Jenna watched him try to be still as Detective Ryan attached the wires to Mitch's chest.

"You know, you're taking your life in your own hands by doing this," Ryan said. He'd come down from Fort Worth as an unofficial consultant to help Kruger out. "You told him, didn't you, Bud?"

Kruger nodded, looking grim. "Yeah, I told him a hundred times. But he's right; we don't have anything on Alan, and bullying him isn't going to do any good."

"Okay, you can button up. Move around a bit, make sure nothing comes loose." Ryan assessed Mitch as he raised his arms, twisted and bent down.

"Snug as a bug on a body," Mitch said.

They ran several sound checks to make sure everything worked.

He hadn't gotten much sleep, but he looked sharp, alert. Too sharp, Jenna thought. There was a gleam in his eyes, the same gleam he'd had when he'd come to New Hampshire to bargain—a baby for the truth.

She and Mitch had gone over the facts and the suppositions until late in the night, both falling asleep on the couch. When she'd woken, long before Betzi was up, Mitch was gone. She'd found a note on the kitchen table beneath her bottles of pills telling her he'd gone out to the gym. He was doing leg presses when she'd walked in. She'd taken one look at that glistening, muscled body and realized he was putting it at risk. Alan could go off. The man was definitely on edge.

Damn Mitch. She'd put aside her anger, and it had opened up the past for her. The past had set her free in one respect: she no longer believed she'd been married to a murderer.

It had also released a part of her that needed Mitch. Deep inside she needed him, wanted him. The thought that she could lose him too . . . she pressed her hand to her heart at the pain that engulfed her.

"You all right?" Mitch asked, bringing her back to the present.

"I want to go with you."

"We've already gone over that. No way. You'll be with Kruger and Ryan." He tenderly brushed the tips of his fingers over the bruise on her cheek. "I don't want you getting hurt."

"I don't want you hurt either," she said on a whisper. It was like that last morning her parents had been alive, when the warnings of unrest abounded, and they'd left anyway to help a woman in need.

He looked at her for a long minute, then he turned and asked the sheriff for scissors. When Kruger handed him a pair, Mitch took one last look at her and disappeared into the restroom. Jenna watched that door while the other men went over their plan. Her hand went back to her heart. She hadn't told Mitch, but since she'd seen the murder scene, Paul's presence was stronger. It was like the months after her transplant, when she'd sworn he was physically there.

When Mitch emerged a few minutes later, Jenna's mouth dropped open. He'd cut his hair short . . . like Paul's.

"All right. I'm ready," he said to the men, not looking her way.

"What'd you cut your hair for?" Kruger asked.

Mitch rubbed his hand across the back of his neck. "Just wanted to be more comfortable." They, of course, didn't know that Paul had worn his hair short over the last several years of his life.

"Mitch, what are you doing?" she whispered as they walked out. "This wasn't the plan."

"I have a better plan." He nodded for her to go with the two men. "I'll see you at the other end."

And then he got on his motorcycle. She slowly walked to the patrol car and got inside. The two men caught up on their wives and kids, and Jenna sat in silence and felt like a prisoner in the back of the cruiser as they followed Mitch.

Kruger waved to the deputy who had been keeping an eye on the White place in case Alan decided to head out.

They parked just before the bend in the driveway, hidden from the house by some scrub pines and underbrush. Kruger and Ryan both put on headphones and Jenna realized she wouldn't be able to hear what was going on. There were only two pairs.

"Jenna!" Kruger called as she alighted from the car and ran toward the house. She wasn't about to give Mitch a choice. Once Alan saw her, Mitch would have to play along that she'd come with him. Certainly he couldn't tell her to get back to the cruiser.

Mitch was standing at the front door when she saw him. From a distance, he did look like Paul, if she didn't consider the broad shoulders. When he turned and saw her coming up, his body went rigid and his eyes went hard.

"What the hell are you doing here?" he hissed.

"We are in this together. So . . . Paul, do what you have to do, but don't you dare tell me to leave."

His mouth started to open, but before he could say anything Alan surprised them both by walking around the front of the semi, a wrench in his black-smudged hands. He stopped short when he saw them, eyes narrowing.

"What are you doing back? Get off my property."

Mitch shot her a warning look to stay behind as he approached Alan, but Jenna walked over with him. "Remember me, Alan?" Mitch had stripped away his accent and the depth of his voice, sounding a lot like Paul.

"Sure, why wouldn't I? You were here Saturday."

"Nope. Haven't been here in a long, long time. And I haven't seen you in a long time, not since that morning ten years ago."

Alan's face went from confused to pale. "What the hell are you trying to pull?"

"I'm trying to put the past behind me. You see, me and my wife, Jenna, we need to get on with our lives." He put his arm around her, pulling her possessively against his body. "And for me to do that, I need the one thing Becky wouldn't give me: the knife."

Alan took a step back, but he still held that wrench in

his beefy hands. "Mitch said you died in a car accident."

"I told him to tell you that. I just wanted to feel out the situation before I came to visit myself. I wanted you to feel . . . safe. If I was gone, then your secret wouldn't be out."

"I don't have any secrets," Alan said, squaring his shoulders. "Get out of here, both of you."

"Not until we settle this. I admit I was drunk that night, and at the time, I was confused about everything." His voice dropped to a sinister low. "After all, I thought I'd killed my own parents. But I didn't kill them. Now I remember what's been bothering me all these years, all the time I was away from my home thinking I was a murderer. Your lighter was in my parents' bedroom. Becky slipped it into her pocket, but I saw it."

Alan's face went even paler, but he said, "You can't prove that."

"No proof but my memory," Mitch acknowledged with a nod.

"I never set foot in that fancy house of theirs."

"The only thing I can't understand is why," Mitch continued. "Because my father snubbed you, left you behind? You were best friends once, but he made some money and left you behind like you were the trash."

Alan's face now went to a fine shade of red. "I didn't give a crap about your father. He wasn't a friend of mine."

"Then maybe it was the way he treated your daughter. How many times did she come home crying because my father had called her a worthless whore?"

Alan advanced on them, and Mitch set Jenna behind him. But he didn't back down, even though she wished he would turn and run.

Alan lifted the wrench. "You were the worthless one! You didn't stick up for my baby. You just let that son of a bitch destroy her! You were a wimp! You broke her heart for your daddy, and she loved you." Alan's voice broke. "She loved you, and you broke her heart."

"How did you know I'd broken up with her? You told

the police that we had been at your trailer all night. If I'd broken up with her, why was I still sleeping with her? What kind of father would you have been to allow that?''

Alan shoved Mitch, sending Jenna back a few steps. ''I was a good father. I was the best father!''

So far he'd given nothing away, nothing of great importance anyway. But the man's temper was running very thin. Jenna's heart was hammering in her throat.

''You loved your daughter,'' Mitch said in a calmer voice, trying to nudge Jenna farther away from him and Alan.

''She was my life.''

''Did you love her enough to kill my parents?''

''No!'' he bellowed. ''I loved her enough to lie for you, to give you an alibi. You killed them. She asked me to lie for you.''

''How do you know I killed them?''

''Becky said she woke up and saw the knife in your hands, the knife covered in blood.''

Mitch took a step closer to Alan, and Jenna wanted to pull him back by one of his belt loops. But she held herself calm and still as he said, ''You know what I think? I think Becky killed my parents, and put the knife in my hand while I was passed out. Then she made me think I'd killed my own parents, thinking I'd marry her out of gratitude for covering my butt.''

''She wouldn't kill anyone! She was a good girl!''

''Would she lie for her daddy?'' Mitch was dancing fast, hoping to trip Alan up.

Alan crossed his arms over his chest. ''There was nothing for her to lie about.''

''Would she blackmail me for her daddy?''

His arms dropped. ''I don't know what you're talking about.''

''Come on, Alan. I handed her the money. One hundred thousand, and then another, then two hundred thousand. I kept moving, but somehow she kept finding me, kept demanding money.'' He glanced over at Jenna, and for a mo-

ment she saw Paul. She felt Paul. Mitch turned back to
Alan. "But the last time, she wanted four hundred thousand
dollars from me. I told her it was the last time. I said I
wanted the knife. But she double-crossed me. She only
brought my father's wedding ring."

"You killed her!" Alan lunged forward with the
wrench. Mitch deflected it, sending the heavy tool flying
several feet away. Alan had his hands around Mitch's
throat. "You killed my baby! I couldn't go to the police
and accuse you because I'd have to tell them everything."

The men fell to the ground. Jenna yelled for help. Alan
kept talking as he tried to subdue Mitch. "I wanted to kill
you, but I didn't want to let Becky down again. So I sat
here and hated myself for what I'd done to her. It's all your
fault! If you'd only loved Becky the way she deserved,
none of this would have happened."

Jenna tried to pull the big man off Mitch. Mitch could
hardly talk now, with Alan pushing down on his throat.

"What happened, Alan? Do you want Becky to pay for
your sins again? You want her to be named as my parents'
murderer? Sheriff Kruger's willing to reopen the case based
on my memory of the lighter—your lighter."

Jenna pulled Alan back and off balance just enough for
Mitch to roll over and gain control. She heard the footsteps
of Kruger and Ryan, but she couldn't take her eyes from
Mitch. The men hadn't seen the officers yet. Alan was too
busy struggling to gain the upper hand again.

"*You* killed your daughter," Mitch said. "You knew she
was blackmailing me. That's why you couldn't go to the
police and accuse me of her murder. You let her keep coming, keep demanding money. You know what happens to
blackmailers, Alan? They die. They always die. Don't you
watch the movies?"

Alan's face went bright red. Between breaths he said,
"I shoulda killed you too! I shoulda killed the whole
damned, worthless lot of you!"

Mitch looked up and saw the men with their guns at the

ready. He let up on Alan's throat, then pulled himself off
the man. With a gasp, Alan got to his feet and prepared to
go after Mitch again.

"Hold it, White," Kruger said, coming up behind the
man with cuffs. "You're under arrest for the murder of
Tom and Lila Elliot." He read him the rest of his rights.

Alan blinked in shock. "I didn't admit to nothing! He
doesn't have any proof! He can't prove the lighter was
there! It was Paul! He murdered them, and he murdered
my baby. Didn't you hear him? Why are you arresting
me?"

Kruger shot Mitch a dirty look, probably for changing
the plan, but focused back on Alan. "That's not Paul, that's
Mitch. Paul died in an accident nine months ago."

Alan simply stared at Mitch. "But how did you know
about the lighter?" Then he closed his eyes when he realized what he'd just said. His body sagged, and he tipped
forward before the officers could grab him.

Mitch ran his fingers through his shorn hair. "Paul told
us. The rest I bluffed."

Alan drooped down to his knees, eyes filled with tears.
"I'm sorry, Becky. Your daddy failed you again. You were
too good for them, honey."

"Paul didn't kill Becky," Jenna said, getting Alan's attention. "She did double-cross him, and he did get mad
and reach for her, but she lost her footing and fell off the
cliff without his assistance." She turned to Mitch. "I knew
Paul wouldn't have killed anyone. There were times I
doubted, but deep inside, I knew he wasn't a murderer."

Alan's eyes had gone glassy, and he stared off into nothing. "Becky was crazy in love with Paul." He laughed
softly. "I was even jealous at how much she loved him.
When he broke things off with her, I knew his parents—
Tom—had forced Paul to do it. He wasn't strong enough
to stand up to his father. It was bad enough that Tom treated
me like trash, but he treated my little girl even worse.

"That night she came home so distraught she couldn't
even stand up. I told her to go inside. I didn't know what

I was going to do, I just knew I had to do something. Becky had left through the front door of the Elliot house, and it was still unlocked. I walked inside and looked around, saw all that money thrown in my face. I hated Tom a thousand times over. I wanted to show him he wasn't any better than me, than my Becky. I found Tom's room. I was just going to scare him. I didn't even realize I'd grabbed a knife from the kitchen.

"All I knew was I hated this man for destroying my daughter, and I wanted him to pay for it. And then I was plunging the knife into his chest, again and again. And when she woke up, that snotty wife of his, I stabbed her, too, before she could scream."

Mitch had gone perfectly still, but his face was a mask of hatred. At that moment he had the same kind of barrier she'd carried with her so long, that wall of anger that kept everyone away.

"Why did you frame Paul?" Mitch asked in a soft, low voice.

Alan was still on his knees, hands cuffed behind him. "That was Becky's idea. She got worried and followed me back to the house. I don't even remember this, but she says I walked out the front door with the bloody knife in my hand. She took control—she was a good daughter, such a good girl—and told me to get home right away, that she would take care of everything. When she returned to the trailer with Paul, she said she'd put the knife in his hand and made him think he'd killed his parents. All we had to do was give him an alibi and nobody would have to pay for it. And it worked too. Except that Paul disappeared and Becky was left alone and heartbroken again.

"A couple of years later, I got real sick. But I didn't have insurance, and the hospital wouldn't schedule the operation until I gave them a deposit. That's when Becky came up with the idea of finding Paul and making him part with some of that money he'd inherited. She'd hidden the jewelry and knife, and since he still thought he had murdered his parents, she threatened to turn it over to the police if he didn't give her money. Then she wanted more, and more. It became her way of punishing him for leaving. Even the last time, when he told her enough was enough, she still didn't want to let him go.''

"All right, Alan, on your feet." Kruger pulled the man up by his arms, then looked at Mitch, who was taking the wires off his chest. "We're going to need to talk to you both."

"Later," Mitch said, handing Kruger the wires and leading Jenna by the hand to the bike. "We'll stop by later."

Kruger opened his mouth to argue, but let it close again. "All right. But later today, got it?"

Mitch didn't answer, just got onto the bike and helped her on. After they put on their helmets, Mitch turned the bike around and headed back to Bluebonnet Manor. He turned toward the stables, past the ring where the elves had left a smiley face for Scotty. Some of the employees looked up and waved, but Mitch just kept heading straight into a thick forest of pines. They followed a horse trail down a winding path that led to a clearing right in the middle of the pines.

When he cut the engine, she got off the bike, removed her helmet, and took in her surroundings. The sun slanted across the bright green grass, casting the small area in an almost mystical glow. Tiny purple wild flowers covered one area, and hundreds of tiny insects hovered over them.

Mitch dropped his helmet on the ground and walked up behind her. "I've come here a thousand times, laid out on the grass and looked up at the sky, wondering what had happened that night, wondering if Paul had murdered our parents. I wanted to come here now that I know the answers." He turned her around, leaving his hands on her waist. "But I don't know all the answers."

All the answers. Was she ready to look within herself to see if she could give him the answer they both sought. "It's beautiful here." She hadn't taken her gaze off him. Most of that cold intensity had left his eyes, but some of it still lingered. She looked at him, at the hair that didn't fall over his forehead and curl over his collar, at the planes of his cheeks, the fullness of his mouth.

"You told me that love and hate are the strongest emotions. Alan more than proved that. Look what happened when both were eating him up." She reached out and smoothed her fingers through his hair. "Why did you make yourself look like Paul?"

"I thought I'd freak Alan out, see if that would push him over the edge."

"And did you wonder if it would freak me out too?"

He nodded, without even hesitating. "Did it?"

"You do look like him. In some ways, anyway. For a second, yeah, I guess you did freak me out. Partly because since last night, I can feel him." She pressed a hand to her heart. "I have never felt such peace. Put your hand here, see if you can feel it."

Mitch pressed his hand over hers and closed his eyes. "Yeah, I can feel it." Even his expression relaxed as he kept his hand there for a few more seconds. He opened his eyes. "It's fading."

She nodded, feeling that too. A beautiful warm feeling swirled inside her, and then slowly departed. Each exhale seemed to release it until Paul was gone. For a moment, she felt an emptiness inside her. "I never got to say goodbye to my parents or to Paul." She looked up into the rays of sunshine and whispered, "Goodbye, Paul." For once, she felt not love, not anger, only peace where Paul was concerned.

She looked at Mitch, and that emptiness evaporated. "You were also right about the truth setting us free. All of us. You don't have the genes of a killer."

For a moment, his body relaxed as that realization set in. But then it tensed up again. "I could kill Alan for what he did to my parents. And for what he and Becky did to Paul."

"They both paid a price for what they did. Becky died, and Alan . . . look at him. He's lived with guilt for a long time, I think. Besides, you couldn't kill anyone any more than Paul could. Let's put the hate aside and focus on the other emotion.''

The pain in Mitch's face evaporated as her words sank in. She lifted her hands, and Mitch automatically slid his fingers through hers. She took a deep breath, feeling everything she had always felt with Mitch—the connection that bound them. It was still there, with no trace of Paul.

''When I looked beyond my anger, I didn't see the emptiness or loneliness I thought I'd see. I didn't see Paul or my parents. I saw . . . you. Only you.'' She pulled one of their entwined hands to her mouth, kissing the back of his hand. ''Do you feel it?''

His fingers tightened on hers. ''The connection? Oh, yeah.''

She pulled their other set of interlocked hands close and planted another kiss on his hand. ''I love you, Mitch. And now I can say, I love you with all of my heart. No doubts, one hundred percent.''

He pulled her close, kissing her until she was dizzy and her knees went weak. Their hands were still locked together, held down at their sides now. His kiss was hungry, as though he'd been waiting a long, long time for it. And then he said the three words that meant more than even the three words she'd said: ''That's my girl.'' After another long, soul-searing kiss, he said three more words that would be added to the new shelf of precious memories she was building: ''Welcome home, Jenna.''

Epilogue

"Look, Sean, the elves came last night!" Scotty tugged on the baby's jumper as soon as Jenna approached the ring.

Sean burped in response, then smiled. Scotty grinned back, more entranced by the baby boy than by the elves anymore. "Shoot, Jenna, when you gonna teach him to say ' 'scuse me'? Mama always makes me say it."

"Well, first he has to start talking. But that'll be on the list of the first words we'll teach him, okay?"

"Oh, okay." He reached down and petted Harvey, who'd accompanied Jenna from the house.

"Hey, there, gorgeous," Mitch said, capturing her mouth in a long kiss that elicited whistles and applause.

Even now, he was breathtaking, the only man to make her heart beat faster by just smiling at her. "Hi, handsome," she whispered, a little self-conscious at the attention. She reached out and ran her fingers through his waves. She'd made him promise never to cut it short again.

"You're not supposed to do that in front of everyone!" Scotty admonished. Then he turned to catch his mom kissing the newest employee of Bluebonnet Manor. "Aw, Mom! Dad! You're embarassin' me!"

Mitch had offered to pay for Tawny's ex-husband's therapy and give him a job if he cleaned up and straightened out. So far, it was working splendidly. Scotty stomped off toward the stables mumbling, "At least the horses won't be smooching."

"They might be doing a lot more than that," Mitch said

with a chuckle. "Wait until he realizes what the mares are really doing when they wink at the stallions."

Sean reached up and wrapped his tiny fingers around one of hers. He had Mitch's brown eyes and her hair, or at least what little he had. Most important, though, he was healthy. "What are they doing?"

"They lift their tail and contract their vulva. You know, I always thought how handy that would be if women were so easy to read."

She nudged him through the fence with her knee. "Like you ever have to wonder!"

"Yeah, well." The wind ruffled his hair, and along with his tilted head, he looked like a little boy. He touched Sean's tiny nose, looking even more like a boy with the expression of awe on his face. "I can't wait to teach you to ride, little man."

"I can't wait for you to teach *me* how to ride," she said. Since Paul's spirit had left her heart, she'd lost her trepidation around horses. But soon after that, she'd learned she was pregnant and couldn't ride.

"Anytime, babe. Anything you want, anytime. You're the Queen of Bluebonnet Manor. But most important, you're the queen of my heart."

"Mitch!" Dave called out, still waiting by the group of kids and horses.

"Coming, mother," he muttered, giving her another long kiss and a peck on Sean's forehead. "Why don't we start your lessons when we return from New Hampshire?" he called as he headed back.

"I can't wait."

Last summer they had spent a few weeks at their home in Oceanside. Jenna had painted horse borders in the office and colts in the baby's room. Sean hadn't yet seen his New Hampshire nursery, but he would soon.

She and Mitch had redecorated the house, and everywhere he had stamped his touch. But in the living room on the mantel sat a picture of the twins. Mitch's idea, because he knew he had nothing to worry about where Paul was concerned. All he had to do was look in her eyes and see that there wasn't room for anyone else in her heart but him and Sean.

To prove that, to herself and to him, she had tied a helium balloon to her old wedding ring and sent it floating over the ocean. Not a goodbye, but a hello. Not an ending, but a beginning.

Her new ring had clusters of diamonds and emeralds that glittered in the sun. As did the four other rings he'd bought her, until she'd finally convinced him that just the wedding ring would suffice. Although she did like the Parmigiani watch he'd bought her to match his own. Jenna watched Mitch work with the kids, falling in love with him a little more if that was possible. She turned back to the house. They'd remodeled that, too, taking out all the gaudy furniture and turning the old master bedroom into a room where Sean could play with his friends when he got older. They almost needed to add another house for all of Sean's toys. Between Betzi, Tawny, Etta, and Mitch, the toddler was probably the most spoiled kid in Texas.

Bluebonnet Manor was her home now, the place where she would spend the rest of her days, would watch Sean grow up, where once she got her education, she'd help with the horses and paint furniture in whatever spare time she could find. Betzi, Etta, Tawny, Scotty, and all the others were the family she'd never really had.

"Sean, they say that home is where the heart is." Jenna looked at Mitch again, who'd been watching her with a wistful smile. "But my heart is where the home is. Right here with you and your daddy."

Survey

TELL US WHAT YOU THINK AND YOU COULD WIN

A YEAR OF ROMANCE!
(That's 12 books!)

Fill out the survey below, send it back to us, and you'll be eligible
to win a year's worth of romance novels. That's one book a month
for a year—from St. Martin's Paperbacks.

Name _____

Street Address _____

City, State, Zip Code _ _____

Email address _____

1. How many romance books have you bought in the last year?
   (Check one.)
   __0-3
   __4-7
   __8-12
   __13-20
   __20 or more

2. Where do you MOST often buy books? *(limit to two choices)*
   __Independent bookstore
   __Chain stores *(Please specify)*
   　　__Barnes and Noble
   　　__B. Dalton
   　　__Books-a-Million
   　　__Borders
   　　__Crown
   　　__Lauriat's
   　　__Media Play
   　　__Waldenbooks
   __Supermarket
   __Department store *(Please specify)*
   　　__Caldor
   　　__Target
   　　__Kmart
   　　__Walmart
   __Pharmacy/Drug store
   __Warehouse Club
   __Airport

3. Which of the following promotions would MOST influence your
   decision to purchase a ROMANCE paperback? *(Check one.)*
   　　__Discount coupon

      __Free preview of the first chapter
      __Second book at half price
      __Contribution to charity
      __Sweepstakes or contest

4. Which promotions would LEAST influence your decision to purchase a ROMANCE book? (Check one.)
      __Discount coupon
      __Free preview of the first chapter
      __Second book at half price
      __Contribution to charity
      __Sweepstakes or contest

5. When a new ROMANCE paperback is released, what is MOST influential in your finding out about the book and in helping you to decide to buy the book? (Check one.)
      __TV advertisement
      __Radio advertisement
      __Print advertising in newspaper or magazine
      __Book review in newspaper or magazine
      __Author interview in newspaper or magazine
      __Author interview on radio
      __Author appearance on TV
      __Personal appearance by author at bookstore
      __In-store publicity (poster, flyer, floor display, etc.)
      __Online promotion (author feature, banner advertising, giveaway)
      __Word of Mouth
      __Other (please specify)_____

6. Have you ever purchased a book online?
      __Yes
      __No

7. Have you visited our website?
      __Yes
      __No

8. Would you visit our website in the future to find out about new releases or author interviews?
      __Yes
      __No

9. What publication do you read most?
      __Newspapers *(check one)*
        __*USA Today*
        __*New York Times*
        __Your local newspaper
      __Magazines *(check one)*

__People
__Entertainment Weekly_
__Women's magazine *(Please specify:_____)*
__Romantic Times_
__Romance newsletters

10. What type of TV program do you watch most? *(Check one.)*
    __Morning News Programs (ie. "Today Show")
      (Please specify: _____)
    __Afternoon Talk Shows (ie. "Oprah")
      (Please specify: _____)
    __All news (such as CNN)
    __Soap operas   *(Please specify: _____)*
    __Lifetime cable station
    __E! cable station
    __Evening magazine programs (ie. "Entertainment Tonight")
      (Please specify: _____)
    __Your local news

11. What radio stations do you listen to most? *(Check one.)*
    __Talk Radio
    Easy Listening/Classical
    __Top 40
    __Country
    __Rock
    __Lite rock/Adult contemporary
    __CBS radio network
    __National Public Radio
    __WESTWOOD ONE radio network

12. What time of day do you listen to the radio MOST?
    __6am-10am
    __10am-noon
    __Noon-4pm
    __4pm-7pm
    __7pm-10pm
    __10pm-midnight
    __Midnight-6am

13. Would you like to receive email announcing new releases and special promotions?
    __Yes
    __No

14. Would you like to receive postcards announcing new releases and special promotions?
    __Yes
    __No

15. Who is your favorite romance author? _____

WIN A YEAR OF ROMANCE FROM SMP
(That's 12 Books!)
No Purchase Necessary

OFFICIAL RULES

1. To Enter: Complete the Official Entry Form and Survey and mail it to: Win a Year of Romance from SMP Sweepstakes, c/o St. Martin's Paperbacks, 175 Fifth Avenue, Suite 1615, New York, NY 10010-7848, Attention JP. For a copy of the Official Entry Form and Survey, send a self-addressed, stamped envelope to: Entry Form/Survey, c/o St. Martin's Paperbacks at the address stated above. Entries with the completed surveys must be received by February 1, 2000 (February 22, 2000 for entry forms requested by mail). Limit one entry per person. No mechanically reproduced or illegible entries accepted. Not responsible for lost, misdirected, mutilated or late entries.

2. Random Drawing. Winner will be determined in a random drawing to be held on or about March 1, 2000 from all eligible entries received. Odds of winning depend on the number of eligible entries received. Potential winner will be notified by mail on or about March 22, 2000 and will be asked to execute and return an Affidavit of Eligibility/Release/Prize Acceptance Form within fourteen (14) days of attempted notification. Non-compliance within this time may result in disqualification and the selection of an alternate winner. Return of any prize/prize notification as undeliverable will result in disqualification and an alternate winner will be selected.

3. Prize and approximate Retail Value: Winner will receive a copy of a different romance novel each month from April 2000 through March 2001. Approximate retail value $84.00 (U.S. dollars).

4. Eligibility. Open to U.S. and Canadian residents (excluding residents of the province of Quebec) who are 18 at the time of entry. Employees of St. Martin's and its parent, affiliates and subsidiaries, its and their directors, officers and agents, and their immediate families or those living in the same household, are ineligible to enter. Potential Canadian winners will be required to correctly answer a time-limited arithmetic skill question by mail. Void in Puerto Rico and wherever else prohibited by law.

5. General Conditions: Winner is responsible for all federal, state and local taxes. No substitution or cash redemption of prize permitted by winner. Prize is not transferable. Acceptance of prize constitutes permission to use the winner's name, photograph and likeness for purposes of advertising and promotion without additional compensation or permission, unless prohibited by law.

6. All entries become the property of sponsor, and will not be returned. By participating in this sweepstakes, entrants agree to be bound by these official rules and the decision of the judges, which are final in all respects.

7. For the name of the winner, available after March 22, 2000, send by May 1, 2000 a stamped, self-addressed envelope to Winner's List, Win a Year of Romance from SMP Sweepstakes, St. Martin's Paperbacks, 175 Fifth Avenue, Suite 1615, New York, NY 10010-7848, Attention JP.